Kieron Smith, boy

ALSO BY JAMES KELMAN

Kieron Smith, boy

JAMES KELMAN

HARCOURT, INC.

Orlando   Austin   New York   San Diego   London

www.HarcourtBooks.com

First published in Great Britain by Hamish Hamilton

Library of Congress Cataloging-in-Publication Data
Kelman, James, 1946–
Kieron Smith, boy/James Kelman.—1st ed.
p.   cm.
1. Children—Scotland—Glasgow—Fiction.
2. Grandparent and child—Fiction.
3. Glasgow (Scotland)—Fiction.
4. Glasgow (Scotland)—Social conditions—Fiction.
I. Title.
PR6061.E518K54 2009
823'.914—dc22   2008020850
ISBN 978-0-15-101348-7

Text set in Dante MT

Printed in the United States of America
First U.S. edition
A C E G I K J H F D B

Kieron Smith, boy

In the old place the river was not far from our street. There was a park and all different things in between. The park had a great pond with paddleboats and people sailed model yachts. Ye caught fish in it too. Ye caught them with poles that had wee nets tied at the end. But most people did not have these. Ye just caught them with yer hands. Ye laid down on yer front close into the edge on the ground. Here it sloped sharp into the water, so ye did not go too close. Just yer shoulders reached that bit where the slope started. Ye rolled up yer sleeves and put yer hands together and let them go down it. Just slow, then touching the water and yer hands going in. If ye went too fast ye went right in up yer arms over yer shoulders. Ye only went a wee bit, a wee bit, a wee bit till yer hands were down as far. Then yer palms up the way, holding together. If a fish came by ye saw it and just waited till it came in close. If it just stayed there over yer hands, that was how ye were waiting. It was just looking about. What was it going to do? Oh be careful if ye do it too fast, if yer fingers just move and even it is just the totiest wee bit. Its tail whished and it was away or else it did not and stayed there, so if ye grabbed it and ye got it and it did not get away. So that was you, ye caught one.

But they were quick, ye had to do it right.

Ye were having to watch it as well how yer body went, lying on yer front, if it was wee bits at a time ye were moving. And ye did not notice till ye slid right down and the water was up yer shoulders, oh mammy. Yer hands reached the bottom and ye pressed and pressed to push yer feet back up and if a big boy caught yer feet and pulled ye out or else that was you and ye went right the way in the water. That happened to people and men had to go in and get them. Daft wee b****r.

On the bottom was all slimy mud, broken bottles and bits of glass and bricks and nails and old stuff, everything. Prams and bike-wheels, and shoes, and then a man's bunnet. I saw that.

One time I was soaking the whole way through and my maw was completely angry, how I was going to die of pneumonia or else diphtheria if ye swallowed the water. My da was home on leave and he gived me a doing. But I liked going to the pond. The men sailed their boats there and had races, and their boats were great. Ye saw their sails and how the boat was tipping right over till it was going to capsize but it did not, it was just picking up speed because the wind was there and it was good, so they were all sailing great and the boys all shouting, and the men too. Go on Go on, Hold there.

Old men as well, if their boat was going to win the race and they shouted their names if the boat had its name and they did. All had good names, Stormy Petrel and Sea Scout. Oh hold there Sea Scout.

I telled my granda. He would have liked it, if the old men were there too, he could have went with me and they had seats, people could sit in the seats and just watch.

My Uncle Billy had a model yacht when he was a boy. He got it off somebody whose da worked in the docks. It was not a toy. Model yachts were real boats and they sailed good. It was just they were wee. If ye could have made a wish and shrunk to a Tom Thumb ye could have climbed aboard and put to sea for treasure islands. Then if ye were getting chased, ye could hide anywhere ye wanted. It would just be a thing like a cat or a dog, ye would have to be careful then, if they caught ye, and ate ye. Or if it was a mouse, they dragged ye into their hole, oh mammy.

Our old house had mice. My maw and me and Mattie were going to have breakfast and there they all were on top of the kitchen table and up on the sink and the draining board, piles of them. My maw went potty and started greeting. Me and Mattie scattered them and chased them but we could not catch them and did not know what to do. My maw was shouting in a high voice. Ohh ohhh!

We went and got my granda. He was not going to come but then he did. My grannie said it was just silly to climb up all the stairs, he would have no breath. Aye I will. That was what he said. I am going.

He made it a laugh. It is a big safari hunt. So then he gived me a joke. How far we going son?

Safari's the kitchen granda.

Our house was three up on the top storey. My granda stopped at all the landings on the way up to get his breath back. When we went into the house he knew where the mice were all hiding. My maw went away out the room. My granda showed us. Oh there behind the chair. See in that shoe. Oh look at the side of the cupboard.

Then he done something, then we had shoes in our hands. We sat waiting for them to come out and when they did ye were to bash them, and if ye got one it was great. They were just wee things, and when they were there ye saw how wee they were, a bit of body at the top, then just with their tails. Ye held the shoe at the ready and had to be quick and ye had to get them the first time. Matt was good at getting them. My granda sat on the chair and told us what to do. Then there were wee wee toty ones. They did not even run so ye just bashed them. My granda said they were babies. But ye were still to bash them, ye were not to let them go else they were going to grow up and it would be a plague of them, so ye had to do it and ye did not want to because if they were just wee and they were babies, but ye had to.

My granda had two cats that were mousers, a big one and a wee one. After we got the mice that was what my granda said, Oh I should just have brought the cats, the cats would have gobbled them up. I was not thinking.

The cats were there in my grannie's house. The wee one lied on the floor near granda's feet. If I went there the cat crawled under granda's chair. He did not like people except my granda. But I could pet him. My grannie did not. The wee cat went to her but she never petted him. Except she spoke to him. Oh what are ye wanting now?

The big cat was a friendly one and rubbed against ye but it stayed in the front room all the time and was down by the window or else on grannie's bed. The sun came in the window on her. But if ye kicked out the wee cat the big one came in. My granda done it. He just said, Oh I have had enough of you. Away and kick him out son.

So I done it. The cat did not like to go. I just took him. Cats do not like cats. My granda said, They like people better.

What about dogs?

Dogs do not like cats.

Do cats like dogs?

Some cats. Dogs are worse than people, that is what cats think.

Cats do not like anybody, said my grannie, they are just selfish besoms.

Oh we are all selfish besoms, said my granda.

No we are not, said my grannie.

Aye but if they are mousers.

Granda said about me getting one but it was my da, he did not like them. My maw did not either, she said they could be dirty. Where had their paws been? Ye did not know except it was dirt, cats were always in dirt. So were dogs.

My granda was great. If he came to the pond with me, he would have liked it. Some boys had poles and men let them steer the boats on their course and they walked round the banks. The men set the sails then launched the boat in a certain way, just pushing it out. They knew where it would land and told the boys. If ye did not know people ye just followed a boat ye liked. Some boys chased ye, others let ye stay. They did not listen if ye asked them a question. Ye could never get too close to a boat and they never let ye sail it.

Uncle Billy's boat got lost, else he would have gived it to me. But my granda said it was all just toys, how in our family it was real boats. He ran away to sea when he was fourteen and told the Captain he was fifteen. He was in the Merchant Navy same as my da except my da's job was better. My granda was just able-bodied. My da said they were ten-a-penny.

I had cousins at sea. One was in the Cadets. I was wanting to join. My maw did not want me to but my da said I could, it was a good life and ye saved yer money, except if ye were daft and done silly things. He said it to me. I would just have to grow up first.

§

There were great smells at the river and big ships went down it, ocean-going. Ye heard the horn and ran to see them. Ye had to run fast so it would not be away. Everybody was cheering maybe if it was a new one just built and here it was launched. Even if it was an old cargo boat or else a container ship. I liked them. Where had they been? They were all old and had been places all over the world. It was great, and ye were walking along and running along beside it then ye had to go round a corner and round a river-street and then back down and there was the river and the boat was there.

Ye heard the horn sometimes and ye were in bed, it was creepy, ye were maybe asleep but ye still heard it, if it was coming out of nowhere, that was how it sounded, ooohhhhh ooohhhhh, ooohhhhh ooohhhhh, ooooooohhhhhhhhh, and a big low voice. Just creepy. One time my da was home on leave and took me and Mattie down dead late at night. It was for a special boat. Other people were there, lasses too. We were all there waiting. It was completely foggy and just as if there was no noise hardly anywhere and everything was thick, very very thick, and ye could hardly hear anything and ye could not see nothing except yellow coming through where the lights were, ye were holding on to yer da's hand, then Look, look! That was my da and in a quiet voice, See, look!

And the yellow was coming out, all bright through the fog, and it was all lights, ye could not even see the funnels or the top parts because with the fog all hiding it. But there it was it was the ship out from the fog, ooohhhhh ooohhhhh, it was the special one. My da was just watching and me and Matt. Ye felt a feeling in yer body and how my da was standing straight so we did it as well. He was

Merchant Navy, but he liked the Royal Navy too. And all the sailors all looking down and waving to us and we were cheering, everybody was just cheering and just ye were greeting, I was greeting. Matt laughed but my da never. Then it was gone and its lights too and just the fog again, ooohhhhh ooohhhhh, ye heard the horn going and it was quieter and quieter and quieter.

I liked the wee tugs best. Some ships were gigantic and needed wee ones to help them, that was tugs. My da did not like me saying boats, if it was a cargo ship or a cruiser else a battleship, an oil container, just to say it right. These big ships needed the wee tugs to help them out to sea. If the wee tugs were not there the big ships would not make it through.

These wee tugs were great, they sailed with their chests out and their shoulders straight, that was what I thought. Nobody would ever say a wrong word to them. Ye could see it. One boat was Seasprite and ye thought of something fast and slippery. Sprites were in a book I read, wee kind of ghosts, they were not friendly but the boat was. Some of the sailors waved. They wore navyblue jerseys and trousers, boots and hats. Ye got the same uniform when ye joined the Lifeboys.

When a big ship was passing we walked and ran along with it as far as we could but there were walls and fences and ye could not go too far. We rushed down to the pier and down the wooden steps for the big wash, the waves crashing onto the steps. One day the pier would collapse, ye could see how its timbers were rotting. At the sides of the steps the wood was soft and with a knife ye could slice it away. Ye went as low down the steps as ye could when the tide drifted back. Then jumped up when the waves crashed in. If yer shoes were slippy ye had to be careful no to fall in, and the worst of all if a ferry was there oh mammy and a person got dragged under. Ye heard stories about that and if there was a boat with propellers it was so much the worse. People drowned in the river. If ye fell in ye could not gulp the water because if ye did ye got poisoned or caught diphtheria.

We watched the ship all the way down. It was in silence it sailed and hardly did not move until then ye saw how it was a distance on, then another distance. How did that happen? Then it had reached the faraway bend. That took a while, if ye were still there and watching ye would maybe be last man, yer pals away home or if Mattie was there he was shouting. Come on you hurry up.

And sometimes I hid from him. My da was all over the world on ships. He liked Brazil the best and Rio de Janeiro.

After he came out he would never ever settle. My grannie said it to my maw. Oh he is used to faraway lands, he will never settle.

My grannie said things that I heard, then if it was to my granda, saying about my da. Oh him! The way she said it, Oh him, talking about my da.

But my da said about her and about people too. He was talking to a man one time and I was listening. It was about my granda and I heard him and he was laughing a wee bit and he says, Wee Larry.

Wee Larry. I did not like him saying that. It was not nice. My granda was not well and it was Lawrence and here he could not stick up for himself, it was just my da saying it, if he did not like my granda, maybe he did not.

My da could speak bad about people and me too. He made jokes. I did not like it. Neither did my big brother, we were watching the telly and he got up and left the room. My da just looked and did not say nothing or else if he looked at my maw but she would just kid on it was okay. He done stuff and she kidded on he did not. That was the same with Matt, if he done stuff, she kidded on he did not, if it was tidying up after him. He just left his stuff, all plates and cups. If it was on the floor, they were just there, he left them. Then if ye stood on them, it was you that got the row. How come? There was a lot of stuff like that.

When I was wee and my da was there ye were better keeping out the way. Him and my maw had their bed in the kitchen. It was a weer bed that fitted in the recess with walls all round except one side. So moan moan moan. That was him. His legs were too long. There was nowhere to put them because it was a wall so they were aye bent. Or if he put his feet away up the wall the blankets all were

7

lifted up so my maw got freezing. He just done that for a laugh. He could not have his legs straight.

The worst was banging his head into the wall. He hit his elbows and knees but it was his head, if he hit that. Oh oh oh or else using bad words. My maw was at her work. She would have given him a row. She hated bad words, swearie words. O for G⋆d sake. That d⋆⋆n bed.

He said it was not swearie words. G⋆d and d⋆⋆n were not swearie words. My maw said they were. But he still said them. But if I said them it was rows or else even ye got hit. I would never say them. But if ye did.

He stayed in bed when he was home on leave. Even if he was awake. He just stayed in it and read books. And moan moan moan. If ye came into the kitchen and made a sound he got annoyed at ye. And ye could not help it, if it was spoons and forks and ye were reaching in the drawer for them. Even if it was a chair and ye bumped it. O for G⋆d sake. O for G⋆d sake.

Sorry dad.

Ye are aye screeching the d⋆⋆n chair.

I did not mean it.

Oh no ye did not mean it.

So he said stuff to ye. I did not like it. Ye got sick of it. He got annoyed or else laughed if ye done something. Oh do not be so daft Kieron you are just a dunderheid.

My maw did not like him saying it. Oh do not call him that.

Oh it is just a laugh.

Dunderheid. My maw gave me rows about if I said heid and not head. But no to my da if he did. So it was dunderheid. Oh it is not dunderheid it is dunderhead. If my maw said it to him but she never. But if it was me, Oh Kieron stop saying heid it is head.

My da never said stuff to my big brother. He liked him the best. People all liked him the best. My granda too. I thought he liked me the best but my grannie said, Oh no son it is your brother.

I did not know if that was true. My granda was the best and he showed me stuff and he said I was his pal, if I was his best pal, maybe I was.

Oh son he likes yer brother the best. He is the firstborn. My grannie said it. Oh he is the firstborn.

I was born second. So they all liked him the best. Except my grannie, she liked me. If everybody liked Mattie she would just like me because that was just fair.

But I wanted my granda. So if my grannie was wrong. If my granda liked me the best. Maybe he did.

My Uncle Billy liked me too, he played with me and gived me stuff for my birthday. No my Auntie May. She gived me kisses but liked Mattie the best. She got him to dance if it was a party. He walked about and did not do it right. Oh come here. And she took him. Oh just stand there and move yer feet.

I was best at it. But I saw her if I danced with her, she gived me a wee look. She would have liked it better if she was not dancing with me. If it was Matt, she would have liked that better. She showed him where to put his feet but no me. But I knew where to put them. But if I did it she did not look. I did not care. She had a boyfriend and was going out with him but then it was a big fight and if ye went to my grannie's there she was. Oh he has kicked her out.

My grannie telled me.

I did not care if she liked Matt the best. Or who else, everybody. But no my granda. I did not think it. He said to me I was his pal and he showed me all stuff to do with everything. Maybe he liked the two of us the best. But maybe he did not, maybe it was just me. If grannie never knew. Maybe he did not tell her, so she did not know. He had a secret wave and showed me it, it was a wee circle ye did with yer hand and when I went home we done it when I was going down the stairs.

The one that did not like me was Matt. Sometimes he did but no to take me places. He went with his pals. They all were big boys. They did not like bringing their wee brothers. But if they had to bring ye. Matt had to take me. My maw said it to him. But he still did not, even if I telled him.

But mum said it, you have got to take me.

Oh tough luck. That was what he said to me. I telled her but she did not hit him.

§

He had books and would not give me them and my grannie would say it. Oh let the boy see the books.

But he did not want to. Oh he will tear them.

I will not tear them.

He was always reading them and I could not. But if he was not there I saw them, if he was at school and I was not. They were libray books. He got them from the libray. It was near our street beside the park. He went most days and would not take me. I was too young. He got all books there and was reading them and I wanted to. He just shoved me. No, no, away ye go.

Then I was old enough to go and my grannie said it. Oh take him to the libray.

So he took me. I was waiting for him. He came home from school and we went.

We waited at the foot of the stairs with other boys and lasses. It was the Junior Libray. The gate was shut. The woman was coming to let us in. It had to be at the time. Four o'clock. All boys and lasses were there. So then she came and opened the gate and we went up the stairs into the Junior Libray. It was just all books. And good smells were there, and wee seats ye could just sit down on. And tables if ye could put yer books on them, ye were just to do it. A lassie went away and did that and she got books and put them on the table and just sat down. Matt was away over too and he was seeing all the books and took one down and was just looking at it.

I was going to get some but the woman said, Oh you have to stay there. Just take the form for your date of birth. You cannot get any books, you will get them when you bring the form back. Your mum or dad can do it.

So it was the next day. My granda did the form. Matt was coming home from school to take me but what if he would not? I just went. But I could not get in. The gate was shut at the foot of the stairs. So if ye were going to skip in, ye could not. A woman saw me. Oh the Junior Libray is not open. Look, it is only two o'clock. Go home and come back.

Oh missis can I just wait?

Well it will be a long wait.

She showed me a chair beside the window and I could sit there.

There was more tables and chairs and grown-ups were sitting on them and reading their books. I could see out the window. It was snowing, and real snow for snowballs. People would be flinging them at ye. Big boys after school. Ye could play at stuff out the backcourt. If people were there to play. Snow was good for chases and making good slides. Slides were great. The big boys made them and ye just had to watch if they gave ye a shot because if ye fell and banged yer head, it was just crack and then ohh ohhh.

Stop kicking the table.

It was a man said it to me. He was an old man like granda. Here, he said and gived me a sweetie. A woman came and I got books to read. She gived me another sweetie. I read the books. It was hot, a radiator was there and what happened, I went to sleep and woke up and people were going up the stairs, boys and lasses. I ran over. A woman was at the desk and saw my form. It was the same woman. Oh that is good Kieron here is your ticket.

She waved round all the books and I was to take ones. I got a big pile. I was not to take them all but I was to get two. I got big ones, they were heavy. I opened my jerkin and put them into my body so the snow would not get them. It was thick falling and people had snow over their heads and shoulders.

I went to my grannie's. My maw was not home till after. My grannie's house was up the next street to us, just across the back. Ye could see it from our kitchen window. When I got there my big brother was sitting on the stool at the fire reading a book. I liked that stool. I wished he was not there.

My grannie made me a piece on jam and I showed her my books. Where is granda?

Oh he is just lying down, he will see yer books after.

I did not want Mattie to see them. He did not look. Sshh. He said that if he was reading. Sshh you. I showed them to him and he would not look. If you are going to read read. That was what he said. If ye wanted the books ye have got the books.

He always read his books, he just sat on the stool and he read them and if ye were playing or ye were doing something, he did not hear ye and if it was grannie saying, Oh Mattie away down the shops a message. Oh Mattie we need potatoes or if it is milk and a loaf.

He did not hear her. She was doing clothes at the sink. But I would go for my grannie. And I said I would and I went to get my shoes and coat but then my big brother was quick off the stool and getting the money and got his shoes on quick and was down the lobby and out the door, banging it shut, so I did not have time to go with him. And my grannie just looking, Oh he will wake yer granda.

Because the noise, granda was sleeping.

§

My big brother was taking me on a long walk with his pals. He said I was to go out the back close to see somebody and just wait and he would come in a wee minute to get me. Nobody was out the back. I looked. I was waiting and he never came. When I went out the front that was him away, he just went away. If I could find him. I ran up and down the street but could not. He was away without me and they went to a tunnel under the river. There was all things that they did and just everything and it was all dark and creepy and ye just heard owls hooting and there were ghosts.

He said he would take me the next time but he did not. It was not fair. I was not too wee. If he was going I could go with him. I said it to my grannie how he just ran away and I could not run after them. Oh take the wee boy son. That was what she said to him.

Oh but grannie wee boys cannot keep up with us.

I said, I will so keep up with ye.

No ye will not.

I will.

No ye will not.

Oh let the boy go with ye.

Oh grannie I cannot, if the other boys are there, they do not want wee boys to come, they just make us slow.

Oh.

So he would not do it. Not for my grannie. But if my granda said it then he would. He only did things if my granda said it. I was wanting my granda to say it but he did not, only to me. Oh son you should play with the wee boys, that is the best thing.

But the wee boys did not play good games and did not go any places, they just stayed in the street. Matt and the big boys went all long walks. It was their travels. Mattie said that, Oh we are going our travels.

So I hid up the close and waited so he did not know and then went after him and he was going to his pals, so then I came out. He was angry. Away home you!

No!

Away ye go!

No!

You better if I tell ye.

No, I am not doing it for you.

Blasted pest.

He came to get me and I ran away. But I just came back again and was hiding in a close. I looked out to see them, oh and they were going. I waited a wee minute more then came out. They could not see me. I was keeping into the wall and if they were going to see me I dodged into closes and was hiding.

I came behind them a long way. But a big boy saw me and telled Mattie and he caught me and punched me. But it was too faraway. He could not take me home, so he had to take me. Oh you, you are just a blasted pest. You are a wee stinking rotter.

So I just went. They were going on the ferry and I went on it too but stayed at the back. I would have liked it better if another wee boy went but they did not. When we got off I followed where they were going and if they were walking fast. Oh Mattie wait for me!

Oh listen you it is Matt, not Mattie. Never you call me Mattie.

If I walked beside them he was going to kill me. If he was talking with his pals and he saw me and I was listening. Oh you wee spy. Stop spying.

I was not spying. If he did not see me I was there and he was talking about stuff. I heard him. It was not my fault. If he was saying bad words. Maybe he was. My da would have battered him, because if I telled my maw she would tell him, that was one thing.

§

My da was away at sea and I did not see him much except if he was home on leave and ye had to say Grace at night for yer tea, For what we are about to receive, may the Lord make us truly thankful. I went to my grannie's. I would have stayed but when it came night-time I had to go back. Make yerself scarce son. That was what my grannie said, You will have to go home now.

But if I went into a corner and just sat still. There was a space between the cupboard and the wall near the side of the fire and I could go in there and sit down on the floor and the light was dark, they did not see me. My granda said, Oh Vera the boy is playing possum.

My grannie looked where I was, and I was just I do not know just sitting or if my eyes were sleepy or what till then my brother came to get me.

My granda was teaching me tricks. He had cards and showed me how to shuffle them and keep ones to the front or else to the back. My brother sat down beside us. My granda brought him into it and showed him as well. Then my brother said I was to go home because maw wanted me to go a message. He gived me a real angry look and with his fist just what he would do to me if I did not go, when we got home, he was going to mollicate me. I hated him. He said things and then I got angry and he just laughed, and he did it when people were there. And he punched me if nobody was looking. That was him. I did not like him or else what he said, I did not care, if he was telling me to go home, I was not bothering with what he said. I was not going home for him, he was not the boss. Till then my grannie says, Ye better go home son.

So then I did but if she said to Matt, You take him son. That was not good because outside the house he would just bash me.

My granda showed me good tricks for fighting. Ye had to be quick, quick quick quick. Because if ye were not ye would just get hit. And if ye went down that was you, they kicked ye with their boots. So ye moved quick, the very quickest. And if they got ye in the belly like a bad punch in the guts, and ye were sick, ye went down with it, making ye bend over getting yer breath. So that would stop ye, ye had to avoid a punch in the guts. Granda said that.

He done the windmill on me, where his hands and arms went round and round and ye were to try and get him. Hit inside, Hit inside.

Punching in at him. But ye could not. My granda laughing, his face going all red, stepping about. Then my grannie shouted at him. Stop! Lawrie stop!

Then him breathing, having to breathe. Oh hooh hooh, hooh hooh, ahooh ahooh, that was the sound.

Lawrie was granda's name, coming from Lawrence, Lawrence McGuigan. My maw's name was Catherine McGuigan before she married my dad. I thought that was a funny name, Smith, and if ye had been called Lawrence as well. So with my name Kieron, my granda's one made it a wee bit better. He did not know any other Lawrence. His maw just called him it.

My grannie shouted at him if he was showing me fighting stuff because he got all puffed out, and sitting on the chair, he could not talk, getting his breath back and just quiet in his throat. Oh Vera I am knackered.

And ye would listen to him with his breathing, hoooh hoooh, ahoooh ahoooh. Then he would give me another wee punch. See that son, ye have to watch for the sneaky ones.

He went to a boxing club when he was young. His pal fought for Scotland and was a champion. Granda showed me how to spar. We sparred a lot, if grannie was out at the shops, or else if he sat down, I just done it. It was jab jab jab and use yer elbow, use yer elbow, tuck it in now tuck it in, get that elbow tucked in and move yer shoulder move yer shoulder, and do not slap do not slap, move yer shoulder move yer shoulder bump bump, bump bump, that is the game son.

My Uncle Billy said, Listen to yer granda Kierie boy, but see for a real fight ye have to go right ahead with them. Ye just rush in and clatter them and do not stop till they hit the deck.

That was what Uncle Billy said, and once ye got them down, ye did not let them back up, ye just carried on till they could not hit ye back. Ye had to stop them, else they would stop you. Even if they were decked, ye still had to fight them. So that was booting yer man when he was down. That was dirty fighting. Uncle Billy gived me a wink. But I did not like dirty fighting. If somebody was a dirty fighter, they did that, they kicked people when they were down. They were bullies. A lot of bullies were dirty fighters and there were boys like that.

My granda called Uncle Billy a mug. He used to say that about people, He is a mug.

Uncle Billy winked at me. When granda was not there he telled me if ye were fighting ye just lifted a brick and ye battered the man with it, that was how ye done it, especially a wee boy like me because if they were bigger, so ye just had to do it.

§

Swimming was the best. My grannie thought it too. She took me and Mattie. She liked going but no all the time. She was a past champion and a best swimmer and was in a Ladies' Club. She was showing me how to swim and when my maw was wee she showed her. My granda made a joke. Oh but yer grannie is a true champion, yer maw only goes to get a bath son she does not like her hair getting wet.

My maw only went on Saturdays. My da came if he was home on leave. Oh I have seen enough water, and now I have to swim in it.

That was to me and Matt because we were wanting him to come. And he laughed at my grannie, Oh she looks like a swan.

We were laughing too but it was cheeky. I did not like it. He said stuff about grannie.

My granda never came to the swimming. I wanted him to come. But he did not. Oh maybe the next time son. Yer brother will take ye.

He gived Mattie the money for us to go. I still could not swim and kept to the shallow end. A rail went round the pond and I held on to it. My elbow was wedged in and got jammed. I had to twist it to get out but it would not come. A big boy came to help but could not get it so the man had to come and get me out.

Sometimes yer feet went under the rail and balanced right, so ye floated good. My big brother did that. He let go with his hands so he went right back in the water just with his head and shoulders up. He put his hands behind his head, so if he was lying down. Oh I am going to have a wee sleep.

I tried it but my feet came out from the rail and I went under the water and back over and the water went all in my mouth and up my nose, choking and swallowing, I could not find the bottom and was nearly drowning. Lucky for me I never.

My big brother could swim good. My granda said he was to show me. I told him that but he just said, Oh grannie is showing ye.

Oh but you have to show me as well.

No I do not.

But if granda said.

Well I do not care if granda said.

You have to show me.

My brother just swam away. I saw him. I held onto the rail and he swam back and said to leave go and he would show me. I would not.

Because if he just ducked me under. Boys done that. If ye were there at the shallow end and they came by, they got yer head and ducked ye and ye could not get out and were drowning. They were just laughing. Matt said he would not do it to me. But then he was laughing and splashing at me and pulling off my hands. He swam underwater so ye never saw him. He just came up at ye or else stayed under and grabbed yer legs or else got up and round yer shoulders, gripping ye over the top and with all his might, so pushing ye off he was just pushing ye off, and ye would go right down and the water was coming closer so ye were kicking him and if he was laughing, then he was angry and just punched ye, trying to loose off my hands again, gripping tight on my wrists and it was sore, squashing them down and pulling them but I would not let go it was just like I could not I could not and I was shouting.

So if I did not stop he really would batter me. Once we got home he was going to. That was what he said. He pulled up my fingers one by one by one. I was kicking him to stop so he would not. He grabbed my trunks to pull them down so I had to leave go one hand to hold them so he was grabbing my other one, gripping the wrist, so he got it loose and I could not stop him so that was me and I went down and down and if ye could not reach the bottom. Not if it was the deep end. And ye rolled to the side and if ye hit the wall oh ye were lucky if ye could touch it so then ye went back up and ye were at the rail and could just grab it, spitting out all the water. It was all down inside ye and nearly if ye were going to be sick, coughing it all out and just spluttering it out yer nose.

Oh you are all snotters! Matt laughing at me. I did not want him and turned away my head. But he swam round. I turned my head the other way, so then he held my chin. You are not greeting?

Not for you anyway.

I swam down with ye.

No ye did not.

I did so. Ye would see me if ye looked. Daft wee pest, just open yer eyes.

If I opened my eyes I would see him, he said that. He was there when I went down and was watching me so I would not drown. If I opened my eyes I would see him.

Oh come on and try again.

But I was no going to so he just swam away. I hung onto the rail. When I wanted to move I walked up the wall so my feet were just down from it and my b*m was sticking out and I could just kick and bounce round the side doing it. People were coming the other way, if they could not swim. They passed their hands round ye or you passed yours round them and they had to stay still a wee minute so ye did not miss the railing cause if ye did ye went under the water and spluttering, ye were choking, and it was hard to find the rail again.

Then if somebody swam over the top of ye, their feet kicking out. Big boys dived in and their arms bumped ye hard, just like a real punch. Then if boys jumped in and it was on top of ye. That happened too. They were not supposed to. They just came running right out from the showerplace and whooshed right in, how they done it with their knees drawn up under their chin, dive-bombers. Haawwwww. That was what they shouted.

So that was you.

If boys were there that were pals they had good games. They stayed in the pond till the men shouted at ye, All out All out.

They wore white jackets. If ye did not go when they telled ye they kicked open the door of yer cubicle and got yer towel and hung it on the iron railing that went between the cubicles and the pond. If it was your towel ye had to get out else the men flung it in the water. Some of the boys still did not go out.

All out! All out! So the men went into people's cubicles and got all their clothes and hung them on the railing and then ye had to get out because if ye did not the men dumped them in the pond. Ye saw them floating in the water and sinking down. They had a big pole to get them out. So if everything was wet, yer shirt and trousers soaking. Yer maw would give ye a right doing or if yer da was there. Some of the boys said they would just take their clothes into the steamie and get a woman to dry them.

The steamie was next door. It had steps up the same as the swimming baths.

When ye came out the swimming baths a big queue was waiting on the pavement outside. If people had more money, if they were allowed, they joined the queue to get back in. Me and Mattie did not.

§

Parks were on the other side of the river. One was one way and the other was the other and they were both good. I liked them. Usually we went to the other. It was a big big walk and ye went different roads and there were closes to go through and sometimes there were good jumps out the back. But if other boys were there and saw ye so it was a fight so Matt and his pals had to watch it. And then if it was big jumps over the middens and back walls, if I was too wee. Oh you just stand there.

So I was just to wait for them. But if it was wee jumps I went and just did them, and sometimes they were bigger and I still jumped it. And if I did not make it and was gripping on and digging in my feet. So if Matt came and helped me. Usually he did, or else his pals. They pulled my hands so I got up.

But if ye done a jump. Or else walking a dyke. I loved it. Then if it was a good one ye did and the big boys saw ye, so if they winked at ye and then to Matt. Oh yer young brother is walking the dyke!

Matt just looked and then when I came down he maybe chased me. Because if I fell and broke my arm or else my head. Boys broke their head. Matt would have got a doing, my maw would tell my da and he would batter him.

Then going in shops. Him and his pals were knocking. I had to stay outside the shop but I saw them and if they had chocolate and gived me a bit. Matt did not. Maybe if he was not knocking, I did not see him, but he went in the shop.

The park where the big boys went did not have a pond but it had a river, just a wee river and no boats went on it. It had smells too but different ones. They were looking for fish. But no baggie minnows like in our own park, the ones here were big and ye could eat them.

Maybe if men were fishing they would give ye one. That was what they said. But ye never saw any. Ye could not swim in the water. It was too slimy and was all soapy. If ye swallowed it ye got poisoned and ye were to watch it if ye paddled yer feet, if ye fell over the stones and drank any because ye would choke to death. Matt was shouting at me.

There were railings to keep ye out. They just jooked through and I came behind. Bushes and trees were there and it was good for games and ye could go down and there was the river and there was all chuck-iestones and ye could reach in and get them and fire them anyplace, even if ye were skliffing them over the top of the water, the boys were counting them and seeing who done the most. They did other stuff or else climbed the trees and all other stuff, whatever it was. I watched or else I could climb a tree too. One tree they all went on a branch and it snapped and they fell down and went in the water. It was just a laugh. It was a great big branch and they carried it and flung it in the water and it went sailing down till then it got stuck. So if they got other stuff and made a dam. They flung in big boulders and were jamming in stuff, old planks of wood and all things lying about. I was just watching. But two men came and were shouting and they ran away so me too because if I was left, if they left me, so I would be lost.

In one place a big wall was there and went right across and under the river. The water gushed over the top of it and fell down, and it was a waterfall. Here ye took off yer socks and shoes to climb down the bank and ye went up and then ye climbed from there up onto the wall to walk across. But the water gushed over yer ankles and ye had to watch it if it dragged ye over and it was all slippy with green stuff twirling over the big stones and if it got yer ankles oh mammy ye were tripped up and that was you over the waterfall so ye were linking hands. The big boys all did it. All link hands.

Could anybody swim? People were saying it. Ones that could would save the ones that could not. Oh you take him and you take you. Matt got me. He was not going to take me but he did. Give me yer hand you.

He gripped my hand tight and it was too tight and even it was sore and his nails digging in but he just did it so I would not fall down. If you go in, I am not saving ye. That was what he said. You will just drown, so ha ha ha.

So then we went and we were just going across step by step and step by step, and a big boy shouted, Do a pee!

So everybody all done one. Even if ye were not needing ye tried a wee bit, standing up on the wall and doing it over the waterfall. It was down from a road bridge. Snobby people were there. Then seeing us peeing and pointing down and men were angry and shouting. Get out of there. Get out of there.

So we hurried up and were going over the wall one by one by one by one and it was all slippery and with green stuff and the water gushing fast oh mammy, Hurry hurry. Because the cops were coming and were going to get us if we did not go faster faster faster Kieron faster. And Mattie was holding my hand tight rushing me and my feet were splashing and splashing till then we were on the other side. Oh and the big boys were all shouting at the snobby people, Hohhh hohhh, and just bad words and all were laughing.

Mattie let go my hand now and we all ran down a wee trail, down through bushes and away up a wee hill and over, all still laughing. Oh I cannot run I am too busy laughing. A big boy said that.

So now there was the gate and we went through it and out the park.

Oh is everybody there? Where is Kieron? Oh there he is.

Matt was looking at me. Oh he was going to punch me, but he did not.

It was a big walk farther down now and then way way along to get to the real river, that was our river, just the biggest one, and then the ferry and that was you ye were safe.

§

Different ferries went over the river. Some were big carferries but most were just wee ones for people walking. There was not a footpath along the bank. Big shipyards and factories were there and ye walked the nearest street to get down where a pier was. These streets were just wee and were a dead-end and ye called it a river-street. Ye did not have anyplace to go except down the steps and that was the ferry. The water was soapy and all colours with oil, and all the big boats getting built. Ye went back and forward on the ferries except no if it was teatime and the men coming home from work, all packed on board and if the ferry was going to sink, ye wondered how it did not and all the men there what would happen? They would all be swimming and ye would see their coats and bunnets all floating and if somebody drowned. People all could not swim and if they were jammed in together and all legs and arms, and feet all kicking then they would just sink down.

When we got to the other side, if we stayed on and went back and then over again, the ferryman did not mind. If it was a cold day or wet ye stood under cover with yer back to the wall. The engine was there and it was roasting hot so if ye touched the wall, yer hand got burnt. Usually ye stood at the front to see the ferryman doing the wheel, even if it was raining and nobody was there, it was just you and ye were just breathing in deep and then getting the smells. And if there was birds, they were sea gulls, gwok gwok gwok. And then up high, gwoak gwoak gwoak. The ferryman wore a black jacket and a navyblue jersey and had a cap. And if they were smoking a pipe, some of them did. They were real sailors and came from the highlands and if they swore at ye it was Gaelic. Ye did not ask to get a shot at the wheel and were to call them Skipper, my granda said it, Oh never touch the wheel son never touch the wheel.

But then my da was home on leave one time and he said ye could touch the wheel and he said it to the ferryman. Oh can the boy touch the wheel?

Aye.

So I could. The ferryman let me. It was the big stick things round it and ye could grip yer hands on it and just if ye pushed it a wee bit. Oh that boy is going to be a sailor, oh he will sail the ocean.

So my da said that he was in the Merchant and him and the ferryman were talking about the seas and who ye worked for.

§

Along our side of the river was a big huge place, all waste stuff full of rubbish and everything all about everywhere just lying and ye could take anything if ye wanted to take it. We looked for stuff that was good and we called it lucks. Oh did ye find any lucks?

So ye said what ye found.

It was near a big shipyard. Fires were smoking and burning. Big boys came here and men too, midgierakers, and ye had to be careful. There were fights if somebody got good lucks and somebody else tried to knock them. Ye did not go beside them. They did not care if ye were wee, if ye were getting in their road, they pushed ye away or even they skelped ye over the head.

Ye looked through dirty old rags and ye were to see for rats if there was burnt newspaper, that was where they hid and ye heard them squeaking, squeeeeek. Big boys chased them. And ye watched for the jaggy glass and melting rubber which stuck to yer hands and was so sore burning ye. Ye found all bits of iron, all different bits. Torn old burnt old magazines with all pages torn out and books too. Oh is there n**e books and if it is a dirty book. Big boys were saying that.

Ye had to walk through high wee hills of red ash, black ash and usually white ash. Yer feet sank into it as far as yer ankles and it got into yer shoes and socks and made it hard walking, having to take them off and dunt out the dust. Then if the ash was too hot, if it went down yer shoes, it burnt ye, and if yer socks got all black and smelled like burning. And all fluffy white stuff that stung yer legs.

Matt and his pals filled a big sack with lucks. They were taking them back to our place. I was going behind them. They were going out to the street. But down at the pier the carferry was coming to dock so what they done, they dragged the sack behind an old rickety fence and planked it in among big weeds then ran round and made it on the carferry. I made it too. They were just going over and then coming back. Halfway across the wee ferry was going too, we saw it. It was keeping out our way. They usually did that to let the carferry go first. So we were looking over at it. It was loaded down with people but then it was all flags and all stuff and it was a band playing oh if it was a circus, it was like one. But it was not. Oh it's the Orangemen! A big boy shouted. They are going to the Walk!

So boys were saying if people were there and they knew them and Matt said, Uncle Billy! And he shouted over, Uncle Billehhh! Uncle Billehhh!

I was looking to see him but it was too faraway for faces and I could not. I climbed on the railing to see. The railing went round the high deck where the people went. All the motorcars went down the low deck. The railing was so nobody fell off. Ye could climb through it. Ye gripped on and went near the edge if ye wanted to see stuff, and then the water down below how the waves were coming and then white and all bubbles, then a next one and a next one and a next one just white and then bubbles and then the next one oh and a man grabbed me oh and he just lifted me right up. Oh you silly wee b****r.

And Mattie was there and his eyes big looking at me.

Is he yours! Well he nearly went for a swim. Keep him in from there.

But when the man went away Matt punched me in the arm but no sore, I would not have fell, it was all good grips. The boys were laughing at the man. Ye could step on the railing and ye would not fall. I did it to see over. The man was not looking. The wee ferry was out in the middle of the river waiting for the carferry to pass. All the Orangemen were jammed together, their arms sticking out and then ye could hear the band playing a tune. Oh it is the Sash. Somebody heard it. I could hear it too but if it was a right tune, I did not hear that.

So the carferry came in to the pier and all the traffic was getting off and we were going to stay on board but then we were not. Oh come on we will go with the band!

So people all wanted to do that. Matt was looking at me but he was letting me come. Uncle Billy was not there.

We walked with the Orangemen for a long long distance hearing the flutes and the drums, and it was great if it was all the tunes and it was the best ones. We went on the pavement beside them and behind then running ahead to see the man that tossed the stick. He was flinging it up high and ye saw it twirling and spinning yet he could catch it when it landed and still be marching.

Then came old men marching then the band and more men then women and boys and lasses and with orange and blue and white. Hullo Hullo, for the Billy Boys and other ones and the boys were shouting toooralooo f**k the Pope tooralooo for the Protestant Boys and that was us. And ye could see the women, if they were tripping up, it looked like they were going to trip the way their toes were, but they did not trip and it was just if they were dancing, maybe if they were dancing. Everybody was just going, what were they doing, just what it was, and ye were not to get in their way. Oh ye better not get in their way! Never get in their way. Oh if it is the Walk just stay on the pavement or ye will get battered.

And if ye went off the pavement they all were marching there and did not stop, the men shouting at ye, Oh get back get back.

And cops were there too. How come the cops were there? But they were not looking at us. They were good cops. One of Matt's pals said it. Oh do not worry, they will not get ye.

We went with them for a long way. It was out on a main road. Other people were there and a lot were boys and some were looking at us and were going to jump us. If they thought we were Papes. We were not Papes. But then they all came to get us so we ran. They chased us through a close and over a back and we were lucky we got over the dyke, and they were shouting, Stay and fight, stay and fight.

But if ye did they would just get ye. I was just running fast but the big boys were getting away and Matt, so I was just running oh where were they, I did not see them and then other boys were there and caught me, and wee boys punched me. It was in a back close. Get him! Just wee boys same as me. The punches were sore but and I was greeting. Bits of sick came into my mouth and I was spitting it out and oh coughing and my belly was sore. I was just sitting on the ground. Boys came and looked at me then ran away.

So when nobody came I went out to see.

Everybody was all away.

Where was I?

I was just walking and then was seeing someplace. I did not have any money. There were shops and they had good windows to look in. One was a big toy shop with all soldiers and motor cars and trainsets, and wee redcoats and kilties too. A chip shop was there and the smell was coming. A woman was looking at me. I went up to her and started greeting, I was lost, and big boys battered me and took my money. If she could give me money. That was what I said. And she did. I bought chips. I was walking down the road and eating them, it was a big pile.

And I saw a street and I knew to go down it then was another street and then another one. And so I went and it was a wee river-street. But Matt was there. He was at the pier, he was looking for me. I did not know if he was going to be angry. I saw one of his pals. Other people were there for the ferry. So if they were watching, so he would not hit me. Oh but he would and I saw him oh mammy I knew his face. Then he saw me and oh he just shouted and rushed right at me for a real doing, he was going to batter me. I just ran away as fast. But he did not come after me, just stayed at the pier. He was waving at me to come but I would not because he was just going to get me so I just stayed up the street and if he came I would just run away. Then the wee ferry came. He shouted on me. He ran to one side and then to the other side and his hand up to his mouth, Kierrronnnn! if ye do not come I am going to go on it. Kierrronnnn! I am going to kill you. Kierrronnnn! Kierrronnnn!

The people all came off the wee ferry and were walking up the street. The ones waiting to get on were now all onto it and it was only Matt there and his pal. Kierrronnnn! Kierrronnnn!

He jumped to make me jump but he did not come. I stayed and watched. Then a wee minute more and his pal ran down the steps and Matt ran after him. The ferry went away. I waited but it did. I was walking just slow if he was hiding and going to jump out and get me. But he did not.

The carferry pier was near and had pillars with chains at the end and I hid behind one to see out. The wee ferry was out on the river, chug chug chug. People were on it but ye could not see the faces. Where was he? Oh mammy if he got me he was just angry and my belly was sore, and all the chips were there, I ate them all up, every one chip, I just ate it, so if I was going to be sick or else the toilet, I was needing. I walked round the pillar and nobody was there. Now motor cars and vans were waiting for the carferry. I sat down on the steps. The carferry was coming. People queued for it and men from their work. But no many. They read the paper or were just whistling a tune or else smoking, it was smoking, I hated smoking and it was cigarettes, if it was yer belly oh ye were going to be sick. When my da was home on leave that was what he did, he just smoked and yer belly felt sick.

The carferry came. The people got off then the motor cars and big lorries. I still was hiding if my brother might be on it. The carferry did not have a lot of places to hide. I could not see him anywhere. I waited till the next motors got on. I ran and jumped on. The men were closing the gates and the chains were dragging. I watched then we were moving. I went to the front. The wee ferry was coming from the other side and would pass us. I went round the other side looking up the river. Once it passed I ran round and looked over to it. Then the carferry was at the pier and the people were getting off and me as well. Matt jumped out and got me. He came in between people. He twisted my arm and I was shouting. Men were looking. Oh I am his big brother. That was what he said, and he was pushing me to walk coming behind and clicking my heels and then kicking them, Oh see when I get you home oh you are for it, I am going to give you a right doing, I will never take you anywhere ever again.

And he punched me in the back and shoved me. He was like a real bully. I thought he was one. I was not to go with him any places. Just get yer own pals. That was what he said.

When we got home we were late for tea and my maw gived us a row. But he did not tell on me and how come we were late, we were just away playing, that was what he said, and I did not say about the boys punching me in the back close, I just went into the toilet and then came out and was washing my hands at the kitchen-sink. My maw was just heating our tea and then we got it, sausage, beans and chips.

§

My grannie's house was nearer school than ours. They stayed across the back. But it was not far to school from my house. It was at the top of my street and then along. Except ye could not go that way. Papes would get ye. Their school was at the top of our street. Ye had to pass theirs to get to ours. The Chapel was beside theirs. So they came out school and went to the Chapel. But the Church was not beside our school. That was what people said. Oh it is all for the Catholics. If the Papes had the Chapel where was our Church? There was not one, no beside the school. It was away way down the road. It was not near at all.

They had Priests in their school. Ye saw them in the playground. Some had big long coats. Then too the Nuns, they were there as well. Wee women with hoods over their heads and their cloaks, black and blue. What did they do? Were they teachers? Maybe if they gived lessons and the Bible. They had different Bibles. Or else if they were nurses. On the telly ye saw Nuns that were nurses. They walked fast and with their eyes to the front. Ye saw them get on the bus and they did not look at anybody except if they knew them, they just stared at the floor. But if somebody knew them first they said hullo back. Ye saw who they spoke to. Oh they are a Pape. Or else in the shops if the Nun was talking to people. So ye saw who it was, who they were talking to, if they were Papes too. Some ye saw in the street and did not know they were Papes till then they were talking to the Nuns. Ye watched for that. Usually Papes had black hair and peelywally skin or else ginger hair and freckles. My da said that, peelywally. But some did not and they just looked ordinary so ye did not know.

We could not go to school up our street because Papes were on the lookout and flung stones. They pelted ye. There were big fights at dinnertime. Boys flung stones into the playgrounds and the janitors and teachers had to stop it and if windows got broke, Oh the cops are coming.

We had to go other streets. Me and Matt went across the backcourt for a short cut. Except ye met boys that were Papes. Ye saw them and ye knew them. Ye jumped down off a dyke and there they were coming up. They just looked and did not do nothing. If they were going to shove ye and punch ye but they did not. How come? My brother said, Oh they think you are one, if ye support the Celtic, and he was laughing at me.

It was my jacket and trousers. My maw bought them and they were a bit like green. Not a real green. I said that but Matt was just laughing. Oh you are a wee Pape.

No I am not.

Yes ye are if it is green, green is a Pape's colour.

It is not green.

Yes it is.

It is only a wee bit.

No it is not it is a big bit.

It is not a big bit.

He said it was. Green was a Pape's colour. People knew that. So if my maw got me a jacket and trousers and they were green. How come? I did not want them. How come she got me them? If it was for me and not for him? How come? If I had to wear them. I did have to. She made me. She was angry. Oh of course you have to wear them do not be so stupid.

I was not stupid. She said I was, if I thought that about my clothes. They were not green, they were just another green and were not Celtic at all.

One time I went to school myself and just walked up our street right to the top and round past the Catholic school. The Chapel was there too and the door was open. I did not see in. I was not looking, and then was past it. Nobody came to get me.

They could not pass our school either. We had stones to pelt them so ha ha and we shouted at them. Catholic cats eat the rats. They shouted at us. Proddy dogs eat the frogs.

They went down the main road then round by our street but sometimes if it was ones ye knew, if they stayed in your street and maybe if ye played with them and ye just passed and saw them looking, so ye made it a secret wee look just if it was a secret wee hullo or if ye kidded on ye did not see them, they did that too. When ye came out to play at nighttime it was okay and ye were just pals.

§

On Saturdays we went to scrambles. So if it was a wedding, ye were looking for weddings. The motor cars drove away and men let down the windows and threw out the money and ye all scrambled to get it. No just boys and lasses, women too. If they saw silver coins they stood on them and ye could not lift up their shoes. Then if ye tried they kidded on they did not see ye or else gived ye a wee kick, but it was hard and made ye stop, so they got the money.

Scrambles were in Chapels and Churches. So if ye went to a Chapel scramble Catholics were there. We did not go to faraway Chapels and had to watch it at faraway Churches because other boys were there and were going to batter ye if it was their scrambles, it was their money, and you were taking it. So they were going to get ye. So ye just would watch it. If it was a faraway scramble ye waited over the street to see who was all there and if it was gangs or what ye just went away back to yer own place.

If it was the Chapel in our street the Catholics saw ye and it was okay because it was your street as well, and if ye were pals with them, sometimes ye were. They acted proud. You were at their scramble so ye had to keep out the way, so ye were not the boss, they were the boss. But if wee money rolled to you ye could get it. I had a pal and he was a RC, Michael Lang, he took me into the

Chapel. I did not want to. I was scared. The big door was there and people were looking. He just walked in and did not worry about any of the stuff. It was to see if the wedding people were coming out. Oh come on with me. Oh you are just feared.

And he was waving to me to creep in, so I just did and then just to skip ben the front and then in the lobby.

Big doors were there and voices and coughing, and big statues, and all people sitting down and women too and all lasses then the Priest and he was up at the front and his hands were up in the air if it was a blessing, maybe it was. Ye got the blessing and then the prayers up to God and Jesus and so it was you oh mammy if people looked round, it was just you there. Oh it is him! See him!

I was needing to get out. The big statues made ye feared and all what was there, what the people all done and their hands giving wee signs that were for secrets and even if it was spells. Priests done it to ye and ye were in awful trouble. A Proddy could not make these signs, even if ye knew what they were. It would go against ye making them and God would see or if it made ye turn into one. People turned into Papes. So maybe if they were Proddies and did the signs and were saying all the stuff, so then that was them and so they were Papes, they turned into Papes. So that was them, and what would happen, they would just have to go to Chapel and if the Priest was there or the Nun, they would just have to maybe see them or talk to them or what it was, I did not know.

Michael Lang was brave because of all what happened to Papes. It was a shame for him. I saw him in my head. He was split in two, the bit I knew and the other bit was a Pape.

He did not have a big brother but two wee sisters. He stayed three closes away. Ye did not get Papes in my close. It was a good close. Papes were in bad closes. It all was dirty and all smells and noises and filfy filfy water. They did not have good clothes and were midgie-rakers. Their das done that, they just raked yer midgie and got yer old rubbish. The boys had no swimming trunks and got borrowed ones. Ye tied them at the sides and they were too big. They came down yer knees when ye dived in the water. People just laughed. Oh he is a Pape. He has not got any swimming trunks.

If ye forgot yer own trunks ye had to get them. Boys did not like wearing them. Oh he is poor.

It was only if ye did not have yer own ones and if it was RCs. I saw them at the swimming baths. They had on their Necklaces with the Crosses that brought them good luck and if they kept the Devil away. Boys wore them as well. How come? They were next to ye in the pond and the Necklace floated behind them, and if a Cross was there on it. That was the worst. When ye were passing ye saw it floating near and had to watch or ye banged into it and then what? Things for Papes were different. If it was good for a Pape it was bad for a Proddy so if ye wore a Cross what was going to happen? If it was burning yer skin. People said that. Oh ye were a Proddy so it would burn ye. Oh it was burning hot.

So it left a real mark like a tattoo. But if ye were a Pape it was okay and it would not burn ye or else whatever. They had Candles and water that was Holy Water. Proddies did not have nothing like that. What did we have? We did not have nothing, no like that. My maw took us to Church sometimes, no much, just if my grannie went. She got us up early and we got a good breakfast and we all went. I saw boys in my school. If my da was home we had to do Grace at teatime. We said our Prayers in bed. My maw forgot to ask if we done them but we did, I always did. So did Mattie. Sometimes he just did it into himself. Because I did not hear him. Oh ye did not say yer Prayers.

I did so.

I did not hear ye.

I done it into myself.

Who did ye bless?

Oh everybody.

Cousins as well?

Just everybody.

One time we went to Church and we got Christened. Other ones were there, lasses as well. We sang hymns. If Catholics sang hymns, maybe they did.

§

My Primary School finished at three o'clock. The big ones finished at four. That was my brother.

My maw was working at her job and did not come home till five. At dinnertime I went to my grannie's. Matt did not. He went to dinnerschool and got big dinners. Steak pie and mashed potatos. Boys told me. Ice cream and jelly. I just got soup and toast. So that was not fair. I did not like soup and a lot of times my grannie burnt the toast. She did not bother about stuff. She put the toast down and it was burnt on one side and no done on the other then she gived ye the soup and it was scalding hot and just watery or if it was a boiled egg and ye cracked it open and it was just gooey stuff like snotters. What ye giving the boy Vera? Is that poison?

That was what my granda said. My grannie's name was Vera. Oh yer grannie cannot cook son.

He laughed at her. But she did not like him doing it. But so she saw the egg, so then she gave me a banana, and it was time up, back to school. My granda took me to the door. He done that most times. In case ye get lost son.

It was just for a joke. I would never get lost. He waved his bunnet at me when I went down the stairs. Full steam ahoy son you show them.

That was what he said, so I was to do good at school. I was going to. It was say yes and not aye, down and not doon, am not and no um nay, ye were just to speak nice. I liked school and it was good teachers, they thought ye were good at stuff, and drawing too, I done faces. Mine was Miss Rankine and she just smiled at ye till then if ye done something and it was bad, and that happened to me oh and then she did not like ye and if ye laughed too much. Oh Kieron, you are just silly.

There was a good short cut where ye went across waste ground. I went it everyday coming back from my grannie's. Big boys played football here and ye watched them. And then ye saw men and they played big games of cards and it was all money and they flung it down on the ground. Then there was angry shouting and men swearing. I saw a big crowd all watching something, oh and it was a fight. Boys from my school were there as well. I got through to see. Two men were fighting. One was on the ground and the other one kicked his shoe into his belly and it went into his low tummy and he was shouting down all bad words, F*****g c**t, cheating b*****d, and thud thud, kick kick.

And the one down on the ground was going, Oh my b**ls oh my b**ls, and he had his hands covering his low tummy so they would not get hurt. But the other one was kicking him again.

The bell went in school and I was still watching. So were other boys. Mattie was not there. He was at dinnerschool.

Me and other boys would not go in the school gate because we were watching. Everybody all was watching, it was just kick kick and punching till the cops were coming.

But the man was still getting battered. It was not fair and the other one would not let him up. He was a dirty fighter and just kicking him thud thud. And the man was all bent up lying there. Oh my b**ls, and water was coming out him, his face and his nose and eyes and he was wiping it. And then Scatter Scatter oh mammy, The polis, a man was shouting.

The cops were there and going to get us and if they booked ye and gived ye a kicking. All the men were running through the backs and round the street and we all rushed over into the school playground. Oh and that man was still lying on the ground and the cops were getting him but no the other one, he ran away.

The door was shut into my class. I had to chap it and then Miss Rankine came and opened it and gived me an angry look and I was saying how it was a big fight with all men and how it was a man and he was getting kicked and booted and how his clothes were all just dirty and mud was all over them, and if he was greeting, maybe he was. B-O-L-L-S. It was just all bad words, I was telling Miss Rankine oh but then she took my hand and slapped it. Oh Kieron Smith do not be so silly. Just go to your desk and sit down.

That was what she said. It was all nonsense in my head. She put it down on a letter and I was to give it to my maw. So my maw read it. Oh Kieron comes late to the class. Oh if he would just stop being so silly and if he is just chattering all the time, he is just a chatterbox.

That was what Miss Rankine put in the letter. My head was full of nonsense and I was silly and a chatterbox. My maw smacked me. Oh you wee silly besom. You wait till your father comes home!

But when my da came home I would tell him, he would hear it, if it was men fighting. I was not silly and a chatterbox. If my teacher said it. I was not. It was just how it was a grown-up man. And it was in front of everybody he was saying it, Oh my b**ls Oh my b**ls. I knew what b**ls was. Big boys called it that. But I never said it out loud and neither did boys in my class. It was funny hearing that man. It sounded funny. It was a bad word. And all us hearing it. He did not care. He just did it. Oh my b**ls, and all people hearing him.

Then how he was greeting. If he was greeting. If it was real greeting, all the water coming out. I thought if it was. And a man doing it, that was a thing. I did not want to feel sorry for him. He was not like a real grown-up. Maybe if he was a worse coward, if he was greeting, that was like a lassie or a wee baby, if ye did it, ye just tried no to. And if it was in a fight so much the worse, that was so much the worse, all people seeing ye.

And that was that man. If he was a cheater, people said he was and so did the man hitting him, Cheater b*****d.

Then if he was a coward. Oh he is a coward. Boys said it in the playground. I was listening. But if he could only be a coward. A big boy was saying that. If it was a man hitting ye and ye were a boy and could not hit him back. Only ye were a coward. If it was a big boy doing it and he was too big a boy. Even ye could not reach him. Ye were too wee. It was not your fault. So if he is not a coward if he only could be a coward. I was saying it to my granda.

Oh do not worry about that son.

Oh but granda if it is a wee boy and the big boy is just hitting him and he is too big?

Never mind if he is a big boy son ye just box him, boof boof boof.

Ye box the mitts off him, that is what ye do. Now hold up yer hands.

Aye but granda if he is kicking ye?

Oh that is a dirty fighter, that is a cheat, cheats never win. That man getting kicked was not fighting, just the other one was kicking him. It was not a fair fight.

But I was thinking about that. If my maw said, Oh do not fight, you must not fight.

So if the man is fighting you, so you must fight him. If a boy was hitting ye, ye hit him back. My maw said, Oh ye must not fight.

Oh but if a boy hits ye, and just ye are shouting at him and he is punching ye and yer hands are up in the air to stop him. So if yer hands hit him, so ye are hitting him, ye are fighting him. So what if that?

Oh stop it Kieron.

But if they are hitting you you must hit them back. Granda would say it and so would my da, if he was there, and my Uncle Billy, if it was them and they were fighting.

§

What if it was yer da and ye saw it was him? He was fighting the man. So everybody was watching. Then you came and saw, Oh it is a fight. And ye saw who it was, Oh and it was yer da. And boys were looking at ye. They knew. Were ye going to fight them? If it was yer da and he was getting a real doing, oh and a kicking, a real kicking. And b**ls, if people said that. My da would never say that. I knew he would not. But maybe Uncle Billy would say it. I heard him saying bad words to his pals. He came back from England and took me and Mattie to the park to see the model yachts. His pals were there and all were talking. F*****g and b*****ds. Oh the boys will have to f*****g beat these b*****ds.

Me and Mattie were listening. If it was the Rangers and playing at football it was a hard game. So then Uncle Billy said it and it was oh the worst bad words. And it was in yer head if he did say it. I did not say it in my head. I tried to and it was only foakoan baaa stids.

I was looking at Mattie but he kidded on Uncle Billy never said it, if I thought he did, he did not, he did not say nothing and it was just nothing.

Then if it was a man greeting? If that man was greeting in the fight. I thought he was. My da would never be greeting. And Uncle Billy, he would not be either. And if he was getting a kicking, if like a real doing, I would help him. I would. I would just jump on the man's back or else fling stones at him. If I had hatchets, boys were making hatchets to hit people and they hit them on the head and split it wide open. So I would do that. Or if it was a dog. Boys had dogs and ye set them on people. That was what I was wanting was a dog, oh a dog if I could just get a dog. People got dogs. Wee puppies. I said to my maw if I could get one. Oh there will be no dogs in this house.

How no?

Because they are dirty.

Oh but if they are clean? Dogs went in the pond. They swam about and then came out and shaked the water, so that was clean, it was not dirty.

My maw did not like dogs. And cats. Oh they are just pests. And where have they been if they climb on the table? Their feet are not clean, just horrible and filfy. They put their paws in dirt.

But they cannot help it, if they had shoes.

My maw did not like pets. A big boy called Derek had a dog and let me clap it. Its hair was long and it was stuck together. But it was hard when ye clapped it and was just looking at ye, what were ye doing, if ye were doing something to it oh mammy it was just maybe if it would bite ye. Dogs would bite ye. If it was your dog and ye said it, Go boy, bite him.

I wanted a dog so if people were going to hit ye or yer da or yer uncle they would soon find out. And ye would never be feared. Never ever. Ye just set it on them, Go boy, bite them. Then if it was Papes and they were chasing ye. So ye just got yer dog. I would take mine to school and show my pals. Ye would just tell it to sit, or else roll over, or if ye threw a ball for it to catch and just said, Stay, stay!

§

Me and a boy were looking at our w★★★★es in the back close and his maw came up the stair and caught us. Oh yous will go to Hell. She shouted at me, Oh you dirty dirty boy, you dirty little pig, and got my arm and twisted it a wee bit. The other boy was shouting. No mammy no mammy no mammy.

She skelped him and took him up the stair and locked him in the house and took me straight round to mine's. I was trying to push her hand away, she was holding me tight. Oh you dirty wee pig, that is what you are, just a dirty wee pig.

My maw was home. She would give me a doing. I was greeting. The woman took me straight up the stair and gived me in to my maw and said things to her dirty and bad words and my maw grabbed me and hit me and was the worst angry she had ever been and a brush was there and she got it and was hitting me with it, hitting my head and my ears and the brush hit my nose and hit my cheeks. Oh when your father comes home! Oh just the worst doing ever you will get my boy!

She was shouting all things at me and shaking me too and when she hit me the brush bounced off my head. It broke, it fell out her hand. Oh my wrist!

She went to pick it up and was pulling me and my head banged into the table, then I was on the floor. It was the worst doing. Then I was in bed. I was not sleeping. It was not nighttime. People were out playing, I heard them shouting. My maw came into the room and was looking at me. I was turned into the wall. She was just there. I knew she was because her breathing, I knew how it sounded. My throat was sore because I was greeting. I just did not care about her, if she was going to hit me or what, I did not care about her. She went away.

My big brother came to bed. It was nighttime. He went onto his side away from me. He knew I was awake. Kieron, what did mum give ye the doing for? Were ye doing dirty things? Eh, Kieron, what did ye do?

But I did not speak to him. I did not turn round. I did not care about him asking me. I was not going to speak to him and not anybody in my house. I did not care about them. Not in that house. It was just the worst house. I hated it, it was just a horrible house and I wanted to go to another one, I had to go to it. If my grannie could take me. Her and granda would like me, if I could go there and just stay with them.

People had better houses. My grannie's house was so much better. Ye could just sit down. My granda read the paper and grannie was doing things and if I had a book I just read it or else sat at the fire and looked into it, the coals burning and ye saw all the caves and ye could imagine how if it was not hot and ye were wee and ye could go inside it and get inside the caves, and the white flaky ash, watching when it fell. Ye could just sit and look into it and it was great. Except Mattie came.

I was there and it was great and then a flap at the letterbox and it was him, I knew it was. I did not want him to come and did not open the door when my grannie told me. I did not like him coming, just when I was there myself. My grannie opened it for him. He came in and looked at me. He wanted me to go away. Sometimes I did sometimes I did not. If he told me something, I did not care. I did not like Matt. Other big boys were better, I liked some, and they were good.

If I could go away, I just wanted to. Children ran away, I was going to. I felt sorry for my maw, she was not a good hitter, even with the brush giving me the doing, her hand got it twisted and she hurted her wrist. She had her troubles. Grannie said that, I heard her and how she got all bad moods with my da at sea and how about wages, it was a worry about that, she was worrying oh if he was not sending anything home, my da. My grannie gived her money. She went in her purse and gived it. I was watching. Oh what are you looking at? My maw got grumpy at me. Then if it was my name and she said it, Oh Kieron.

It sounded funny, I heard it in my head how she said it. Oh Kieron. Maybe I was another boy.

§

I was going to sleep and I was awake and just a wee voice. Oh it was Mattie talking. I turned over to see but it was all dark. Oh if we are all on trial and getting tested for true valour, maybe if it is God but maybe no, maybe just intelligences, if they are intelligences. And if ye pass the test for true valour ye will come hither, oh we beseech ye. They would bring ye if it was sure and steadfast and if it was you and ye were worthy, Oh come hither if we beseech ye.

It was Matt and he was saying about it. It was his voice. Sometimes he said stuff and it was in bed. If he talked to me that was when. Maybe if it was books out the library. So if it was intelligences away in outer space and they came down here and if ye passed yer tests something good would happen and ye would get a prize. If it was in the Lifeboys, ye got the lanyard and the white cover for yer hat, how ye did good behaviour. Matt got it. He was in the Lifeboys. There was all games ye played and he told me about them and if they went places for picnics and then on adventures that were just like yer travels but they were just better and ye could go on boats, just like canoes the Indians had. It was just adventures and ye went down rocks and canyons. I would get going too.

Ye were on trial and getting tested. If ye had true valour and were sure and steadfast. If ye did ye got whisked away to a far-off planet. That was yer real home so that was where ye went. And ye maybe were a Prince in yer own country and ye were to get the throne so you would be King.

So ye were a Prince, that was what ye were. It was the same as

Bonnie Prince Charlie who was a RC. We got him at school. I liked him but Mattie said how he was a Pape. The kilties too. They were all Papes. So that was them, if ye were going to fight with them, they were all Fenian bees. That was what Mattie called them. So away and fight for them, if ye wanted to be a Pape, well same with them, and William Wallace too, if ye thought he was a Proddy he was not, he was a Pape. So if he was he was Irish. The Irish were true Papes. So it was the English, that was who ye were if ye were Scottish, that was what Mattie said, ye were just a true Protestant and it was the Redcoats ye liked, if it was true Protestants, ye must be for England. RCs were for Ireland. So if I liked Bonnie Prince Charlie and the kilties then if I was a Pape, I must be one, if I was Irish. I did not care. And if I was a Prince. Maybe I was. I did not care. And if really I was a Pape, or if it was a RC I did not care.

The teacher was reading us a story. She read us it before the bell rang every afternoon. It was about a boy and a lassie and they were adopted and how it was not happy times for them with a wicked stepfather but then their auntie sent for them and they went on a cruiser ship and went to Italy. That was where the auntie lived and she had a house beside a lake and rooms each. The boy had one away up the stairs in the highest place, there was no place higher except Heaven and it was his own wee place and ye could just look out the window and away way down ye saw the big lake with trees and bushes and oh a wee rowing boat ye could go on and just do the oars swoosh swoosh, swoosh, and ye just glided and it was over to the wee island and then just a wee Chapel, and the teacher was showing us pictures and that was what we saw, it was a real Chapel and a Priest was there, Oh my son you have come home.

So if they were Papes. They were. That was their home for the boy and girl and they did not know. So I could be one too. If really I was one. Maybe I was. I just did not know because they had not told me. My maw and my da got me as a Protestant and put me as a Protestant but all the time if I was not one, if I was a real Catholic. Kieron was for Catholics. People said it. I did not care. I would just do all the stuff. If it all was horrible, I did not care.

Oh Kieron is a Pape's name. They said that. Oh ye do not get

Proddies called Kieron. So if it is Irish, you must be Irish. Oh you are a Pape.

Well so I did not care. If it was my maw called me Kieron. I told her what people said. She said not to be daft and that was the end of it. But I asked Mattie and he said I was a Pape, that was what he said, Oh you are a Pape. So then we were fighting but he was just kidding and laughing, and would not fight he would not fight, he was just laughing oh I would kill him I would just kill him if he was laughing at me. I did not want him, if he was a brother, I could get another one, so if he was a RC, I did not care. So if he was my brother. Well, I did not care.

I asked my granda. If I was not a Pape how come I had a Pape's name, it is a Pape's name. So my granda said, It is not a Pape's name.

But if it is to do with Catholics?

Do not be so daft son.

It was not daft. It was not daft. And it was not fair granda saying that. If it was to do with Papes how come they called me it? How come? Except maybe if I was one. I was not daft.

Oh it is nothing to do with Papes, just a name yer mammy wanted to call ye, maybe it is a filmstar or something, ask yer grannie.

My grannie just looked at me. That was what she done, and she breathed deep so ye knew ye were not to say it, what ye were going to say, it was just something and she did not want to hear it.

Only from school, my grannie liked it if I told her stuff that was funny, if lasses were there and playing with us and if things were funny, Oh he pulled her hair and she slapped him on the gub.

Slapped him on the gub! And my grannie would be laughing, Ohh hoh hoh hoh, and my granda too, just laughing, and if I told them more stuff and just made them laugh. Oh the boy is a comic.

But Kieron was not a good-sounding name. Some names were. They were hero-names. Johnnie or Luke or else Jimmy or Danny and a boy was Mac. If ye were Mac ye would be a best fighter. Oh there is Mac, and ye would not be scared of nobody, if they wanted to fight ye, well, you would just fight them. That was Mac.

My da was home on leave and if I stayed out late it was smacks on the b*m and skelps on the head. His hand skliffed up the back of yer head and it was sore. And if it was a right thump and ye went flying.

We were telling creepy stories on the first steps in the close. The light was on but it was quite dark and shadows were there and if ye had to go out the back close to get something oh mammy nobody wanted to. Lasses were there too. The one beside me was Elizabeth Dunlop and if ye saw her eyes looking at ye. Oh what is Kieron saying? She was just listening and her eyes just looking at ye, Oh what is he saying.

Ohhh ohhh they are coming to get ye mammy daddy mammy daddy, and all just laughing.

Oh but if ye were shivering too because what ye were saying and it was creepy so ye were feared to go out, no just the lasses, and it was time to go home, somebody was shouting. Oh Kieron it is you.

Oh if it was yer da. Time for bed and it was doings if ye did not. Whose close was it? Maybe it was away along the street and ye just had to go and oh there was the Chapel too and if a Nun was there and looking at ye oh and the gate was open and what if the door was open and ye got dragged through and it was just all everything there oh it was just even if it was devil monsters. Mattie said about them. And if it was time to go home and it was out the back close ye were going and it was all dark and just the darkest and that was where they were hiding in all the shadow bits oh and the midgie there and in the corners, black hoods over their heads, and getting ye and all just creepy with bones pulling ye and not skin, just all stringy and gripping ye tight and just pulling ye away away.

I ran round the front and just ran ran ran and then into my close but ye were going up the stairs and round the landing and oh if a bad man was there ye thought he might be and him dragging ye down and down into the ground oh and it would be out at the midgie too if there was rats there, that was where they went and ye heard if they were squeaking, squeeeeeeek, oh mammy rats could bite ye and if they chased ye ye just ran ran ran and ye were up the stair and nobody could get ye.

§

I came home from school with all my pals. There was lasses there as well. I said how it was my birthday, Oh we are going to have a party, and my granda had balloons. My grannie opened the door and I brought all them in. Oh what is this?

It is me grannie.

Oh it is you.

My granda was there. His hair was all sticking up and his braces were hanging down. How many is there son is it the whole class ye have brought?

No.

The bedroom door was open and so was the door into the lobby cupboard. My pals all were looking to see what things were there and oh there was the lavatory door opened and they were looking in, if there was a smell and granda was there. They were going ben the kitchen and my grannie had a loud voice. Oh no, do not go in there, do not go in there!

She took them to the parlour and went away herself to the kitchen.

Their house was very high up and I was showing my pals out the window and how if ye looked way way to the side ye would see the park just at the edge near where the library was. That was the library there and then too ye could see the wee chip shop way far along. And if ye opened the window and leaned out ye would see how the Church was there, where ye would go to the Lifeboys. I was joining. My big brother was taking me.

My pals were going to go as well but no the lasses, they had the Brownies. They were going to them and did not want to go the Lifeboys. They said that. Oh we want to go to the Brownies.

My granda came ben now and he was all washed. Oh close the window Kieron son. Oh everybody all just sit down on the floor. Now are ye all in the same class? Who is good at their sums and who is good at their reading?

He said if they were all doing their lessons and what was their names, Oh that is a nice name.

And what team did they support, if anybody supported the Celtic. Two boys did. My granda was laughing. Oh who was good players, did anybody go in for the boxing? I put my hand up.

Oh I know about you.

When it was the lasses he said, And what is your name hen, where does your daddy work? Oh it is the shipyards.

My grannie came and gived them all a piece and jam and cups of water then I was to bring them back out to the street and play a game.

It was not my birthday at all. My grannie said it. Oh you are a fly wee besom.

§

My grannie and granda lived across the back. From their house ye could see my kitchen window. My granda showed me. He saw me at the window and waved to me. That was what he said. But I could not see him.

Oh ye were there.

Oh I did not see you granda.

Oh ye were not looking, if ye need specs, maybe ye do.

Did he stand at the window or was it farther back. What was I doing when he saw me? The sink was at the kitchen window. If I was washing my hands or if I was getting my hair washed. My maw did it there and the water went down my neck, and if my head bumped off the taps or else the cold water came out by mistake and went all over my head into my ear and down my neck. Aaahhh. Maw! She did not like me calling her maw and never to say mammy. Mammy was the worst. Mum or mummy was the best. The same for heid. Oh mum you banged my heid! It is not heid it is head.

She always banged it. Ye just had to kid on it did not happen. And the edge of the taps was sharp and could cut ye. After yer hair got washed ye looked in the mirror to see and ye were all soaked.

Oh you are a drowned cat. That was what she said.

But she did not like cats. My grannie and granda had two cats and my maw had cats when she was wee but she still did not like them. Oh they are dirty and all fleas.

I would have liked a dog. I was not feared of them. A big boy called Derek had one and I clapped it. If he was going to the park he let me come and I could take the leash then in the park he took the dog off the leash oh and away it ran and oh just ran about everywhere and ye threw things and it ran after them. But if people were running it ran after them and Derek shouted at it. And if it was boys playing football, the dog ran to catch their ball, but it could not go in its mouth, lucky for them.

We played football in school. Matt went early to play before the bell rang. I was too wee to play but if wee boys were there we could play, if we had a ball. Ye were tired and sat at yer desk with sore legs and feet. At playtime ye were not to go out the school gate but ye could get a game in the playground. If the ball went over the big railing ye had to climb over or else skip through the gate if a teacher was not there or the jannie. The balls were wee and they could burst. We played on with a burst ball, it skliffed across the ground, and was sore if it hit ye on the ankle. Some of the big boys picked it up and threw it and it hit ye.

I burst my shoes when I was chasing the ball and kicking it. My maw was angry and gived a letter to my teacher. My teacher read it and went away out the classroom and when she came back she did not look at me and was angry. She did not like me because of what my maw wrote. I told my maw and she sat down on a chair, and she was angry.

The playground was up high and with a high fence, and barbed wire at the top to stop ye climbing over. The big boys could get up to the top. If the ball got kicked over the fence and landed way down below it was a bakery and there was men there and they kicked it back but sometimes they did not. The smells of baking came into our classrooms and we were starving, it was bread. When ye climbed the high fence ye could see all loafs, stacks and stacks. They were on wooden boards and the men were putting them into vans.

§

It was me got the bad doings in our house except one time Matt got one. Him and his pals were away knocking and the cops got them and took them home in the cop-car. There was a loud chap at the door and it was me opened it. Oh it was big cops there. They came right in the lobby. Oh where is yer mammy son?

Oh but she was not in, tough luck for Mattie it was just my da, he was home on leave and he just came out with a angry face. The cops told him stuff. It was not good. My da was talking to the cops. Matt started greeting. He was just greeting loud and the big cops were looking. They were just going to go away now and what was going to happen. Oh it is out of our hands Mr Smith, saying that to my da.

The cops went away. And here my da saw me, Oh what are you doing here away to yer room!

But I was not doing nothing except just there, I opened the door and the cops were there. Oh away to yer room.

I did but my door was open and I heard. Matt gret louder, if he was going to get a doing. Oh and he was, he did. My da was talking and then he stopped and Matt was going, No daddy no daddy no daddy.

And ye knew what he was doing, just getting Matt and holding him so he could not get away and just whack whack whack.

When my da gived me a doing he always talked but here with Matt he was not. With me he was skelping and talking and if I jumped away he caught me. Oh how many times have I telled ye and oh skelp skelp skelp. But do you ever listen? no, skelp skelp, you just never never listen, skelp.

But no here. And Mattie was shouting, No daddy no daddy no daddy no daddy, and my da was just smack – smack – smack – smack.

Matt never got hit hardly at all so now he was. It was a bad one and I did not like it and just hearing him, it was awful and I did not want to hear him, no greeting like that. It felt funny in my stomach. What was my da saying? His voice was too far.

Where was my maw? She was at her work.

I felt sorry for Mattie but I could not say anything to him, he would not let me, he just went to his bed. It was maybe half past seven.

I went into the living room where my da was reading the paper. He was sitting on his chair and smoking a fag and his face was all red. He did not look to me but he saw me.

I just took down the cushion and sat where I sat at the side of the couch, no far from the telly, that was where I used to sit, if he forgot I was there and maybe was speaking to my maw and saying stuff, ye just listened but he did not like ye doing it. Oh go to bed. But this time he did not say it.

It went on and on not speaking. I got up and went to the door. My da was looking at his paper, his feet under him. He had a angry face. I went away out the room. But there was no place to go, so I just went to my bed but Matt did not want me, I knew he did not and he was just lying and if he was sleeping, I do not think he was. It was a hard doing and I heard low down in his body, hoh, hoh, hoh, hoh, and if maybe it was just if he was still greeting or just breathing. He was not sleeping, he was awake and just thinking about stuff, if he wanted to run away, he must have, that was what I wanted if I got doings, I got a lot of doings. He did not so just it made it worse.

§

People all supported Rangers. Their pitch was away up the road and along. On Saturday ye heard big big roars coming, Ohhhhh, Ohhhhh, so a goal was scored. Two boys out my class were going to see them. Terry and Ian. I went too. Terry's big cousin was taking us. He did not know me and Ian were coming as well and looked angry at Terry. It was just you to come!

But me and Ian just went and he let us.

It was a long walk and ye had to go where there were gangs against ye. They were midgierakers and were Papes. They had sacks and went round people's midgies looking for lucks. If they came down our street ye shouted, Midgierakers Midgierakers. My da said how one had a Yankee motor car and was a millionaire. We went through their place to go to the Rangers. There was all men walking and ye walked beside them. The boys that stayed there just looked. If ye were not with the men they jumped ye. They were tough fighters and ye did not want to get caught.

Coming out of there ye passed a wee football park where a wee team played. It was beside a railway line. Ye could look down at them playing football when ye passed over the railway bridge. Ye could skip in to watch their game. Ye climbed down a wee hill and across the railway tracks and up the other side and through the fence or else under it.

There was not a way in like that for the Glasgow Rangers. It was big big walls, cops on horses. Big railings and high gates. Ye could have climbed them, but the cops would see ye. So ye could not get in except if ye had money to pay at the turnstiles or else got a man to lift ye over. That was how me and my pals were getting in. Terry's big cousin was telling us but I knew because my Uncle Billy said it. He done it when he was wee. And that was what he said, Oh you just do that and ye will get in.

It was the biggest biggest crowd, all men there and boys too and then cops and some were on their horses, big big horses that came close up to ye and ye had to watch out for their feet kicking ye. If ye fell under their belly, that was you and ye got trampled to death.

The horses just done the toilet when they were standing there. It just came out and ye had to watch it. Ye saw the s***e on their tails and b*ms. It was funny looking and people all were laughing.

We were waiting there and Terry's big cousin shoved me. You go over to that f*****g queue.

I did not want to but he said I had to. He shoved Ian to go to another one. It was all queues and all men waiting in long long lines and all going inside the wee gates, it was turnstiles. Then boys were getting lifted over. I saw it. Ye just went to the front and men would lift ye. Terry's big cousin told us. Ye were just to watch for the cops and if the serjeant was there. Oh mister, going to lift us over?

I knew what to say and if men just laughed and did not do it. Oh away ye go son. But if one gived ye a wink so ye were just to stand there beside him and then just nearer and nearer, nearer and nearer. Some men had beer and the smell blew over ye. Oh Mr I have lost my money, can ye lend me any?

If he was a drunk man sometimes he gived ye money or else just laughed at ye, Cheeky wee b*****d.

Cops got angry. They had red faces. Boys were getting lifted over and it was beside them. One cop was swearing. Do not come the c**t! There is the serjeant.

Ye were hoping they would not look to see. If ye were faraway they let the man lift ye but then if they shouted, Hoy you stop that, and chased all the boys away.

When they done that the men all laughed and went, Boooo.

Some big boys screwed up bits of silver paper and flicked them at the horses' b*ms and one shouted, Stick a pin up its a**e.

So if ye done it what would happen? The horse had a very big b*m and maybe would not even feel it or else if it did and was a bucking bronco so the cop fell off.

All men were saying bad words and so were the boys. And the cops too, if ye came too near the horses. Get out the f*****g road!

If it was just wee boys they got lifted easy. But if it was too big a boy the cops waved their hand so the man had to stop or else it was hard for the man to lift him over the gate. Some men were wee so when ye were in mid air their arms were high up holding ye and ye had to walk yer feet over the gate. The man taking in the money could not stop ye because he was in the cubicle and could not come out. But if he was angry at ye and shouting at the man, Oh what are you playing at! Do you think I am a mug? I am getting the f*****g polis!

The man lifting ye over was angry back at him. Aw shut yer f*****g mouth he is just a boy.

I will put you out as well you f*****g b*****d ye.

Just f*****g try it.

F**k you.

Oh f**k you.

I will come round there and batter yer f*****g c**t in!

Away and f**k yerself.

And ye were getting nearer and nearer and people all shoving then it was you and the man taking ye just winked and if it was a big man it was just wheeeecchh and that was you, ye were over and jumping down the other side. Ye had to watch it so ye did not fall back or else yer head got banged on the gate or the brick wall. So ye were on the ground and ye just ran round and jooked through the men going up the stairs, some walking, some running, and if ye got into there nobody could get ye.

I was looking to see Ian and Terry and the big cousin but they were not there. I waited a long time. Maybe if the cops came and got them. I waited and waited. Everywhere it was all men and big boys, all crowding and going fast. If the game was going to start, it was, men were saying. So then I just walked in with them and was just going along and on up the steps and ye could not stop even if ye wanted. And the steps up were steep as steep and men were hurrying up and if ye were too slow, Oh get out the road. Oh for f**k sake look where ye are going!

I was watching down at my feet because if I tripped and fell, so I did not fall, and I saw three pennies there on the ground and tried to get them but the men were pushing ye and ye had to walk on, ye could not stop. Other boys were there. I saw them. They were getting stuff, empty bottles and dowps to smoke, getting matches off men to light them. Boys had bags, and that was for the bottles. Their bags had all empty bottles and they would get money back on them. They were just picking up all the bottles and it was money back. How many bottles did they have? Just piles of them. But if you were there and took them they would batter ye.

I was at the top of the stairs and the best thing when ye looked down, just the best ever, seeing the pitch, oh and it was away way far below, just all the green grass and the lines round it and then the goals and the nets all just there and the best ever ye could think. Men were shouting and bawling. Then the biggest roar. They were coming out. The players all were coming out. I could not see. If it was them, if it was the Glasgow Rangers. People all were cheering. Oh come away the boys!

I was having to jump up to see. And I did, and it was not boys just men! People were saying boys but they all were men. Big ones and wee ones, and some had baldy heads. Their blue jerseys and white shorts and their thick socks all pulled up to their knees and them just jumping up and down, slapping their hands.

The other team was just quiet and looking down at the grass. They were skinny and if they could not fight, maybe they could not, they were so just skinny, that was what I thought.

People all were singing now, more and more, and shouting, Oh oh oh and all what they were singing, all the words and ye just felt the best ever ye could feel and with them all being there, just everybody, crowds and crowds, all different and all the boys too, oh just it was everybody, that was what ye felt, it was just the greatest of all. And ye were just laughing, ye could not stop laughing and then oh it was shivering too if that other team wanted a fight well we would give them it, anytime, anyplace we would fight them fight them fight them, oooohhhhhh till the day is done we would and just fight them and never never surrender, we would never do that if it was dirty Fenian b★★★★★ds, well it was just them and if they wanted their go we would give them it till the day is done, we would just follow on and never surrender if it was up to our knees and that was their blood we never ever would surrender if we were ever cowards, we would never be, never ever.

It just made ye angry, if they thought that, if we would be cowards oh we would never be cowards, and it was just everybody, oh who wants to fight us because ye shall die, we will kill yez all we will never give in, never, never never, never shall there even be one to give in. We would die first and all people were with us if it was big boys and men and who else just if they were there, and everybody if it was the wee boys it was just everybody there and all helping and you would be beside them all and yer pals too if they were there and it was for King Billy too and if it was for the Gracious Queen oh against the Rebels if we are, oh we are, if we are, oh we are. So what is the cry? a man was shouting, Oh and we were all shouting back, The cry is No Surrender, No Surrender or ye will die.

It was for our hearts and shields, we would never surrender. If they wanted to beat us they just could not, if it was all the Papes and Fenians and they were wanting to fight us well we would just fight them back. Who did they think they were? If it was just Papes, if they were going to fight ye, ye would just fight them back. We would not be feared of them, we would just kill them if it was all Rebels, if they were going to get us, they were not going to get us, they were just a Papish crew and were cowards.

Ohhh.

A man was pushing my shoulder. Stop f*****g kicking.

I am no kicking.

Ye are f*****g kicking me you silly wee c**t.

Oh he is just a boy.

Well tell him to stop f*****g kicking me!

He is not mine, I do not know him. Son, who are ye with?

I did not tell him but just went away along and was jumping up to see to the pitch down over the heads. I loved seeing the pitch, all the grass and muddy bits where the goalie was and in the middle line at the centre circle, and ye could see where to go with the ball and how ye would be running if the men were chasing ye they just would not get ye because ye were a quick quick runner and would just jink about if ye had the ball and ye were kicking it good and could score a goal into the net and the goalie could not catch it, a big grown-up man and he had a cap on and he was diving to save it but yer kick was just hard and ye scored the goal and they could not catch ye ye were just running and jumping over the wall and then away up fast out the road so the cops would not get ye.

Everybody was all singing, and ones were jumping up and waving their arms and punching, oh it was big punching and oh the men's faces all angry angry oh for the Fenian b★★★★★ds oh for the Fenian b★★★★★ds. Celtic would know about their troubles, we would fight them fight them fight them, till the day is done, oh if they thought we would be beat by them, we never would be beat, no by them, never never never, no against them and all the Irish and the Papes, never never never, if we would ever surrender, never never, we would always guard against them, we would just chase them away and they could just go back to Dublin and we would follow on, if they were just running away, not staying to fight and we were the bravest Protestant Boys, we would fight to the death, we would just kill them because if they hung themself oh for the Sash well we just would wear the Sash too if it was for our fathers and King Billy and then if it was the Gracious Queen, we would fight till our dying day. Oh and they were playing. The game had started. A man was chasing the ball, it went out for a shy. A man beside me was smoking and it was going in my face. He was smoking it fast and laughing and what he said, Follow follow, and a man beside him was just looking and he said it, Follow follow, and then he spat down on the ground and did not watch for people's feet.

It was hard to move and the men were going up and down and up and down and it was steps so ye had to watch it ye were going back with them, and yer knees were bending and heels hitting men's feet and then if ye were falling forward and ye just caught on a man and a man was saying that, Oh watch for the wean, watch for the wean.

And it was me.

Oh where is yer da son? The man said it to me and was grumpy. Is yer da here?

No.

Oh ye better go down the front.

And he pushed me out to where there was a walk down all the steps down to a wee white wall. Boys were standing and ye could get in there, squeezing in but one saying, Heh you watch it, if I was shoving him but I was not, I was not meaning to, I was just getting in. Then people all were pushing and a man was angry and shouting, Oh for f**k sake ye are crushing us! It is weans here, watch the weans.

They were crushing into us and yer knees were against the wall and ye were shoving back. I was looking to see Terry and Ian but they were not there. The ball came. It was kicked high and was coming over our heads. Ohhhh and people all were cheering.

One man was getting the ball now to take the shy oh and his thick thick legs and all the men too how their legs were just the thickest, if ye got a kick off them they would just kick ye up in the air. And the one taking the shy was giving deep breaths, and going now taking aim and oh throwing the ball. And he done it far and then was chasing after it and so were all them.

§

I was out a message and a big boy grabbed me. He got me down and his young brother was there. Oh that is him.

The wee brother said that.

I did not know who they were. The big brother kneeled down on my arms so I could not move. I was trying to wrestle him off but I could not and was throwing my chest up and shouting. It was the worst dirty fighting. His hand now over my mouth and I was smothering, could not breathe, rolling about and he punched my stomach. Get that Get that, shouting to his young brother.

It was a big boulder, a right jaggy one, wee bits sticking out. The big brother pressed his knees down hard on my arms and then back holding my legs and I was trying to push him off and twisting my head and he slapped me on my face at my ear. I am warning ye, you stay away from my young brother, ever hit him again and I will kill ye.

But I did not know the young brother and he was there with the boulder in his two hands gripping it, holding it to his chin, getting my face in full view and taking aim and then he dropped it and it was full force how he done it, landing it on my nose and face and there was blood all over, my nose burst. They ran away and I got along the street, where I was, I cannot mind, through a back and up the stairs to the house and my grannie and granda were there and my grannie took me out and along the road and slow slow, Oh careful son careful, holding my nose. Oh hold it together if it is broke and it moves oh the broke bits would come out the skin.

So if she did not hold them right, my nose would be in a bad state forever and she was holding my nose and taking me on the street and way way along by the picture-house and the park and away way to the hospital.

The nurse was there. Who done it son?

I did not know. I had not seen the boy before. If he went to my school, I did not know, maybe he mixed me up. If he was in a gang from another street. There were battles with people in other streets. But ye did not know who they were, if it was one face, ye were just fighting and running or if ye were tossing stones or what. I had never seen that wee boy. He did not go to my school. If he was a Pape, maybe he was.

My nose got stitches sewn in by the doctors and was twisted up with a dent at the side and bandages were on it and a thing not to make it worse. People were laughing. Oh you are a real boxer.

Oh do not worry, said the nurse. The doctors said it would heal up because my grannie did a good job, she was the one that did it. People would just think I was a boxer.

That was right and my granda said it too. He was sitting in my house when me and my grannie came in. My maw was onto her feet and seeing my nose. Oh my oh no oh no. And she was grumpy and poking at it. Oh why do you have to fight Kieron. Why do you always have to fight. Then she was cuddling me but banged the bandages a wee bit.

Aahh mum.

Oh Kieron I am sorry.

The boy is scarred for life, said my grannie. The stitches leave a mark.

Oh it is only a wee mark, said my granda.

His nose is bashed and twisted, said my grannie. The wee soul, look at him!

Oh no. My maw cuddled me again. Oh I hate all this fighting why do ye have to do it. I am just fed up with it. It is not fair. Oh Kieron.

Mum it was boys done it to me, I was not fighting.

Who did it? said Mattie.

I did not speak back to him. I did not look at him. He said it again to me, Who did it? I did not want to speak to him. He never stuck up for me but just punched me. I did not care about him.

Oh living here is horrible, said my maw.

My granda was looking at her.

Oh but dad, it is.

It is no use talking to him, said my grannie.

No because my brains are scrambled listening to you all day.

Your brains are just scrambled. Imagine marrying you, I must have been thick.

No as thick as me.

Oh you are thick. Just look at that boy.

They all looked at me.

It is not my fault, said my granda.

Yes it is, said my grannie, you and yer stupid boxing. Oh what a nose! Look at the wee soul!

Oh wait till his father hears, said my maw.

Oh well son now ye are a real boxer.

My granda said how ye would never feel sorry for a real boxer, except if he got injuries to his head and passed away in hospital. That happened to a boxer and my granda was watching, it was maybe a punch to the side neck or above his ear, if it was a foul blow, maybe it was. My granda said it was but the referee was cheating and kidded on he did not see it. Then the other one that was the dirty boxer, he just hit the boy again oh just the hardest and how his knees just were jelly and ye saw his head spinning on his neck. Ye could see it just where ye were sitting. It just spun round so it went off his spine, and that was him.

Oh dad, dad. That was my grannie saying it, dad. She said that to my granda, Oh dad, shut up with that nonsense.

It is not nonsense Vera.

Hohhh, and my grannie just breathed hard and looked at my maw with her eyes big.

There was a place where they had boxing matches and my granda went. He did not go now but when he got better he was going to take me. It was not faraway and was always busy. Ye were lucky to get a seat but he knew the people and could get seats just whenever he liked.

My brother said if he could come as well. He liked boxing.

Oh but my maw was angry. For Heaven sake dad have you not had enough fighting? Look at him! Just look at him! Oh Kieron why do you have to fight fight fight?

It was not me that was fighting but I did not say it. If one person was fighting the other person was, that was what she thought.

But if somebody shoved ye and ye were just walking. So if that was fighting, that was not fighting. Or if they just kicked ye. Ye were walking past and they did it. You did not do anything to them.

My maw was making toast but I did not want any, just bed. My grannie and granda went away home.

Mattie came the same time as me. Who was it that did it, if I knew who it was. I did not talk. I was thinking who it was and all what else I was thinking, oh I did not want to talk to Mattie. No. And I was not, I did not want to. He said, Oh if ever ye see him tell me.

Big brothers went after ones if they battered their young brothers. Maybe if Mattie would. Maybe he would.

If I ever saw that big brother again. Big brothers stick up for the wee ones. I was thinking of his face but could not see it right. He was just looking down at me, gripping me and doing all what anything, I just could not move, I could not move and his wee brother there, Oh just get it, and he would just drop it, just a jaggy boulder, if it was coming on my nose, I could not stop it and do anything.

I did not see faces right. If it was my da, if it was his face. I thought about him and he was sitting at the table. Oh you stop that, angry voices and just grumpy, Oh away to yer bed. I could not see his face.

My nose was sore and it was a funny sore how it went, if everything came out it and just was nothing left and was only a bone, if I took off the bandage, my nose would all be white and people would just laugh, they would. But if I went on my side it was another way it was sore and I did not do it. Matt was away to sleep. I was glad and shifted to the very very edge, if his feet touched, I did not want to touch them, I did not want him and anybody.

§

A big boy showed me how to make hatchets. I liked making them. When ye were fighting gangs ye had them for close-in fighting. Ye got tin cans out the midgies and then wooden sticks. Ye bashed the tin down with a boulder then put in the stick and bashed it down again till it was stuck. Ye tried to get good ragged edges. A big boy said, Oh your hatchets are good. He said they were tomahawks. Oh Kieron makes good tomahawks.

I planked them round the side of the midgie. A big boy wanted one. I gived him it. It had a right raggedy edge and was good. He took it and split a boy's head open. It stuck in his scalp. Somebody pulled it out and the blood soaked all his hair. His hair was soaked with it. All black and flat to his head but then at the other side his hair was sticking up and ye saw it red.

Oh if the cops were coming, somebody said they were, and if they got me, I was thinking that, oh because I got the hatchet.

People all were talking how it was going to be a big fight. Oh it was a pitched fight, if it was pitched, a pitched fight. Their gang would come and ours would be there and then ye would just be fighting.

And if they had knives too, their gang had all knives and people were going to get chibbed. So if we had knives we could get them or just if it was hatchets. Big boys were saying how their das had hammers and if they could get them or else screwdrivers for stabbing. Mattie was there and he was looking at me, if I was going to tell or what was I going to do. Other wee boys were there and we were just waiting, what to do, Oh make hatchets.

The gang was coming. I told boys in my class. They were in gangs too and if it was their gang coming to fight ours. They did not know.

But a gang did come and we got all stones. I did not know these boys. A lot of them was there. They chased us and we were all in a close and could not get out. They were at the front and firing in at us and we were diving up the stairs, the stones firing off the walls and hitting into our ankles. We rushed out the back but ones were waiting there and pelted us. They had a lot of boys oh and were just firing in at us and a woman's window got smashed in and a pram got hit and the cops all were coming.

Men came and were shouting at us. If stones were hitting motor cars. They did. People did not care. A man was running to get us, he was a bus driver. The stones hit his bus and he jumped out and came after us but boys were flinging stones at him so he ran into a close and just looked out. So then the cops came and chased us. But it was just the big boys they chased. They all ran through the close and over the dykes to get away. The wee ones were just standing there and the cops passed by giving ye looks but that was all and ye just stood there because ye were wee. What were ye fighting for? The cop said it to us.

It was gangs, that was what we said, they came to get us so we were just fighting them back. My big brother was there and he got away. How he done it, when the cops were chasing him, he just walked up the stairs and the cops did not get him, they did not go up the stair, they just ran through the back close. If the cop said, Oh where is yer big brother, and if I said where he was they would have got him and took him to jail and if they gived him a right kicking. They would. Lucky for him I did not tell them.

Mattie was angry. Oh shut yer mouth.

Oh but I could if I wanted.

Well if ye did I would batter ye.

Well I do not care.

You are just a wee cliping little pig.

I am not.

Well if ye tell the cops.

I am not going to, I just said if I did.

Oh shut up.

§

Matt went to Church for Sunday School. He had to for the Life-boys. Mr Simpson was the teacher. He came from the posh houses near the park. My da called him skinny malinky Simpson big banana feet. Oh he is not Mr Simpson he is Mr Sampson, the strongest man in the world. See his arms. His arms are just pipe-cleaners but his feet are just bananas, the biggest bananas in the world. Oh he is big but just if the wind rises, Oh a man is down, a man is down Mr, I hope you did not huff and puff.

My da talked funny about people. He done it about all what was at sea, it was stories. He done it in funny voices and if he was at the pub. We would be eating our tea and he would say it and we were all laughing. Oh if it was the Cape of Good Hope, if they call it the Cape of Good Hope? So how come? and it would be a joke and all laughing.

Spit came out yer mouth and went on people's food. Oh if you are spitting in my food, oh be careful if you are spluttering. My da would push yer shoulder, Oh look at him.

But he would just be laughing and so would we all, and if it was darkies. My da saw all darkies, and chinkies too, they all were there and just all what they were doing, even if they fell in the water, Oh I am velee solee, and how all what they done and if they did not eat stuff, Oh I eat this I eat that I do not eat yours.

Aye well ye b****y better no eat mine's.

My maw would be laughing but she did not like him saying the bad word and she would look at me and Matt. Oh you will not do it, it is just your father.

They eat all porcupine pie and snakes wrapped in sausage rolls and for mince they eat all maggots and dead flies. For fish, any kind of fish, they mash up their bones and eat that too. Everything in the fish, they just eat it and if it was a white man ye would just be Ohhhh my stomach is sore-looking.

The ship's cook just gived them wee plates of food but if it was you ye got big plates. So if they saw the food. Oh he has got big food we do not.

Oh you are just a cannibal, you only want heads and arms chopped up in soup. So then if the men spat in their food. Oh watch the darkie eating the food and it was mixed in their gravy.

My maw did not like him saying it and put her fingers in her ears, her eyes were shut. I am not listening I am not listening I am not listening. Oh do not say that Johnnie it is just horrible and disgusting.

Well if it is true.

I do not care, do not say it.

Oh but

Oh do not say it, not with the boys.

My da would look at Matt and just a wee smile. If he looked at me. He did look at me. If I did not know what was he saying. Oh did ye get it son?

Sometimes ye did not get it, ye just saw him and he gave a wee laugh and ye knew what it was. So you were laughing too. And he said it to ye. Oh ye like that one, he likes that one, pointing his finger at ye.

And Matt would be laughing.

But if it was grannie, saying jokes about her. How come? That was what he done. Even she was swimming, Oh she is like a swan.

And he did a swim with his arms and how grannie kept her head straight in the water. My maw heard him and did not like it. Oh but she does not want the water on her hair.

Well how come she goes to the baths! My da laughing. If she had an umbrella, then she could swim with the umbrella.

Then if you were laughing, maybe ye were. He said it and it was funny, but I did not like laughing. If it was yer grannie and ye were laughing about her. She took me swimming. She was a best swimmer, my granda said it, and she was a past champion. I would stick up for my grannie. How come my da said things about her? He just did.

He never went much to her house. She was my maw's mother and he had his own one. If my da liked her the best. She was my other grannie, Grannie Petrie Smith. She stayed in Dunfermline and did not come to Glasgow. Oh they are all sinners, they are thieves and murderers, they will cut yer throat. That was what she said if it was Glasgow people, Oh they are just keelies.

She stayed in the same house as my big cousins and my Uncle Eric and Auntie Maureen. It was an upstairs-downstairs house and had a garden round the front and round the back. The back bit had a shed with all stuff inside it. They were quite rich.

My big cousins were lasses. I liked their voices. Oh ye do this ken. Oh if ye ken this. We did not see them except at holidays, we went on the train to visit. Sometimes it was two trains.

Grannie Petrie Smith had bad feet and if ye were going to kick them, oh she was always worried, Oh my feet my feet. So if ye were running past, Oh watch my feet watch my feet, and she poked ye with a stick.

Grannie Petrie Smith had the worst name. Oh I am not an apple I am not an apple. Oh you have not to call me Grannie Smith but just Grannie Petrie Smith.

Petrie was her name before she got married to Smith. Smith was my da's da and passed away when my da was a wee boy. He was my other granda. So we were Smiths from him. Auntie Maureen said how me and Mattie would have liked him but Uncle Eric said, Oh ye would not, he was just a crabbit old b****r.

She did not like ye if ye were noisy, if ye were talking, she did not like ye doing it, if it was too loud. Oh he is too noisy, oh tell him to be quiet. Oh he is just a wee keelie.

She did not like my name. Oh is it Kierrunn? Oh you must be O'Malley and McGlinchey or if it was Kelly and Reilly. Oh is it Kierunnn you must be O'Reilly. Oh if you are Oirish you are from Rome, oh if you are a Roman Catholic.

Oh and if she poked ye with the stick and ye said it to her, Oh Grannie that is sore, she just went, Aww graaaaanie. Oh you wee Glesgie keelie.

My da was laughing.

But my maw had a big red face. She was giving angry looks to me. And it was how I was talking. Oh you do not say this you say that. If you are talking to people you are to say this and not that oh it is just a showing-up if you speak like that, it is not awww graaaanie it is oh grannie, listen to your brother.

I looked for Matt but he was not there. He went with my big cousins, they had a room up the stairs and had records.

Please may I go out to play?

Yes you may.

Ye had to say it like that when my da was there. So if ye were at the table at teatime and finished yer food. Oh please may I leave the table please can I go out to play?

Grannie Petrie Smith was like a witch ye saw in books and her face too, it was like it except she was old old. She was older than a witch, she was just a real witch. I said it to my big cousins and they were laughing. Matt was there. They were out in the garden. I went looking for them and that was where they were beside the shed in the garden. They just talked and Mattie was listening. Grannie Petrie Smith was a moaner and did not like if they were putting their music on. Oh thump thump thump, thump thump thump.

But she did not poke them with her stick. And she did not poke Matt. Oh she pokes me, I said.

It is just your face, said Matt.

Well you are her favourite.

Oh shut up.

Well she likes you the best.

She did like him the best. I did not care. I did not like her. I said to my big cousins about our other grannie that stayed in Glasgow. But she was not their grannie. They had their own one and she lived in Fife. She could not walk and was in a chair. They had all uncles and aunties living there, and a lot of cousins that were boys. I wanted to see them. Mattie said, Oh they are not your cousins.

Well if we just visited them.

But it is not our family.

But if they did not have any cousins that were boys maybe they would want us. If we just visited them. I would visit them. It would be great. Ye would just get the train. What was their name? I did not know their name. Even just ye were pals. We could go their pals. Maybe they did not have pals.

I would have loved cousins, and if they were in Glasgow. People in my class had all cousins, and some were best fighters and ye could just say Oh he is my cousin, so then he would stick up for ye if ye were having a fight.

Uncle Billy and Auntie May did not have children. That would have been our cousins. We only had cousins off my da. He was my big cousins' uncle. They liked him. Uncle Johnnie, that was my da.

They had their maw, my Auntie Maureen, she was his sister. Our grannie was the same, Grannie Petrie Smith. They had to call her that as well. My big cousins were talking about it then they went away. Matt was away too. I was looking for him out the back and front. Weer lasses were playing skipping ropes. I just was watching then came in the house. I needed the lavvy but the lavvy door was locked. Grannie Petrie Smith was in. I heard the coughing and knew it was her so I went ben the parlour. My maw and da were there but, I heard them outside the door. My maw talked funny, and a quiet voice. Oh but my da was just angry and ye could hear it oh and angry to my maw. Then he looked and saw me. Oh what are you doing? Are you listening behind doors? What are you doing? What – Are – You – Doing?

My stomach was just sore and I was rubbing it. But he just reached and skelped me on the leg and I fell down and he waited for me to get up and he skelped me on the b*m.

Oh so you are listening to people's conversations. You wee sneak. Away out and play.

I was greeting. Oh but da I need the toilet I need the toilet.

You are just a wee sneak.

Oh Johnnie, my maw said, do not call him a sneak.

Well he is one, listening to people's conversations. If I catch him doing it again I will give him a good skelp.

So I was greeting. Oh but I was not doing nothing, I was not listening behind doors. I was just needing the lavatory and I was bursting for it.

Oh away out my sight.

I heard the plug getting pulled and Grannie Petrie Smith coming out. I did not want her to see me and just ran out. I hated that house and she was not a real grannie. I went away out and in the back garden and I just stayed in it. Then the wee bushes were there and I saw them. I creeped over and lied down on my side just lying along, and I done the lavvy there on the dirt oh and the pee was on the dirt and coming closer and closer but I was still peeing and some pee went on my leg. It was just the worst. My clothes were dirty and my maw saw them. I went away out the road and just walked about. They did not know where I was and were waiting to go home on the train. My da was just looking at me.

My maw said it in a low voice, Oh Kieron hurry up, where were ye?

I gret. How come? I just started, it was horrible, them all there, my big cousins as well, just looking.

§

Big boys could be bullies and not just if it was brothers. A boy in my street got doings off people and he did not have a brother. He was the same age as me but just wee. Big boys punched him and it was not fair. One time a dog bit him. A boy set it on him. Boys done that. They shouted to their dog Get him boy, and the dog would chase him, or you if it was you.

They flung stones at that wee boy and it was not fair because he had nobody to stick up for him. A big bully hit him with a plank of wood and just laughed. I saw him. The wee boy was greeting and the snotters were coming out his nose. I was thinking if we could get the big bully, maybe we could. We could put him in a sack. Oh and just fling it in the midgie and when the midgie-men came they would take him away, they would put him in the dumps and all the seagulls would come and peck him. I said it to the wee boy that was getting hit, Oh if we grow up, we will just get them and give them a doing.

If I was a big brother I would have stopped that bully. I hated all the bullies. Big brothers were the worst. I just was wanting to hit them, just fight them and oh it was just maybe hitting them.

It was just all the big boys, if we could fight them. We said we were going to and went and got all the wee boys and I went to my grannie's street and up for Terry out my class. Come on out, we are going to fight the big boys.

Terry came. So then we went the next street to get our pal Ian and coming back Michael Lang was there with his pals, Catholics. I saw their faces but did not know them. Oh we will come with ye.

And we all were just laughing and oh just laughing, it just was good. We all came down the street and were picking up good stones. We took them out the back and planked them. Somebody said it to the big boys, if we were going to fight them.

Oh but they were not going to fight us, and they were laughing. Oh away ye go, wee lasses.

I made hatchets and two big big ones ye could swing. Ye just needed long sticks to make them and it was two hands to hold them. Big boys could not get close-in if they were trying to get ye.

We had our hatchets and stones all ready out the back and were waiting. But the big boys did not come, they were out the front kicking a ball about. So we just went to start it. We got their ball and kicked it away down the road. Oh what was that for, cheeky wee b★★★★★ds.

So we flung stones at them so then they got angry and were just, Oh we will f★★★★★g batter yez, you wee c★★ts.

They chased us through the back close and over to the midgie but they were coming too fast and we were just getting chased everyplace. A big boy chased me but I just was able to lift a big hatchet to hit him but it did not work good. He chased me into the midgie but oh the head fell off the hatchet so it was only the stick left. I climbed up the midgie roof to jump up on the dyke but the big boy was catching my feet so I jumped away and there was a good boulder there and I flung it at him and then stepping back because if he was going to get me, but stepping into nothing and straight off the roof and landing smack into the ground crack my head. The big boy was shouting he was going to get me, oh get me oh and his eye was all bleeding, I saw it all and his face all oh looking at me but I was just could not get up oh and my head I could not get up, I was to get up. I could not.

The big boy was there and I was seeing out at him, then up to the sky. Nobody was there. Then voices were there. It was just the sky and if my maw got me and if my da, if she told him, when he came home, he would just get me, he would just oh if he did, he just would.

I was sleeping.

Then there he was, my da, oh it was him, he was not at sea but home on leave.

A boy told Mattie and Mattie told my da and here he was. He kneeled down on the ground to lift me up and carry me, he carried me across the back and up the stair. He was talking to me. Oh Kieron ye are going to be alright, ye will be alright, do not worry do not cry, and other things, I do not know what.

We were in the house. My brother was there. My da was angry at him and then to me, Oh but you are a silly wee fool, oh if ye do not look out, broken noses and oh silly wee fool if you are climbing up on that midden do not ever climb up on that ever again, just never ever ever do it oh if ever I catch you oh it will be so much the worse.

My maw was at her work. My da took me to the hospital and I was walking and Mattie there too.

Oh my da hated waiting. My wee boy's arm is broke. The people all were looking at me oh poor wee boy. But we were just to sit. Oh Mr Smith the nurse is coming.

He hated waiting and it was ages. Ye just had to sit. But out came the nurse to get me. Oh who is this boy, we know this boy, oh his arm is broken. Oh poor Kieron.

And she took me ben the room. Then there was the big boy that I flung the brick at. He was with his maw and sitting beside a stretcher but he was not on it. His head had bandages.

I was into a wee room and the nurse was looking and my da was rubbing my head.

So it was a stookie on my arm. The bone would get better. If it knitted. The bone was knitting. The stookie was round it to keep it straight and if it was straight it knitted. They tied a white sheet in a sling round my shoulder and elbow. I was to keep my elbow in the sling and if I did not the bone would not knit.

When we were walking home my da stopped at the chip shop and got bags of chips. I could not hold mine. I had to just eat out his and Mattie's. Up in the house my grannie and granda were there and I was to write my name on the stookie but it was the wrong hand and I could not write. My da got me to do it, he held my hand with the pen then got my fingers to do it the right way. Everybody was laughing.

Then da and granda wrote their names on it but my maw and my grannie would not. Matt did not want to write his name on it. I would have let him. My da said to do it, so then he did.

Me and him were in the same bed and he was banging my arm. He did not mean it. I woke up with it happening. I was kept off school. My da went back to sea and I went to my grannie's till my maw came home from work. I had books from the library. When I went back to school people wrote their names on the stookie. The lasses laughed. Ones that I liked were there and I wanted them to write their name but they did not.

Yer fingers poked out the plaster but not enough so ye could write. Ye were not supposed to do anything except sit at the desk and listen hard to what the teacher was saying. Ye tried writing with yer left hand. My granda got me to try. Ye gripped the pencil tight but yer fingers could not work it.

I could run but not for playing football. It was too sore. I took my elbow out the sling so my arm was hanging down. My fingers fitted into my trouser pocket but it was too sore.

When the stookie got taken off my arm was skinny, white and blue. Oh it is Rangers. My granda said that.

He showed me exercises. He pushed my fingers back and forward. Then I was to hold his fingers, if I could grip them, just tight as tight then slack then tight then slack. Other things. And holding stones. My granda had special stones and all smooth. He was good at sharpening and he did all knives and scissors. He did it for the women up the close. I saw a woman when I was going up the stair. Oh take this knife to yer granda son.

He had the stone and just rubbed the knife hard and being careful with it. He showed me how to, and it was special stones that were good for it. He kept them in a drawer and I was not to take them out the house. I was to hold them and squeeze them then slack and then squeeze. My grannie said he was not to, it would not be good but he said it would be good and I needed to get back to my drawing. He knew about all exercises because of his training, he did all the training. My grannie said, Oh I will take the boy swimming that is the best thing. You can just come and watch.

Oh I will come.

My granda said that but he did not.

I knew how to swim now and grannie was taking me. I ran up the stairs to get her. Their house was up the top flat. I bent down to see through the letterbox. My granda came to the door. Who is it?

Me.

But he knew it was me, laughing to grannie. Oh there is the boy Vera no escape now.

The swimming baths were the busiest on Saturdays and the noisiest ever ye could get. My grannie gived me a look when she saw all the people. Her eyes went big and from side to side. Oh Kieron, but she did not blame me. She went up the stair to the ladies' changing cubicles and I went to the boys', then was into my trunks and out in the pond swimming about.

But where was she? She still did not come. I swam and swam for ages. If something had happened. I did not know. How come she was not there? I done more swimming, diving down to touch the bottom. I was good at underwater swimming. I learned it before I could swim on the top. Down at the deep end big boys were diving for stuff. They chipped a penny out to the middle then diving off the side and staying underwater till they picked it off the bottom. The men attendants did not bother so all the boys diving, it was great, except ye had to watch out if the penny was too near the deep end because people were diving off the dale, and if they landed on top of ye, their arms would have smashed into ye, if they would break their arms or what if it was head to head, them diving down on top of yer head like that yer heads would both be smashed, ye would be dead, they would just crack. Heads cracked, and it was like eggs. Then the blood all spilling and it would be into the water, and it would be yours. Then my grannie, if she saw ye and ye were just lying there on top of the water or else sinking to the bottom, maybe ye would, if ye cracked yer head, so what would happen then? If ye might be dead so ye were away to Heaven or else Hell, and then yer grannie seeing ye. Oh poor wee soul, he is my wee grandson, oh poor wee boy if he is dead.

Where was she? She still had not come out the ladies' door. I was swimming for ages and she still had not come out. And ye could not see her up at the ladies' changing cubicles, then seeing the clock, then the divers up the dale. I was going to do it again. I tried it once and hurt myself and I had not tried it again. No many wee boys done the dale. It was my head I hurt, my arms were not straight out right so the water smacked it and it was just like the worst punch or else if it was a hammer, just plohhhh, plohhhh, and I was coming up and up and I got on the rail, my hands on it, I just held on a minute till then I went up the steps onto the side and into the showers and was just dizzy and sat down at the wall. Matt was there and he saw me. I just sat there. After I got up I went to my cubicle and sat on the wee seat and did not go back in the water, and then my face felt hot.

I wanted to dive it again. It was just to get it right and yer arms the gether and straight out. What some boys did was go steps at a time. Ye started from the second step and so on till ye reached the top. I could do the steps. It was only the dale. I needed to try it again. But no the now, no with my grannie. Then I saw a wee boy. He climbed the steps right up. He saw the dale was clear, took a wee run and dived straight off. I had not seen a wee boy do it like that before. He was weer than me and his swimming was just like splashing about. Then he done it again, just ran up the steps onto the dale and dived right off. He was dripping wet too so ye thought he could slip but he did not. And he did not hurt his head. Maybe I could. Yer hands had to be touching. If they were too apart the water smacked ye. I was shivering. Sometimes it was cold. Oh but I wanted to try it. Who was that wee boy with?

His pals. If it was his grannie or his brother they would not let him.

The dale was empty. I could just run up. Ye could go on the dale just to look. Ye had to watch it if somebody came and bumped ye.

Oh but I wanted to do it. But what if my grannie saw me?

Where was my grannie? Maybe if something bad had happened,

I wanted to go and see but could not because it was through the ladies' door and ye could not if ye were a boy, if they saw ye it was just dirty, ye were trying to see them so if they had no clothes on. Some boys tried to look. I did not. Ye were trying no to. They came down from the upstairs. They had their cubicles round the upstairs, a railing went round the edge.

That railing was higher than the dale. Ye could stand on it and dive off. People said that. Except if ye crashed on the ground below. Ye would have to fling yerself way out to miss it. But what if yer feet caught on the edge? Ye would just break them.

Then my grannie was there in her costume, walking slow out the ladies' door her arms down straight and no looking anyplace, her shoulders going a wee bit side to side. She wore her cap. The women all wore their caps, so did the lasses except if they were wee.

She did not see me, only in front of her feet. All boys and wee lasses were running about and ye had to be careful they did not bump into ye. I was waving to her. She saw me but kept walking to the steps at the shallow end. That was what my grannie done. She walked down and started swimming straight away. A lot tested the water, if it was too cold, they went a wee bit at a time, flicked up the water on their body till it got warmer. Some went back to the showers for a heat. My grannie did not, she went down the steps and stood on the bottom and then was swimming straight away. She done breadths and not lengths and did not put her head under the water.

My grannie was a good swimmer. I swam beside her but she went ahead. She was slow and I was fast but she beat me, except she did not race me. I raced her. She did not talk and kept her mouth shut tight so the water did not go in. After a wee bit she climbed out and that was her. I waited a wee while longer then I went out too.

I got dry and my clothes on and waited outside for her. It was ages till she came. There were steps up to the swimming baths' door. The next one along was for the steamie. Women went in there to wash all their laundry and clothes. It was heavy stuff to lift. The women carried it in baskets and prams but some could not lift it up the steps so boys helped them up the steps. The women paid them. The boys that done it knew each other and did not fight. But if ye went near the steps and they did not know ye they swore at ye or else just stared and if ye did not move they smacked yer head.

These boys were old. They got the money off the women and played a game for it against each other. They chipped the coins against the wall, and the one that got the coin nearest lifted all the money. It was a lot of coins lying there and all shouting and laughing, no much fighting. All the boys smoked, they gived each other draws of their fags.

§

In a backcourt a building had fallen down. Men shifted away the big stones and all stuff. Along from it was big jumps and high-up dykes. Mattie and his pals went here. He did not like me coming because I would just fall off. But I would not fall off. Oh away and go with yer own pals!

But my pals did not go to the big jumps. If he was not there I still went. The big boys let me. Ye climbed up on the midgie roofs to start. Then ye reached over to a wall, and that wall was the dyke. Ye climbed on to the top of that.

The dykes were big walls made of bricks. They split the backcourts. It was them or spiky palings. Ye climbed up on the dykes so ye could walk them. There was spaces in the wall where yer feet could get grips. Bricks fell out. That made the spaces. Ye got in yer hands and feet. If ye could not manage to the top big boys helped ye. Ye got yer hands up as far as ye could then the big boy just pushed ye till ye got yer elbows on the top, pulled yerself up. Ye got yer knees on it and balanced. Ye stood up bit by bit and with yer arms out, steadying, then coming up a wee bit more and so more and more and then ye were up and if ye could stand, that was you and ye were standing, yer arms out, and ye could bring them in slow and slow till ye were just standing and could look down and if a big boy was seeing ye. Oh he is up.

That was you.

The top of the dyke was for walking or sitting. If ye were on one and wanted to help somebody up ye could not. It was not wide enough. We just walked along and saw all the big jumps and if there was good buildings to climb.

Some dykes were not good for walking. They had tiles at the top that came to a point, or were round. The round ones were okay, ye could walk along them, ye just had to walk in the middle. The pointed ones were no good. We called them pointed. Tiles sloped against bricks to make that point and all went along in a line so it was like a tightrope. Ye tried to walk it. Ye put yer feet on the sloping tiles beneath the point. Ye bent yer legs and took wee toty steps. Some could do it but no for long. It was just for a laugh ye done it. If ye slipped and fell it was between yer legs and ye had to watch it. Oh my b**ls. People shouted that.

The way to do the pointed ones was sitting down and bumping along on yer b*m. But if ye done it hard it was sore. The other way was getting yer knees on the sloping tiles then doing it. But I never done that. Boys said ye could.

The ordinary dykes were easy. I could run them. I was telling my pals at school. Then if it was the big jumps, ye could do them too if it was a straight-across jump and ye got a good run-up. But if there was no a good run-up ye had to stand still to jump and it was hard.

If ye jumped to a high dyke ye had to fling yer body and get yer elbows on the top and then up. On some dykes the bricks came out when ye stood on them or else shifted and ye had to watch because if ye fell that was you and yer feet would be up in the air so it was yer head first, and that was the worst, clunking against the dyke then smack on the ground. If ye were falling ye got yer hands down first so yer head did not crack. Ye had to try it or it was tough luck for you. Oh he cracked his head. People said that. Yer head cracked open. Oh his brains spilled out on the ground. Yer brains were just there on the ground. It was all bricks and boulders, all glass and stuff. The ground was like that if ye fell. Ye would have to twist yer body in mid air. Oh where would ye land? Ye would just try and see. But it was a worry. I was thinking about it and my teacher hit me on the head with her ruler. That was what she done, she just hit ye. Oh Kieron Smith wake up you are sound asleep.

Please miss I am not.

Oh yes and do not snore, if you were snoring, you are not to snore in the class. The teacher just said it to make everybody all laugh. So if it was funny, all everybody laughing at ye. But I was thinking about if the wall caved in and all went on top of ye so if it was a whole building ye got buried alive. People got buried alive, ye just saw their hand sticking out and ye came and rescued them but maybe if they were flattened, and their heads as well, just like a flat pancake, so that was them, they were just squashed to death and their heads just mashed. Their whole bodies, they would be mashed in and it was all just it would be horrible,. And who was it oh if ye knew him. Maybe ye did and it was one of the big boys and even if it was yer brother, imagine just if it was Matt oh ye could not it was just oh no, ye could not even, ye could not.

So ye just had to watch it. Some backcourts had wee outside buildings. They had caved-in roofs and tile chimneys broke off and all smashed windows. Ye climbed up them as well. Ye could run and jump along the roofs. If ye could not do the next jump ye just dreeped down and ran along the ground and up the next one.

Dykes could be high up and ye had to watch because there were spiky palings down below and people fell onto them. One got killed when the spike went through his belly. He was older than me but younger than Mattie, but he did not play with us. If he was a RC, maybe he was. He had all cousins in America and they sent him stuff. A baseball jacket that was shiny blue with white sleeves and a big red bird on the back. He had a good haircut. Boys said that, just short and sticking up.

There were shops along some streets and the backs of the shops stretched into the backcourt. So ye were over the top of them. When ye walked a dyke it was a big big drop down. Right up the top. Ye were looking down to the street and saw all motor cars and people, so if they saw you. Oh look at that boy! Oh he is going to fall!

One high-up dyke led to the back wall of a picture-house. Big boys were pointing to it. There was a pipe going up and that was what they saw, if they could climb it. So if there was a window they could get in and watch the pictures for nothing.

Grown-ups chased us. Women hung out their washing on the clothes-lines and did not want ye near it. Sometimes ye were running and ye ran through it and if it was a wet sheet it just stopped ye and got dragged on the ground. The woman saw ye out the window. Oh you f*****g wee b****r.

They were going to chase us but we were laughing and ran away.

§

I could join the Lifeboys and it was great. All the troops had their own number. Ours was 168, if somebody said What troop are ye? ye said it, The 168.

So we were the 168. If ye saw boys at school or at the swimming ye just gived a wave or hullo and just maybe if ye shouted, Ye going on Tuesday? Everybody went so ye knew it, ye just said it and maybe even if ye went up and were talking to who it was. Some boys done a Lifeboy salute. So if people were looking, Oh we go to the same Lifies, and sometimes it was my grannie if we were at the swimming. Who is that boy son?

Oh he is in my Lifies.

It was great. And if he went to yer Sunday School. Ye had to go to it and if ye did not it was woe betide ye. There was two classes on Sunday morning and if ye were a new boy ye went to the first at half past nine and were not to be late. People were late. If ye did not want to go ye just walked slow. But the Sunday School teacher did not like it. His name was Mr Beaton. Oh it is the Sunday School ye go to and it is not the Lifeboys. That was what he said. Oh do not think about the Lifeboys, here is the Sunday School. It is not important for the Lifeboys but if it is God, that is the Sunday School.

He was angry if ye could not say the stuff. Oh for our dear Saviour, if that is what happened to Him while others walk abroad. Oh how come how come? It is just Iniquities because if it was the Gospel and ye did not know it. Oh who will save you who will save you. You will just be in Anguish. So if the Lord forsakes ye, oh it will be a sad lookout for ever and ever for the Lord sakes for ye.

If ye could speak words out the Bible. Matthew, Mark, Luke and John. Say Deuteronomy, Deuteronomy, we all were to say it. Oh it is not Deuteronimo, do not say Deuteronimo. You will be in Anguish and it is complete Anguish if you rot in Hell, it is just the worst horrors.

Then if it was the Young Defenders. If we knew about them. And if it was Truth Concealed. Oh if the Devil gets ye oh you will be in Anguish and cannot go to Heaven, Oh pity you pity you, for ye will but Languish evermore. So if it is yer Fate. Mr Beaton was angry how people were so blind and would stay blind, if that was what they wanted, well so be it, if it is tough luck for them, and all Icons and Painted Images. They only were Concealers so it was Truth Concealed. So they were just Blasphemers and Craven Idols with all Painted Images and Mother Mary if she was a God, that was just Blasphemers and ye were going to Hell for evermore and yer Soul was rotting. And ye would see in there how all the faces were screaming and bawling, all crammed the gether in a big pit with the fire underneath ye, and devil creatures were shifting the wheel round and round and ye were tied down on it and were over the fire getting toasted and getting yer body all stretched in agony.

He had bent-over shoulders. If ye saw him in the street. Hullo Mr Beaton. He just looked at ye and did not want ye calling his name except only in Church. He gave ye homework, if ye could learn all the Books and say them, Matthew, Mark, Luke and John, if it was the Devil and ye burned in Hell and were in Anguish with Iniquities.

Mattie had a Boys Brigade Bible and was showing me it. And it was the same name as him, Matthew. Matthew, Mark, Luke and John. I was saying about the Sunday School teacher.

Oh it is Thomas Beaton, he is a serjeant in the BB. Matt was laughing. Oh if ye see how he marches, he just does it funny.

Big boys made a fool of him because how his arms stayed straight. That was when he walked. The BB officers looked at him but he did not change it. People laughed at him. That was what Matt said. Oh but do not you do it or else tough luck.

Because maybe he would just hit ye.

We did not like him. But ye had to go to Sunday School if it was for the Lifeboys.

After it was finished ye could just go away. I went up to my grannie's and got toast and cheese for my breakfast.

The Lifeboy uniform was a navyblue hat the same as sailors, navyblue jerseys with collars and blue trousers, shorts or longs, and black sandshoes or white sandshoes. If it was raining ye went in ordinary shoes or else wellingtons and ye carried the sandshoes under yer arm.

Only Protestants went. Catholics had another thing, it was the Boys' Club. They all went there. Michael Lang too. They had a football team. The Lifies did not have a team.

The Leaders knew me because Mattie used to be there and he was a good boy, that was what they said, Oh you are Matt's wee brother and then they smiled, they liked ye because it was him.

Mrs Milligan was the first Leader. She was great and did smart salutes. People said she was fat. She was not fat. She always had a cheery face but if ye were being cheeky she stopped ye. She had a wee child. Oh but if ye swore or used bad language. Oh woe betide ye, that was what she said. Then yer prayers for every night ye started, Oh God, Whom we cannot think and do anything right, oh kinder our hearts and lead us into truth for Thine is the kingdom, the power and the glory, amen, and then a smart salute.

Fall-out!

And oh everybody running and getting set.

Ye had to be smart to go and ye had to be clean and then yer uniform and to speak good, not umnay didnay and willnay but am not did not and will not. Before ye went ye had to have a big wash in the house, face and neck, hands and knees. My maw did it because if ye wanted to be good. And when ye were on parade it was all inspected and that started the night. Mrs Milligan was just waiting for ye to get ready and she had her whistle and was going to blow it and was going to blow it. And quick quick quick because then she did it.

Fall-in! Tallers to the right, shorters to the left, single rank siiize!

And ye were to jump to it as fast as ye could, getting into line, and yer sandshoes thumping and skidding, shuffling to your bit and the boy next to ye was just a wee bit weer and the other one next to ye a wee bit bigger, right down to the weest shorter from the very biggest taller and yer arm out stretching the space from him to you.

Stand Easy!

Hands behind yer back.

Ohhhh Atten-Hunnnn!

So it was the inspection. Ye all got inspected. Mrs Milligan came down the lines with Mr Hope and ye had to hold out yer hands palms down and then palms up and then if ye had on shorts it was right knee up, left knee up, and the Leaders would see they were clean and then yer wrists and the backs of yer knees, that was what people forgot. Then yer sandshoes if they were clean, they were yer good ones and ye just kept them for the Lifies. Some did not, and if it was poor, ye knew if it was poor, if the boy's maw and da did not have money. Billy Williams. He was in our group and was scabby, I did not talk to him, but it was a shame. But because yer sandshoes, if they were dirty, if it was a point off yer team, so ye were just to try yer hardest. Some boys wore them out the house and they were not supposed to. Billy Williams had his on at school so if it was raining, ye went through puddles. He was in the class above me but people laughed at him.

So if ye had anything bad, Oh you have dirty knees, it was points against and yer group was looking at ye, Oh see him, and some boys always got points against with dirty knees or else wrists if it was their hands and necks and what, it was their own fault if they just got a right wash before they came and ye saw them and ye knew

Oh they are going to fail inspection. So if they were in your group, that was you, and ye got fed up with it. Oh if it was Billy Williams. Oh it is short trousers, he should just wear longs, then they will not know if his knees are filfy. But Gordon Fletcher said, Oh it does not matter because then at games Mr Hope sees when he wears his gym shorts.

People never pumped, just never never, but sometimes ye got smells. It all was points if ye done it good. Ye done it the whole night for all games and all what happened. Mr Hope counted it up. Points went for good attenders, if ye were a regular attender. If ye went all the nights. Ye would go all the nights. We all went. So ye got a prize at the very end. If it was Perfect Attendance that meant the Sunday School as well, and ye got a Bible book except just with the Psalms.

The two Sunday School teachers came to the Prize Night. Ours was Mr Beaton and we were seeing how he walked. I wished he would do it good. They had on their BB uniforms and leather gloves. They marched up to Mrs Milligan and gived her the smartest salutes. But she gived a smartest one to them and we thought she was the best at it. I got my Bible book. It was a wee one but it was good and I liked it, how all its pages were just all new and just crispy, and ye smelled it, it just smelled good and how the pages all fell blue and white and it was all just yours with your name.

Everybody split into groups and ye had leaders in each one. The top boys got a special white cover on their hats and white lanyards and white sandshoes. Mattie had them when he was there. They kept them white with clay. He used to do it and I watched him. Our top boy was Gordon Fletcher. He was good at all the things. Just everything, and he had all stuff sewn on his jersey, it was badges. Ye got them when ye done good stuff and yer maw sewed them on. Gordon Fletcher was just the very best. The races started and I was running and he said, Oh fast as ye can Smiddy.

That was me, Smiddy. It was my turn to go out in the race and I was sitting waiting ready and oh just waiting and just ready. And he said it to me, Fast as ye can Smiddy.

So that was me, Smiddy.

Oh if your name is Smith, you are Smiddy. That was Gordon Fletcher, he said it to me. You are Smiddy.

I said it to my granda, if I was Smiddy. Oh aye son if yer name is Smith then ye are Smiddy.

I said it to Matt but he just looked and did not say anything back.

So that was me now Smiddy. Smiddy Smiddy. I was glad. People did not like Kieron, that was how they acted. I liked it. So Smiddy. Other boys said it. The same in school. Oh Smiddy! Oh there is Smiddy.

And it was me. It was just me, Smiddy. I wanted people to call me it, lasses as well, they just looked, Oh Smiddy. I liked lasses saying it.

The Lifies was the best of all and Gordon Fletcher and if ye won yer race he gived ye a wink. So you were the best wee boy, that was Gordon saying it, if he just winked, so if ye done a good race or what if it was good points for the team. He said that, team. It was just a team like football, ye were all just playing and ye all were men, Oh is that man in your team? Whose man is he? Is he your man?

And they were just talking about you or another boy. Who is next man? Oh it is me. It was you, you were next man. Ye called them man.

They were relay-races and ye had wee bags to pass to the next man and they were beanbags. They changed the team about. If fast boys were in one then they switched them so ye got close races. If ye had a slow runner second in yer group then ye would have a fast runner for yer third one. If yer first man was a medium runner maybe two of the weer ones would be fast. It got evened up. Ye saw the way one group might have a long lead after three rounds. Then other ones were catching up. So it was the last round and the weest boys in the whole troop sitting and waiting and all just ready. And everybody cheering and yer own group would be shouting yer name, whatever it was, Smiddy Smiddy Smiddy. And even if yer last man was not a good runner ye would still be cheering because sometimes boys ran faster and ye did not think they would and they just beat the good ones and it was great.

Some ran faster and other ones slower. Boys had too skinny legs or else if they had a bad leg or maybe there was something wrong with them so they could not run right. Or if they were too lanky, just lanky skinny malinkies. Or else too wee. Wee boys could be good racers and so could skinny malinkies but no fat ones, fatsos if ye called them that. A man in my street was a fatso. My da said that. Oh there is fatso, if we saw him out the window.

The best racer usually was just if ye were medium. But then for the other competitions ye might get fatsos or skinny malinkies being the winners if they were good at other stuff. Ye did not get football because there were too many boys but ye could get games with balls and I liked them, if it was keepie-uppy or else if ye had to dribble yer ball down to a marker and then dribble it back. Some boys could not do it and their balls would go flying everywhere and maybe your team was the winner and other ones still had men out running. When yer team finished ye all sat on the floor with yer legs crossed and yer hands on yer knees or else arms folded and yer back straight. That was how ye were to sit, and if Mr Hope took Mrs Milligan down to see ye ye all were sitting straight.

At the end of the night Mrs Milligan said, Oh Mr Hope, please read out the points!

So then Mr Hope would read out the points and have them all added up. So who has won this week's competition?

And oh if it was Gordon Fletcher's team well that was us. And all people would cheer ye. Ours won it a lot of times. So then it was eyes closed for the prayer to our gracious Queen. Oh we beseech ye oh God and we pray to ye for thy servant Elizabeth our Queen, her husband and their children. Oh grant ye we will stand steadfast on the side of right for them and spread goodness and happiness where'er we go, for the Lord's sake we ask it and it is in the power and the glory, amen.

Dismissed! We all saluted Mrs Milligan and Mr Hope and they saluted us back.

So that was us. We just had to go home.

But if ye helped to tidy up. If ye could. I tried to, I liked it. It was benches and mats lying on the floor, and then if it was the storeroom and it was all jumbled, beanbags and all balls lying and ye were just to put things in their place. The top boys all done it. Gordon Fletcher. And after ye finished ye just said cheerio to everybody and Mr Hope would lock up. He had the keys to the Church hall and all Church places. If ye went in there where the Services were it would just be the Church and all the lights out, all just dark.

Me and Terry ran to catch up another boy. Usually we done that. Terry stayed three closes down from my grannie. We came round that way from the Church and there was a chip shop on the corner.

If I was by myself and it was dark nights I went round the streets to go home. If Terry was there or else it was light nights ye could cut through the close across the backcourts and over the dyke.

But it was different in the dark. Lights only were coming from the back windows up the tenements and ye could not see where ye were going. Ye had to watch no to step in mud or a puddle or else in jobby, dogs were aye doing jobbies, or else ye watched for broken glass. That happened a lot. If ye fell ye sliced yer knee. Or nails in yer sandshoes, if it was rusty. One went in Terry's and a woman pulled it out but his maw took him to the hospital. He went off school because of it.

Then if ye ran in the dark and if ye met a dog, oh ye would frighten it and it would bark and run away or if it growled and would go for ye so ye had to stay dead still, just wait. Sssh boy, sssh, sssh, sssh, just whispering and the dog would just be looking, Oh sssh, sssh, and then maybe if it just went away, well so could you.

Men frightened ye as well. If they did not mean it, usually they did not. But if it was a bad man.

People said it to the wee ones and laughed but it made ye jump. Oh it is a bad man going to get ye. Or a bogie man was like a ghost. There is a ghost. Oh mammy, there is a bogie man. Or if it was a phantom strangler. My brother said it. Oh a phantom strangler is going to get you. But I just laughed back, he was just saying it.

A boy always got money for chips. Me and Terry went with him. He shared his chips with us. But if he gived one to me and no to Terry or if it was two chips and he gave them to Terry and no to me. That was what he done.

Oh there is a big chip. Oh take it Terry, here is a wee one for Smiddy.

So ye got sick of it. So he held a chip out so ye were to take it and then he would bring it back quick and just eat it and laugh at ye. I would have belted him. I thought I would, but I did not, and ye always thought Oh here is the chip now and sometimes it was, he just gave ye it. Oh I am just kidding. That was what he said.

We ate the chips at the corner. I walked home after and ye were sad, just how the Lifies would not come again and it was away next week. Up in the house ye had toast for supper. Sometimes my maw made it, usually it was me. I liked making it.

§

I did not know we were moving to a new house and then we were so that was us. It was away away and ye needed the subway and then the bus or else ye could get a train and then too if ye wanted the ferry, the ferry took ye instead of the subway and it did not cost ye nothing.

My da came home from the Navy for good, he was getting a job on dry land. He was tired out and it was his holiday but my maw did not have the holiday and was getting all ready to go to a new house. That was where we were going. Uncle Billy was back from England and was helping with the flitting. I was to keep out the way and was at my grannie's. Her and granda did not like us going away. She was saying it to him. How could they travel all those miles to see us? They could not. And what about the boys? That was me and Matt. Running up and down the stair every ten minutes? Once we flitted that would be us and we would not come back.

If we were too faraway, they would never see us because we would never come to visit if it was a train to take. We would never come and see them, that was what my grannie was saying, how it was my da's fault. If it was not for him and just how he wanted the new house, it was him to blame if he did not wait and see if there was something better. Why did he not just wait?

My grannie was shaking her head and granda was just looking. Oh but it could not be my maw's fault. She would not want to be miles away, it was too far. It was my da's fault. He knew it would be hard for her and granda. Granda could hardly get up and down the stairs, that was his breath, so he did not go places, just stayed in the house, so they never went places, just seeing the walls of the house and my grannie got sick of it, oh she did, that was what she was saying. Oh we just never go anyplace, and she was sad saying it.

It is not my fault Vera.

It is like a prison. Except for the messages I would never go out.

Aye but it is not my fault.

It is not mine.

No, no. Granda lifted his newspaper and was reading it and my grannie turned on the tap at the sink and was seeing out the window, her back to us, ye could not see her face. My granda was looking at her. She would not say anything. My grannie done that and just did not say anything and ye were wishing she would.

And you would do it for her, whatever it was, ye would just do it, if it was her messages, Oh grannie I will go yer messages. Can I go yer messages?

My grannie turned to see me.

I always went the messages for my grannie and would always go them, so if it was a train to take, I would still go them. I liked going them, only if it was a heavy pile of potatos and all vegetables, carrots and turnips, it was just a heavy bag and it was two hands going up the stair. The shops were round the corner along the road and I knew the ones to go to, if they gived ye good food, some of them did not. My grannie said the ones that were not good, Oh do not go there he is a cheat if his potatos are old and how his carrots are just soft.

Grannie I can go yer messages.

I forgot the wee boy was there, she said.

He is in his hideout, said granda, he is playing possum. Sure ye are son?

Well I am no a wee boy.

Ye have got big ears.

Oh but I can go grannie's messages, even if it is the new place, I can just come back.

See what I am saying? said granda. The boy is never away from here. He is not going to stop now. His big brother too.

But we will never get to visit them.

Aye we will.

Oh Larry.

We will.

My grannie was looking at me and was sad. Ye will need to go home soon. Then to granda, I forgot he was there.

It is his memory, said granda. Everything ye say, he is taking notes, that is weans for ye.

Granda said weans but my maw did not like it. Oh it is children, they are not weans they are children. And if it was words the same, oh she did not like it, aye and cannay dae. Aye but I cannay dae that. My granda said that. Aye but I cannay dae. It is not aye and cannay dae it is yes and cannot do.

Take an apple son. My grannie touched me on the shoulder. I got the apple and squashed back in at the side of the grate.

My seat was here, it was a stool. A big cupboard was at the side and my head went against it. I liked it here how ye could just see everything and were out the way. If ye were reading, ye could just read. Sometimes I was sleeping, if I woke up, it was time to go home, my grannie just there, she done things at the sink and the table or else the cupboard if she was making soup and had all the onions and carrots and stuff and all just was chopping it up.

My granda sat on his chair no faraway. He read the paper or else with the wireless on. He did not like television. If he just read and the wireless was not on ye could hear his breaths. My grannie did not care about the wireless. If he went ben the front room she just turned it off. Oh a wee bit peace son.

My grannie's house was better than ours. I just liked it, except if my big brother was there, so if he was, I just came home or maybe out to play. Usually I went to my grannie's every day. My maw telled me not to. Oh it is too much. But I just did. I telled her I was going for new books to the library. I ran fast to the library and got the books then went fast to my grannie. She liked to see the books and if I was talking about them. So did granda. What is the story son?

So I told them if it was adventures and just saying all what it was, if it was in a woods and children were straying oh and what happened if it was a bear going to get them or else a wicked man who had an axe and how he had funny shoes if they went up at the front where his toes were, and his trousers too. His legs were just skinny and funny knees sticking out. Oh I am going to get you, oh and ye were hiding if it was the boy and girl and behind a bush.

My grannie was laughing. So was granda. But my grannie's laugh was funny, Ohhh ohhh and her hand covering her mouth. Granda pointed at her and she still laughed, Ohhh ohhh.

§

Uncle Billy came home for the weekend to help with the flitting. His old pal was there too. His name was Chick. He got a van from his work. He could drive it and was doing all the lifting for our furniture, him and Uncle Billy and my da. My da did not have pals here, he had them in all other places and through in Fife, that was where they stayed.

Matt could help but I was not to, I was too wee and would get in the road so just stay in yer grannie's. But I would have been a help. I would have carried wee stuff. My da said I was to go and hurry up because it was going to rain soon. I had to stay in my grannie's till my maw came and got me.

My maw gived me a piece on cheese but I did not feel like it and flung it in the midden when I was going over the back. I went slow up the stairs and sat down on the steps for a wee while. I was fed up with stuff and did not like how it all happened, and just because ye were wee. If I could have helped, I would have carried stuff too.

There was a lot of things. It was not fair how my da done stuff. My maw too. How come it was always Matt? Everything was for him. That was what I saw how he got everything. That was if ye were the oldest. The young ones did not get anything. If Matt only was to do things. How was that fair? It was not.

I went up the stair and chapped the door. I gived my own signal. My Auntie May let me in but then she went away over to help my maw. That was her sister. My granda was ben the parlour. The wee cat was in with him. I looked to see and it was on his shoulders. That was where it went. My granda was reading the paper and it just jumped up the chair and lied round them. I was saying how Uncle Billy's old pal was there for the flitting and Matt was helping but I was not to. Granda was tired. Oh would ye just go ben the kitchen son, see what yer grannie is doing.

My grannie was at the sink. She done that and did not talk much, just looked out the window. Ye could see the sky over the building across the back. It was our building. If ye looked hard ye could see our kitchen window.

My grannie was washing clothes, it was my granda's socks. I did not have any books and was watching her.

The big cat was there and I played with it. I could drag wool over the floor and under the bed and it chased it. I dragged it fast but ye were to let it catch the wool sometimes. It was training for the mouse. One time it just stayed under the bed and did not come back out. It was lying down and having a sleep.

My maw came a lot later and I woke up, I was lying on the bed in the recess. My grannie was going fast now and looking at us. Oh I will make a pot of tea, I will make a pot of tea. Oh no mum there is no time, the men are ready to go.

Oh but a pot of tea.

Oh but the men are ready.

Yes but you can stay a minute.

Oh no mum I have to go. May is down there too.

My grannie was just looking. Now my maw was greeting and she went and gived my grannie a cuddle. My grannie was her mother. When we were going down the lobby my grannie did not come. I

was going to give her a cuddle but she did not want to. My granda
came out the parlour, he went to my maw. Oh come here hen!

Him and my maw had a big cuddle. He smoothed my hair and
gived me money. Now that is for you. And come back and see us.

So that was us and we went away. We were to go on the subway
and the train. Only us. Matt was to go in the van with the men. My
maw took me round to see them driving away. It was all packed
inside. My da was waiting with Uncle Billy and Chick, they were
smoking. Matt was up the street with his pals and saying cheerio.
When he saw me and my maw he came running down. Him and
Uncle Billy sat in the back on top of a carpet and squeezed in beside
stuff. I was not thinking anything. They were laughing and Uncle
Billy was making jokes. Chick slammed the door shut. Ye still could
hear them. Oh where is the candles? Where is the candles! Uncle
Billy was shouting.

My da went in the front of the van with Chick that was driving.

Matt's pals were there and waving when it went away. They said
cheerio to me too.

Me and my maw were just going to the subway station. It was a
long walk. A bus went but our family did not catch it. There was
not the money.

It was a different walk from the ferry. I liked it okay because there
was shops ye could look at. One was a bike-shop with just all bikes
and different bits, wheels and frames and saddle bags and all different.
People always looked in the window. And a good toy-shop was there
too, away along from a close with high dykes and big jumps. Matt
and his pals used to go here and I came with them. I went with my
own pals now, but not much. The toy-shop had all model yachts and
model soldiers in the window, and the best trainsets. A boy in my
class got one of the trainsets for his birthday. He could go to this
toy-shop and get wee bits to go with it, a new carriage or else other
things. He was a only-child and got pocket-money, so he saved it up.
That was how he got it, his family was well-off. My maw telled
me.

The rain was starting and she was wanting me to hurry but I still
was looking in it. There was farm-animals in the window. That boy

in my class bought farm-animals. Pigs, cows and sheep and wee ducks, that was what he bought and it was just for weans and wee lasses. I said it to my maw.

Oh it is not weans it is children. Oh Kieron, it is children and girls, do not say weans and lasses.

My maw was sad if I did not speak right. I would have to start now I was going to the new school. It was all different there and just all nice and very faraway from the old place. Oh if I would just stick in at my lessons and stop all the nonsense. My head was full of nonsense, the teacher said, if only I buckled down. Oh Kieron you will buckle down, will you?

Yes mum.

She did not like me saying aye, and if I said maw, maw was awful and just horrible, she hated it. If I said it to her, Aye maw. Oh she would have hated it. I could never have said it. Aye maw. I said it into my head, Aye maw.

But if it was my pals and I spoke to them, I would just say it then if it was my mother, Oh it is my maw. And they would say it to me. That was how they spoke, and their maws and das too, some of them, that was how they spoke. I said it to my maw.

Oh yes Kieron but they are keelies. My maw said, Do you want to be a keelie all your life? That is what they are, just keelies. They will be stuck here till they are dead. They will never go anywhere and never amount to anything. You are not a keelie. Not in my house. And if you buckle down. Oh Kieron will you buckle down? Promise you will buckle down.

Matt could go to his Secondary School now and it was the very best kind of one so he had the very best chance in life. He was lucky. How did he get in? It was my maw done it. So when it was me she would get me in it too. I could go to it after. She said it to my teacher.

My teacher said, Oh Kieron has got it in him except his head is full of nonsense. If he would just stop being so silly.

I liked that teacher but she said stuff about me. I did not care. But if I did go to the good school. Well I wanted to go, if my big brother was there. So if people were picking on ye, a big brother stuck up for ye. Matt could stick up for me. I did not have a new school to go to. I would get it after the holidays.

Me and my maw were walking up from the railway station. She knew how to get to the new house.

The rain was on but not too bad. But it was a long long walk up and ye were getting soaked. Away over a big long hill and our house was way down the street, ye had to go away way down it. It was all quiet. Me and my maw were walking and ye heard our shoes. Ye could not see lights in many houses and could see in some windows. My maw said, Oh do not look, but she done it too.

All the furniture was shifted in, the van locked up and nobody there. Then a noise up above and a big voice shouted on us. It was my da looking out the window. Uncle Billy was waving down to us. Hoy yous two!

My maw was smiling but saying yous, she would not like it. You not yous, you not ye. Head, not heid. Dead not deid, instead not insteid. And not isnay and wasnay and doesnay. When I said doesnay my da said, Walt Doesnay, you do not.

My maw was laughing.

It was the very top stairs. That was smashing. I liked so ye could see out and just be over the top of everybody.

My da was there and he gived my maw a kiss then she went in the bathroom.

A cupboard was there for coats and jackets with all pegs and hooks. I was to put my coat on a peg.

Then the new bedroom for me and Matt. But only the same old bed. We were getting our new beds soon. Ye would get one to yerself and just kick out yer feet if ye wanted. He was lying on top reading a book. He was on the side near the window and his stuff all spread out. My side was the door and my stuff was there. Who put it there? That side of the bed was not my side in the old house. If it was my old side I would have been at the window. So who done it like that? It was him.

I was going past to see in the cupboard then the first drawer but he shouted at me. Oh that is mine. You take that other one. Oh ye see that chair, it is mine, is not yours. You get yer own chair.

You are not the boss.

Shut it.

I ran to see out the window. Oh ye better not walk there too much, it is my side of the room. That is yours at the door.

Away ye go, I said and just went out the room. He wanted me to. I went down the lobby to see the bathroom. The door was open. I went in and saw the bath. I turned on the water and pchohhh, it gushed out and splashed back on me. Then a wash-hand basin. It was beside the lavvy bowl. I done the lavvy and washed my hands. There was no towel but and I just had to use toilet paper.

My da was with Uncle Billy and his old pal Chick. They were sitting at the window drinking beer and sherry wine. Uncle Billy was laughing, Oh the old sherry wine is a good friend of mine.

I went to see other house bits. My maw and da's room was there. I pushed the door and went in. My maw was standing near the bed and all clothes were there on top and she was hiding her neck and chest. Oh Kieron, she said, Kieron. Oh do not do that Kieron you must knock the door. Knock the door before you enter. You cannot just come in.

Sorry mum.

You must knock if it is a bedroom and someone is there.

Sorry mum.

I went in to see the living room again. There was no many seats. I was just sitting on a cushion on the floor. Chick was saying about something then was a bad swear word. Uncle Billy laughed but my da saw me. What are you doing here?

I am just sitting.

Well sit somewhere else.

Uncle Billy said, Oh Kierie boy! Do ye like yer new house. Oh Kierie boy!

I went into the kitchenette and was looking here and then the door to go out and that was the balcony.

The door out was locked. The key was in the lock. I opened it but oh the rain was coming hard. But I just looked out. It was smashing, it was just smashing. I was going to get my coat to go out but my maw came in. She opened her message bags and got out the bread and cheese for sandwiches.

I helped with it. She was happy and saying how it was a great house.

Then was a loud tune from out in the street. I went ben the living room to see. It was a ice-cream van. Everybody looked out the window. There it was and people were queuing to buy their stuff. Oh we will make it a feast, said Uncle Billy. It is me and I am paying, do not worry.

Oh but, said my da.

No. It is me. Uncle Billy was laughing and he held up his glass. It is for the new house.

Chick was laughing as well. My maw was there and writing it down on paper. It was all sweeties and two bottles of ginger, six packets of potato crisps and two ten packets of cigarettes. Then she was laughing too. Oh Billy what about my sandwiches?

Oh we will eat them and all.

We are starving, said Chick.

I did not see her laughing much but now she was. Matt too was there and he was laughing too. What for? I did not know what for. If it was the ice-cream van and we were all getting stuff. I do not know. My da was looking over at my maw.

Uncle Billy went into his pocket and piled money into my hands. Oh Kierie boy.

My da said, You go as well Matt. He cannot manage it all on his own.

I can, I said.

Oh you will make a mistake. Matt, you go as well.

Put on yer coat, said my maw.

Heh son give yer brother the money, said my da.

Oh I can take it, I said.

Give him the money.

Now Uncle Billy got more money. Chocolates as well Matt, that is for your mother. Oh you are my darling big sister and I lo ye dearly.

Uncle Billy winked to all us. His old pal Chick was laughing and looking at my maw. I did not see him where we used to stay. He came from a street near the library and used to work beside Uncle Billy. Not now he was in England. Uncle Billy was staying in his house for the night. If he got drunk sometimes, my grannie and granda did not like it. Uncle Billy was saying it and making people laugh.

No my maw but, she just shaked her head.

Uncle Billy was good and ye got stuff off him. Ye just watched it when him and my da were drinking. One time he pushed me. But he did not mean it. I was walking past the couch and he leaned and it was a push on the shoulder for a joke. I was just wee and I fell on the floor. Oh sorry son sorry son. I did not mean to do it.

That was near the fire, said my maw.

Oh sorry.

Ye do not know your own strength.

My da was laughing. Oh he was just playing.

But that was a drink in him. My grannie said it, Oh if Billy gets a drink in him.

If he had money he gived ye it. In the old place he took me and Matt to the pictures. He just used to come up for us and said it, Coats on boys, and that was us away. Then two times to see the Rangers. That was great. I loved it. So did Matt.

My da did not take us many places. He needed a good job first. And if he could not get one. Well, he would have to. He did not want to go back to sea. Except if he had to that was that. Uncle Billy was saying to him about how it was jobs in England, if ye were getting big money and just all overtime, yer digs money, and ye saved it all up and that was you. He came home a lot of times. Ye got a bus down there and it took ye all the way back. Ye just got big money then came home and bought stuff. Ye just worked for it and ye got it, because the jobs were down there. My da was looking over at my maw. Then he was looking at me and Matt and we went down to the ice-cream van.

§

Our family and another one was first up our close. Ye had all the smells. Stones and concrete and everything that was going, all new, we had it, it was smashing, and ye were wondering who was going to be yer neighbours. I was wanting to go out and see stuff, just how everything was all new and all people that were new. But there was nobody to play with. Matt did not know boys either. When he went out I went with him and saw stuff all roundabout. But if he stayed in the room, usually he did, he was doing lessons all the time and just swotting. It was my room too but he did not want me in it. Oh it spoils my concentration.

My maw said it too. Oh Kieron it is his concentration, if you can just be quiet, he is doing his homework. Oh it is a ink-exercise, your brother is doing a ink-exercise.

I was not to go into his side of the room. Oh it is a house rule, it is a house rule.

Who said?

Me.

Who is me?

Him. He made the rule, and it was for the complete house. Then came the new beds. But the way they fixed things all was wrong and just not fair. It was the exact same sides. He got the window and I got the door. So if my side of the room had the door he always went in it when he came in. Then he went out, so that was him in my side again. But I was not to set foot in his. Oh keep to yer own side, do not set foot in mine.

But if his side had the window? So how come? I was not to look out the window. What if it was mine? If he had the door and I had the window. He would have wanted to look out. But if it was me coming in the door and it was his side, how did I come in. If I was going to my bed. Oh you cannot come in my side. Oh if ye get a ladder to climb up.

Because he would not have let me through. That was my house.

How bad it was. Going to yer bed at night, ye would have to go outside and climb up a ladder.

I did not care about his side except the window. How come he had it? It was not fair at all, I could not even look out. If I just wanted to see. If it was getting dark, or raining, if it was pelting down or what. I just wanted to look out and I could not, so that was not fair. How come I could not just look out? That was all. How come I was not allowed to? Oh away ben the living room if ye want to look out the window.

That was what he said. Oh away out on the balcony. Ye love the balcony. Away out on it.

I did love the balcony. So what? If he had the bedroom, so the balcony was a place for me. If I was not even to go in my own bedroom. If it was his. The whole bedroom.

I just got let in to go to bed. That was my house, it just was not fair. He made all the rules, he just made them up. He kept his school books and jotters out all the time. They were even set on the window-sill. If he was out the house and I was looking out the window I had to watch no to bang into nothing. It was all there. The books and stuff, jotters and pads, and all in order. He kept them in order. The pages for reading all were marked. He took them off the window-sill at night but one time he forgot and left them there the whole time and when it came morning every single one was soaking wet. All the pages, pages and pages just soaked through all stuck the gether and tearing if ye opened them and Matt was just jumping about and all angry. Oh he was angry, and bawling and shouting. But no me. How come it was me? He was just looking at me. It was not me. I did not do it. Oh it is all ruined it is ruined.

Well it is not my fault.

Oh away ye go.

It is my room.

Oh shut up.

My da saw all the wet. Oh it is just the damp, the water comes down off the windows in these houses.

I just went out the room. I was glad the balcony was there. The door went out from the kitchenette. If ye were waiting for yer tea ye could just open the door and go out. Even it was raining ye could stand in at the door and the water might not get ye, if it came down over yer head, past yer shoulder. Only if the wind was blowing hard, it blew the rain in on ye. Ours was the top floor so ye saw people over the back if they were in their balconies. A boy lived three closes along from me on the first floor and if he was out on his I saw him. He was out a lot. We kidded on we did not see each other.

The balcony was made out of bricks and had a wall round it but ye could not climb up on the wall good, it had a round bar along the top, it was made of iron. If ye sat up on it ye could not balance. If ye got up on the wall to stand ye could not do it right. That round bar hit into yer ankles so yer legs could not go straight, so if ye were going to walk, ye could not. I thought how to walk along the bar, it was like a tightrope. But if it was yer bare feet gripping, maybe they could.

There was no dykes in the new place, not real ones. Ye looked over the balcony wall and saw the backcourt. It was all stones and bricks, mud and big puddles. But the great thing was the balcony. It was mine, that was what I thought. If Matt got the bedroom, well then. My maw and da had their bedroom. They all had the bathroom. I never got the bathroom. They always were in it. Oh it is a bath, I need my bath, that was what they said. In the old place we did not have one except the swimming baths and they were for everybody. My maw loved the bath. She always was saying it, Oh I am away for my bath.

My da just laughed. Matt done it too, he always was wanting a bath. My da said, Oh is he got a girlfriend?

Matt did not like him saying it and went into the bedroom. He did not like me coming in except if I was going to bed. I heard him saying to my maw about a snib for the door.

Oh but what if yer brother needs to come in?

So if he snibbed the door, how could I get in? I could not. It was my room too.

Oh but it was all his lessons, his lessons his lessons his lessons. He needed to get peace and could not if I was there. I made all fidgeting noises and just was a complete pest, that was what he said.

But how come? I was not doing nothing if I was just in bed reading a book. Oh but he hated that too. If ye turned a page, Oh you are doing it too noisy.

I am not, I am just turning a page.

Well do it quiet.

Then if ye were going to sleep. He needed the light on. Well keep it on, I do not care. That was what I said.

Oh but I cannot do it right if you are wanting the light off and I have to be quiet.

Well I do not care if I need to go to sleep.

Oh you are just a blooming pest.

I told my maw but she just went with him. Oh Kieron it is so important for your brother if he is doing his studies.

Oh studies, it is just swotting. I fell asleep and I woke up. It was him turning a page. Or a wee cough, he done all wee coughs, so that was me awake.

Oh I did not mean to wake ye.

But he still done it, if he coughed. If he coughed he coughed. But I did not care if he woke me. I liked noises and listening just to what it was if it was outside, motor cars or what, if it was music from through the wall or big boys shouting in the street or maybe just heels walking, oh that is a woman, cullick cullick, cohhhhh, cullick cullick.

But I found how I could read in the bedroom and not lie on the bed. It was a wee place down between my bed and the wall where the door was. The bed was pressed against the wall but ye could just squash down and under. My da kept all suitcases under my bed but I shifted them the gether and it was easy to squash in. But when I came out it was all fluff and oose stuff down my pyjamas. My maw was shouting. Oh Kieron it is filfy it is just filfy.

But it came up from the floor under the bed so it was not my fault. It was all dirty under there. I got a brush and just brushed under.

If it was after tea and Matt was going in to swot, I just went in first and got my place comfy. I had the book against the wall and it got the light. When he came in he knew I was there but he did not say nothing. Because if it was my side of the room.

I liked it there. Nobody saw ye and it was yours. But Matt did not like me doing it. Oh I am just reading.

Oh well ye can read in the kitchenette.

So can you.

Oh shut yer trap.

No for you.

I was not going to for him. He wanted me to go to the kitchenette all the time but people went in there and the chairs were not comfy. If I went into the kitchenette I just went out on the balcony.

It was my balcony. I thought that and it was. A pipe was beside it and went up to the roof. Ye could lean over and touch it. Sometimes ye heard the ice-cream van but our family did not get stuff except if it was fags for my da. It was all too dear. They all just put their prices up because it was out in the scheme. Other vans done it. Butchers, fish shops, bakers, fruit and vegetables. They all were there and they had dear prices so we did not buy stuff off them. My maw went into town every Saturday morning then came home in the afternoon. She done a big shop. When she came home she was loaded down with message bags. How could she carry them all? She could not. Me and Matt went down to wait for her off the train and we carried them up and over the hill and way way along to our street. Sometimes it was not that train and ye had to wait for the next one. Then ye saw her getting off and if a man was giving her down the messages, so me and Matt ran to get them.

§

I wanted to go out but it was just raining all the time. When it went off I saw boys outside playing. They were kicking a ball. I went down and got a game. They were playing heidies. I played the winner. Pat and Danny, they were quite good players. The rain started. We sat in a close and were just talking how about the old places where they stayed and I stayed and what like everything was and if they had good dykes and places to go. They did not know about ferries but they had good stuff in their old places. It was smashing and I was telling my da and he was laughing, Oh Saint Patrick and Saint Daniel, that is who he is playing with.

There was Proddy boys round our bit but they were just older or younger or just did not go about. Ye saw them up at the window looking out. People stayed in the house. They had games and read books.

The Protestant Primary School was high up and had a real-size football pitch but the workies were still in doing stuff and it was not ready. After the holidays special buses were taking us to other schools till it was ready. The RC Primary School was ready. It was weer than ours and made of tin same as ours. So if a stone hit it it would make a tinny noise and what would happen.

Matt was going to his same Secondary School. There was not a Secondary School in the new scheme. He was getting a train to go. That was lucky. I read a book and the children went away to school and with their suitcases all packed, saying cheerio to their mothers and fathers at the train station. Boys to one school, girls to one and they just met up for hols. Some were sisters. They were with the boys at the seaside and had all adventures. If they were swimming and the lasses did not have their swimming costumes they just used their underwear and the boys just looked away. It was just all living together, doing yer lessons and then games and big dinners, ye saw them in the dorms and it was cakes and buns. They were posh and were in England but they were still like pals and ye thought if ye met them, well, they would be okay, and ye could show them places. My maw would have wanted it. It was posh people for her, she liked them. My da did too, a wee bit.

My maw was at the same work like in the old place but he was in the house all the time and was just grumpy and looking out the window.

One day was sunny and Matt was going a walk so I went with him. Outside our house ye crossed the road and went down a big hill to a field. Away over we found a burn that stretched the whole way and ye had to find places to cross. There were stones ye could step on one by one. We found a place with a big pond flooding. Big boys were there. We were watching them. They knocked planks of wood off the workies and tied them together. They made a raft and it could float. They went on it a while and gived us a shot. Matt got a big stick and pushed it on the bottom, it was smashing and just wobbled out. Oh but then the planks came away and we had to go in the water. Matt jumped away but I could not and fell a wee bit so my side went under but I got my hand down to get up. Matt was going back on the raft. So did I but it was all slippy now and ye had to watch it.

There was a lot of spare ground roundabout, some was fields where they were building new houses. Once ye got there it was a walk up a wee hill and out to another flat bit where the workies were making a road. They had tractors and bulldozers. There was going to be new houses up and over the hill as well, thousands of them.

Some workies talked to ye. Others just chased ye and said they would give ye a boot up the a**e if ye went near their tools. One time they shouted at us, Wee Squatter b*****ds. So they thought we were the Squatters. I told my maw and she was angry.

They left all stuff lying about and ye could knock it if they were not looking or after teatime when they were all away home. Matt got pals with a big boy that builded the raft. He was called George. He had a young brother Jim and had to take him. So Matt wanted me to go as well so if I went with him and then Matt went with George but I did not want to. Jim was weer than me and was not a good runner and moaning a lot. George just punched him but it made him moan louder and then he was greeting. But it was not a hard punch. I did not want to go if the young brother was there.

Ye better, said Matt, else ye cannot come.

Him and George went ahead and left me and Jim so I just took him and we went with them. We knocked all nails and stuff off the workies. It was all in our pockets and too heavy so was pulling down yer trousers. Ye had to keep yer hands in yer pockets to hold them up. And the nails stuck in the cloth and tore it. Jim was saying to George, Oh mum is going to kill me. Oh that is your fault.

Matt and George had a hammer, a saw and chisels, and planked them down the field. I saw where they put them. Then Matt brought the hammer into the house. It was under the bed. He told me no to tell dad and no even to touch it else he would batter me. When he was out I got it. It was big and heavy and I could hardly hold it up, it just toppled.

Him and George were going back down the field. They went through the fence across from our houses and down the hill past the big boulder. I went after them and George's wee brother followed after me. They ran away so we ran after them. Once ye got to the big boulder ye were running fast down the hill and could hardly stop and ye were flying down and then thumping along the flat bit yer knees nearly hitting yer chin and then when ye stopped ye looked back to see how much ye had done. Back up the top of the hill was the houses, I saw my window.

The big boulder was smashing. It was gigantic. Ye climbed it and sat on the top. How come it landed there? Who could have rolled it up? No even a real giant except if he was the biggest of all. So if people were getting chased by him, maybe getting away, then he flung the boulder at them, he just picked it up like a wee stone. But lucky for them he missed when he flung it, but there was the boulder.

After that was ferns and the long grass and ye had to slow down and watch where ye walked, it was swampy and yer feet splashed through. Even if it was sunny and this day it was. The ground got too squelchy and yer shoes got stuck if ye were slow running, and yer feet came out and ye fell or else just ye were hopping, yer socks all soaked and muddy and if ye fell ye were just filfy. Jim would not go through the swampy bit. I showed him to go round the outside. He said, You come too.

I am not coming, I am going through the long grass.

Well I am telling.

It meant telling on me to his maw and da so if they would tell mine. I did not care, he was not my young brother and I did not have to look after him. Matt and George were away way across now and walking way to the gun-site hill. It looked like that. I telled Jim to hurry up and just come with me. He always thought about snakes, oh mammy daddy if snakes were there and going to get him. People said there was adders. Ye just had to watch.

I went through the long grass and the swampy bits for speed. Ye could go if ye did it careful. Ye looked for clumps of that long grass and ye walked on it. It was not good grass, ye could not eat it. The stems were hollow with a wee bush thing growing at the top. It looked like a bee.

I liked the swampy bits. Ye got deep puddles for frogspawn. Ye put yer hands in and lifted it out but it was very slippy and going through yer fingers. If ye had a jar ye put it in and took it home. Ye just smuggled it in and kept it under yer bed. The frogspawn went into wee shapes. The wee shapes started moving about, then with their tails. That was the tadpoles. Ye gived them names then put them back down the field into the burn so they could swim about. Then they came frogs. When ye saw frogs down the field ye called their names so if they came to ye, well, that was them.

There were other patches of swampy stuff and we went through it, then jumping the burn. In some places it was easy and ye got good stepping stones. When it was too heavy rain the burn ran very high and wide and ye could never jump it. One time Squatters were chasing us and we were having to jump the burn but the last one doing it missed the top. He was a big boy and quite a slow runner. He could not get a grip up the grass and his feet were on the sandy bit and it was too too slippy and muddy cause everybody's feet had all been there and dragging in the water and his feet could not get a grip. So he slid back down into the water, and there were the Squatters. Us up on the bank shouting on him, Hurry up hurry up. The Squatters were firing stanes and we were firing back till the big boy just got out in the nick of time.

The Squatters would have battered him or else captured him and took him back to their camp, it was over the gun-site hill. People were feared of them. They hated ye if ye came from the scheme. My maw and da did not like them. Oh they are just Tinkers and have no right to be there.

Their camp was way over the other side of the gun-site hill. Ye crept a long way past the barbed-wire fence, watching for holes in the ground. Ye could see down to the wee roofs of their camp, all tarpaulin and corrugated iron. They chased ye hard and were smashing runners. Lasses were with them too and they all were best fighters. The leader was Cochise. People called him that. He was like a man. What would happen if he caught ye? He would kill ye. He only wore his trousers and did not wear any jerseys or shirts even in winter, but stripped to the waist with things round his arms and sometimes with his bare feet and things round his ankles. He had a real hatchet tied into his trousers and then warpaint. That was what he had. He was the best fighter and would beat men if it was a fair fight. If they captured ye, they had lorries and caravans and took ye away, and ye were tied up.

The gun-site was on the very top of a big big hill stretching wide as streets. When ye looked out the living-room window of our house ye always saw that hill and were wanting to go. It was all grass and thick bushes up there, high bushes, ye could not see nothing from faraway. All guns were there from the war, big guns for shooting down airoplanes and wee stuff like ammunition and bombs. People talked about all what was there. It was hidden under the ground down secret tunnels with trapdoors and with grass over them and stanes and twigs all in disguise. If ye fell down one it would be all guns and stuff, and ye could bring them home. If there was a rifle there, that was what I wanted or else hand-grenades and tommy-guns. Some stuff was on top of the ground and ye would find it under tarpaulin sheets. Barbed-wire fences were round it and soldiers stopped ye getting in. They carried machine-guns and rifles. They wore long coats and no hats so ye did not know who they were. But if they gived ye chewing gum, if they liked ye, maybe they would. So it was Yanks if it was chewing gum.

At the foot of the near side of the gun-site was where the workies were and ye had to dodge through the new houses and then walk way way over. Berry bushes and jaggy nettles were here, dead thick and ye had to hold big branches up to get under. We passed it and on through all the ferns and jaggy nettles and bushes. Now Matt and George walked away on fast and did not wait for us. It was not fair. And Jim was just girning all the time. I telled him to shut it.

Ye could hear the noises from the workies but it was in the distance and there was no other sounds except that, and then the buzzing if flies were there or else grasshoppers how they clicked their knees. I caught one, ye just went to the noise and parted the grass with yer hands and there he was, he just was sitting and ye grabbed him with yer two hands.

Jim was sitting for a rest. I was seeing the way to run if the Squatters came. I said it to Jim but oh he was just moan moan I want to go home so I stopped and just sat down too.

Ye could see way far far over to our houses, it was right away over. My da might have come to the window, he would not have seen me, I was not even a wee speck. It was just bushes and bushes. It looked safe to go. But if Squatters were there and could see ye and then were creeping to get ye. So if they were, all ye could do was run. And people did not run the same, and if a wee one was there ye got slowed down because ye were holding his hand. That was Jim but he could run himself, I was not waiting for him.

Ye looked farther up the hill and ye could not see the gun-site. That was funny. It all was there and ye could never see it. Not till ye were there. Ye went over one hill then another one was there higher up, and higher up again, so ye had another rest. Big ferns were here. Ye thought ye had reached the top but ye had not, there was aye another hill to go, then another one, till finally that was you and there it went flat, and ye saw wee bits here and there so ye knew. The sun was hot on my head. I saw good grass and pulled a few stalks. The inside ends were sweet and I chewed them. I looked for the wee plants with the soor leaves. They were best. Oh and then shouting. Kierronnn! Kierronnn!

It was Matt. Me and Jim went through big ferns to get to them and George shouted about snakes, Oh be careful, it is full of them.

Matt said, Oh it is poisonous vipers.

It was just tormenting Jim because he hated them. Snakes were all in the ferns, that was where they hid. I never saw them but I went careful and just watched it. They slept there under the ferns. And if ye stood on them, well, if ye did, that was you. I lifted up the ferns but never saw them. Matt and George were laughing. I did not care. Then Jim was wanting the toilet. Oh well away and do it, that was what George said.

No, I am wanting to go home and do it.

You cannot.

I want to.

Well away ye go then!

George and Matt just ran away now and I was left with him. I told him to do the toilet as well but he would not because it was in the open and what would happen if something bit him?

If a snake came I would capture it. That was one thing, a pet snake, if ever I could get one.

Matt and George found the barbed-wire fence round the gun-site. It was a trail through thick thick bushes. Ye had to get through the fence, climbing or else underneath where there was holes. The holes were there, ye just crawled under. Jim was moaning how he did not want to and oh oh oh oh. George was telling him to shut up but he would not.

Matt went under the fence. He lied down on his back and his hands pushed up the bottom ends of the wire with George holding it up. He got through easy then held it for George. But they did not help us. George said to Jim. Oh you wait here.

You too, said Matt and they crept away fast through the bushes.

But I was not waiting. I was going under the wire same as them.

Oh do not leave me. That was Jim. It was good if he went first. If I held the wire for him then him holding it for me.

Oh but he would not, he was too feared, he was just nearly greeting, oh oh oh, and snakes too oh they were coming and going to bite ye, oh oh. Oh please wait here Kieron please wait here.

No, we have to go under the wire.

Oh please do not, please wait here, oh oh.

And now he was bursting for the toilet and he had to go and he could not wait and just had to do it. Oh but if there was no paper to wipe his B-U-M, where was the paper? If there was no any.

Well ye just use leaves to wipe. It was docken leaves, ye just found them. I said it to him. Away into the bushes and do it.

Oh no no I will just do it here.

No, away into the bushes.

Oh no you go into the bushes.

But I am no needing it is you.

Oh but I can do it here.

Well I am just staying.

Oh but you will just watch me.

I will not watch ye.

Oh ye will, please go in the bushes.

No.

Please Kieron please.

So I had to go in the bushes. I went away a wee bit, if I could look over to see Matt and George. But I could not so I just sat a wee minute, watching out for stuff, if snakes were there, maybe they were. If it was real adders or else grass snakes. Grass snakes did not bite, that was a pet I wanted. Even if it was a adder and the adder knew ye and you were its owner, it would not poison ye then. People had snakes. They wrapped them round their arms. Boys said that. I did not see them. I did not see any snakes. George said it to Jim, Oh it is all snakes and they come out and poison ye with just their fangs poking out, they jab ye.

I did not believe him. He said it to make Jim scared. So if it was big ferns where ye were sitting, what if a snake came out? What if they did? If ye stepped on one or else sat on top of it. People said that. Oh he just sat down and the snake bit him right through his trousers, the poison just went right in.

The big ferns is where they hid and waited for ye. Thick bushes were there too, with all jaggy nettles so ye could not go through. The Army put them there to stop ye, ye could not go in them even if ye were wee. If ye wanted to go in them, I did not. There was no any space. Yer feet would just get trapped and yer body too, ye would have to be a ghost. Ghosts could just slide about into mid air. If ghosts were here. Ye could get dead spirits from the war if it was soldiers and their ghosts came. Sailors went down to the bottom of the sea. Their spirits were all down there except if they went up to Heaven, but some did not, they just waited. If they had to stay down below. If God would not let them in. Maybe no, if He was angry. God got angry if ye done bad stuff. Then if it was soldiers. They all got shot but if it was blown up and they were smashed to smithereens so they did not have a body, it was all bits everywhere. Where did they go?

I did not like the bushes where I was sitting. Ye could not see in. It was just leaves and leaves and all thick branches all fankled, all stuff poking out, fuzzy stuff and poison too, so ye could not go in, ye could not, even if ye wanted to but I did not want to, never never, there was no space for ye, ye could not go in, I would never, and never try it. Ye would just get stuck, how yer foot would just get twisted in and trapped, ye would just get trapped, and ye could not move, ye could not move.

Oh but I did not like it here. I did not. I just did not. I was shivering, how come I was shivering oh but I was oh but I was, I was I was I was and could not stop it if I was scared, my teeth hitting against each other. And it was just loud and louder, and now I needed the toilet, I really was needing and just had to go and it was just now I just had to and I looked and where was docken leaves if it was diarrhoea oh I felt it coming but it was just fern leaves to wipe, I could not find dockens.

Then came talking. I heard it. I hid down. Oh if it was a Yank or a soldier. Or else a Squatter, oh a Squatter, that was what I thought and if he captured ye and took ye away. But then it was not it was Matt and George. I saw them away over. They were smoking. They were there and smoking. George was, I did not see Matt doing it. And nothing else, I did not see nothing else. Except away far far. That was rich people's houses. Big boys went knocking out their gardens, apples and stuff. There were all fields there in the distance. Ye could get turnips out farmers' fields. George said that. Him and other boys went. He was taking Matt but no me. How come? I could keep up easy, I was a fast runner and could jump good if it was the burn and we were getting chased. I said that and Matt said to me, Oh just get yer own pals.

But if my maw found out he was smoking he would get a real doing. I could tell on him. If I did that would be him. So how would he like it?

Oh and then he nearly saw me. Him and George were coming. I ducked down and went back through the bushes. Jim was there waiting at the fence. But what happened, Matt came right to me. Take Jim home.

What?

Just take Jim home.

No. What are yous doing?

We are just going a walk.

I am going with you.

So am I, said Jim.

Kieron is taking ye home, said George.

I am no.

Yes ye are. Matt gived me the punch sign for a secret warning. That was what he done and he would just get me after if I did not do it. Oh you are getting a secret warning.

That was what he called it.

The gun-site was no good so they were going away someplace else. And if I tried to go with them Matt would batter me. Brothers did that. George done it to Jim. It was just the same. So if it was brothers, that was what they done, it just was not fair. And people did not know. They done it behind their backs. If it was yer maw and da watching the telly, he came in and just gived ye a look or else if he held his hand up and in a punching grip showing ye, Oh you, you are going to get it.

That was the sign, so that was you and ye were going to get it. If it was Matt, he just went back out the room. So ye were feared to go out the living room, so if it was the lavatory, ye did not want to go because if he was waiting ben the lobby. He would be and would get ye.

If ye did not know about brothers ye would not see the sign. Some of what Jim got off George I knew because with Matt.

It was not fair a first brother and a second brother, because ye were not the first ye did not get stuff and because ye were weer ye got doings. Nobody bothered because it was brothers so it was their business and kept out it, even if it was bullies and they were punching wee ones. They done it so ye would not come. Well I just did. I did not care. So if they said, Away ye go. I just followed them. I done it the next time and they were going a long walk. Jim was not there. I was glad.

George was there with Matt, and another big boy. I did not know who he was. I followed them right away over the field and away over and across at the edge of the gun-site hill then away down and out on a country road. There was no pavements to walk on and bushes and trees at the side of the road. Ye just had to watch it, and if motors came, sometimes an old lorry.

They were smoking again and drinking ginger. George had a job as a paperboy and made a big wage and it was him bought all the stuff. Me and Matt did not get much. Matt was wanting to get a job too. My da thought it was good but my maw did not, only his studies. That was what she always wanted was studies, Oh do yer lessons do yer lessons.

I kept way behind and was just hiding a wee bit. I did not care if they saw me except Matt with smoking, he would be angry, if I was going to tell on him. Maybe I would.

I saw him now and he was going to chase me. I knew the way he done things. He would just wait and wait and go a wee bit slower and a wee bit slower and then oh running and running to catch me but he would not catch me. He would not. Except if he did. So I ran back. I saw George laughing to him, saying something. That was about me. I waited before going. I did not see them round the bend, then round the next one I did not see them. Maybe they were just hiding.

It was miles and miles away. I knew where the scheme was but ye could never have seen it from where we were, it was too faraway and then all hills and roads were in between and now cows but mostly sheep. We were coming out to hills and big hills. I saw the sheep there and if ye looked high up they were way way up there.

But I could not see Matt and if there was a tree I would have climbed it because with Matt, he just would sneak up on ye and then jump out and get ye.

It was funny how sheep, ye saw them and they did not look good, but they were and were smashing climbers. If they fell down a mountainside the shepherd had to go and find them, he lifted them on his shoulders, wee lambs.

I found good grass and was looking for soor leaves. There was a wee gate with a step fixed to it and ye climbed up and over and into the field. Cows were there and were looking at me, if they were going to charge me, maybe they were, I went by the side of the field and away over from them. There was not any trees anywhere, not good ones. A wee loch was. I just came on it. I went over a wee hill and there it was. Ye could have went for a swim. I was going to but I did not. The water was not blue but black-looking and big long weeds were coming out. I felt the water to see but it was freezing cold. I took a wee sip and it was good. Maybe if I paddled out. If it was not deep, it did not look deep. I was going to take off my socks and shoes but I did not, because if it was deep after all, even just the deepest like a big big hole right in the middle or else a big fish nibbling yer toes or just if it bited ye if it was very big or if it was like a Loch Ness monster, it could have been.

It was all quiet roundabout and big boulders, if baddies were hiding behind them. It was a laugh but what if they were? Ye thought about it. And if ye were the cavalry ye were getting a drink of water, ye were having a wee rest and the horses too, then the Indians were coming to get ye, just quiet and creeping up, knives in their teeth to scalp ye, and ye were just lying down to get a drink of water and the arrow thudded into ye or else the one standing beside ye, he was yer old pal oh and the arrow thudded into his back, Oh I am done for. So ye ran quick to hide, just for cover, and drawing yer gun except if ye did not have one, only a rifle. Soldiers just have rifles and ye left it over beside yer horse so ye had to run to yer horse but the Indians were there and stole yer horse and were here coming to get ye and with their knives or else their spears.

If my pals from the old place came here they would love this place. If I got Terry and Ian and boys out my class they could come and see it. I would just bring them. I could easy do it. Just if they had money for the train, that was all. Oh they would love it and all the good games ye could play they would love it.

It was all smashing for playing. Except how the big boulders and stuff was all quiet, it was quiet. Ye could not hear nothing only maybe the wind, just a wee bit. So if it made ye feared, ye could see how it did, if it did, ye were just there and nobody else. There was no any sounds, there was just no any sounds. Oh but birds, high up, ye saw them, whirling about, wee specks. Then just the sheep and they were just away high up, right away at the very top, ye looked and there was one farther up, and the wind making the grass shiver. I liked the sheep. They were just how they were and did not look good but were the bestest climbers. They were not fat, their coats had been sheared off.

I went home. It was a long way away but I knew how to go, it was easy. I just went to the road and that was it and I would just get it easy. I sat down for a rest and got some good grass to eat but none of the soor leaves. I liked them. Ye just chewed one. Ye were not to swallow it, and ye got the juice. Ye spat it out after. I was starving and if ye got turnips. I did not know how to. It was best just walking. I could not see the road and was looking away over the hills and went up high to look but could not see anything. It was all just in the country. If I found the road I would go on a bus if buses came. I had no money but just say to the conductor, Oh please Mr I lost my money.

But I could not find the road so just kept walking and walking and having wee rests and just getting to where I saw it looked the way to go and I was just going there and I got to a road but it was not the same road, just a wee one. It was all dried out so if no motors came, just a ghost road. I was walking and walking. It was windy and steep down so ye went round and round and down and down and were running a wee bit. I came to a wall and a house, and a pile of pigs behind a fence. Real pigs. They were all running about and squeaking when they saw me, just real pigs and ye saw their wee eyes and they were just manky all where their mouths were, they had been eating food and it was all dirty. Farther on all the big houses started where the rich people stayed and I just went on and came round a bend and down a long big hill and there saw the bluebell woods. When ye saw them ye knew ye were nearly there. It was smashing to get to my close and up the stair. When I chapped the door my maw came and she saw me. Oh Kieron.

Then my da's feet down the lobby, Oh is that him now and he grabbed me at the wrist and gave me a skelping, just hard, I did not care. I saw Matt was there and did not care for him either, none of them at all, and my maw, I did not care about any of them and just was wanting away, just getting away from that horrible stinking b****y house just to get back to the old place and my old pals and my school just in the classroom and my grannie and granda and the street going up and just everything.

§

Pat stayed two closes along from me. I went pals with him and Danny McGuire. I went into Pat's house a lot. The walls had Crosses hung up and pictures of Jesus and a big one where was all the Disciples in Raiment and it was the Last Supper. Jesus was killed on the Cross. It was just the same story and ye saw Judas, Oh he is the one and the Pieces of Silver, Oh do not forsaketh me, but he does.

Pat had one wee brother and one big sister. Her room door was shut so ye could not see in it. She had big fights with their maw and da. So did Pat. They were not feared of them. Pat's da worked in the railways and was aye sleeping on the chair when ye went in his house. Pat did not like him. If ye went on the train ye saw him waiting at the gate to collect the tickets off the folk coming home. A lot did not have tickets and just skipped past him. Pat's da looked at them but did not say nothing. If he was scared to, if he was a coward. If Pat thought that. But I liked his house better than mine. He had a good room, it was just his wee brother with him.

Danny McGuire came up and we were talking and I was saying

about the ferry and how ye could just do stuff. They were wanting to go and see it so I took them. I did not tell my maw and da. My da did not like me talking about the old place and if I wanted to go to my grannie and granda. Oh this is yer house now, ye have got to get used to it. Ye are not running to them all the time.

We went on Saturday morning. Pat knew a way to go on the train so ye did not pay much money. We got to the river and oh they loved it and on the pier showing them the steps down and how ye went right down the bottom one and then the one next to that was under the water and how ye just could stand on it when the waves went out and then jumped up when the waves came in. A woman was up the top watching us. Oh come away from there!

We were just laughing. The ferry came in and I showed them how to do it, jumping aboard and standing ready to jump off and doing it before the ferryman jumped ashore with his rope. Ye called him Skipper and ye had to get up the stair before he tied the ferry. That was what we always done, it was just like a race and the Skipper tied it fast so he could beat ye. They were real sailors from the highlands.

The ferry was out in the middle and ye could see right down the river. Ye leaned yer elbows on the side and just looked over and saw everything, all the boats, big ones like my da sailed in and went round the world and wee ones too and then the ones getting built with all the big planks and poles way up high where the men walked along the sides. They could just look down and did not fall off but if ye waved they did not wave back. I liked wee boats the best. I would have loved one, if ye could have yer own boat and just go in it and sail about wherever ye wanted. I was going in the Navy when I grew up. I was telling them how my da was a real sailor and that was him.

Oh but what if it sinks? said Danny.

Him and Pat could not swim. I showed the lifebelts to them. Danny touched one. Oh you are not supposed to touch it, I said.

How no?

It is bad luck.

What happens?

I did not know what happens. Except Danny should not have

touched it. I never touched them. It was not good to do it. I did not think so.

We got to the other side of the river. I thought to take them to my grannie and granda or else the park to show them the pond, maybe if the yachts were out and it was a race. Then we were saying about football, how they had not been to a real game. I said how with Rangers ye could go and the men would lift ye over. The cops were there but ye just knew what to do. So if they were looking ye just kidded on ye were not doing it and then if ye waited and just ye got a man and he whisked ye over and that was you and ye saw the game and it was smashing. So we would go now. It was Saturday. So I told them. I will just take ye.

Oh no, it is Rangers. Danny said, Rangers is just for Protestants.

Oh but they will not know, we can just go.

But what if they find out?

Oh but they will not, we will not tell them.

Oh but if they know?

But they will not know. Nobody will see ye. So if ye do not tell them. It will be okay.

Danny had a worried face.

Him and Pat did not look like Catholics. Catholics had white faces and black hair or else red hair and freckles and white faces. Only their names. Their names were Pape names. If ye said their names. Ye could not say their names. If anybody heard them. Oh do not say yer names out loud, I said. Oh and mine too, do not say it.

How come?

Oh it is a Pape's name, Kieron is a Pape's name. If they think it. If they think it is. It is not, Protestants are called it too.

Pat said, I know a boy called Kieron Ramsay, he goes to my old school. He is a Catholic.

Protestants could be Kieron too. But I did not know a Proddy called Pat. And a Pape called Billy. But if there was, maybe there was. Or Danny, I did not know about Danny, maybe it was Saint Danny. My da said that.

But we would not say names.

I took them the long way so past my old house just to show them.

I did not show them the Catholic School and the Chapel. I took them past my school, and through the houses where the midgierakers stayed. It was all Papes lived here. But it was dead quiet. People were there but were not watching us. They were just doing stuff, kicking a ball and just what, playing games and stuff, talking. If they looked at us, how come we were there and walking in their place, if they were going to chase us. Oh but we are RCs. I would say it.

We got to the Rangers but nobody was there except just wee boys playing heidies on the pavement. It was a big wide pavement. Two cops were there but not chasing them.

All the gates were locked. A man was walking with a dog, a big beauty and just skinny with a long tail. I said it. Oh Mr we were looking but where is Rangers, is there no a match on?

Oh no boys they are not at home today, they are up in Dundee.

Oh.

Danny said, Is that a racing dog mister?

Yes.

Where is its races?

Faraway son.

The man walked away with the dog. We were looking and the dog walking and his head just going up up, up up, and too how his shoulders went. Whish whish, ye could see it. It was a beauty.

Danny said, That is a greyhound. It is a real racing dog. A racing dog is a greyhound. In my old place ye could see them racing, it was a dog track and my grandpa went and he took me.

But that was us now and we went back for the ferry. It was a very very long walk and we did not have any much money. No for chips and we could see a chip shop. The rain started. It got heavier and the wind blowing. Ye felt cold too. Down at the pier there was a roof to duck under. So we were there waiting and watching the rain bounce up. It was the heaviest. Ye could see too how it hit the water, straight in and it was just a complete blanket.

On the ferry we stood under cover beside the engine. A lot of people were there. It was very hot and the engine smell was strong and that sweet smell was in it and I did not like it. Sometimes it was there and ye wanted out to the fresh air but if ye could not get out, the rain pelting down and everybody just there and men smoking and ye did not get good air off the wind. Danny felt sick, oh and was going to be, and he was, the sick splashed down and on a man's shoes and on his trousers and he did a swear word, F**k sake.

Danny went out the sheltered bit and was more sick. The man was shaking the sick off his trouser bottoms. He had a girny old face and ye thought he was going to hit Danny. Lucky for him he did not. We would have waited off the ferry and fired stanes at him. We would have.

§

My granda was not keeping good. Uncle Billy was back from England again, staying with him and grannie. Auntie May was away someplace else and was getting married. Me and Matt went over to see granda. We walked a long way to get a bus. We done it to save money. The bus did not come so we did not go. But we were walking and found a canal. We were used to the big river so this was just wee, but still good. Men fished in it and so did some boys and they were catching fish but we did not see them. After that we went a lot. If Matt would not go I went down myself or sometimes Pat came. Danny did not go away much from the street.

The canal was good. Ye watched the boats coming down through the locks. Other people went, lasses too, but ye had to watch it with other boys. Ye were wanting to make pals but if they were wanting to fight, I did not want to, so ye were ready to run.

Wee boats went on the canal, cabin cruisers and barges. They sailed across Scotland and came out the other side. At these locks the water changed, it was high and low. The boat went in high up and then sat in between the locks till it went low, it got lowered down. And the boat was on top of it and when they opened the gate the boat sailed out and it was hurrehhh, I shouted it. I loved seeing them come out. The sailors let ye help to wind the handle that set the height of the water. The handle was for a big wheel and ye had to watch it did not spin, ye could not do it yerself unless ye were a man. But they were not real sailors, no like my da.

If ye were jumping across the gangways over the locks ye got chased by the lock-keeper. Oh you wee b★★★★r. But ye would not fall in. He said ye would but ye would not.

Along the sides of the canal were reeds and ye could get them out the water. They cracked when ye bent them and were hollow inside. In the olden days the kilties were hiding from the redcoats and they sank under the water with the reeds in their mouths poking out the water, getting air to breathe.

If ye went the way east the path stopped and ye had to go down on the road and walk that way to catch up. Then there was the railway and ye walked along the tracks. There were men there and they chased ye. If ye listened to the line ye could hear the train coming. There were bushes there and ye could hide in them and if the train went by oh ye were just there and hiding. Matt was saying how there were foxes and wolves too, they came from the country.

§

After the summer holidays everybody from our scheme got special buses to a temporary school. Mostly we did not know people, except if they lived beside ye. Papes were there too but their schools did not go on my bus. The bus I got stopped at the same place so I stood there to wait. People did that. Ye saw ones from your bus and stood near them. I saw two lasses from my class at the temporary school but they did not talk to me. I did not talk to them. Julie Michaels and Lorna Buckle. People shouted her name to her. Oh beltbuckle, tie my beltbuckle. She got a red face.

We got the special school buses down behind the shops. A lot of other buses were there. I saw Pat and Danny and gived a wave. Some days the bus did not come for ages. People said about going home and some did. But then if the buses came. I just waited till the end. Nobody was in my house. I had my doorkey but I did not like if it was just me in the house. My da had got a new job. It was in a factory and quite faraway. He got a train into town and then a bus and the same back.

We all got tickets for schooldinners. It was great. It was in a separate building and they did not care if ye came for second helpings. Ye got steak pie and other stuff, mashed potatoes and cabbage, it was just great and then sausage pie, it was all pastry with sausages sticking out except sometimes it was burnt but ye still ate it, it was great. Some big boys got their dinner and then joined straight on the back of the queue. They ate up their dinner quick while they were waiting and then it was their turn again, so they had an empty plate and just got second helpings. At morning time ye were just sitting. I could not wait. What were ye getting? Steak pie and potatos or what. On Wednesdays ye did not get a dinner, just a soup then ice cream and jelly and if it was Friday ye got fish. Fish on Friday. That was for Papes, a boy said it, if we were getting it, how come?

But I did not get on good at this school. That was what I felt. I did not know boys and did not have pals. How could I not go to the old school? In the old school people liked me. Here they did not. In the old place it was me said things, Oh we will go to the park or jump the dykes or maybe if the lasses were there and it was dark nighttime we all telled stories. It was good fun, sitting on the stairs under the lights and saying about creepy stuff and if one had to go home we all laughed about ghosts getting them or if bogie men were there. The lasses liked it and so did we. But in the new place things did not work the same. I was not a best fighter. Boys just looked at me in a wee way so they thought they were best fighters. But if they did not see me fight. How come they thought they were better if they did not see me?

Even if I was the best fighter in the whole class? If ye did not have fights ye could be. So if ye were not, nobody knew ye were not. So ye could have been, so how did they know ye were not? Ye could just have said it, Oh I am the best fighter. But people would just laugh, or else fight ye.

One day it was freezing cold and ice was there and we were waiting ages, stamping about for yer feet to get warm. People were down at the corner to look out for the buses. Boys were flinging stuff about for a laugh. I did not know them. A thing hit me. What was it? Just a scabby old cloot thing like an old towel but complete filfy. The boys acted like they did not see it hit me. But if they thought I was daft or what, if I could not fight, they would soon find out. They flung something else and it hit a boy beside me. It was John Davis. He wiped it off his coat and looked over at who flung it. The boy looked back at him. John Davis just was watching him and with a look on his face, and he kept looking at the boy. He wiped his coat again but the other boy just walked over to another bit so then ye knew he was feared of John Davis, I thought that. How come? John never done nothing, just looked. So that was that and people knew, Oh watch it, if it was him, and they just left him alone. He had on a Rangers' tie. That was what he wore. So I said it to him, if he supported Rangers, and he did. I was talking to him and the buses came. I sat beside him. He did not go to my school. Him and another boy and lassie stayed on after we all got off.

If ye spoke to him he did not speak back but was watching ye hard so ye were careful. Ye did not try anything with him. If he lost his temper, ye wondered maybe if he would, what would happen. Boys looked at him but then they did not and just looked someplace else.

He did not have pals much. I went home with him one night after school. His maw opened the door and took me in. She did not speak, just smiled. It was Rangers everywhere. Even the living room. It had all blue and orange for the curtains and carpets and all pictures, it was King Billy and the Queen on their horses or else just standing. My maw did not let King Billies go on the wall but she liked the Queen and we had pictures of her. The biggest one was in the living room. Her and the Duke wore the Sash and had on Army clothes. My da put up Rabbie Burns. He liked him. Oh my love is like a red red rose.

John Davis had a big brother that was like a man. Ye did not see him except just coming in or going out and he did not speak to ye.

And he did not speak to John. Ye saw him and he just walked past. They had the same bedroom and it was Rangers Rangers Rangers and all the players were on the wall and calendars and all stuff.

His maw was a wee woman that just went about. I was bigger than her. She did not talk, just looked at the ground and was smiling all the time. How come? If she was thinking about a joke. They had a wee dog that lied in its basket under the kitchen table. He had quick breathing and steam out his mouth and dribbling all the time and it went on the carpet. My maw would not have had it.

I was in with John and his da saw me, Mr Davis. He had funny teeth that stuck out. Oh and what is your name son?

Kieron.

Oh, Kierrunn, that is a nice name. Then he said it to Mrs Davis, and he was looking at me. His name is Kierrunn. Is that not nice?

John did not talk to his da or his maw except if he was looking for stuff if he could not find it and was crashing about flinging open the drawers. That was when he shouted and it was dead dead loud and oh it was just really shouting, Oh where is it where is it! Oh where is it!

If he was getting angry. Ye thought he was. It was a worry. Ye were just there and looking. But then he was okay again.

They were in the Lodge and if there was a Walk ye saw them. His da wore the Sash and the round hat and with the umbrella under his arm. So did his maw, and she wore a hat as well and a handbag. Mr Davis walked first and then John and her. She took funny steps when she was walking as if it was all wee puddles on the ground and she was wanting no to step in them. John walked a wee bit the same as her and he looked at the ground too. I said to him. Oh hey John look at the sky!

I just done it to get him. But maybe it was something, if it was birds flying, so then he was looking. And if it was a big flock of birds and how they all went flying high and if it was a shape and ye saw one bird flying off by itself. That happened. Then other ones following and other ones staying behind then they would all come the gether and ye watched them flying on and on and would keep looking and keep looking till yer neck was sore and they were wee toty wee specks and ye did not know if ye could see them or what. I would say it to John. I can still see them I can still see them I can still see them until then I could not. He was looking too and waiting for me to say it. Then if clouds were coming and they flew into them. They all went to Africa for the hot weather. And ye got ducks. The ducks flew as well. I said it to John. One time we came off the school bus at four o'clock and I was going home with him. Other boys were kicking a ball and putting down their schoolbags for goalposts. These boys did not go to my school but I knew them because of the school buses. Papes were there too. Any chance of a game? I just shouted it.

Aye.

So I got John too and he came on. They picked sides and me and him were last picked. The very last was him, just how he looked and did not talk or else bother. But then we were playing and he was a best tackler, bestest, he was, and I did not know and was pals with him, so how come? I was just looking. Whohh, ye just could not get past him. And his knees banged into ye too and just how he was tough with his tackles or else in shoulder charges, ye bounced off him. Ye were running at him and he just stuck out his foot. Trying to dribble him, ye could not. How did he do it? He just stuck out his foot and got the ball. And then of all was heidying the ball, he would have beat men.

I could not heidy the ball right. My granda showed me and showed me. Oh it is the front of yer head son do not close yer eyes. Attack the ball Attack the ball.

If it was the middle of yer head it was no good. Yer head had two bits and then there was the middle. If the ball hit in there it was where the two bits joined, and it was softer, so that was how it was sore and the ball did not go the right way because it was the two bits, one one way, one the other and the ball hitting in, so where did it go, that way or that way?

And ye had to watch how ye done it. It happened to me, the ball just plonking down and ye were dizzy and ye had to wait a wee minute and could not run. If ye did not heidy the ball right and it was too many times that would be bad for yer head, just like what happened to boxers so it was punch-drunk.

Uncle Billy was there and he was laughing when granda said it, but it was right enough. My granda shook his head at Uncle Billy. Oh never mind him son he is a dumpling.

I was telling John Davis about it but he did not bother if it was the front or the back or what, if it was the middle of his head, he just jumped and got it and the ball went sailing away. His heidying was better than some boys kicking. He was just good at it.

Except I was a fast runner, John was not. He was big and ye thought he was too big. Some boys tried to be funny with him, if maybe he was daft because people might think that. So now they did not and if me and him were coming off the school bus and the boys were there for a game, well, they just picked us in the teams. Oh John you kick that way. Smiddy you kick that way!

That was me, my name, it just was Smiddy now. If somebody said it to me. What is yer name? Oh it is Smiddy.

I just said that.

But then what happened. John stopped playing. How come? It was his feet or else shoes. I was saying it to him and he held his feet up to show me. If his shoes got all bashed, maybe that was it. Mine did too. My maw got angry because I played with my school clothes on. Yer trousers too, how they got manky and one time were ripped all up the leg right from the bottom. How did that happen? I did not know till I was running and then my trouser just flapping. My maw sewed them. She just grabbed them off me. That was my good trousers. Oh no! and she was angry. Oh do not you ever do this again Kieron Smith you will come home from school now and change.

I said it to John. We will go home and change first. Put on yer old stuff and yer old shoes and that and I will see you there in a wee minute!

I just rushed home and changed and back out, just with a piece on jam and a slug of milk out the bottle. My maw did not like me doing that but she was not home. I lived away farther from the shops than John. But then I got there and was on playing but where was he? He never came back. I went up to see but he would not come out. If he went in his house and changed out his school clothes that was him, he did not come out.

I said it to his maw. Oh if he has got old shoes.

She just smiled.

John is the best player Mrs Davis if he can get his old shoes and then just play.

She was making their tea. It smelled good and my stomach was rumbling.

Oh can I look in the pot?

Mmhh. She nodded her head to me.

It was mince and potatos and there was big thick onions, that was it I was smelling. Oh I was starving. My maw did not make onions. My da had a bad stomach and onions were not good for it. And if it was fried. Oh no. And for an egg, poach it or else boiled, that was my da.

But John did not come out. I liked being pals with him but it was only sometimes ye saw him, that was all. He did not like climbing. There was a good wall near the shops and people climbed it. He only watched. He kept watching till ye made it to the top and his face was worried, if ye were going to fall, he thought ye were. I walked along the top of it and done funny steps. He was glad when ye came down. I just laughed. Oh John it is dead easy. See the ones we climbed in the old places! We had the biggest jumps and the biggest dykes. This is just nothing.

He could have climbed it. I said to him, Go and do it.

Some big boys were not good climbers and it was fat too, but John was no fat. And he was not a daftie, if people thought he was, he was not.

Ye watched for ones that were. Some dafties were no feared of nobody. They would just fight who it was. They did not care. So if ye laughed at them they would get ye.

Ye had to be careful in the new scheme. Ye did not know who was who. Then too if it was Papes, who was a good fighter and who was not. And if the Pape was a daftie, ye did not know.

And people walked at ye. That was what they done. Ye had to get out the road. But if ye did so they could walk then they were the boss and you were just nothing. So ye had to watch it when ye were walking. Ye were aye ready, so if ye saw boys coming to ye, and it was a long way away ye were thinking what to do. Maybe ye crossed the street. But if ye stayed on the same pavement what would happen? Ye had to think what to do. Because if these boys were coming to ye, ye could not bang into them. And they would not get out your way. No unless it was just one or two and they were younger or else wee or just if they were not good fighters. Ye had to act tough. Men done it too. They all just acted tough. Boys were walking down the street and I watched to see. So if it was a man coming, what did he do? So if he crossed the street well maybe he was feared.

People just tried it with ye to see if ye were easy and ye had to do something back to them. If they punched you you had to punch them. If they stole yer school bag or clicked yer heels and tripped ye, you done the same to them. Ye acted tough. I was not near getting bullied and nobody made a fool of me except if it was a laugh and ye all were doing it. Even the best fighters, they did not get me. If it was football or what, I was good at stuff, if it was games or running. People knew that. Then if it was climbing, I was a best climber.

§

My maw said it was good if I started Sunday School. She heard people saying about it and I should just give it a try. I did not want to but my da said, Oh you will meet other boys and stop moaning.

Oh but dad.

No.

They were going to make me go. I did not want to except if it was the Lifeboys and ye had to. I went in the old place and it was horrible except ye saw yer pals. The Sunday School teacher was always angry. If he thought ye were making a fool of him, but we were not, I was not. I did not want to go except if it was the Lifeboys.

My maw said, Oh but there is going to be a Lifeboys.

Well I can go then.

You will go just now.

Well what about Matt?

Oh he is too old.

My da said, He will get Bible Class when he goes back to the BB, so that is enough. You need it and he does not.

How come?

Ye just do.

How come?

He did not say anything more. He stuck up for Matt but he did not stick up for me.

If it was the Sunday School for me it was the Sunday School for him. But they did not think it.

But my maw was making me go. But what happened next Sunday I wanted to go. She left my collection money on the kitchen table. I was making toast for my breakfast and I just thought about it and I just wanted to go. That was funny. I thought that. If it was the Minister. Just on Friday morning he had been in our class at the temporary school, he was saying stuff about Jesus going into the Temple and he just got everybody out that was doing money-lending. It was good how he done it. They were in His Father's house and should not have been doing that there if it was the ways of the world and it was not as it is in Heaven. Jesus was just young when He done it. They were all men but He could just do it. God helped Him for His strength.

I liked that Minister. He had another voice and was a bit like my cousins in Fife, oh ye ken. He had a red face and he smacked his hands. Now boys and girls, will ye sit up straight now and then I will tell ye and it is a story, it is a real story.

And so he done it and people all liked the story.

So it was good it was me. I went and looked out the living-room window and was glad it was, I just wanted to go. Matt was still in bed and so were my maw and da, they had a long lie on Sundays. So if I went into the Church, if they were still in bed. That was me in the Church and they would still be sleeping.

When I went out I closed the door very very quiet so not to wake them up.

And walking along the street, I liked it, and away round the long road and over the hill. Nobody much was there and ye could just see all stuff. Then there were people and they were going to the Chapel. They were just walking. I went on the other side of the street. I looked at them but they did not look at me. I did not know any ones that were there. RCs went to the Chapel at all different times, at nighttime as well.

I did not care if it all was Bible stuff. I was just myself here going. I liked it and could just do something if I wanted to. Except if I had a ball I could have played it down the road, so for the next time I would get a ball, even just a tennis ball.

It was a wee old Church down near the railway line and all leaves on the ground, piles and piles.

But who only was waiting. Two wee boys out the infants' class and four lasses from Primary 4. That was who was there. They were just looking at me. If it was the wrong Sunday School. I walked over a bit and stood beside bushes. There were trees here too and ye could have climbed them. Matt said there was chestnut trees.

I could see the railway line way down a bit. Imagine there was a train could take me someplace. Just away to the seaside then ye could swim and go on the sand. But I could go to my grannie's.

I had not seen my grannie and granda for ages. It was great in the old place, ye could just cross the back and go up the stair. I saw them all the time. Mattie as well. But I went more than him. I just liked going. In the new scheme ye could not.

Ye just could not do stuff. I did not like it in the new scheme. Maybe I hated it. If I did hate it. And I did not have any pals. Except John Davis. Then if it was Pat and Danny, but they were Catholics. Ye did not see Catholics much. They went their other places. So I did not have any pals. John did not come out much. His maw and da did not let him. He could have come to Sunday School. But I did not say to him. He would not have wanted to come. He did not like going places. I went up for him but he just stayed in. He took me in but I wanted to stay out. Oh we will go down the field and jump the burn. I said it to him plenty of times. I can show ye the gun-site, come on we will go and then if it is the Squatters, we can see their camp.

No.

Oh but just a walk after tea.

He just said no. That was John. He would not have come to the Sunday School.

But I thought if other people went so if ye got pals, if boys came I would get pals with them. I thought that. But here was nobody except lasses and two wee infant boys. I just waited.

An old old man was there. He came in the gate and opened a wee door at the side of the Church building. He brought us into a shady room. And then funny smells and all black clothes hanging down. What were they for? The Primary 4 lasses were looking and so was I. Maybe it was the Church Minister's stuff and he changed in here, it was his cloaks and stuff. Our School Minister wore a black cloak but no when he was out on the street, then it was a jacket and trousers. But no Priests and Nuns. They had their stuff on all the time and just went about everywhere. They did not care. Papes did not care. Ye saw them and they just were going their places and if it was Chapel they just went in the door. Look at them going in. People said that. But they just done it. In the old place we went to scrambles and if it was a Chapel ye saw them all going in and just talking or else laughing.

Black cloaks. How come it was black cloaks? Maybe other colours were there too. If it was purple.

That smell but. What was it? Maybe sweaty feet. But oh like sugary stuff too, it was horrible and maybe even if it was yer eyes. I felt it. That smell was making my eyes nippy.

The old man was waving at me. Oh boy if ye just lift down a chair. He said it to me, oh boy, and there was the chairs all piled up on tables.

I was to help get them for the two wee infant boys and the Primary 4 lasses. He passed them to me and I put them on the floor. Oh but if it was the wrong Sunday School class? Maybe it was, maybe there was one for older people.

Oh mister is there another Sunday School? I said it to him but he did not speak back. Then he was looking with his face all wrinkled up. Oh mister is there another Sunday School for big ones?

What?

But a woman was there, just come in the door. Oh no, this is the Sunday School, she said. Do not worry, boys and girls your age will be coming.

She got a seat and put it down to look at all us. She had white hair and a quite snobby voice. Hullo boys and girls, I wonder what your names are and what school you go to.

The two wee boys were saying it to her. Oh Miss my name is Andrew.

I just was standing up. Oh please Miss I will come next week.

I beg your pardon?

Oh just I will come next week Miss.

I needed to go and went over to the door and if she grabbed my shoulder, maybe she would, I would just run, she would not catch me.

Oh but sit down.

I just walked and it was out in a corridor. I kept on but I was feeling funny and it was just an awful feeling in my head, if it was going to blow up, if my body was getting bigger and bigger and blow into smithereens else what would happen what would happen, I did not know, just to get out and I was just walking getting away.

I went down the road, then the next one, and the sign was there for the train station oh and I had my collection money, I had it in my pocket. My maw gave me it for the Sunday School. I could just go on the train. I could, I could just do it. The stairs went up to the train station platform. I just went up. Nobody was there. I walked along to the very end of the platform. All bushes and big big weedy bits, and bricks and boulders and then sweetie papers and all litter stuff.

Foxes and wolves came at nighttime. Along here it took ye to the canal. Boys ran over the railway track. They just done it. Ye listened to the lines and if it was all clear then ye did it. It was good. But what I thought, ye could just run along if ye keeped into the side and just at the bushes so if a train came, nobody would see ye and it would just be you looking out, ye would see all the people on their seats, but they would not see you.

A bench was there and I sat on it. It was funny how it was just me and I was at the Sunday School and nobody else was. Out of everybody that was all my age only it was me. How come? It was just a thing and I was thinking about it. Then all other stuff. And a secret wee thing how really if I was a Pape. That was a wee thing I used to think. If I was one and did not know it so I was not going to Chapel but just to Church. I should have been going to Chapel but was not. Because I did not know. Because nobody told me. If I did not know. So I could not do it.

If I did know and did not do it that was different. Except if it came to me in my head and it was just there. So if it was just there. That was like knowing. So really I knew. So I did not go but I knew to go.

God would see me. God saw into yer soul and knew everything ye did and ye had to confess. So if I was a Pape God knew I was one. And I was not doing the stuff, all what ye had to do if ye were one. If it was the Sign of the Cross, God would know I did not do it and would be sad and would not like it.

But if I did not know I was one, so that was why I did not do the Sign. God would know I did not. So it was not my fault, He would forgive me. If it was a Trespass. Maybe if it was and not a real Sin. But if really I knew I was a RC, if I was one. So it was a Sin I was doing and God would be angry. If it was a Sin forever. So I would go to Hell and get damned for all Eternity except if it was forgiveness. God forgived ye. It would be alright but just ye would have to start doing it. Because if ye knew ye knew and could not not know ever again. So if it was God, He knew ye knew. He did. Ye still would be alright but just if ye done it from that very moment. Oh but ye would have to and have to. And it was all the stuff.

When ye went into Church ye walked down the passage and sat in the pews. But if ye were a Catholic it was a Chapel and ye gived a bow and kneeled down and gived the Sign of the Cross too. Ye just took yer thumb across yer chest. Ye dragged it up and down then across and back across. If what it really meant, A Cross. So ye took yer thumb A Cross yer chest. And ye done it sore with yer thumb and felt it on ye and it was the biggest nail jagging in. It was like that and that was for Jesus so if He was on the Cross. I saw it in Pat's house and then His Heart was the Bleeding Heart.

Ye came in the Chapel door and walked down the passage where was the Altar and the big statues. It was maybe Jesus or else Mother Mary or God. Ye gived the Sign to that and then walked down to yer pew. That was what the RCs done. Their football players done it too, first when they ran on the park then if they scored or dived to save a penalty. I saw games on the telly and ye kidded on ye did not see it. Oh if he was one ye liked especially. Oh he is a Pape, that was what ye thought and they all were Papes. Darkies too. My da just looked right at the telly and did not say nothing but maybe a loud breath, hohhhhhh. So if it was a Priest in a picture on the telly, he did not like that.

But how come they done the sign? My da said that. If they wanted a special favour off God and it was to help ye win the game. That was just Blasphemy. They kissed their hands as well. How come? Ye saw it on the pictures if the Pope was there else it was other ones and kissing their hands, oh Father I am sorry. Boxers done it too. If it was for good luck and they would fight good and not get beat. What happened if they did not do it? If they ever did not do it so they got beat or if they missed a penalty if it was football. So about the ones that did not do it if they were Idolaters or if they were the Protestants. It was funny seeing darkies do it. My da laughed if it was. Oh the darkie is a Pape.

So then Mass. Mass. Ye went to Mass. And if it was special Mass, ye got Special Mass too. If it was dead people.

So I had to do it. If it was me and I was one. And if it was in the Church maybe I still had to, and just so nobody could see me doing it, if I just came in the door and the top of the passage and just stopped for a wee minute, a wee wee second. I could see me if I did, and just there and doing it quick. It was me doing it. If it was. I could not see if it was me. If it was my face there, I could not see if it was. It was smudged, if it was a face. Whose was it? It could only be me.

Ye thought ye knew yer face, but when ye tried to see it in yer head ye could not. It was just the old one from Auntie May's photographs. She had them in a bag. The one of me was when I was three. It was wide and round and it was smiling. I was a smiling baby. Auntie May said that. But it was not like my face at all. Only in the old photographs. Oh ye were a smiling wee boy. Oh why do ye not smile? Smile.

So then they took yer photograph and ye were smiling. Because they telled ye. Say cheese. Oh he is smiling now.

I was not smiling. It was just my face. And Matt was looking, I did not like Matt looking.

§

The pipe that went up the wall beside the balcony was a ronepipe. It came down to the backcourt. People played there. The family on the ground had two wee lasses and usually they were there with their dolls and stuff. Sometimes I climbed the ronepipe a wee bit. There was the elbow joint there and ye could stand up on it. One time over the back I saw a boy climbing higher. I watched him. Up he went, whshuuuu, the first-floor landing and he jumped into the balcony there. Hoh. Who was he? His back building faced over on to our back building and was faraway so ye did not know who it was except he was round that street, that was where he stayed.

Then I was down the backcourt and I saw up our wall, how the ronepipe was fixed. It came down the side of the balcony. It was one pipe and two wee pipes joined into it, one to the kitchenette and one to the bathroom. That was what the boy was climbing. Ye just went up the big ronepipe. But where did his ronepipe come from? It came from the balcony up above. Whose was that? Mine. Where did mine come from? The roof, and it passed right by them all, right down to the ground, and the wee bits just went off into the houses and they took the water down from yer kitchen-sink and yer bathroom, when ye flushed the lavatory pan, ye could hear the water. I was showing Pat and Danny and saying about the boy climbing up.

Pat called it veranda, ye were out on the veranda. Other ones called it that. No just RCs. So if it was a kitchenette balcony it was a kitchenette veranda. My maw did not like veranda, it was balcony to her. So I just said balcony. Some houses had front ones, they came out the living room at the front of yer building. But back balconies were best, people all said it. I was going to climb mine. I was showing Pat and Danny and came a big gushy noise down the ronepipe and Danny made a joke. Oh that is old Craig doing the lavvy.

Mr Craig lived one-up and was the neighbour above Danny. He was awful crabbit and if ye were sitting on the stair, Oh away out the back.

We are just talking.

Well this is not your stair, away out the back and talk.

It is my stair. That was Danny saying it.

No it is not, you do not have a stair.

Because Danny stayed on the ground floor. So he was not to go up the stair. He did not have the stair. But if we were just sitting on the steps up, they were just at Danny's door, so they were his too so we could sit there. Oh ye have no right to sit there, not on these stairs.

Aye but that is his door there, the steps are just at it.

Oh you shut up you do not even stay here.

That was to me because I said it. He did not like people up the close. Oh away out and play!

Aye but if it is raining.

Oh I do not care if it is raining.

Mr Craig was wee and skinny and his braces were there to keep his trousers up but the braces hung down over his shoulders. And if he was just back from the bathroom, that was what it looked. Imagine him on the lavatory pan. What if he fell down? Imagine ye gived him a fright, ye just went up and kicked the door and oh he was sitting down and pohhh that was him he fell down the pan. He was skinny enough, he could just go down it.

Pat was saying that and we were laughing but seeing up the rone-pipe, how the wee pipes went and there was another gushy sound. So if a woman was there and doing a washing, emptying the sink, the water just skooshed down. Ye saw the stank on the ground next to where the ronepipe went into the dirt, so that was where it all went. I was saying to my da about it. Oh that is the sewage.

Where does it go?

Into the sea.

Into the sea?

Everything.

Everything meant all jobbies and all what came out the lavvy pipes and the kitchen-sinks, it all went into the sea. And if ye spat in the sink, my granda did, he was aye doing it. My grannie did not tell him off but my maw did, if she saw him, Oh dad do not do that but he did, so then that went down the pipe in the sewage and all every-thing, if it was a spider or a eariwig or just a fly if ye killed it, if ye put it down the drain. And yer fingernails too if ye cut them, and yer toenails. It all just went it was just horrible to think because if ye fell in, ye were on a boat and ye just – or else ye went swimming, people just went swimming, and it was in the sea.

§

The new school started. It was up the lane next to our close. In the morning I kept the kitchenette door opened and listened for the bell. It rang and I was out the house down the stair and round the corner. My maw shouted at me for doing it. But she was getting ready too and was too busy. She went to her work after me. She gived me a tie to wear but I took it off when I shut the door. I belted up the lane. Everybody all was lined up in the playground, I sneaked in beside them. On the first day there I saw John Davis. I thought he would be in the class above me but he was coming into my class. That was great. But how come?

Oh it is just my lessons.

He did not know his lessons and was getting put back. Sometimes he looked at me if I said about my lessons. How come I knew them and he did not.

I was glad he was in my class and I sat beside him. I did not know many people. Some knew each other from their streets or their temporary schools. Two lasses were there from my one, Julie Michaels and Lorna Buckle. Lorna Buckle did not like me. I never done nothing to her but she did not. One time I was behind them at the queue for schooldinners and I heard her saying, Oh it is him.

And if that was me. I did not know if that was me. How come she said it. Julie Michaels was her pal and did not look at me.

Ye were just seeing everybody in yer class and mostly all it was new people. I liked that. Because I did not like the temporary school. In my new school there were boys I saw from playing football and just walking about. I thought they were Papes but here they were not. I saw a boy that flung stanes at me one time. He was just a wee boy. I kidded on I did not know him and so did he.

Oh and then a boy w****d. He sat at the back of the class. The teacher was out the room and he just started doing it. He had a look on his face and if ye saw his eyes he did not see back. I knew about w*****g but I did not know about other people except just boys laughing. It was a complete shock and everybody was all not knowing what to do but just all if they were talking, nearly talking or else just sitting but jumping about and in low voices saying, Oh what is that? What is he doing? Is he doing that? Oh he is not doing that? Is he doing it? Then the word got said, w*****g. People were saying it, Oh he is w*****g.

Now people were wanting to see and looking round then pointing at him. But he was just doing it and no seeing nobody. Lasses sat facing the front so they would not see him. One dropped her pencil on the floor and reached down to get it but then she turned her head and was looking past her arm, that was how she done it. She got a big red face, Oh he is oh he is!

Others lasses did not look and were acting angry, Oh he is just a child, he is just a child. Oh that is awful. I am telling the teacher.

Some boys laughed at the lasses and were seeing if one looked to see him w*****g. Oh she is looking, quick, see her?

But he did not care about nobody looking. His name was William Mitchell and he got called Mitch. He just done all stupid things, and what he wanted, he just done it. Then if ye dared him, he done it all. He was a best fighter but and people did not joke much to him.

The teacher set us a test to put ye in place. Miss Cooney. When she read out the marks we went to our new desks. John Davis got put in the worst dunce's seat.

There was four divisions in the class and eight double desks in each. The first division was the brainiest one and the top seats for the best two pupils, Sarah Wright and Isobel Hartley. Oh Sarah is always Wright.

The second top row was for the next best then the next then the next. The fourth division was the lowest. But the teacher done it different at the front rows. She kept the front row for dunces so for the front desks in the four divisions it was dunces, so in our class ye got eight real dunces.

The boys in the dunces' row were not good at their lessons or else were not good in another way. So if they were absent all the time or were talking and laughing too much or if they done something bad. The teacher said it. Oh I want to keep an eye on you.

None lasses were in the dunces' row. If one had been there people would have looked at her and felt sorry but not boys. Boys did not care. They said that. Maybe they did. John Davis was the worst dunce in the lowest seat. He did not come much to school. When he came he stood near me and I spoke to him. Other boys did not and were looking.

The teacher put me in the top division. Lucky for me it was the low-down row. The one below me had two dunces. I sat beside Ruthie Grindlay. She did not eat blood-oranges. Her maw gived her one in a poke and she was going to throw it in the bin, Oh it is all black.

Oh but it is not, I said, it is just a blood-orange.

Ruthie Grindlay did not listen to me, so I got the orange and opened it and people were looking, Oh it all is bad it is black, but it was not. I ate it up and gived some to a boy at the desk across the way.

Ruthie Grindlay did not talk to me and hid her work. I was not trying to see it, if she thought I was, I was not going to copy her. So I was third top boy in the complete class. Two more boys were in the top division, one was posh and one was Samuel Ross at the desk above me. The posh one was top boy and in the second row. I never saw him except at school. He just went by himself in the playground and did not play any games. Second top boy was Samuel Ross. He did not talk to me. I did not talk to him. After the test people said, Oh you are in the top division, you are brainy, Oh Smiddy is brainy.

But I was not brainy. It was just the test and ye wrote down the answers. My maw was glad when I told her. She wanted me to stick in at my lessons. Oh maybe you can go to the good school. Only if you stick in. Oh Kieron you must stick in at your lessons.

My maw was saying about the posh boy but I did not know him. If people were posh my maw liked them. Oh he is a nice speaker.

There was a dentist's house and a doctor's house and that was what my maw wondered, Oh maybe it is the dentist's boy or the doctor's, is he a nice boy? Oh he will be a nice speaker.

My da said, The dentist and the doctor do not stay there it is just where ye go to see them. They have their own house someplace else, miles away.

I did not tell them my pals. They would not like them. One was Gary McNab. He sat at the desk below me. He was the top dunce. If he done better he would get out the dunces' row and into the fourth division. I got pals with him. He did not say the answers if it was a test. He just laughed. He saw me writing fast and just shaked his head, Oh Smiddy, teacher's pet.

If he copied. I showed him my test paper and he only looked at it and made a face. So he did not want to do the answers. So if he knew them himself, maybe he did. But John Davis did not write any answers and was the worst dunce.

Gary McNab made people laugh. And if the teacher was not looking he turned round in his seat and stole yer stuff. He skited it over the flair maybe if it was a jotter and it was you to go and get it. He did it to Ruthie Grindlay and she told the teacher. He called her fat bum and if he f★★★★d he said it was her, Oh smellee pong, that was you.

One time she was greeting, Oh I did not pimp I did not pimp.

So she did not like me. It was not me that said it but it did not matter. I did not care anyway. Boys would not tell the teacher else it was hard luck for them. Sometimes me and Gary were pals. His big brother was a best fighter. Everybody knew him. But if Gary thought he was a best fighter. He acted it. But he was wee so maybe he was not. I did not think he was. One time he was walking down the street with his big brother, I waved to him and he did not wave back. Ye thought ye were pals with him then ye were not. That was Gary. Then he would laugh at ye. How come? He just laughed, as if ye were not something, whatever it was. Oh what ye laughing at Gary? I said it to him.

Oh I am just thinking about something.

He was pals with Podgie. They stayed in the same street and shared their stuff. So if they had sweeties, they did not give ye one. And if it was a fag and they smoked it, they would not give ye a draw. Only one draw and they would not give ye it. That was to me and Mitch, and another boy Peter Wylie, if we were with them. I did not get fags. But Mitch got them and he gived us draws. He stole them off his da and his big sisters. My stomach got sick with smoking. I was in the class and I went dizzy, Oh please miss, and I had to leave the room. I just went to the lavatory and put my head down the pan and just was there. Podgie told me to fling cold water on my face. That was what he done.

But when Gary McNab done something to me I done it back to him so then it was a laugh and ye made a joke, so if ye were out on the floor and ye did a daft face or a daft walk. Miss Cooney caught me and grabbed my arm and went to give me the belt. I hit at her hand, no meaning to do it but just because she grabbed me. But then she thought I was more cheekier so got more angry. Her hand was shaking, she got the belt out her desk and gived me four. Two went up my wrist. Usually ye just got one of the belt for what I did, a daft face. Four of the belt was too much.

Gary was a good laugh and other ones near the dunces' row, except no John Davis. He did not do stuff except football maybe if we had a game in the playground. He did not come knocking. We asked him to. If he was one of the boys, he could come with us. It was not a gang, just the boys, that was what we called it. Maybe if it was a gang, some thought it. We just said the boys, ye were one of the boys. We went about the gether and played football or what, if we went down to the shops.

One shop was easy, we used to get chocolate biscuits and sponge cakes. Mitch was not good at knocking but he was good at helping ye. One time we were w*****g he put his hand to do it to me. He done it funny and it was sore. Podgie was laughing. Mitch did not care. But he was feared of Podgie. But he was still a best fighter, except for Podgie, if ye laughed at him he would batter ye. That happened to a boy that was bigger than us, he laughed at Mitch to do with how he was talking. People said he talked funny. He was saying words and it was how he said them. That bigger boy was getting Mitch to say the words then he was laughing at him so Mitch just kicked into him, oh he just rushed him and kicked in. That boy was beat and had to get away.

Podgie was not so big as Mitch but with a thick body. People said he was the best fighter. Maybe he was not. But he went after people. He did not go after me but if he wanted to go after me. I think he did. Ye were going up the road and he shoved ye in the back. Oh what was that for?

Ha ha. Nothing.

He done it to Mitch too and Mitch did not stop him so that was how Podgie thought he could beat him. At football he booted into ye. So if you done it to him he just done it back and the ball was not there. It was not your fault, ye were just playing the game and it was not a real kick. So he kicked ye. Oh what was that for?

Well you kicked me.

But that was the ball.

Then how he looked at ye, seeing what ye would do. If ye were letting him get away with it and then he had a wee smile. And if you did not tackle hard the next time that was you, he did not bother with ye. So if he could beat ye any time, that was how he acted. Even if ye were pals with him. So if he done it to ye ye just acted it was nothing, ye did not even notice or else ye laughed like it was a joke. Sometimes he punched people and then got the ball. Oh I did not f*****g mean it, I was just running.

Oh but then he caught a wee Primary 2. He was just a bully. We were down at the shops and he caught him. That was the worst. Open yer mouth till I see yer teeth. The wee Primary 2 done it and Podgie spat right in. A greaser down to his tonsils. Podgie said that, Oh it is a big greaser.

The wee Primary 2 could not get it up. He was choking and choking and went down on his knees choking and pulling his lips out with his fingers, pulling them out. Podgie grabbed his head, Wee b*****d.

The wee Primary 2 was greeting and trying to shut his mouth. Podgie pulled his chin down and got his nose up so his mouth was open and spat in again so then the boy fell down and was just choking.

That was Podgie, he was just a bully. Maybe Gary was one. He was if Podgie was there. He tripped people up when they were walking. If he done it to you ye had to act something, just whatever ye done. Boys laughed when he done it to them. But they were no really laughing. Podgie punched me on the shoulder and I said, Oh quit it.

What will ye do if I do not?

Oh Podge, just quit it.

Podgie laughed but he stopped doing it. I called him Podge and no Podgie. So when ye said it it was better sounding. Other ones started saying it. But they were still feared of him. But I do not know with John Davis, if he was too. Or if he did not think about it, maybe he did not. John just looked at people. I thought if Podgie and Gary McNab were going to jump him. So if they did, what would happen? It was a worry.

Miss Cooney did not like John. She picked on him, Oh you, John Davis, if you just listen and stop being so silly.

When she gived him a row for no doing stuff Gary had his head on the desk and laughed round to me. But I did not laugh back. I saw him make a joke to Podgie and it was about John. Oh if they were making a fool of him. I kidded on I did not know. But what would happen if they jumped him? If John was my pal. He was my pal.

Miss Cooney said things to him and he was just looking at her. In the playground he stood near me. But he did not come to school a lot. A boy said to me, Is John Davis a good fighter?

Oh if he loses his temper.

Have you seen him do it?

Aye, he done it on the school buses.

Oh but really, he did not. John did not hit people. I saw him as if he was nearly going to but he never did. But if he did ye would have to look out. Anybody would have to. John was just big and strong as well, I thought he was.

Another time people were saying who was best fighters and who could give ye a good go. Some were looking at Podgie because if he was the best fighter in the class. He was just standing with a wee smile. But it was my turn to say and I said, Oh John Davis would give ye a good go.

John Davis?

I think he is a best fighter. A boy hit him on the school buses and he battered him. He just lost his temper. I think he is the best.

Oh the best, said Gary McNab, in the complete class?

That was a trick. He was trying to trick me. If it was the complete class, so that was everybody, Podgie and everybody. I said, Oh well I am no saying he is the complete best.

But really I was. Podgie and them were looking at me. Nobody thought of John Davis but he was the biggest in the class. If he fighted ye he could knock ye out. Just if it was one punch, because if it just catched ye right and it was yer jaw, if he lost his temper.

People could lose their temper, if ones were laughing at ye. So if people laughed at John maybe he would lose it. If they done things to him. If he let people do it and did not fight.

Some boys done what ye telled them but John Davis was not one of them, I knew he was not. Mitch was a bit like it. Podgie telled him stuff and he done it. It was dares. Podgie would say it, Oh Mitch I dare ye to skelp that lassie on the b⋆m. So Mitch done it. Ask that lassie does she know what a Gerry's Helmet is? So Mitch went and asked. The lassie did not know and everybody all was laughing. She looked and saw us and got a big riddy. But so did Mitch, so we all were laughing more. But one time a man slapped him because he emptied a dustbin out on the pavement. Then the man ran out the close and got him. The man shouted at him, Weans are playing there you dumbcluck b⋆⋆⋆⋆r, I will get the polis. We threw stanes at the man and Mitch got away. We were laughing about it, dumbcluck b⋆⋆⋆⋆r.

It was only Podgie that done stuff to Mitch. If other ones tried Mitch would batter them. He was no feared of anybody. Except for dogs, he hated dogs and would not go near them. If he saw one he would walk out the way from it or even run away, I saw him running away and the dog just chased him. But dogs aye done that. I telled Mitch, ye just had to walk and it would be okay.

But it was no just Mitch that Podgie done stuff to. He got ones to go messages too. Away to the shops and get me a packet of crisps. Go and do this and go and do that. He did not say it to me. I would not have went. But if he did say it? He would not. If I was his pal. I did not know if I was his pal.

He thought ye were trying to get in with him and ye were not. He just gived a wee smile. I did not like it. I did not try to get in with him. People thought we were pals but we were not.

It was you went pals with him, he did not with you. He was not really a pal. Because you were not his. Even if he was yours.

If ye went up for him he came out, but sometimes he did not. Oh I am watching the telly.

I did not like him bullying people. He done it when I was there and I did not like it. Podgie saw me looking but still done it. He done it a lot to a Primary 4 boy. Other ones picked on this boy because of how he walked funny and what he wore, it was stuff people laughed at. One time he falled in the canal and was caught in the weeds, his feet got fankled up. He was dragged down and down and going below the surface but a man was there and jumped in and got him. They thought he was passed away but he came to and was sick, all the water gushing out. It was in the paper and his photograph was there. My da was reading it. Oh here is a boy in your school. He nearly drowned in the canal. He was playing on the locks, I hope you do not do it.

The other boys made him do it. They made him run over the top of the lock and go faster and faster. Everybody all was talking about it. His maw kept him off school the next day. If he was at the hospital. People said he was. But he was not. His da had a tree in his garden and people climbed it then if his da came they just called him names and ran away, they did not care about him. Ye would not like it if it was yer da.

A boy said to me, Do you do boxing?

He was looking at my nose, if a punch done it, that was it. Oh I done a lot of boxing in my old place. They had a boxing club and my granda took me and my big brother. They were teaching ye. It was just how ye done it, just throwing yer punches and putting up yer guard, jab jab and then with yer uppercut. I loved it. My granda was a great boxer, he knew a lot of tricks and used to show me and my big brother when we stayed there. Boxing clubs are great.

I hope they will start a f*****g boxing club here, said the boy.

Me too, said Mitch.

Was yer granda a real boxer? said Podgie.

Oh aye.

If they start one here I am going, said Gary McNab. I bet ye my big brother will come too.

Other ones were saying it now and then it was brothers, if ye had a big brother, what like he was. Gary McNab's big brother was a best fighter in the complete scheme, people knew that. One boy did not like his brother. Oh mine is a b******d, I f*****g hate him.

And then it was a football team. We talked about that. Maybe they would start one here. Schools had football teams.

§

My da did not like darkies and if they came on the telly or if they were tough and in a boxing match he just watched them, no saying nothing because if they were good fighters, if they were winning the fight and the white one was getting beat. Oh look how he is all cuts and bruises but see the darkie how he is not, his skin is just leather it is so thick and he does not get cut and bruised, that is why they aye win the fight.

So if it was the white man ye were wanting him to win. But then ye were watching and ye liked it if the darkie won. Just cause of yer da and it was against him. I was glad. And if it was a wee darkie so ye wanted him to win. I wanted the wee ones to win. Except if the big one was Scottish but the Scottish ones usually were wee. My maw said that, Oh the Scottish men are always so wee.

No they are not, said my da.

Oh well usually.

My da did not like that. Other stuff too. Oh that is a dirty punch, that is below the belt, oh look at that the solar plexus, oh he has hit the solar plexus, oh ohhh, moaning moaning, moan moan moan. He was a true moaner, just always moaning.

Oh and if one was a Pape and giving the Sign. My da hated that. Really really, he did. He kept the newspaper on his lap so then he lifted it up and kidded on he was reading it. So if he did not see the white one making the Sign. He acted like that. So if he did not know the white one was a Pape. He could say the white one was good. But no if he saw he was a Pape, if we saw he saw, so then he could not. If the Pape won then my da just looked at his newspaper, Oh I think God answered his prayers, he prayed to God to win the fight and God just done it for him, oh is he not just good, that is Papes for ye.

My maw said, Ssh.

Oh but God is a Pape, he must be, the Papes must just be the best.

Oh ssh.

It just annoys ye. My da said it an angry voice but no his loud one, it was just quiet. My da got loud angry too. If it was quiet angry ye still done what it was, if he said it. Kieron, go to bed.

Ye just went. Even it was half nine and it should be ten o'clock, if he telled ye in the quiet voice ye just done it. Matt too, if it was him he would have went. Except it was never Matt, just me. My da gived rows for nothing and it was to me he done it. He was moaning about his job. Oh I hate that damn place, it is all just slave-drivers, I am going back to sea.

I wished he would. He worked late and that was him, ye were not to talk when he came home. Oh you are a wean you should be seen and no heard.

He said wean. My maw heard him but kidded on she did not, ye were not to say wean just child. She put out his tea and he ate it up. Then his cup of tea and a fag, then it was okay and ye could talk. What is coming on?

What on the telly. If it was something you wanted he did not, so he got what he wanted. Things all were ordered for him. The complete house. But you were there too so ye got sick of it. I sat on the floor at the side of the settee. Ye could look up and see them but they could hardly see you. Sometimes they thought ye were away to bed and said stuff about ye. Did that boy do his homework?

I shouted, Aye.

Oh it is not aye it is yes, said my maw.

I thought he was away to his bed? said my da.

No, ten o'clock is his bedtime.

Oh.

I waited a wee minute then counted up to thirty and got up to go to bed. That annoyed them. I hoped it did. No my maw really but my da. And Matt too if he was there. So if it was a good programme on the telly and I just jumped up. Goodnight!

Oh ye do not have to go yet, said my da.

Wait till the end of the programme, said my maw.

Oh I am just tired.

You have watched most of it, said my da, ye might as well see it all.

No, I am just tired. Goodnight.

And away to my bed. They did not like me doing that, Oh if we watch that programme and he does not, how come? Maybe he does not like it. But we do. He is just spoiling it going to bed.

I did not care. I went to the bathroom to do my teeth and just was laughing. And into the mirror. Except sometimes. If I did not like seeing my face, how yer eyes just looked back at ye. It was funny how they done it. Yer own eyes. Even like somebody else's, it was like that. Ye could get creepy feelings. I did not want to see in the mirror. If ye could not see except yerself, if somebody was there behind ye. You were just blocking it. Who was there behind ye? Ye could not see.

Even if ye could see but did not see them, they could still be there, if they were invisible, so if it was a Dracula, they did not have their reflection but still creeped up on ye.

They heard ye coming and were waiting. They came out to get ye. So pulling the plug if ye done the toilet. It was a loud noise. So if it woke them up, all ghosts and just evil spirits, all in the coffin, if they came out to get ye, oh mammy daddy I did not pull the plug except if I opened the bathroom door first. Then I jumped out into the lobby and tried to switch off the light before they grabbed my shoulder and got me back in. They could not get ye with the light on, they could not come out in the light. They hated it if it was light. A lot of times I left the light on and I did not pull the plug. And even if my da said it, Oh who was last in the toilet?

Well I just said it was me, Oh sorry dad I forgot.

Ten o'clock was my bedtime. It was too early. I said half past to people. Other ones did not have a bedtime. If they were saying in school about what was on television and it was late on I acted like I saw it or else just said something. Oh I went to bed early last night, I was just tired.

Gary McNab watched to see who was early to bed. He got staying up late. It was just up to him when he went. He made his own supper just for himself. If he wanted a piece he just made it and no for anybody else. In our house it was supper for everybody at nine o'clock. It was me made it. No all the time but usually. If it was not me it was my maw. My da and Matt never made it. I did not care. I liked making it cause it was just yours and ye got what ye wanted, toast and beans else toast and cheese. I went through at nine o'clock and started. My da did not like it if it was too early but I still made it. Oh it is too early. I did not care.

But then if it was a bad temper, even just his voice and ye got jittery. I wished he was back in the Navy. How come he left? If he did not like his job how come he did not go back to sea? When he was in the house he got the living room. My big brother got the bedroom and my maw got her bedroom and the kitchenette too. I just got the balcony. If it was raining or just cold I still went out. I saw people in other balconies. One smoked a lot and if his maw and da were watching the telly he used to go out for fly puffs. I waved to him and he waved back. David Sinclair, boys called him wee Sinky. But ye would never call him wee Sinky just Davie. He was older than me but wee for his age.

Sometimes I just went out to see if anybody was there, so if ye saw a head sticking up and they shouted across to ye. Hoh Smiddy!

My maw blamed me if somebody done it. Oh who is that shouting and bawling, that is terrible, children are trying to sleep, come in from there Kieron.

§

One time I came home from school and the trapdoor up to the roof was open and ladders were there. The trapdoor was outside our front door on the landing. I went up to see. I just looked then the man was coming, a workie, he was whistling coming up the stair so I just came down fast and into my house and shut the door. He went up, he was doing work up in the loft. I heard his footsteps. It was TV aerials, he was putting them up.

My da had step-ladders. I thought to do that. I could get them out and go up. Mitch could come. Sometimes he came home from school with me and I took him in the house. Matt did not come home till quarter to five. My maw came in from her work at quarter past. So I said to Mitch and that was what we done and we done it a lot of times. It was a real den. I made pieces on jam and we ate them when we got up. It was just great. We just had a look about and found another workie's ladder beside the skylight. It was a slanty window, but ye could not get through it. But maybe ye could. Imagine ye got out on the roof.

We just walked along on the rafters. Ye could go a far way over other people's ceilings and ye thought about that, if ye made noises like a ghost so they heard ye. Oh there is a ghost up there! Oh oh.

It was a laugh. Mitch had fags and we smoked one up there.

But I was worried if the neighbours saw me and ye had to watch so ye did not put yer foot through the plaster because it was some-body's ceiling. But if ye could not help it yer foot slipped off the rafters and went down between and kicked the plaster but lucky for me it did not go through and make the ceiling come down. But then that happened, it was not me but it was thiefs. They broke into yer house and that was how they done it. They climbed up and kicked in the plaster till it broke then the ceiling came in and they dreeped down into yer house. So then they robbed ye. It happened to us when we were away for the day. They did not close our front door. Other ones could have come and stole everything out the house. That happened to a family in our street. They were away at the seaside and when they came home their house was empty, everything all was took.

Oh but when they done it to us my maw was greeting and my da was the angriest ever. If he got a hold of them he would just murder them, they were just thiefs and scum. We were looking to see what was robbed but could not find nothing. The cops came and said it. Oh check all yer stuff Mrs Smith.

So my maw was looking at everything again. But all it was was cheese. Oh it is just cheese, they have took the cheese.

The cops said, Oh they must have been disturbed. It is boys on the run. They are running away from Borstal. If they do not find stuff they just take food.

After the cops went away my da was quiet to me and then he held onto my arm. Were you up in that loft?

Oh no dad.

Because what about my step-ladders, somebody has used my step-ladders, did you ever use my step-ladders?

Oh no dad no, I never did.

Well if ever you go up there, if ever you go up in that loft my boy never ever you go up there or you will get a hammering.

But dad

I am warning you.

Oh it is not Kieron's fault, said my maw.

Well somebody has shifted these step-ladders. Who done it? My da said, Was it you Matt?

Oh no da.

Well somebody has used them.

Oh we were lucky it was just cheese, said my maw.

But how did he know? I did not think how he could know. Him and the man next door got a padlock and they put it up on the trapdoor so the thiefs could not get in again. But I knew where the key was so if I got it I could still get up, but I did not because with the step-ladders, if ye did not have them, how could ye do it?

Except the landing wall. It was outside our door where ye went down the stairs. Ye got up on it easy, but just usually to sit. But if ye stood on it and reached up. Ye could, if ye balanced right. I said it to Mitch. Just if ye climbed up on the wall and balanced. I could do it. He could hold onto my legs. I could get the key in the padlock and open it. Maybe I could.

Oh but ye had to be careful standing up on it. Ye got up sideways and just sat with yer legs over then on yer knees and just kneeled a wee while. Nothing was there to hold on. You just balanced. Ye got up a wee bit at a time, just a toty bit. Ye kept yer arms out, quite stiff out. Mitch was wanting to hold my feet there but that was no good because it was trapping ye. I telled him no to but he done it in case ye fell.

Oh leave go my feet Mitch.

Oh but if ye fall!

But you are tripping me.

He was just scared if I fell over the wall down on to the stairs at the window landing. And if it was head first, ye would break your skull in two. It would just crack like a big egg.

But I would not go headfirst. I would twist my body in mid air so I could get my hands and my shoulders round a bit and that would make it better for landing. It would not be headfirst. But I would not fall anyway.

Mitch was going to hold onto my legs again but I did not want him to because it just stopped ye. Just let me do it Mitch.

Oh but Smiddy if ye fall.

But I would not fall, only if he done it. It was just slowly slowly, ye done it just slowly, a wee bit a wee bit a wee bit, both hands doing it, till then they touched the roof. Now it was good. Ye pressed up yer fingers to balance and got them up on the trapdoor. Then I went on my tiptoes and got the key in the padlock, and got it off. He passed me up the brush and now he could hoist me, so I shoved up the trapdoor. Ye could not reach to do it yerself, ye needed a brush or else a stick.

I had to do the climb up now else if I did not close the trapdoor people would see it. I was worried about the neighbours because they would just tell my maw. But it was quite easy. Mitch hoisted me a wee bit more and I got my hands gripped on the sides of the wood where the trapdoor came down. I pulled up on my elbows. Now it was kicking my feet in mid air, swinging them up and up. Ye could not fall now. I got up and found the workie's ladder. I could let it down for Mitch to climb. Oh but it clanked and clanked and I worried if the neighbours heard.

It was smashing up in the loft. I loved it. Ye could make it into a den and it was like a hideout. Me and the boys looked for dens and hideouts and were wanting to make one. Maybe if we got a good tree or else a cave. A lot of times we looked for caves down the field. People said there were and ye could find them near the burn, but ye had to go away far along. There were rabbits there and ye could eat them. Me and Mitch went looking for caves a lot of times but never found them. But the loft was great. If ye put planks over the rafters that was like a floor. Ye could take up stuff too, a chair and books and ye could just sit down and read them or else do any stuff and ye could plank any stuff. Mitch had n**e books so if we took them up. Just anything. Nobody would know so ye would not get bothered. It was just a room to yerself, that was what I thought. But Mitch had one already. Oh a hideout is better, which would ye rather have? If it was a hideout, ye would not get bothered. People would not come into ye. That was what he said. He hated them coming in his room so ye had to chap the door first. But I would have loved a room to yerself, just the complete room, what would ye do?

The workies had a ladder up in the loft and I could let it down for Mitch to climb up but I did not want to in case if somebody found out. If Mitch was no there I could not climb it. I did not do it much. My da would murder me if ever he catched me doing it. He said it. My maw heard him. Oh your father is just worried you will fall and break every bone in your body.

§

It was just how Matt was always there and swotting all the time. That was all he done and it was the bedroom, that was where he done it and ye were not to go in. Oh no. It was just your room but ye were not to go in it. Because he was going to college and every-thing was just to be for him. Oh do not put on the wireless if yer brother is studying, do not turn up the television. Oh it is ink-exercises, it is for his Latin. Oh Kieron if you are whistling, do not whistle too loud if your brother is studying.

I was just sick of it. I would have went to my grannie's except it was travelling all the time so it was more money and ye got home late. I went on Saturdays with my maw or else Sundays with my maw and my da. Matt usually went himself and done it straight from school. His school was near the river so he could just run down and that was him. But no with me. If I went straight from school I did not get to my grannie's house till quarter past five or else half past.

Coming home was worse because nighttime and no as many ferries and then if it was the train and ye missed one it took ages. People went and got a bus but no if ye had a return ticket on the train, ye did not have money for something else. Then if it was cold or it was raining, ye did not want to go, I could just have stayed. And ye got sleepy. Granda would tell me, Oh ye better away up the road son. Oh Vera I will take the boy down to the subway.

Oh no dad. My grannie said he was not to because he was too tired so she would take me instead.

In my grannie's house ye did not have to bother about stuff. I loved it. Her and granda did not watch much telly. But if ye wanted to ye done it, if it was football she did not mind. Me and granda watched it but not to the end because I had to go home. Usually ye were just reading if stuff was there and it was all quiet and nobody doing nothing except if my grannie was at the sink or the kitchen cupboard oh and she banged a pot and ye all jumped. Oh Vera ye would wake the dead! That was my granda and just laughing and making big eyes. She would wake the dead son, that grannie of yours.

They were all in their graves, all the dead bodies, then coming out and it was nighttime and there was the moon and a wolf howling at ye, oh mammy, and it all was creaking so the waking dead. And ye just thought about it and if ye were going home ye walked down the road and passed the corners of streets and who was going to jump out at ye and there was the pavement and away ye could see a man coming to ye he was walking down to ye and oh ye better get out his road and just walk into the side of the building so he will not see ye he will not notice ye but just walk straight and his eyes no seeing ye if it is a murderer or who, a waking dead. Matt said it. Oh it is the waking dead!

When I was wee he said it to be creepy and make me feared. Just when he put out the light to jump into bed. Oh the zombies are here! I pulled the blankets over my head and he was just laughing. Oh there is the waking dead going to get ye! The zombies are here. Oh and they are going to get Kieron.

My grannie and granda asked about him. Oh where is Matt we have not seen him? Grannie said it. But granda was looking as well. Aye son, where is that brother of yours we do not see him.

Oh he is swotting all the time, that is all he does.

My Auntie May was back staying with grannie. She had troubles. Auntie May never spoke much to me but now she did, a wee bit. Oh now Kieron give me a kiss. She said stuff about the new house and if my mum was keeping fine and how was my dad? So if Matt was doing good at school was he going to College? People said it. Oh Matt is a brainy boy and he is going to College. He will do well for himself. People wanted to know if he was going to College. My granda as well. If Auntie May was saying it ye saw him and grannie were listening. Oh Matt is going to College. Oh that is smashing. Oh is he top of the class? Well he must be. He is just clever and good at all his lessons.

I could have been good at my lessons. They did not think it. Auntie May said, What about you Kieron, are you getting on at your lessons?

The boy is good with his hands, said my grannie. She said it to me, You are good with yer hands son never you worry.

But I could be good at my lessons too. But I did not want to be. But my grannie did not know it. I did not care.

Except she did not think it. How come she did not think it? I could easy have done my lessons, easy. So could Gary McNab and he was a dunce. He just laughed at stuff. I did too. My grannie did not know everything. People thought she did. Oh if yer grannie says it son. That was what my granda said. Oh she is the best.

But she did not know I could be good too.

§

A thing happened. Me and other boys were talking about stuff. I was saying how a boy climbed the ronepipe. It was the same street as Billy MacGregor. He stayed across the back from me but it was faraway and hard to see his house. He did not know who the boy was. So I was going home from school and that was it. I did not think I was going to climb the ronepipe. But then if I did. What if? I started running. Because if I did. Maybe I would.

So if I was going to do it. Well I would soon see. Maybe I would not. But I went fast in the close and up the stairs in the house and into my old trousers and sandshoes.

I did the lock on the kitchenette door and left it open. So I was going to do it. I was. And I did not go out on the balcony, just back down the stairs again.

Out in the backcourt I looked up at the ronepipe a while, just to see. The family below us had the same one. When ye went up ye passed their balcony and could put a foot on it but if they saw ye, ye had to watch it, because they would just tell on ye. So if ye just passed it and went up to yours. I was the top flat. So if I went up past the bit where the wee pipes joined.

I was looking and looking and then I just done it. I was thinking what to do and could not think it all, so I just got up on the wee pipe at the ground and then just up and up and it was the greatest thing. I did not do anything except go and did not look down except at the balcony below mine. I put my foot on the edge for a wee second and saw down then. But I just went back on the ronepipe and up again and there was my balcony wall and I was climbing beside it and up to the top of it and getting my elbow onto the wall there and then a grip on the wee bar that went round it and it was easy and I was over and jumping down into the balcony floor. I leaned back over to see down where I had come but just a minute. I went into the kitchenette and ben the lobby into the bathroom. I done the lavvy and was washing my hands. Wee scratches and bits of bleeding were on my knuckles, the skin was tore. It was the greatest thing, just the greatest thing. Maybe Pat had seen me, if he was looking out the window, or somebody, maybe the street across the back, if that other boy saw me. I went back out the balcony and looked out, seeing down. Somebody was out at a midden away closes along from me. If they had seen me, maybe they had. Then the kitchenette door, somebody was chapping it, Matt was home from school.

I wanted to tell him, I was going to, lucky for me I did not. Then my maw came home and I was to set the table for tea. Matt did not have to because he was doing his homework. I did not care. That was me now and I had my whole place that was just my whole place and it was a complete place. That was the balcony, it was my balcony. I looked out the living-room window to see if Pat and Danny were out with a ball. They were not. Usually they did not at this time, they were getting their tea. I could just go up for Pat. I could just wait for him. I looked down the field and saw people away down over the burn. Who was that? If it was Squatters. Even if it was Cochise. Could he even climb the balcony? Maybe he could not. Who else could? I was going to do it again. Not tonight. I could never do it if people were in but after school I could and I just would do it. Except tomorrow was Saturday so only it had to be Monday.

I went into the kitchenette. My maw was making the tea. I got the rubbish bin from under the sink. I am away down the midden.

Oh thanks Kieron.

I ran downstairs. Out at the midden I emptied the rubbish and looked up to see where I had been. It was good seeing it. The wee pipe went into the kitchenette. The other one stretched over to the bathroom. But ye could not get to the bathroom. It was too far, there was no grips. It was only the window, so how could ye get to it? Oh it did not matter, the balcony was just great and I was seeing how I done it and it was so high. How had I done it? But I had. I had just done it, it was just the greatest thing. And seeing how ye got to the balcony. Ye reached yer hand to the wee round bar on top and gripped it tight to take yer weight. Inch by inch ye could leave go the pipe with yer other hand, then yer elbow on the top of the wall and ye hoisted up and ye were over and jumping down to the balcony floor. That was how ye done it. And if ye looked and somebody was watching ye, ye could give them a wee wave.

So that was me now and I climbed it a lot of times. I just thought about it in school so if the teacher was talking. Oh stop dreaming Kieron Smith.

That was me and I was just thinking about it. I telled the boys. Gary said, Oh Smiddy is a boaster.

I was not a boaster, just if I did it and I said it.

Mitch came home with me after school. It was raining but and I did not do it. So the next time it was dry. Him and Peter Wylie came with me. I did not take them in the house but just went to get the kitchenette door. Ye had to watch it was not locked else ye could not get in. Only if the wee window was open. There was the big kitchenette window and then a wee one at the top of it. Only the wee one got opened. Ye could crawl through but it was the side of the sink down below and ye slid in, so ye had to catch the edge of it and then be careful coming through, if yer legs banged and yer shoe crashed the window and then if it broke.

If my maw and da caught me climbing the balcony I would get a doing. I knew I would.

But then what happened, Matt knew I done it. He just said it one day to me. How did he know? Somebody telled him. He would not say who, but somebody.

He did not climb it. I said to him but he did not want to. What other boys done it? I did not see them, except him from the street across the back. Over here it was me, I was the one that done it. Danny's house was on the ground floor so he did not have a balcony. Ground-floor houses got the wee garden at the front so that made up for it. Danny's da put in flowers and wee bushes. Pat's house was up the top flat and he did not fancy climbing it. When nobody was there I climbed his to show him. He was on the balcony looking down at me and talking all the time. Hey Kieron, Kieron!

But I did not look up at him. If ye looked up ye just got dizzy and oh ye were going to go back the way or if the ronepipe came away in yer hand. People said it would, the nails popped and that was that and ye just went over and would get a broken back or if ye landed on yer head ye would just pass away. Big George said that, Matt's pal. Oh ye would get killed, yer head would just smash open. Or if it was yer face landing and getting flattened.

But if ye held on tight. I did not look up but I could look down. It was best just climbing and no looking anywhere except just the pipe and the wall next to ye. Ye knew where to put yer feet and did not even look, just up up. I was fastest. I would have raced Matt. If he went up the stairs, I would have climbed it. I would beat him, no unless he ran. But if I could still beat him, maybe I could.

Then I found how to do the bathroom. That was the hardest. I did not like doing it much. Ye were past the join and had to stretch yer hand over and ye were sticking close into the wall. Ye had to do that. And ye could not see because yer head was the same way facing, that was into the wall. And ye did not want to move it. Ye could not because for the balance. So it was just yer hand and it was inch by inch and just yer fingertips oh just reaching over just reaching over till they touched the wall at the ledge and ye could hardly see, because ye were looking into the wall. Ye set yer fingertips there and then yer one foot inch by inch, it was yer knee, so to get that, ye were wanting to get that to the ledge if ye could get yer knee there, just at the edge and if ye could do that oh just a wee bit inch by inch and if ye made it, oh, and the wee top window had to be open so ye reached to it and got a good grip to pull ye up onto the ledge. And when ye done that it was easy, ye could trail yer leg over and if people were looking up and seeing Ohh! and they would see it and Ohh maybe he will fall, but it all was easy now and ye were doing it for a laugh. Usually people left the wee window open on the bathroom because if there was a thief he could not get up to it. How could he? People thought that. My maw and da thought that. I said to my da, Oh maybe people can climb in.

Ye just put yer hand through and down to get the handle to the big window then ye opened it. But I did not say it to him.

The balcony was the best place in the house. Ye got peace there. We were high up, but no so high as in the old house. But it was still high. I looked out and thought if it was water down below, if ye could dive in, it was like three dales up at the swimming baths, that was how high.

Even if ye were up on the roof, imagine diving off. Some ships my da sailed in were like that, ones as big as our complete building, sailing through the ocean. The sides of the ship was as big as it.

§

The Squatters' camp got flattened and they all were sent away. People were saying about it. And the Army was coming to clear the gun-site hill. We were waiting to see it but the Army lorries all came in the middle of the night and done it when everybody was asleep. Hundreds of lorries. People said that. It was going to be new houses, just houses and houses. Ye looked over at the fields and up to the gun-site hill, and it was all going to be houses, houses and houses. That was what my da said. Ye would not see nothing but houses. He sat at the window and looked out. If ye were watching the telly that was what he done, just smoking a fag. My maw said to him, Come and watch the programme, but a lot of times he did not.

I knew what it was, he was missing the sea. Uncle Billy told us. One night after tea me and Matt went over to see grannie and granda. Uncle Billy was there and took us in to see granda. He was not keeping well and in his bed. Oh boys ye should have said ye were coming and I would have got up.

He was too tired now. I saw him lying in bed and his face was just thin.

Oh what about the new house, so we were telling him. Then about school, Oh how is it, what like is yer teachers? Are they all horrors?

Grannie was laughing. Oh dad!

Well mine were all horrors.

Oh but do not say it.

Him and grannie liked hearing about school. Matt said about his lessons and what he was doing. He did not talk about stuff if I was there so now he was and I was listening. He had a teacher he liked and it was him said it about college, Oh you are good at science.

So he was going to go, just if he done his lessons good. He was going to do them. My da was going to make him a desk so he could put his books. Granda told him to stick in, Oh you stick in son.

Oh he is always swotting, I said.

Matt just looked at me.

Grannie did not want us to stay long. Uncle Billy was there. Come on we will go to the pictures.

But grannie said, No Billy do not take them it is too late. Oh boys you better just go home. Come on Saturday or Sunday the next time.

Uncle Billy walked with us down to the subway. He was asking about my da's new job. Oh he does not like it much, I said. It is too cramped for him.

Matt was looking at me. He did not like me saying it.

Oh he is missing the sea, said Uncle Billy.

The bike-shop was there and we saw in the window. The man that had the shop was a champion. The bikes there were the best of all. Oh I will win the pools, said Uncle Billy, then I will get yez one.

Matt said, I do not want one.

Oh well, said Uncle Billy but that was all.

So I did not like Matt saying that. Uncle Billy did not talk after it and we were just walking. This was a windy street. It was dark and the lights were not good. In the new scheme ye saw the sky and there were stars but here ye did not. I was glad Uncle Billy was there. If ye saw boys they picked on ye. At the subway station he gived us money. Alright men, cheerio.

When we were on the subway Matt said, Ye should not talk about dad.

Oh but Uncle Billy.

But ye should not anyway.

Matt could say these things to me. When he done it I wanted to say something back but could not. If me and him went places, he did not like taking me places. I liked going myself to grannie's. If ye went with him something happened.

§

I stopped swearing. No because of nothing. It was just if it was a laugh. Gary McNab was turning round in class when the teacher was not looking and he was saying stuff, T***e b*m k***h s***e d****e f***y b*m t*t. I was laughing too and he was saying in a low voice, You say it You say it.

If I would say it. Usually I did. He said it and I said it back and we were just laughing but this time I did not so he was saying, Oh what is wrong with you, how come you are not saying it. Say it.

No.

Aye.

No.

So then Gary said it again, T***e b*m k***h s***e d****e f***y b*m t*t.

And we were laughing. And Ruthie Grindlay that sat beside me was going, Oh tch huhhh, and turning round to see the lassie behind her. She did not like me laughing and talking to Gary McNab, if he was a dunce and we were in the top division. So he was whispering to me and the teacher looked and saw us but only me she said it to. Oh Kieron Smith, stop being so foolish.

When playtime came we went out to the playground. It was raining and a lot of us were in the shelter talking and laughing about the teacher. Gary McNab was making people laugh and saying how I would not say the swear words, and he was looking at me, and then he went, Well say them now.

But I was just laughing at him till then Podgie said it. Oh Smiddy, say the words.

No.

Come on.

No.

Come on, say s***e.

No.

Say it.

No.

Now other boys were looking.

Say t***e.

No.

You are just coming it.

I am not.

But that is not swearing, said Gary and he said the words again,
T***e b*m k***h s***e d****e f***y b*m b*m.

Other ones were saying it too. Oh what is Smiddy doing? It is not
swearing. Bad words is not swearing.

Some is swearing, if it is dirty words.

So other ones were shouting, Say s***e.

No.

Podgie said, Say f**k.

No.

C**t.

No.

People were laughing. Say jobby?

Jobby.

How come ye say jobby?

Because it is not swearing.

Look, said Gary, he has got a big riddy. Say k***h.

No.

K***h is not swearing.

Yes it is.

It is not.

Say f***y.

No.

Is f***y swearing?

Yes, because it is a dirty word.

Aye but it is no swearing.

Yes it is.

No it is not.

It is, if it a lassie's.

A boy out the class below said, How come ye do not swear?

Other ones were looking at me. I said, That is my business.

Say f**k, said Podgie.

No.

Mitch and other ones were there and looking at me and I felt how my face was and it was in my head to stop and just speak a bad word, whatever it was and I was waiting for Mitch to say it or if it was somebody, Billy MacGregor or Peter Wylie, if they said something so if I could just laugh but I could not. I thought I would. But then my face was sore and was just funny and I was rubbing it, and oh my cheeks and my bones felt funny. Mitch said it, Oh Smiddy does not swear.

Podgie said, How come?

I do not know.

Gary said, I have heard him swear.

Yes, I said, but I have stopped now.

And I did. I did not swear again or else bad words and dirty words, I tried not to, so people knew it.

It was funny how I done it. I felt it was funny. But I wished I had not started not swearing. Other boys did not swear but they were posh or else just if they were swots. So now I was in the top division and was one who did not swear.

My maw hated swearing. Even if it was my da and he said bloody. Oh Johnny.

Sorry.

Me and Matt never done it if we were the gether. If other boys were doing it and it was the two of us there, well, ye wished they did not and maybe kidded on ye did not hear it.

Then I took red faces. Gary McNab watched me and shouted, Oh Smiddy has got a riddy.

And that started too if somebody was saying a joke and if it was dirty or with a bad word people looked at me to see what I would do, so if I got a red face and they all were laughing. Smiddy has got a riddy.

But some ones that did it were watching because if I got them, Who are you laughing at?

When it came after school or holidays and I was kicking a ball with Pat and Danny I swore same as them but then I stopped doing it there too.

So in the class people had a different look at me. Some liked it. I thought that with Gary McNab and Mitch but no with Podgie, it was just another thing and even ye thought if maybe he wished he did not swear or else what could it be? Podgie did not like it if things happened with other people it was only to be him, him him, he was the big man. He thought I was trying to be big. Mitch was saying to him about me climbing and Podgie just went away so he could not hear, he did not like me if I was a good climber.

I did not know about the lasses, if they thought I was good for not swearing. They would. Most lasses did not swear but said the first letter, You are a dirty b. Some just said it, Oh you are a cheeky b★★★★r.

But people said, Oh he is in the top division, he does not swear.

But that did not matter. I would not swear if I was in the dunces' row. So what? It would not bother me. People there did not care about their lessons but ones in the top division did, and they did not fight and they did not do stuff except if the teacher said so. People thought it about me. None of the boys played with ye in the top division. But the ones there did not want to play. Usually they had ties on and were snobby. Ye thought that about top boys. The teacher let them go messages out the room and they just came straight back but if it was me I just waited, so then she did not ask me. I was glad.

§

One Saturday morning Mitch came up for me and it was only seven o'clock. We were going to play football but no till ten o'clock.

But now seven o'clock and the bell rang. I was sleeping and did not hear it but my da was there, just going out the door to his work. He took Mitch in and waked me up. What is that boy here for at this time of the morning?

I do not know dad.

Do not wake yer mother.

No dad. I took Mitch into the kitchenette and made toast and tea for breakfast. I said to him, Oh Mitch it is too early. We all were sleeping.

No yer da.

Oh aye but he is going to work.

After breakfast we went into the living room but it was too early for the radio or television. I had cards and we just played Pontoons for kid-on money. Me and him done it a lot and kept scores, who owed who, ye would pay back when ye were a man and got yer wages.

Mitch had three big sisters. I was glad I did not have. But maybe it would be good. If they done stuff for ye, sisters usually done it, if it was housework. Mitch thought a big brother would be good but maybe it would not. I telled him.

He came up for me a lot of times. I took him in. My maw said it too, Oh take him in Kieron.

If Matt was there he let him in too. But if Matt was in the room swotting I had to take Mitch into the living room. But if my da was home it had to be the kitchenette or the balcony, or just the landing stairs outside the door, he did not like Mitch. Oh he is just a dunder-heid. He called him that. I did not like it. My da called people names.

Me and Mitch just sat on the steps and talked about stuff or else played cards. If we were all away out and Mitch came up for me he just waited till we came home. He sat outside the front door or else at the foot of the close, on the steps to the pavement. My da did not like him doing it. Oh has he no home to go to?

Then if it was too late at night. Once it was after ten o'clock and it was my time for bed. We had had our supper and were watching the telly. Matt was in the bedroom swotting. The bell rang and my maw and da were looking at each other and were worried. Oh who could that be?

I was going to answer the door but my da said, Stay there son I will go.

It was Mitch. Is Smiddy coming out?

My da was annoyed and gived him a row. Oh what time do ye think this is? A boy of your age should not be out at this time of night. It is far too late, away ye go home. And he shut the door on Mitch and came back and was saying about it to my maw and laughing. Is Smiddy coming out? Oh he had a ball too! Ten o'clock at night and he is looking for a game of heidies. A boy at that age, it is a disgrace.

My da was not saying it to me, only to my maw. But I was there and it was my pal. So how come? How come it was not to me?

I jumped up from the floor and rushed to the window and opened it to see down. My maw said, Kieron, it is too late at night for that.

Oh but I am just looking out.

Do not lean out the window.

Oh but I am just

Shut that d**n window, said my da.

Oh but

Shut the window.

I did shut it but was still trying to see out and down for Mitch.

Come away from that b****y window!

Yes but dad

What is it with you? My da was sitting up in his chair and looking straight at me. Eh? I am asking you a question?

Answer your father, said my maw.

Well if he is my pal, if it is Mitch.

It is after ten o'clock at night.

Yes but if he is my pal.

Ten o'clock at night, said my da, and he is out looking for a game of football!

It is far too late, said my maw.

But it is not my fault.

What are you talking about? said my da.

Well if he came up for me.

We are not saying it is your fault, said my maw.

Do not be so stupid, said my da.

Well I am not being stupid, if he came up for me, it is not my fault.

Oh away and give us peace, said my da. What is he doing up for ye at this time of night? Ten o'clock! For a game of b****y football! There is something wrong with that boy. He is just a b****y dunderheid.

No he is not.

Aye he is. And do not talk back to me.

My maw was looking at my da and I knew what it was, it was swearing and saying aye. He kidded on he did not know.

I was just going to wave to him, I said.

It is too late at night, said my da.

Yes but I was just going to wave.

Oh for Heaven sake. My da shaked his head and lifted up his newspaper. He kept it at the side of his chair and just read it when he wanted.

William's mother and father will be worried, said my maw.

They will not.

Of course they will.

Of course they will not.

What? My da leaned out of his chair now to look right at me. His face was the angriest. I was sitting where I sat at the side of the settee but I could not go behind with him speaking to me. Oh what did you say? Eh? What did you say? Are you being cheeky to your mother? Do not you ever be cheeky to yer mother! I am warning ye.

I was not being cheeky.

What!

My maw said, Yes you were Kieron.

Well I did not mean to be.

Well it d**n well sounded like it to me! Get to yer bed.

Yes, I am going.

Aye well go, just b****y go, afore I lose my temper.

My maw was looking at my da because all what he was saying. But I just got up and went to the door and right out. I was glad, glad glad glad, just glad. I did not want to stay there with them. It was just not fair and I was sick of it. If it was my pal I should have went to the door. It was my pal if it was Mitch. He came up for me. It was not up for them. He did not come up for them. So if he did not, if my da said it to my maw and not to me, he should have said it to me. Oh your pal is at the door. He should have said it to me. I should have went to the door just to see Mitch. Oh it is too late, I cannot come out. I would have said it to him.

Oh yer pal is there at the door. My da should have said that. It just was not fair, because I was young. If it was Matt it would not have been, he would have said it to him. My da always said stuff to Matt, no to me. That is what happened in this house. I was sick of it and I just thought it was horrible, just all things ye were always not allowed. How come ye were not allowed? And if it was something even just if it was yer pal, if he came up for ye, how come ye could not see him? It just was not fair. Because he came up late, it was not my fault.

I saw Mitch at school and said it to him, Do not come up for me too late, that was too late, my da was just angry.

What for?

It was too late.

Oh did he give ye a doing?

No, but he nearly did.

Oh if he does ye should just f*****g run away. I would go with ye, we will just go to England, I have got cousins there and they would help ye.

Mitch wanted to run away a lot. I said I would go with him but just no just now. He still came up for me, even if it was rows. The doorbell rang and my maw went to get it. Oh is Smiddy coming out?

My maw did not like him saying it. Who is Smiddy?

This is his house.

Oh his name is Kieron, it is Kieron, you must say Kieron. And it is not hoose it is house, you must say house.

House.

My maw took him in but she did not like him in the house all the time and no if we were having our tea. He kept looking round to see us. He was sitting on the settee and doing it. Lucky for him my da was not home. My maw got up and left the table, she carried her tea ben the kitchenette. She said it to me after. Oh William is watching me eat, tell him not to, it is awful rude.

My maw did not like people watching her. Sometimes she thought stuff and it was just daft. But Matt said it too. Tell Mitch no to watch us eating.

So after me and Mitch went out I said to him, How come ye were watching us eat, my maw did not like it.

Oh I was not watching yez eat.

Aye ye were. Matt said it too.

I was just looking.

What at?

Everything.

My maw thinks it was her.

Well it was not.

So after that if we were having our tea he just sat in the bedroom and waited. My maw said to Matt about his books and jotters because if he had them all out and Mitch was there but Matt said, Oh mum it is okay.

Oh but you do not want him touching your things.

Oh he will not touch them.

That was Matt saying it. I was glad. Because Mitch would not. So it was good Matt saying it. If it was Podgie but, Podgie would touch everything. I took him in and that was what happened. I did not like taking him in because ye just had to watch yer stuff all the time. But no Mitch. He loved my house. Oh Smiddy I would stay here. That was what he said. He hated his house and the most thing was his da. When he was a man he was going to kill him, that was what he said, I am going to poison him to death, he is a horrible old stinking b★★★★★d.

He would do it. Mitch was Mitch. I did not go into his house much. His maw did not mind but he did not like me going in. If it was his big sisters. Boys had sisters and did not like people going in their house. So if they saw something. Oh I saw yer sister's k******rs.

He was good at spitting. He done it through his front teeth, tthhhh. And he was a smashing whistler and did not use his fingers. Ye would be away at the end of the street and ye would hear him. Even across the field and down at the burn, oh there is Mitch. I could only do it with my fingers but no loud.

Some boys laughed at him. It was a funny thing in his voice and they mimicked him too but no if he would hear them. He was very very good at fighting. He was a best fighter in the school. He did not care about stuff. If it was a boy in a higher class. He did not care. He was in a big fight with a Primary 7. All people were watching. The Primary 7 was a best fighter. Then Mitch was greeting. We saw he was, and it was loud greeting, he was making a noise and it sounded just funny and people were looking. The Primary 7 boy's pals all thought stuff, if Mitch would give in. But we knew he would not and he just still was fighting, and he bashed the Primary 7 hard on the ear with a real hard punch and the Primary 7 just stopped and was holding his ear and going, Ohh ohhh and moaning, then went down on the ground and was still moaning.

Mitch ran away. Me and the boys ran after him. You won the fight Mitch!

I thought Mitch could beat Podgie at fighting. Other ones did not. Podgie done stuff. I did not like it. He dared Mitch to do stuff and Mitch done it. Go and skelp that lassie's b*m.

I telled him no to but he did.

Oh away and throw a stane at that window. So Mitch went and done it and Podgie and Gary laughed. Mitch hoped I would laugh but I did not. Oh Smiddy it is just for a joke.

But I did not like Podgie doing it. If it was me I would not have done it. So how come Mitch done it? I did not know.

Then in the class if Podgie said it, Oh away out and touch the blackboard. So Mitch ran out and done that too. And if Miss Cooney saw him, Oh William Mitchell what are you doing?

She shouted at him and gived him the belt. Mitch just looked. She belted people all the time but did not do it good. People laughed at her. So if ye were chalking a sum on the blackboard ye did a daft face or stuck yer tongue out. Then if she gived ye the belt. One time she done it to Gary McNab and he said, Oh please Miss that was dead sore, and he held his hands out and just flapped them so everybody was laughing.

Then people spoke rude to her, just saying all slang words, aye and doon and aw I cannay dae that miss, whit is it ye says miss. One time Podgie grabbed a lassie's school bag and emptied it on on the floor and Miss Cooney saw him but kidded on she did not. But I saw her and she did. The lassie got a big red face and was going to greet but she did not.

Miss Cooney was boney and with skinny legs and a yellow skirt and then the same jacket, she did not change it. Her back was bent over and she had black hair in a funny way stuck up. Gary McNab said, Oh that is not hair it is a hat.

Oh it is a wig. Podgie said, It is a wig to cover a baldy head.

Everybody all was laughing, lasses as well. They did not like Podgie but still were laughing. But some thought if it was true, if it was a wig. Imagine it. Then what happened, she dropped her chalk on the floor and went to pick it up. But she put her hand on her head. So that was to stop the wig falling off. So really it was a wig, it could be. Out at playtime people were talking about it. Oh if it is a wig. Maybe it is. Maybe she is a murderer, if it is a disguise. Oh what are we going to do? People were saying that.

So Podgie dared Mitch. Heh Mitch you lift it and see.

People did not think he would but he did. Miss Cooney was chalking stuff at the blackboard. Mitch ran over and pulled her hair hard. She fell down and was shouting in a high tiny voice, ohhhh, ohhhh.

Mitch was just there standing and people all were looking and just quiet.

Ohhh, ohhh.

What was going to happen? We all were watching. But she just got up and was holding her head. She saw a book and grabbed it, she bashed Mitch right on the head with it, oh and the book fell and she got his neck and choked it and then bashed him again and he was fighting to get away and done it. He ran to the back of the room. She shouted and went to get him but he dodged roundabout. She could not catch him. It was funny to see but everybody all was quiet and just looking to see. Ye could hear Miss Cooney breathing, Huh hoh, huh hoh, huh hoh, huh hoh.

Then ye saw how Mitch was getting near the door, he was just going with toty wee steps, getting there. He was trying to. But she saw him. Oh do not dare leave this room William Mitchell. But he did, just dived to the door and flung it open and away. Miss Cooney chased out after him.

What would happen? If she caught him or if it was the headmaster or else what? If it was the cops and the Approved School. Boys got sent to the Approved School or else Borstal. People all were talking till then a teacher came in, Get on with your work.

Another teacher came in and sat at Miss Cooney's desk till the bell went to go home. Me and the boys were walking down the street talking about it. Then there he was, he was hiding in a close. He came out and walked in the middle of us so nobody could see him, Oh if the cops came. Gary said it.

We went down the shops. Mitch told us he did not see Miss Cooney. He just skipped out the front entrance and then out the gate when the jannie was not there. But the next day Miss Cooney did not come in and she did not come back again to school. Mitch's maw was there, she went into the headmaster's office. Mitch got a bad doing off his da.

But he was not good at football. He hoped he was and he was a fast runner but he did not hit the ball right and could not dribble. Usually he went in goals. He was good at diving and did not care about it, no even if it was raining and he got soaked. On the school pitch it was puddles puddles and down the goalie's end was worse, and then muddy. So who was in goals, if he had to dive, he got soaking wet and all muddy clothes. My maw would have killed me.

If it was too heavy raining ye did not play.

That was the worst. It just was. It was only football ye wanted.

Sitting in the class and just waiting for the dinnerbell to ring then dinnerschool then getting a game.

Usually it was Billy MacGregor had the ball. The ones to carry it lived beside the school. If they were too far away they did not carry it. If ye carried the ball ye had to be first back. Billy did not go to dinnerschool. His maw was home and made his dinner. He got soup and toast and cheese but if his maw was late he just got a piece on cheese. Wait for yer soup! That was his maw shouting. No, I am not hungry. Billy told me. He just rushed out and back to school.

If ye were late back with the ball people moaned at ye. If ye were dead late that was the worst thing, if yer maw kept ye in and the boys were out on the pitch waiting and there was not a ball. That was the worst. Who is carrying the ball? Oh it is Billy. Where f*****g is he!

How come he was not here! Then ye saw him running up and he gived a big kick of the ball. We got the sides picked and then were playing.

It was not Billy's ball really. It was a boy called Wotherspoon, it was his ball. He gived it to Billy after morning playtime. Billy kept it under the desk or if somebody else took it. I did too, sometimes. Ye just squeezed it under. If it jumped back out, sometimes it did, so ye pushed it in or if it bounced out on the floor and the teacher thought ye were laughing at her, ye were not, ye did not mean it. I will take that ball!

But she gived ye it back at dinnertime and just was smiling. Oh well ye better have it I suppose.

After school some of us got another game and the boys out Primary 7 played with us and weer ones out Primary 5. Sometimes it was only a wee drop of boys. We played crossing the ball and heidies, or three-and-in, so one boy went in goals and who scores three goals out the other ones, so it was your turn in goals.

Oh but it was the worst if it was heavy raining all morning and ye heard it against the wall and then the roof, just lashing down, so if ye could not play. Ye tried no to think about it. If ye did it stayed on but if ye forgot about it it might go off. Then it did but a wee while later it was back on again. The school was made of tin. It was loud loud pattering, and the teacher could not do the lessons right. Oh for Heaven sake!

At dinnertime ye all went under the shelters, standing there and seeing if it was going off, even a wee bit so ye could try it. Boys went out and gived the ball a long kick down the pitch then ran after it but it was through all the puddles and it was hopeless. Usually ye just got Primary 5 boys to do it. They wanted in with us so we could let them play. But if it was me and Billy MacGregor and we went out, we passed the ball to test the ground. If it was no any good, the ball stuck in a deep puddle, it was just a laugh, people splashed through to kick the ball and ye all got soaked. But if ye could still play. Maybe ye could. So if somebody under the shelter shouted to us, What like is it?

Billy looked up at the sky and held his hand out to test. Oh I think it is going off a wee bit.

More people came out to see. Podgie and Gary. Oh s***e it is too rainy. They ran back under the shelter. It is f*****g pelting! What did ye say it was going off for?

Sometimes me and Billy MacGregor just stayed out passing the ball and if Mitch was there he came too but a lot of times he did not come to school.

The other one that came was Peter Wylie. Him and Billy were pals. Peter liked bikes and said how ye got real racers, maybe if it was a Flying Scot. Or if it was an Italian one, they were the best. Peter was wanting one for his Christmas but did not think he would get it. He said how Rona Craig's big brother was getting one for his birthday. His granny was getting it for him and it cost a mint of money.

People all talked about stuff. Some were getting good presents at Christmas and then if it was their birthday. But ye knew if they were boasters, a lot of them were.

Oh but then if the rain went off and still time before the bell Podgie and other ones came and we picked sides fast. There was a big slope on the pitch. It was aye best to shoot down the way. Ye tossed a coin and if ye won the call ye shooted down the first half because most times ye did not get a second half, the bell always rang too soon.

In the winter it snowed some days. People liked the snow for big fights, lasses too, and it was great fun, maybe if it was boys against lasses, and it was just all the lasses out the complete school so all wee ones too running about, Oh mammy daddy mammy daddy. It was just a laugh.

Just for football it was hopeless how the ball turned into a snowball. But it was a laugh too, ye could not run for laughing and then the goalies, if Mitch was there he was like a snowman walking because he just dived for every ball. John Davis was looking at him too. See Mitch! See Mitch!

Mitch did not care but, he just done it. But he did not laugh, he just done it, sometimes if he looked at me. If it was a good game. I just said it to him, Good game Mitch.

Oh aye.

§

The carnival and circus was on and the boys were going. I tried to get money but my maw did not like giving me it because my da was not working. I would not even ask. They would never give me nothing. Mitch said to go into my da's pockets. But if he has got no money.

Oh he will have some.

But he did not have a sausage. Him and my maw argued about it and I heard them. That was what he always said, I do not have a d**n sausage.

Well what about her purse? said Mitch.

But I did not want to go into her purse. I done it when I was weer but did not like it. I got too nervy and all worried. I went into the bathroom and it was diarrhoea because of it, just my stomach.

So then if ye got caught. A thief was the worst. What if it was off yer mates? Yer mates was the same as family. More so. My da said that. They were the lowest of the low and just scum when they done it. If my da's shipmates caught a thief they flung him overboard. That was what they done to one bloke. Things went missing on board. Who would have thought it was him? It was one nobody would have thought. They expected a Chinaman. Chinamen were on the boat. But it was not, it was just Scottish. What all the men done was trap him. They all were waiting. So then they caught him and the next thing he went missing. Man overboard. Because they flung him overboard and it was out in the ocean. That was harsh justice. That was it if ye were at sea. They done it to a darkie once. The men did not like him and he went missing.

I sometimes done it for fags, I went into his packet and if he had eight I took two or if it was four I took one. Mitch said, Oh just take three. But if ye done that yer da would know. One time I took a fag and got a bad feeling in my stomach. I was on the toilet seat and just seeing the fag and thinking how him and my maw were watching the telly. I broke the fag up and flung it down the pan. But I pulled the plug and it would not go down. The paper came away and the tobacco all was floating. I kept doing the plug but it did not go down. It was a worry the whole night.

Mitch knocked money out his house. His da kept his money in his coat pockets so he just dipped him. Mitch said that, I just dipped him. He done it with his maw too. Oh I dipped her purse.

But I did not want money off my maw and my da. Nothing. I did not want nothing off them. They just talked and talked about it. I got sick of it. Sometimes ye forgot and just asked, Oh can I go to the swimming baths after school tomorrow?

Oh no, there is no money, it is too dear, how many times do you want to go there. It is dear and so is everything, all just too dear. Oh if ye want to go to the swimming baths, ye were only there on Saturday if it is more money for the pictures and then if it is the circus.

I only went sometimes to the circus. The boys all liked the carnival the best but it was the worst out the whole lot for money. It is just a bunch of thieves, said my da. Carnival people are just tinkers and then when ye are on the roundabouts all the money falls out yer pocket and they all get it. They just fling ye about to steal yer money.

It is just a fraud, said my maw, shots on this and shots on that. I do not know how their mothers can afford it. Oh they must be rich for that.

My da did not like his job and just left it. He came home in the afternoon. Me and Mitch came back at four o'clock and he was there. Lucky for me I did not climb the balcony. When my maw came home it was a fight. I was reading a book in the kitchenette and their voices were loud. I did not hear what it was. My maw came in and then back out when she saw me. But her face was red and she did not speak, and away into the bathroom. She was greeting and did not come out for ages. He came in to put on a kettle for tea and stood with his hand on the handle waiting for it to boil. I wished I was not there but Matt was in the bedroom and it was raining heavy, I could not go out on the balcony. But then my da switched off the gas and just went away to him and my maw's bedroom. He got on his coat and shoes and went away out. He did not say where he was going. My maw came out the bathroom and through to me. Where is your father away to?

I do not know mum.

Oh did he not say anything?

No.

Her face was all red, she had been greeting in the bathroom. That was what she done. When Mitch said to go in her purse, I could not. He hated his maw and da but I did not. I just wished I had a job, if I had my own money, that was what I wanted.

§

Podgie thought he was the best at football. We were playing up his street one night and his da was watching out the window. The streetlights came on, it was dark. So he came down and was shouting for Podgie to run and score a goal. Podgie was doing it. He played better. His real name was Derek and his da was shouting that. Go on Derek go on Derek.

Podgie did not want ye saying Podgie if his da was there. So if ye just let him beat ye because his da was there, if he was wanting that, but ye did not. I did not care if his da was there. So what? If his da thought he was the best player, he was not. Podgie just could tackle and boot the ball, that was all, and if he scored a goal it was just easy and he kicked it. And then if he did a dirty tackle on ye his da just shouted, Good play good play!

It was not good play it was just dirty. People just s★★t it when he tackled. So they let him win the ball. He never picked me. Him and Billy MacGregor were captains. Billy was the real best player. Him and Peter Wylie were in the second top division. Billy would have wanted to be in the top but he was not. He looked at me no swearing. His maw and da all went to Church. Billy always picked me for his team.

But Podgie was too slow. I could play him easy, ye got the ball at yer feet and ye just ran with it because he could not catch ye. So he stopped running. He told us what his da said. Oh Smiddy would be good if he remembered the ball. Smiddy runs fast but he cannot dribble, ye just stick out yer foot and get the ball off him.

His da took him to the Rangers' games. I said how I got in when I was wee. The men lifted us over the gates, we did not have to pay. So we got in for nothing, we just dodged the cops. Podgie went away and told his da then came back. Oh Smiddy you are a lying b★★★★★d.

No I am not.

Ye f★★★★★g are.

No I am not.

My da said ye could never have done it because that was the olden days.

I did so do it. I done it a lot of times.

Podgie did not believe me. Him and Gary were pointing at me and laughing. Two boys from the class below us were there. They were laughing too. What were they laughing about? If they thought they could laugh at me. They just went with Podgie because they wanted in with him. They were feared of him.

But if it was fighting he would beat ye. I thought about how ye would fight him and what my Uncle Billy said. Oh ye just grab something and batter him with it, if it is a brick or what, a bottle, ye just batter him with it and the best place is the nose, hit him on the nose and he will not get up. Or else boot him in the b**ls. If it was football it was rupture. Ye could not move if the ball hit ye there it was just the worst agony. So what if it was a boot? Ten times worse, a hundred times. Yer b**ls went all black, that was what happened to a bad rupture, ye saw all the football players if it was Rangers or who, Celtic or Thistle, and it was a free kick, they all shielded their b**ls else what would happen, it was a rupture and that was you.

Podgie acted tough with me all the time. So if I was easy he was going to take me any day. I thought how to fight him. Podgie could bash ye. He was not fat but just with a very thick body so if he did punch ye, ye would just fall down and that was you if ye were knocked out. A knock-out punch. Ye saw that in boxing.

If ye just did not do nothing, that was the worst thing. Boys done that. Somebody was battering them and they were just holding themselves, Oh stop stop stop, oh do not hit me, do not hit me. But they just got belted harder and then down on the ground, if it was a dirty fighter, they got a kicking. People shouted that, Oh let yer man up!

But a dirty fighter did not let his man up, just booted into him on the ground and the boy shouting, Oh give us mercies give us mercies.

A dirty fighter did not give mercies. The big boys were like that at football. They just booted ye. Two times they let me and Billy MacGregor play with them. They just booted ye off the park. They were in Secondary School. RCs played too, well if it was Sunday. So for Billy because he was good, it was just boot boot boot but Billy just dodged them. If it was me I just ran fast to get away, then they shouted at ye, Oh Smiddy is a wee s***ebag.

No wonder if you are just going to boot us!

But that was all they done. Ye heard somebody say, Oh he is a great tackler. But he was not a great tackler just dirty. I thought that. Then if they had thick legs they just crunched ye. Some of the big boys' legs were very thick, and if ye were trying to get into them they just banged ye and ye fell down. Even they did not mean it, they just caught ye or if it was their knee it cracked ye. Oh and it was pure agony. Yer leg was away and ye could not stand on it. Ye had to go and sit down till it got okay again.

So it was not good playing with them even if they let us. Ye just liked it because they were big. We got our own game and it was best. Big ones played with us but only Primary 7 up to First Year Secondary. In that big Sunday game ones had left school and were working. I did not play good with the big boys. Podgie and Mitch did not even play in their games. They just sat and were smoking. Gary McNab was with them. Gary did not play football much. One time he said to me, Football is p★★h.

His big brother played and it was him and his pals brought the cards. He just left the game and went over behind the goals. So did other ones. Then the football finished and they started cards. Pontoons. Ye had to get to 21s or ye got bust. It was for money, so only them with money played. If ye did not have money ye just watched. I liked watching. But if there was too many wee ones and just all talking all the time, the big ones got angry, Oh stop f★★★★★g yapping. Oh f★★k off, wee c★★ts.

But if ye were just there and quiet and just were watching then it did not matter. Or else if ye helped and went messages. If one was playing and you were not he would just say to ye, Oh will ye go to the ice-cream van and get me five fags and a bottle of ginger.

So ye just went. I went a lot because I did not have money. Ye got a drink of ginger or else a fag for going. If that one won a lot of money he could give ye something, threepence or sixpence. Sometimes he did not give ye anything, no even a fag. Just if he was flinging away the dowp he gived it to you so ye got the last draw before it burned too low. Some big ones did not give ye nothing. Ye ran round to the icey or else down the shops for them. Then ye came back and they laughed at ye. So ye stopped going their messages. Oh he is too miserable.

Some boys made pieces for ones that were winning the most money, and they said, Oh I am starving.

Do ye want a piece on jam?

No, a piece on cheese.

This was what Podgie done. He stayed near. He would run away up to his house and make a piece on cheese and then back down and give it to the other one and he would get money for doing it. So then if he played cards with the money he got, so if he won. Most times he lost it quick.

I lived too faraway to do it.

In my house ye did not get money. Matt got a job but then stopped it with his studies. A lot of the big boys had jobs. They done deliveries, milk or papers or what. Gary's brother worked on the milk. Another big boy there was George who was pally with my brother and had a wee brother Jim, he was a paperboy. He spoke to me. Oh I do not see Matt these days, what is he up to?

He is doing his studies. For his exams.

A lot of times George lost his money and was dead angry. He tossed his cards away and one time he tore them. Gary's big brother was looking at him, so if it was going to be a fight. But George won sometimes and if he gived me money. Do not gamble it now.

He called me Kieron. Some of the boys looked at me. Smiddy is Kieron. Then Podgie and a wee smile to Gary McNab, oh it is a Pape's name, I knew what he was meaning.

Somebody said Podgie got a doing off a Pape. I did not know if it was true. Just if he was going to pick on ye, that was what worried ye. One time in class me and Gary McNab were talking and he telled me Podgie had a wee t****r. Gary done a w*****g sign with two fingers and was laughing. I telled Mitch. Mitch said it back to Gary but Gary said he did not say it, so if I said he did I was lying. I was not lying. He just laughed. That was what Gary done, so if it went back to Podgie, what would he say to me?

Podgie said stuff to people. Oh your maw done a washing and I saw her k*****rs hanging up. He done it to Mitch about his sisters.

Oh do ye see their clothes hanging up? Have they got k★★★★★rs? Oh do they wear k★★★★★rs? Oh do ye see them going to the bathroom? Do they wear their knick-knacks? Do ye see all their legs? Oh come on and tell us! Podgie made w★★★★★g signs with his hand and felt yer d★★k. Oh Smiddy has got a h★★★★n.

I have not.

Oh ye f★★★★★g have. Oh Mitch see yer face, ye have got a big f★★★★★g riddy.

Mitch let him say it. How come? I did not like it. If he done it with me. He did, he did do it with me. But Mitch could have hit him. I think he could have. I said it to him. You could just batter him.

Oh but he is a pal.

Podgie did not act it with Gary McNab because of his big brother. Ye saw him walking about. Everybody did. He could fight anybody. He carried a blade, people said it. A blade was a knife. One time the Squatters captured him and he escaped out the camp. Gary told us, he just had the knife and they were feared, the ones that were guarding him. He was getting a big gang from the whole of the new scheme to go and fight the Squatters. He was not scared of them, even if it was Cochise. Gary said it. But I did not think it. The Squatters were all away now. Me and Mitch went to see their old camp. Peter Wylie came with us. But nothing was there except the new building site and all muddy tracks and everything, bricks and bricks and just piles of stuff. We went in and got piles of nails and one tool that was an iron bar. The workies were not looking at us. We planked the stuff in swampy grass near the burn.

The iron bar was good. Ye used it to open stuff, just wedged it and then forced what it was. It was dead heavy but felt good in yer hand. And if it just tapped ye on the head ye would be knocked cold. Imagine having it and somebody claimed ye so it was a fight and ye could just use it. What if ye had it in yer pocket? If they would not leave ye alone. Ye could just take it out and batter them. Podgie done it, he came up and shoved ye in the back. He done it to me. Or else clicking yer heels and it was a joke but if you done it to him? Well ye would not do it to him. It was sore when he done it. It just made ye angry and I got angry and what to do, ye wanted to do something but could not, ye could not do nothing. And all people seeing ye, and if ye were with the boys so it was yer pals, and if it was Gary and him laughing.

My face just went red and ye just got worse angry and they were laughing at ye. I would have battered Podgie. If I was John Davis I would have. I would have got him down and booted into him. Or else just punched him. The first time he said anything to me I would belt him, calling me names or what, I would not be scared of him.

§

My da told me to sit on the settee. How come he did it? Just because he picked on ye. Ye were there no doing nothing and it happened. Worse if ye talked. So if ye were not allowed to. It was your house same as them but they did not want ye talking. Matt said stuff. I could not.

I did not like sitting on the settee except if nobody was there. If my maw was there or Matt ye could not see the telly right because their face was in front of ye. That was all ye could watch was their face. Ye could not stop it, and if it was my maw, she did not like it and looked round to see ye if ye were. But I was not. I did not want to look at her face but ye could not help it, just how ye were sitting on the settee.

My maw told me to sit nearest the television but then if it was your face they were seeing. Ye were just blocking the way and ye were not to move. Oh why cannot you sit at peace?

But mum I am just

Oh would you just stop fidgeting.

Ye could not do nothing. Then if ye picked yer nose, that was the worst. Oh go and blow your nose Kieron that is just very bad manners.

Then if it was other ones doing it. Matt picked his nose too but he kidded on he did not. Me and the boys were talking about it and Gary McNab said about his auntie, how she done it and that was the worst of all. But if it was yer maw, imagine yer maw done it. I could not. I had not seen her ever do it. But I saw my da and it was his middle finger. People were talking about ones that done it but I did not say about him. But his face went funny and he did not wipe it anywhere. People done it and then if ye shook their hands, I would never do it and then if ye made the supper. It was horrible.

I did not like watching people. Ruthie Grindlay was in the second row at the desk across from me and always scratched her head, and it was all dandruff falling down on the desk. The teacher was talking and she was doing it. I had a wee dream and it was caterpillars falling. It was not a real dream in bed, just at my desk in the class and she was doing it, all caterpillars falling out her hair and on the desk.

Then she looked down to see it and blowed it away and gived a wee look to see if people were watching. It was just horrible and clatty. Imagine yer mouth was open and ye were eating yer dinner if it was dinnerschool and it landed on yer plate, just her dandruff, it sickened ye and then if she f★★★d. That was worst. Except if she was fat. I thought if it was a fat person because all the wind was packed in their body, it would just be like it was not their fault, if they were just so big and jampacked with wind so if only they had to move an inch and something jumbled inside their stomach, they would not even know they were doing it. My grannie done it, she was just walking and it came out, but she did not make a smell. But she was not fat.

§

No many people from the scheme went to Matt's school. The ones that did stayed on at school and got their Highers, then it was the best jobs. My maw said it, if ye could just do that, that was you and it was not a dirty job, ye worked with yer brains and not just yer hands. White-collar jobs were the best ones to get, and if ye could get one as a clerk. People were clerks, they did not get their hands dirty and it was short hours. My da worked in a factory and did not like it. Oh but Matt would never work there, said my maw.

His school was all posh and snobby. My maw liked if he was saying stuff about it. I came into the kitchenette and he was talking oh and my maw's face, ye saw her eyes all big and just laughing, oh she loved hearing it.

But no if I was there, Matt did not want me hearing. So if I came in and he was talking to my maw he just stopped and was waiting for me to go back out. He did not want me there, just so he could talk to mum and tell her stuff, he did not want me hearing. Because it was all snobby stuff. I knew it was snobby stuff. I did not care. So if he was saying all about his lessons and what the teacher said.

Oh and who is in your class, if they all are good speakers and oh just if they are good. My maw liked all good stuff.

When the boys were talking about big brothers and saying about best fighters they did not say about Matt. He did not do much fighting here. He did in the old place. If it was gangs, if our street was fighting them, Matt charged into them. He was a best fighter. He was. I saw he was. He went with his pals and they just all went places. Now he did not. He just stayed in his room, he read books and swotted. If he went out it was Saturday and Sunday and he got the train to meet his pals. They were in his school and did not live in the scheme.

Mitch liked him. He wished he had a big brother but I told him how they might not be good. Ye could still get doings. Not real doings, but punches. Then if they wanted something they just took it and if it was the biggest dinners, they always got them, if it was potatos on yer plate ye aye counted more on his and they were just always bigger. Sausages too. Oh he got three sausages what did you get? Two and a half. Else yours were skinny and his were fat.

Or what? Stew and mince. He got the most meat, yer maw always gived him it. You just got carrots and gravy. And he got the biggest puddings, bigger than my da as well. How come? My maw gived Matt the biggest in the house. My da just looked. The same if it was a piece, if my maw was making us one, he got the thickest slices. So if it was a piece, I made my own so I could get good ones, I just looked for the best slices, I just dug down inside the loaf and I got them if they were thick.

And I made the supper. He never made it. But I liked making it. Because I just gave him the weest, toast and cheese or else scrambled egg, I gave him the weest plate and then seeing his face, he used to see what everybody was getting. So if it was my maw's and da's, he could not say nothing because he should get the weest. But if it was mine and he saw it was bigger, oh ye just felt like laughing. I sat down with mine and I nearly was. If I had laughed he would have got me. He would have punched me on the back or on the shoulder. They would not have seen him doing it. Usually I took first bites out mine so he could not see the size.

He would not make the supper. He was lazy. I thought that. He did not do stuff except if it was studying, and my maw and da did not make him. With me they did. Oh away down the shops for milk and potatos, oh take that rubbish bin down the midden or else peel the potatos. Oh Kieron you peel the potatos and will you please set the table. If Matt set the table he just put down the placemats and the knifes, forks and spoons. I done everything, cups for tea and milk and sugar and all plates and then salt. Oh but if it was Matt, oh no. And then all his stuff in the bedroom, all just lying under the bed, and his socks and pants, he just threw it all under, and my maw had to get it for the laundry basket. So that was not fair, if I had to get mine myself, he never got his.

Or else the window side. How come he had the window side? He just took it. I would have loved sleeping there and then at nighttime maybe with the curtains open for the moon and stars. Except when the light was too bright coming in because it kept ye awake. Or else if it was a loud storm with thunder and lightning. Although that was alright, ye could just lie there and think about things. When my da was in the Navy they had the biggest storms and thundering gales, the waves coming over the bows of the boat and if ye were not careful they seized ye and carried ye overboard. Men were lost at sea. Some of his pals went overboard and if that happened they could not survive, no even if the Captain and everybody knew they were overboard because they could not turn the boat back, it took too long, it had to go on a big wide circle to do the turnabout so the ones that fell off were already drowned and lost forever.

Or if it was up north at the Arctic Circle and it was too cold if it was winter and they were dead in ten minutes. Or even one minute. It was exposure. And how cold it was too, so they would be a block of ice. Nobody could dive in and save them, their body could not take it. It had to be lifeboats and maybe they did not work if it was too bad a storming wind and ye could not launch them or else if they capsized. The Captain would not waste more men for the sake of one. That was what happened. And ye were there in the water and yer feet just going up and down and oh what about sharks or what. Ye were just having to watch it, and seeing the boat too, getting farther and farther away, the lights getting lower and lower, going into the distance, if ye tried to swim after it and yer boots were too heavy, all the water getting in, if ye were wearing big wellies, the water filling them up and dragging ye down for a horrible death, so ye had to get them off, just treading water, keeping yer head up, unless ye just dived down to do it, that would be the best thing, so using yer two hands to pull them off.

Or no wearing wellies at all. Ye would not wear them because why, because what good were they? Ye had to wear them when ye were wee. I hated them except for going in puddles but they gived ye hacks and it was just sore the whole day. They were hopeless for other stuff. Ye could not play football with them and never climb an inch. Imagine wellies and climbing a ronepipe? Even a tree. Ye could not. So the same if ye were a sailor. If they could not grip the deck ye were best wearing something like whatever it was, just the best for gripping and so if ye fell in they would not fill up and drag ye down.

That was what ye wondered, ye saw somebody drowning, they had not the strength to keep up. Yer legs just gived in and that was you, ye sank down, having to take in the water once yer breath ran out, right down fathoms and fathoms right to the bottom of the sea.

Or else if ye just floated, if yer body had no life left in it, it was all gone, so maybe it went back up to the surface. Ye saw some bodies like that, other ones just went to the bottom.

Some did and some did not. So how come, if one body did not float and another one did? Matt asked my da that. I cannot mind what my da said. But maybe if seaweed dragged ye down, all twisting round yer ankles and ye were trying to escape but ye could not and ye were just making it tighter and tighter and ye could not breathe and the water was there and just waiting to fill up yer lungs. It was a horrible death.

I liked it when my da told stories but he did not do it much, only when we were wee and he was home on leave. Most times now he did not speak or else just got angry at stuff on the telly, if darkies were winning all the boxing or if it was Papes in the pictures, all the time it was Papes how ye never saw Protestant Churches on the telly, just Chapels, he got annoyed with that or if he made jokes if it was Priests or else in a Chapel and people were all lighting their candles and kneeling on the floor.

Stories about boats were good. I liked hearing them and reading them too if it was an adventure story and people were sailing ships but no if it was submarines or the war, I hated stories about that. I liked them about pirates and the olden days, treasure islands and the Coral Sea. I was telling the boys how ye could swim down so deep and the water was just so clear, even at the very bottom ye could open yer eyes and just see what was there, fish that were just how they were, and all the sizes and big big mouths and the skinniest bodies, just thin but with the sharpest kind of shark's teeth. And all shells ye blew into and were like bugles in the BB band, and if ye found old hulks and boxes of gold coins that were pieces-of-eight and skeletons were there guarding them with all scaly fingers if ye had to push them to open the box and the seawood all trailing.

§

Climbing was the best thing so if ye saw a good tree or what. If it was a different building. The Church down the hill was great-looking and had wee different roofs for jumping right up to the Cross at the top. Imagine ye could climb it and get on with both hands or if ye could stand up on the top of the wee toty bit. Oh but how would ye balance? Just one foot on top of the other, ye could maybe do it that way.

Even going someplace with my maw and da I still looked for the best buildings, and if the roof looked good, what was the best way up? If there was not a way ye got a funny feeling, so the building was not friendly. Some buildings had a face and were friendly. The school building's face was a robot, ye could not see if it was friendly. But the back of my building was friendly, ye saw that, it was just friendly, ye would never fall off it because it would not let ye, it did not want ye to fall.

But then the Chapel too, it was friendly. How come? The Chapel only had one roof but it did not have a pointed part, it was complete flat but with a wee slope. So if ye climbed it ye could run about. There was a lot of windows up high. If ye lied on the roof and looked way over the edge ye would maybe see in a window, if some-body held yer feet. Imagine ye did and people saw ye? The Donnellys were up my close, they were Catholics, so if they were there and just looked up at the window it would be me. Oh there's Kieron!

Or Pat and Danny. What a laugh if it was them seeing up. But a funny thing how the Chapel roof went on a wee slope. It was not a big slope-down roof, just a wee one. But ye could run down and do a jump, except there was not a place to jump to.

The new scheme was no good for high-up jumps. Me and the boys were talking. They knew about dykes and jumps from back in their old places. We could go and see them. They could come to mine and I could go to theirs. I wanted to see them, and if we done them, maybe we would. I said it, if we could go on Saturday morning, we would just maybe go, but only Mitch wanted to come with me.

There were no balconies in the old place, it just had windows, so if ye climbed one, ye would just go in there. Usually the window was left shut but so there would not be draughts. My grannie was aye saying about draughts, and if ye left the door open, Oh shut that door son, because granda got cold. He put on jerseys and a cardigan. My grannie laughed at him. How many jerseys is that?

Never you mind woman. Or else Vera if he called her Vera. Never you mind Vera it has got nothing to do with you.

My granda was good at saying stuff and if my maw was talking to Auntie May they would be laughing about him and all what he used to say. My grannie gived him rows but then she just looked at him. He pointed back at her with his thumb and then just a wee whisper, Wheesht son, danger signal, no sparring the night.

My grannie's ronepipe window was the kitchen window and if ye climbed in there she would get ye. She was always at it and doing stuff. She kept the window shut except if it was old bread for birds, ye heard them clucking and she put it out on the ledge for them. Me with the cats and her with the birds. My granda said that.

My grannie did not like cats much so if she left the window open and granda's cats went for the birds and chased them right out and over the ledge, Oh I would laugh, said grannie, but he would not.

So if ye were going to do the ronepipe ye would have to open the window first. But ye would have to ask her and she would never let ye. Oh we are three storeys up if ye fell and broke yer neck or else yer back.

People said that, if a workie fell off a roof, Oh he broke his back the poor man.

Another roof was my new school. The building was made out of tin. Matt laughed, Oh your school is made out of tin!

Oh but it is good inside.

Well no outside. What if the wind blows it will fall down. Then if you are up the top floor. How would ye get down?

We would just climb down. Primary 7s and 6s were up the top. That was us. So ye would climb down. But if the ronepipes were not there. Just dreeping down and swinging. So if the walls fell down, ye could still make it, and just helping down the lasses.

The ronepipes were on the wall. If ye climbed it ye would not get a right grip with yer toe. In stone ye got wee toty holes and stuff, but tin was slippy and yer feet would skliff off. But if ye wedged them in. Ye could, in behind the ronepipe at the wall, ye would get a grip. But if ye went in too far and yer foot got stuck, it got twisted. That happened. Ye were wearing sandshoes and they were skinny so that was how they got stuck. Shoes were not good for climbing but they did not get stuck so that made them better. If ye climbed the school wall ye would watch what shoes and maybe sandshoes were the best. But maybe they were not.

We were talking about it at Friday dinnertime. It was pelting rain so we could not play football. There were two big shelters, one for boys one for lasses. If it was raining hard some lasses came into ours or if we went into theirs, sometimes we did, just for a laugh. So instead of boys and lasses Primary 7s and 6s went to one shelter and Primary 5s and 4s to the other. Wee ones just tried to get in anywhere. If there was no room in one they went to the other or else just got left out, so tough luck, they went to the lavvy. But if Primary 7s and 6s were in smoking that was them and they had to get out. Some big boys were bullies, they booted wee boys up the backside, Get to f**k, so it was not fair if they just needed the lavvy.

People were saying about good walls and trees, there were good trees roundabout, so who was best climber. Ones looked at me and a Primary 6 said, Smiddy goes up the top of the ronepipe. So other ones were looking at me then at Peter Wylie because he done it too but his house was only one storey up. Mine was the top.

Oh but Smiddy can touch the roof. It was Mitch said that. I did it one time for a laugh. But Peter knew I done it.

Billy MacGregor said, But if ye climb it ye climb it, even if it is not high. Ye still climb it.

Him and Peter were best pals. The lasses were looking over and hearing what we said. Julie Michaels was with Rona Craig and Lorna Buckle from our class, so were other ones. Boys talked loud so the lasses could hear, just showing off, punching boys and shoving them.

No for a fight but just a laugh, except if Podgie spoiled it. He booted the ball at people. A lot of times he kept the ball. It was not his but he still did. The boy that had the ball acted like he did not care but he did care because whose ball was it, it was his, but he was scared because it was Podgie.

Podgie just wanted to be the boss. He said how ye got great dykes and jumps back in his old place.

Oh but mine were great too. I said how they were just the best and some were really high up, ye had to balance going along and it was just like a tightrope. Imagine ye had a tightrope and could walk it, if ye put it between yer houses, if ye stretched it right across the back and then ye could just run across and no touch the ground and all everybody was down below. Gary McNab made a joke and people were laughing. It was a wee bit dirty and lasses heard. We looked at them but they were just laughing as well, some of them.

Imagine a lassie climbing. Lasses could not climb if with dresses on because ye could see up. It would be with one hand because for a lassie it was a dress and she would be holding it down so it did not blow up. All people down below would see her k★★★★★rs, they would, and just her legs to the top, just if they looked up, they would see, they would, so she would have to wear trousers except no in school, lasses were not allowed to because it was the uniform and it was skirts, lasses had to wear them and if the wind blowed, ye just waited for that, it was a laugh.

The bell was going to ring. But bang, Podgie booted the ball into the lasses. One hit Ruthie Grindlay. They were angry shouting at him. He was laughing and done it again. They were having to jump so if it smacked into their legs, it was sore. And mucky too, how it was making their legs all dirty and then if it was splashing their skirts, it was grey skirts they wore and that was just not fair. Boys were laughing. Mitch too, and Gary McNab. They thought it was good what he done but other boys did not. Peter Wylie and Billy MacGregor, I saw them give a wee look then they went to the edge. The lasses were angry and going out the shelter. I went to stand next to Peter and Billy, just looking out at the rain.

Podgie was still kicking the ball and boys were laughing, a lot of

Primary 6s. They just wanted in with Podgie. Julie Michaels, Rona Craig and Lorna Buckle had gone over to the edge of the shelter with other ones out our class. Isabel Hartley shouted at Podgie, Oh you are just a child, you should just act yer age!

Podgie and Gary were laughing. Mitch was laughing too but it was daft and I did not want to. It was what wee boys done. So if Podgie was yer pal. But he was not a real pal.

Now the ball got booted out the shelter. It travelled right the way down the playground. Oh for f**k sake. I heard somebody saying it.

Who was it thumped the ball? Podgie was asking. Whoever thumped it would have to go and get it. That was what he said. But we knew it was him. We all were looking. Who was going to get it? Nobody, no unless a wee boy, if Podgie made him. The rain was bouncing off the ground.

Billy MacGregor said, Oh Smiddy, did ye hear about the Lifies? They are starting soon. They telled us down the Church.

They are going to have a football team, said Peter Wylie.

Oh that is smashing.

You joining?

Aye, I said, we had a great Lifies back in the old place.

So did we, said Peter and was telling about how all the things they done. Me and Billy were saying about it too. I saw Julie Michaels looking at us. If she was listening. She saw me seeing her and turned to Lorna Buckle.

Then Podgie was there and saying about climbing. He was just butting in. How come he was talking about that? He thought we were talking about it but we were not. Podgie did not like climbing. Because really he could not climb. So how come he was saying about it?

Except just getting in with us, he did not like us talking because he was not here. He wanted to stand with us so we would be with him. It was to be the boss.

He was looking at me. How come? I did not care. Because I did not like him booting the ball into the lasses. Because I went with Peter Wylie and Billy MacGregor.

If he said about climbing, that was just stupid. The other one that did not climb was John Davis. Podgie hated it because then it was him and John Davis and that put them together. Even a wee wall. Oh climbing is s★★★e. I cannot be bothered climbing. That was Podgie. But if he climbed a wee wall then he could climb a big one. I even said it to him. Climb a wee wall first then do a big one. It is just the same.

No it is not.

It is. Ye just do not look down, no till ye get good at it.

That is right, said Peter Wylie.

Is it f★★k, said Podgie, what if ye fall off?

Aye but ye do not fall off, I said.

Oh you are always talking.

No I am not.

You think you are the best climber.

No I do not. I do not.

I saw other people looking. But I did not say I was the best climber. I was not a boaster, if they thought I was, I was not. So if I was a best climber. But no the complete best. I did not say I was.

But so maybe I was. I did not care. If I was I was. If I wanted to climb something I climbed it. If I wanted to. It was up to me. I would just do it. It was my business. Even if it was my da. I did not care if it was my da. I said it. Oh if I want to climb something I will climb it. I just want to do it.

Well what if it is yer da? said Podgie. If he f★★★★★g catches ye.

What about it?

Oh ha ha, said Podgie. So he gives ye a doing!

Well that is his business.

So if he batters ye?

It is his business.

Ha ha.

Well I do not care either if it is me. Mitch said, If it is my f★★★★★g da, and he catches me if I am doing something I do not f★★★★★g care. I would just kill him.

People were looking when Mitch said that.

Other people now were talking about their das and what like they were. Lasses too. Then Rona Craig said about her da, how he got killed in the Army. I knew that because she said it before. It was her maw and her grannie in the house. I liked that, so ye just could do things, if yer da was not there. She had a big brother too. Me and the boys knew him because he had great bikes and showed ye how to do stuff. I liked Rona Craig. She had a wee face and brown hair and just how she had a quite loud voice and was aye laughing and playing with other lasses. She was quite cheeky. Her voice was there now and ye heard her, she was saying about her uncle and auntie. They were taking her and her cousin to the circus for a Christmas present, it was to the Kelvin Hall, the circus and the carnival were coming. Oh I am going too! shouted a lassie.

Oh my da worked in the carnival, said somebody.

Donald MacDonald said how his uncle was a great football player with Rangers. But he did not play for Rangers, it was just trials to play for them. A Primary 6 boy's uncle played for a team down in England. Another one shouted about his granda played for Clyde and got capped for Scotland. I did not know who the boy was. I thought he was Primary 5 except Primary 5s usually were in the other shelter.

Now people were saying about their grannies and grandas. I could have about mine and how he was a good boxer, his pal wore the amateur vest for Scotland and was a champion, then my grannie too and how if it was swimming, she was just a great swimmer. But now all people were talking and just loud so ye could not hear one because they all were doing it. The wee ones too, Oh de de de de de de, de de de de de de. It was seagulls out the shelter, goh goh goh goh, quoh quoh quoh. All their voices.

The rain got louder now and pattering off the roof, bouncing off the ground. People were watching it. Podgie said, Oh Smiddy, I know a wall ye cannot climb.

He stepped out, pulling his jacket up over his head, and pointing up at the school roof. Ye cannot climb that. Ye can never climb that.

How no?

Because ye cannot.

How?

Just because ye cannot.

How?

Oh are you trying to say ye could? Oh are ye? Are you trying to f*****g say ye will climb it?

Maybe.

Well do it?

No.

Because ye f*****g cannot. Ye cannot. If ye could ye would.

Maybe.

Do it!

No.

Because ye cannot.

Maybe I can.

Well go and f*****g do it.

No the now if it is raining, it is pelting.

Well do it after. Do it at four o'clock.

Podgie was talking in a loud voice. So people all were hearing. Lasses too. All watching. So if ye were going to climb it or ye were just a coward? Did ye just do what Podgie told ye to do? That was Mitch. Go and skelp that lassie's b*m and he would go away and do it.

Podgie was laughing at me. How come? I never done nothing to him. It was just jealous.

Oh he was the best at everything. That was what he wanted. Okay if it was fighting and throwing stones and stuff, or if football, sometimes he was good at football and ye said that, maybe, maybe if he was. But no climbing. No running. No swimming either, he never went. I said to Mitch how he never came to the swimming baths, just because he cannot swim!

But even if it was yer da. Podgie had the best da. Oh my da comes here with me and goes there with me. Oh if my maw says that to me. Just leave the boy alone.

That was Podgie's da. He got Podgie the Rangers strip so he was going to play for Rangers. Ye just got sick of it.

Then Gary McNab said, Ye going to do the school roof Smiddy?

Maybe.

When? said Podgie. Do it the f*****g now.

No.

So when?

At four o'clock. No if it is raining but. I am no doing it if it is raining.

§

It was a flat roof. If ever a ball went up it would stay up. But none went up. People said they did but it was too high. I thought that. How could ye kick one up? Ye could not. Except if ye threw it. But ye could not. No even a wee one. Even if ye batted it up. Unless maybe a golfball. I did not care about balls on the roof. Better if there was none. I did not want nothing on the roof. It was the highest. Nobody would see ye up on it. Ye would just be there and that would be that. So if ye were up ye were up, seeing down over all the roofs, right the way over and then there were the hills away way over the gun-site and up to the highlands. That was us in the new scheme. The Minister said it at Friday Assembly. Only thank the Heavenly Father because where we were, it was the beautifullest place if ye would want to be anywhere. Imagine ye were stuck in the middle of the town and could not see any single thing except tenement buildings, would that not be awful? Only give thanks to the Heavenly Father.

Reverend Christie had a baldy head and a tough face but people liked him because he told stories from the Bible and good ones about the Army and stuff. Oh there was this young man who saw slaughter with a heavy heart. One day we would all grow up.

After he finished and sat down Mr Reid stood up, the Head-master. Thank you Reverend Christie. We do not want harum scarums at this school. We are a new school in a new scheme and we are new people, we are all ourselves new from what went before so here is new chances and a new life and we all are so so lucky to get it.

Mr Reid had an angry temper. So if it was mischief-making, there would be none of that in this school and if it was breaking windows or climbing buildings or doing any single last thing he would be completely angry and maybe expel ye.

That was what he said. People would get expelled for climbing stuff. Oh and what would yer mother and father say about that? Your mother would be crying and your father would just be so upset and angry and you could not blame him if ye got a real leathering, it was only to be deserved.

Some were looking round to see. And it was me. But how come? If it was. If somebody told the Headmaster. Maybe they did. Oh if they did. So if I could not climb the roof.

Reverend Christie was on the chair beside the Headmaster and his head was nodding up and down.

After Assembly we went to our own class and Ruthie Grindlay was beside me at the desk. Oh uh Kieron what did ye do?

Nothing.

Oh uh.

I did not do nothing at all.

Oh are you climbing the roof?

I did not say things to her because she just would tell people.

And Gary McNab too. Oh Smiddy ye going to climb the roof?

My stomach was just ohh ohh. I could see out the window, the rain still coming, but only spitting. So if it went off and the wall was dry.

But I was not doing it. What about the Headmaster? So if I was a coward. If people thought that. How come they did not climb it? If it was only me. How come?

Because Podgie. Podgie made ye. That was what he done. He got people to do stuff.

But if I climbed it I climbed it. It was my business. If I done it, it was me. Maybe I would maybe I would not. Only I would see. If I did I did.

What like was the roof? Maybe I would do it.

At four o'clock people went to the shelter. No many lasses came. Ye could see them over at the school gate looking back to us. The rain was still spitting, it was too slippy, I was not going to do it, except what if I did, it was just my business.

Then the jannie was there. He came walking out a wee side door. He had his coat on and his hands in his pockets. He was not looking to us but if ye went to the building he would see ye. He had a wee smile on his face. Usually he did. Mr Thompson. He was a BB Officer and people liked him. If he saw ye doing something ye were not to he just said, Yes boy! So ye stopped. But he did not tell the Headmaster.

Now he was standing by the school wall. But he would go away soon. Mitch and them were beside me, Podgie as well. You going to do it? Eh. Eh Smiddy?

Maybe.

So if I did it. If I did it I did it. A lot were there and looking at me.

At the top of the building ye could see the roof the same as mine, how ye reached the top and the edge stuck out. That was roofs. It was the gutter and then the slates sloping down. Ye could not get on to my roof. Ye got stuck underneath, I just touched it thinking about if I could, maybe I could but I did not think so.

I did not like looking up if the roof was near, so all ye saw was the sky. Ye felt funny and yer head, even if ye were dizzy. So if it happened I put my hand in between the pipe and the wall, twisting it. And my knee too. I could press it in better if it was a wee bit sideways. But still if I looked up at the edge of the roof a funny feeling started oh if my shoulders went back and my hands came loose, if that happened.

How could it? Except if somebody done it and pulled me back. An invisible ghost. But if it was a new building ye would not get ghosts, but a bad angel, if it was pulling up my fingers or just it was happening and nobody was doing it, just them themself, all popping out, pop pop and it all comes away.

I was seeing my fingers there and what like they were, no mine's. Whose were they? They were keeping me up. Imagine somebody pulled them up one by one. If it was one complete hand came off.

But I could do that easy. Ye had to else ye could not climb. One hand on and one hand off, that was how ye done it. One touched down and the other came off. So for that wee split second, if none hand was holding the pipe. It could. Ye could just whizz it so none was touching. Just for one wee tiny toty wee second. So if ye did. And ye would not fall. How come?

Or if ye just leaned in tight, moved yer belly in or yer shoulders and yer head, just move right up close, and if ye done that then take yer hands away, if they were holding the pipe, take them away, because ye could, ye would not fall. Ye would not. No if ye had it right. Ye would still hold yer balance. I could. I did not need my hands, I could just climb even just with my knees and my feet, that was all I needed.

So then at the top, if I was underneath and the roof jutting over, so then I would just go back a wee way, just very very wee, reaching back behind my head, just putting up my hands to get a grip, maybe there was not a grip. But there would be. So my hands would get there onto the top and my body holding on below, so then if ye just pulled up a wee bit by bit by bit so then up ye come and yer body could just swing out a wee bit and coming up and so then what, getting on yer elbow and it would just be yer knees now, oh mammy, and ye were having to, oh mammy, I could not do it except maybe I could, if I could. If I could I could. My feet would be there and it would be just my knees, letting them go one by one if my elbow was on, if I got my elbow on because then I could do it and could take my weight, that was all I needed. Because ye could not just go to the wee pipe where it met the gutter because it was not a real pipe, it was just a bit of one where it joined the gutter and the rone-pipe down, so if ye held on to it it would just come away in yer hand, the nails would pop and it was not welded, welded was like glued the gether so the two bits did not come open.

Oh I did not know, I did not know.

Most ones had went home already. It was just me and the boys now and ones from Primary 6. But the jannie was still there. He was standing then just marching a wee bit one way then the other. One time he came along and looked over at us but he did not say nothing. His arms were folded.

Oh I am going f*****g home, said Gary.

Are you doing it or no? said Podgie.

Oh I will do it another time, I said.

§

It was me had to switch channels on the television. I was nearest. I sat on the floor beside the settee and could just crawl over and do it. I liked sitting there. Ye did not see people and could just watch the telly even if it was a s**y bit. If it was just my maw and da, I would be there and the s**y bit was on and they would not say nothing and maybe even ye saw the woman's t*ts, if it was the shadows and they just sloped down if she was sitting and the man was looking and she is just sitting down and the man goes over to kiss her but then if he kisses her just where her front neck slopes down and that is her t*ts. I was waiting for my maw, Oh Kieron would you turn that over please.

But she did not say it. I waited to see. My da never said it. But ye just knew he wanted ye to do it. I used to. So a s**y bit came on, I just went and switched it over without them saying but if ye got a row. Oh what are you doing!

So now I did not. I just waited. Even the weest thing to do with it, the man just kisses her. Oh turn that over. So then I had to do it but no if they did not say it. But if it was going to happen, ye knew it was going to, oh darling darling. And if anything was dirty, just if it was s*x, that was worst of all. Oh it is dirty it is dirty.

I was just waiting to see because it was me to turn over, I always had to do it just because I was nearest, it was not fair.

My da just sat how he was sitting, no moving, with his newspaper there but he was no reading it. And my maw too, sitting how she was sitting, with her magazine. She read them when she watched the telly. I waited a wee minute more because if the s**y bit passed it would be okay. The man was kissing her.

But it was Matt, because he was there. They waited because of him, if he was not there my maw would have telled me already. So now she said it. Oh Kieron would you please switch channels.

So I got up to do it.

Oh what are you sighing about? said my da.

I am no.

Yes ye are, if yer mother tells ye to do something you just do it.

I am doing it.

Aye well just do it and none of yer nonsense.

So I just done it and that was that. But Matt got up and left the room. He done that a lot. They did not like him doing it. My da was angry, ye saw how he was sitting. I sat back down beside the settee. I wanted to get out the way but I could not, if I moved an inch it was me too. I sat still, no moving a muscle and it went on. My maw kept her head down. Was Matt going to come back? So in the distance the plug got pulled, Matt coming out the bathroom, down the lobby and straight into the bedroom and the door shut. So ye knew that was him, he was not coming back. It was because they changed the programme. My da was angry. Matt doing it made them feel stupid.

Oh it is not family viewing, said my maw, if they know families are watching, why not put on something decent, not just dirty things.

Yes, said my da. It is b****y ridiculous what they get away with.

My maw made a wee noise but did not speak. She did not like swearie words or bad words. If he said b****y it was not a very bad one but if he did not say sorry. In my house if ye said a bad word ye were to say sorry. But he did not, my maw was huffy with him. She did not look at the television, only the magazine. My da was reading his paper so now it was only me watching. It was the news. After a wee minute my maw said, You can switch back now Kieron.

It was to see if the s**y bit had finished and it was on to something else. The worst was if the woman and man was in bed and it was worse s*x so ye just had to switch right back again. I done it without my maw saying. But now it was okay. Then Matt came back in. Sometimes he done this, just to see if we had switched back. But my da was still angry and it was against Matt. Oh he is just spoiling everything. That was what my da thought. Then he said, Oh Kieron is it raining?

So I had to go and look out the window. It was raining heavy.

I did not like it. If we were all against Matt, that was it, but I was not against him.

People were waiting. If somebody would talk to Matt or him to us. If my maw would. She did not care if people were not talking she would just say something. She thought what to say, but could not. My da would not speak and neither would Matt. And they would not look at anybody except if my da might look at my maw. He gived her a big look so people knew he was doing it. But him and Matt did not look at each other. Then it was all quiet till a big sniff from my da.

But if I said something. If I wanted to I would, but I did not. If it was me with my da it would be worse. Matt did not get the same trouble. I would have got sent to the room if it was me. I even would get hit. If it was a argument, it would come to me. I would just be sitting out the road. It was not me but they made it me. All them just sitting like that. Oh Kieron it is time for bed. But it was not time. Matt was there and just sitting and it was him started it with leaving the room. It was not me done it but it was me got the blame.

I just waited and stayed beside the settee. No supper was made but I was not going to make it.

I did not talk but just sat. If I talked and done it ordinary I would get a row. Matt would not get it. He spoke the proper way. He never got a row, he was the goodie. It was me was the baddie, even if it was him.

Ye just got sick of it, so if they were going to pick on me, I was not letting them, I just got up and went to the window then went straight out the door, and ben the kitchenette. It was raining heavy out the balcony. Out the front and out the back.

Then what I done I made the supper. That got them. Where did

Kieron go. So they came in and here I was making the toast, and for them too.

That was me, I just went and done it.

If it was not me it was my maw. If I did not and she did not ye did not get any. Matt ett all what he got and so did my da but nothing else. They did not even rinse their cups. My maw done it or else left it till the morning. A lot of times I done it. If I was there and cups were lying, I just rinsed them. Maybe if the toast was on and I was waiting. I done any dishes. I did not care.

§

I had a plank under the bed and I kept money there. My maw did not go under the bed much except if she was brushing the floor. Sometimes she did that, getting angry, Oh the house is a complete pigsty, nobody does a stroke in this house. That was what she said. But if it was just me she said it to? That happened a lot of times. She got angry and it was only me there. My da was at work and Matt was not in. How come it was me? She was getting on to me, if I was lazy. That was not fair. I was the one that helped, so then ye got rows. How come she did not do it to Matt or else my da? It was me that helped with the tidying, no them.

So if I done something for somebody, that was the same. If I got a row for that. That was not fair. If it was a woman round our street maybe if she forgot her key and was locked out the house. She was down the back hanging out a washing. Then the front door slammed shut, Oh I am locked out I am locked out. Because she had forgot her key. That happened. So if I could climb the balcony for them. It was the boy or lassie came and asked ye, Oh Kieron my maw's locked out.

I was quick up the ronepipe and it was easy except it was wet ye had to watch it. But I aye wore sandshoes and got a good grip on the jaggy bits behind the pipe. Ye got yer hand more in it, tight, yer knuckles got scraped. But it was not sore. Ye did not notice till if it was bleeding but it was only a wee bit.

If it was just the wee top window open at the bathroom it was hard, ye had to reach across and it was just yer fingertips and ye were having to be just quiet and not hardly moving. Ye put yer hand through and reached down to get the handle for the big window. When ye done that ye were seeing down to the ground and there was the woman's face looking up at ye and her hand at her mouth, or if she was smoking a fag.

Then the big window open and I got in and my foot down on the toilet pan. But ye had to watch it there if ye kicked the top bit and it fell off. Sometimes I done a pee in the toilet before going out. Ye opened the front door and the woman came in then the wee children. I liked doing it. People looked up to ye. That was what I thought. And then ye got money. If she did not give any it was bad. It was because she forgot. I said it to the wee children, Oh tell yer maw did she give Kieron any money for climbing the balcony?

So then she sent them up with it. So if they chapped the door, I had to go and get it so my maw would not see. Oh if you are getting money. How come?

But the real worst was if the window was shut, if ye forgot to look before ye climbed. So all ye could do was go back down. And if ye ripped yer trousers, that was when ye did it. Oh you are always ripping yer trousers! That was a row off yer maw, she had to sew them up. I hid them and took them over to my grannie's.

But that was funny how people thought ye could still get in. The kitchenette door was locked and the windows all were shut and they still thought it. Ye climbed back down and they were looking at ye. Oh what is wrong? Why ye did not go in?

The kitchenette door is locked and the windows are shut.

Oh but could ye not open them?

But they are all shut, even the wee ones.

Oh ye got in the last time. Oh my man will kill me, oh I have got to make his tea, oh the baby is there, what will happen? Oh why can ye not go in?

So if it was my fault, that was what they thought, Oh he is not opening the door for me. But it was not my fault.

Then if ye got caught and yer da gived ye a doing. If they asked and my maw and da were there I did not do it. They did not know I done it.

But if the people did not give ye any money. Some did not. Even ye told their children. They still did not. So how come they did not climb it themself if they thought it was easy and it was nothing? If ever they asked me again I would never do it, that was what I thought, I just would not do it and did not care who it was.

Except my grannie. But it would never be my grannie.

But what if it was my maw? If she was down at the midgie with the rubbish and forgot her key and that was her and she could not get back in the house? Oh Kieron I was just down at the midgie.

She did not say midgie it was midden. I was down at the midden and forgot my key and I am locked out.

Oh well it is not my fault if I am not to climb the ronepipe, da just gives me a doing.

Or else Matt, if he forgot his key. I might have climbed it for him but maybe he could do it himself. Maybe he could not. I never saw him climb the balcony. Maybe he done it when I was not there. Usually he was in the bedroom, swotting. My maw did not like me saying swotting, Oh it is studying. You should be studying as well.

We had a new teacher, Miss Halliday, and she was a true moaner. That was all she done. If ye were drawing in yer jotter and she catched ye doing it, Oh stop that drawing, jotters are not for drawing.

She only liked the top division and if ye were up in the high desks. Ye had to speak right all the time, Oh it is not cannay it is cannot, you must not say didnay it is did not. If it is the classroom it is not the gutter. It is the Queen's English, only you must speak the Queen's English.

I was in the top division but in the low desks. She did not like me. I sat beside James McCulloch now. He made a lot of smells and ye said it to him. Was that you?

No.

Oh aye it was you ye made a smell.

No it was not.

Oh away, it was.

So then he got a red face. So it was him. It just annoyed ye when he done it. People thought it was you, Oh Smiddy f****d. That was Gary McNab. He just said it out loud so everybody looked.

It was not me, it was McCulloch. He always did it. Lasses were there too and they smelled it. Imagine doing a f**t with lasses there.

Then if they thought it was you. That was McCulloch. How could ye say about that, ye could not.

How come he did not keep it in? People tried to unless for a laugh. But McCulloch was just

Imagine being his pal.

People did not say f****d in my house. It was a bad word. But not a swear word. Bad words were not as bad as swear words but quite like it. Gary McNab thought f****d was a swear word. In his house they said pumped, his big brother too. Other ones said pumped. But that was a funny one because if it was a lassie, if a lassie got p****d, so it was a swear word. Oh he p****d her, that was swearing.

But if it was a smell, Oh he pumped, then it was not, it was just bad, but not too bad and ye could say it.

In Podgie's house it was f****d. His maw said it too, so he just said it. In Mitch's house it was pooped. When Mitch said it people laughed. Who pooped?

Ye got rude words as well. Some rude words were bad words. But some were not. Belly was rude but not bad. Ye could say belly. Sometimes I did. Only if I was out the house. In the house it was stomach or tummy, my maw only said tummy. There was some bad words I could say. T***e and k***h, b*m, d****e and c**k. But I never said them. The same with f****d. Out the house people said f****d but I did not. I just did not.

There were other bad words I did not say even out the house. S***e, a**e, p***k and f***y.

Some bad words were like swear words. F****d was funny because a lot of grown-ups said it, Oh who f****d? One time on the train a man said it to his pal, Oh some c**t has f****d.

Who let off and did not let on? that was what my da said.

Some lasses said f★★★★d. When I was wee I said it to my maw, Oh is f★★★★d a swear word?

She got angry and said I never ever was to say that word again. It is pimped, you have to say pimped, Oh I pimped, pardon me.

I never said pimped. Matt did not either. We just said made a smell, Oh somebody made a smell.

Ye could never say pimped out the house. Imagine the boys hearing. It was just complete stupid. Nobody said pimped except lasses. Lasses said it in the class too. Oh who pimped? Who pumped? It was just daft. Imagine ye had a pal said it. Who pimped? Well ye would no have him as a pal.

Some words were not rude, just bad, nearly as bad as swear words. If it was yer thingwi, yer p★★★k or b★★ls ye could not say any words, no in the house or if it was the class, except thingwi, Oh he hurt his thingwi, if the ball hit ye for a rupture, oh my b★★ls, ye could not say it, just yer thingwi.

F★★★y was a swear word, a lassie's f★★★y. So was h★★e. Oh did ye get yer h★★e? that was swearing. So for a laugh we used to sing

Oh I want my hol
I want my hol
I want my holidays

People looked to see if lasses heard us singing. Then if I was singing it too. I was. I could sing it if I wanted. Hol holidays, that was not swearing. If it was a hole in the ground and ye were digging it. So I just sang it too, it was just a laugh.

§

Matt got an old bike off Uncle Billy but my maw would not let it in the house. Oh that dirty old thing, it is filfy. He had to keep it out on the landing on top of newspapers. My da said if ye were just to clean it up, that was the first thing.

Oh but it was very very heavy. Ye carried it down and it was sore on yer shoulder. The wheelguards were not working good. The front tyre was hitting in and rubbing. Ye could see it was all scraped. The chain came off if the wheels spun round too fast. Ye could get it back on but it just came off again and yer hands were total manky. It was a thick sticky dirt, all greasy, it went on yer jersey and trousers.

Matt got fed up with it. Oh it is just blooming useless. I telled him how Rona Craig was in my class at school and her big brother was great at bikes and what if we showed him it? But Matt did not listen to me. He kicked it on the back wheel. Oh do not kick it, I said.

I will kick it if I want it is my bike.

Well it is not the bike's fault.

Oh shut yer trap.

When he carried it up the stair it was all dirt over his trousers. He got angry at it. I am going to sell the blooming thing to Joey Johnston. It is just a fawnti.

Joey Johnston kept old bikes. He got bits out them or done them up and selled them. People said they would not buy a bike off him, but some did. He stayed round the other side of the scheme from us. His house was on the ground floor so he had the wee garden at the front. He kept a lot of stuff there. The neighbours did not like him doing it but if it was his garden. He covered it all with old blankets and tarpaulin. What if ye jumped the fence and knocked something? Oh but ye would not, ye would just be too worried to try it because if he catched ye he would batter ye. There was other Johnstons too, that was cousins. So if ye ganged up on him they would just gang up on you.

People said he stole stuff. Maybe he did. I did not like him. He was not old but grumpy grumpy all the time. If ye went to his close to see his stuff he just swore at ye and telled ye to f**k off if ye were no buying nothing. Gary McNab flung a stane at him one time and he was going to grab us.

I did not want Matt to sell the bike to him. Rona Craig's big brother was good, he showed ye how to. He did not mind if ye watched. I went with Billy MacGregor and Peter Wylie. I said to him about Matt's bike and how it was not going good. Oh just bring it and I will see it.

That was what he said. I telled Matt but Matt just was moaning. Oh to pot with Rona Craig's brother.

He did not like him. It was because he was good with bikes. He did not know him. They went to different schools. Rona's big brother had three bikes and worked on them out in the back close. He let us see his best one. Ye could lift it up with one hand. Even just with yer pinkie. It was a real racer and cost a right mint of money. His grannie got him it for his birthday. It had a green and white frame so it was Celtic but he did not bother about that. Oh it is Italian, it is white and green.

He did not care about football and even who the teams were, and players playing for Rangers, he did not know who they were. Oh but bikes and who was racing champion, that was all he wanted.

He put them upside down and picked into the chain and all the wee inside bits with a toothbrush, and then the spokes too, getting them all spick and span. Ye needed it right for racing, so if it was spick and span, that stopped the rust. And then with the oilcan, ye oiled in all the wee bits. Oh anything that moves ye just oil it. He showed us.

He had two other bikes and kept them in a fixed wheel. Fixed wheels made ye crash so ye had to watch it. We got a shot on one and it was hard. Ye had to keep working the pedals and if ye took yer feet off – oh well you should not take off yer feet because trying to get them back into yer pedals, ye could not, the pedals were just whizzing round and round and yer feet banged into them and could not do it. A motor car was at the side of the road when Billy was going and he crashed into it, the handlebars skliffing along the side. A man saw him but he got away.

Rona's big brother went long runs on his bike. He went away down to Loch Lomond and over the hills. Lots of people went. They made fires and boiled tea. Men were there too, and it was a good laugh round the fire and all having yer tea and people brought pieces with them and sometimes if it was a frying pan, somebody had one and they made sausages and just gived ye one. Rona's brother had all pals that went. It was a club for cyclists and they joined it. Matt could have joined it too. I asked. But just if he got his bike good, then he could go.

I told him. My maw was listening. Even an old bike, ye could get it good if ye fixed it. Ye got it clean and oiled and if it was spick and span. I would take it to Rona's big brother. So if he just done something and showed me and we could fix it. Maybe we could.

But it is my bike, said Matt.

Oh but we can clean it all up.

Well it would be nice to see it clean, said my maw. Your father is sick of seeing it so filfy.

Well it is too old, said Matt.

It is not too old to be cleaned.

But mum it is falling to bits.

Oh he only wants to sell it, I said.

Well you just want it for yourself, said Matt.

Oh I do not.

Yes you do.

Well I would go it. You do not go it.

Because ye cannot go it, it is a fawnti.

It is not a fawnti.

What is a fawnti? said my maw.

Falling to bits, said Matt, that is what it is.

Oh Matt it is not fawin it is falling.

I said blooming falling.

You did not, you said fawin. You can surely speak better than that.

Oh well if I want to. If I want to I want to. It is not blooming fair. It is my bike.

Oh Matt.

She did not like him saying blooming. But it was not a swear word and it was not a bad word.

Well I would clean it, I said.

Matt looked at me but I did not look at him, then he made a signal. He was going to get me. It was a punch. I did not care. If he punched me for nothing. Brothers done that. They done it on the shoulder. Ye walked by and they just punched ye. I would not have hurt a young brother like that. No unless if he just really really needed it. And it would be a wee skelp, only a tap, so he knew no to do it the next time. But Matt done it for nothing.

Oh well if Kieron can get it cleaned, said my maw.

Matt shaked his head and went away out the room. That was him. Now it was a right bad temper with me but I did not care.

After teatime me and him were in the kitchenette doing the dishes. I washed and he dried. He hated washing but I liked it because ye were first finished. But sometimes he just stopped before everything was washed. Oh I will come and dry it after. He did that to be first finished.

He was not talking to me because of the bike but I was talking to him. He kidded on he was not listening. He whistled a tune, and was clinking plates and cups. I did not care.

But that is what he done and it annoyed ye. So if ye were just trying to tell him something and it was clinking clinking and then whistling, he done it loud.

I was just saying about the Milano bike. That was Rona's big brother's. It was a real racer and a lightweight. No like Matt's. It was the opposite, it was not thick and not heavy and its wheels were thin and just sparkling clean and all straight spokes and just clean and the saddle too was a racing saddle, it was slim-line, and wee tiny mudguards, white and green the same as the frame and the wheels too, just no like Matt's, squeaking all the time, squeak squeak squeak, that was all his done.

The blooming wheels are buckled, said Matt.

But if Rona's big brother looked at it and could fix it. Maybe he could. He had good tools. He kept them in a wee satchel and could change a tyre in two minutes.

I do not care if it is one minute or no minutes. Who cares? I do not.

Oh but he is good and shows ye how to do it.

I do not care if he is good. I can change the tyres myself. The blooming wheels are buckled.

But if they are oiled?

But they are buckled.

But Rona's big brother

Oh Rona's big brother

Well he can do it.

I do not care, I am selling it.

It is not yours to sell.

Yes it is.

If Uncle Billy gived ye it.

Uncle Billy gave me it.

Well if he did.

Now my da came into the kitchenette. Oh it is loud voices the night, what yez arguing about?

It is my bike, said Matt, Uncle Billy gave me it. If I want to sell it I can sell it.

That old thing, who is going to buy it? My da laughed. Yer Uncle Billy fished it out the Clyde.

Oh but dad, I said, if it was just cleaned.

Well if it was cleaned, that is a start, it needs to get cleaned.

But there is no point dad if the wheels are all buckled. Matt said, It is falling to bits, it is just falling to bits.

Well if it is falling to bits who is going to buy it?

Joey Johnston.

Who is Joey Johnston?

He buys old stuff like bikes. He does them up and sells them.

Who to?

People.

What people?

He steals stuff, I said.

Who steals stuff?

Joey Johnston.

How do you know? said Matt.

I just do.

No you do not.

Aye I do.

Ssh, said my da, then to Matt, That fellow will not give ye much money.

Well he will give me something.

Bikes are dear son, how no let yer brother have a go? He wants to try fixing it.

But he cannot.

But he wants to have a go.

Matt was just looking at the sink.

Eh? said my da.

I know a big boy will help me, I said.

Oh well if he does, said Matt and he tossed away the dishcloth. He went straight out the kitchenette and into the bedroom. He shut the door, but no slamming it. My da did not like slamming doors and was looking after him. Then he looked at me. Who is the big boy?

Rona Craig's big brother. She is in my class at school. Oh but da he has got a smasher, it is a Milano racing cycle and just light as a feather. His grannie got him it. She just got him it and it was a mint of money. That is Rona's grannie. She stays in the same house as them. I will take it round to him.

Well give it a clean first.

Oh yes dad I will.

I started cleaning it right away. On Saturday morning I carried it down the stair and walked it round the street. Rona's big brother was not out the back close. Usually he was always there. Maybe he was still in the house and would come out soon. I waited a wee bit then was going to go up the stair and chap the door. But what if Rona was there and she came?

Oh well if she did, I would just say what it was. I liked Rona. People did. She had a funny laugh. It was hee hee hee, hee hee hee, and she put her hand up to her mouth. If somebody done something in the class ye would hear it. The teacher did not like her doing it. Oh Rona would you please be quiet, if you are giggling would you please stop it.

But then if somebody done something she would do it again. Oh please miss I cannot help it.

I flapped the letterbox on the door. It was her grannie came, a wee lady with a hat on. She was the only one in. Oh they are all out, she said, you will have to come back after.

I walked the bike back round to my own house and carried it up the stair. Oh but it was just so very heavy. Matt was away seeing his pals from school and my maw was up the town shopping. But my da was home from work. He was in the living room reading the paper. I told him and he said, Oh wait and I will have a look.

He came out to the landing and turned the bike upside down on top of the newspapers. Oh it is b★★★★y mawkit.

Oh but dad I cleaned it.

Well ye did not clean it enough.

He went away and got old cloots to wipe it, and a bucket of hot water. Now you just watch, he said, this is how ye do it.

So he started wiping it and it was the same as Rona's big brother. Oh I used to have a bike myself.

He cleaned right into all the wee bits to get the worst dirt. He moved the wheels to see the wheelguards. It is mudguards, he said. He went and got tools, spanners and pliers. He screwed things about and then after that he lifted the mudguards right off the wheels, he just took them right off, and he turned them up and inside it was just thick dirt. Oh they are all bent to shreds, they are just b★★★★y useless. Dump them son just dump them.

Then he birled the wheels and they went round, only sticking a wee bit. See that. Better already. Oh but a wee drop oil, he said.

He had his own oil and he squirted it in. He felt the tyres. These tyres are fine.

Now he turned the bike the right way up and gived it a wee bounce. Will that do ye?

Oh dad, aye. Can I go and try it?

Well just be careful, it is yer brother's bike. And come up the stair if it is raining. The mud will fly up on ye. Mind ye have got no guards now cause we have took them off.

Oh aye.

And do not go out on that main road. Now I am warning ye!

Oh no dad.

I went away and got ready then carried the bike back down the stairs and out the front close. When I was getting on it I looked up at the window to see him watching, I knew he would be. He made a wee signal like a wave. That was my da.

The bike was going good. I went it down to the shops, so if people were there, just who I would see. But nobody was there. Oh but John Davis, he stayed near the shops. He would love the bike. There was grass outside his close and a wee wall. I stood the bike at it and ran up the stairs, rang the bell. But nobody was in. I chapped the door and rang the bell again. I looked through the letterbox and it was all dark. Saturday. People went places. Sunday was better. I came back down the stairs and out the close and the bike was no there. I looked about. Maybe I put it someplace else. Or if somebody moved it. But it was nowhere. It was just nowhere. I went to the next close, I kept looking. Where was it? Oh if somebody had took it for a shot, if any boys were there. Wee lasses were playing at the next close. I said to them, Did ye see a bike there?

No.

My bike was over at that wee wall.

Oh that bike. A man took it.

Who was it?

The lasses just looked, they did not know. It was just a man. He went on it past them. They did not know him. He just stole it. He was just a thief that stole it. I started running up the street where the lasses said. Nobody was there. I went round all the streets. The rain came on but went off again. I went round them all again. Joey Johnston's too, I hunted all over. Nothing. Nothing nothing nothing. I did not want to go home. I could not. I went back to John Davis' close. Maybe the bike was there again. Maybe somebody just took it like a wee trick.

But it was not there. The wee lasses were away. I walked along the street.

But if the one that stole it did not live in our scheme. Maybe he did not. If he was a stranger. He might have been. Maybe from the new houses away over. So I went away down the field and over the burn, away way over the other side and round by the new scheme where the Squatters used to be. I passed all new houses and some people were there.

Oh but if I saw the one that done it. Well if I did I did. I would just shout at him. So if he had a blade, he could not get me. I would tell people and see if there was a cop or where if he stayed in a house, if he did, I would see the number and just tell the cops.

I was hunting roundabout. Then it was dark, or just nearly getting dark. I asked a woman and it was past eight o'clock. Eight o'clock! Oh and I never knew. My tea! My maw would kill me.

But I did not want to go home. I did not, I just did not I did not I did not want to go home.

I could not go to my grannie's. It was too late and I did not have money.

I could not run away. I could not. I had no money. I did not want to run away. Not if I had no money. You could not run away if ye had no money. It was dark too and it was raining. Ye just could not.

Oh but I wanted to, I needed to. What could I do? I did not know. Oh but if Mitch was there. Mitch wanted to run away, he always was wanting to. So if I could go with him. But Mitch was no there, he was no there he was just away, he was staying at his auntie's.

He could have smuggled me into his house. I done it for him. Pals smuggled ye into their house. Ye done it if yer maw and da did not like the boy. If it was Podgie in my house and my maw was there, she did not like him. For my da it was Mitch, he did not like Mitch. How come? Oh he is just a dunderheid, that is what he said, my da. Oh my da, my da was going to kill me, he was, he just was going to. But what else? Nothing. I had to go home. I just had to. Oh but my stomach was sore. How come he was there and no just away? If he was back in the Navy, I wished he was back in the Navy. It was just so much the worse when he was here. How come he came home? And if he did not like the factory and was always moaning if it was dry land, well he could just go away again to wet land if it was the sea. How come he did not? It was just so much the better when he was away.

I crossed back over the burn and up the field, up to the scheme.

Boys were inside a close. They were Papes. I knew them and they shouted on me. Hoh Kieron, your da is out looking for ye.

Out looking for me. He would just be someplace, wherever he was and just angry.

It was the worst ever. The very very worst. Since I was a wee boy nothing ever was worse. I could not remember nothing worse. There was not anything worse.

And Matt too. Oh Matt, I was not thinking about him but it was his bike and he would blame me because it was just me, he would say that. Touching his stuff. Why did I not get my own stuff to touch? Matt would say that. It was his bike. Uncle Billy gived it to him. Not to me. He did not give it to me. So how come I took it out? It was not mine to take out. How come I did?

So if he hit me, he could hit me. I did not care. If he did not want me as a brother. Maybe he did not. I did not want him either.

But it was just a man done it. A man done it and was a complete thief. I would never do nothing ever ever again, just never ever, never never ever. If something ever happened to me and was ever ever good. Nothing ever could be ever again. If God would save me. It was not my fault. I would make a promise.

I was at my door and had to chap it, usually I flapped the letterbox. Now I just chapped it. I done it quiet. But the door opened and it was my maw. Oh Kieron Kieron, where have you been? What happened what happened?

I started greeting. Oh mum a man stole Matt's bike and I was looking for it.

Oh Kieron. My maw came and cuddled me. We were just so worried, your father is out looking for you. He thought you were run over by a bus.

I was away looking for the bike.

Oh you should have come home and told us.

I did not know.

Oh Kieron. My maw stopped cuddling me. You are just so silly. You are. Your teacher says so too. You are just so silly.

But mum it is not my fault.

Oh no it never is.

But mum

I put your tea out a while ago and now it is ice-cold.

I do not want my tea I want to go to bed.

Kieron.

Oh but mum I need to. I am just tired and I am just

Look at you! You are filfy. What have you been up to? Away and get washed and I will heat up your tea.

But mum I just

Your father will be up the stair soon.

Oh he will batter me.

He will not batter you. Do not be so silly, he will just be glad you are safe and sound.

I want to go to bed.

Well you cannot, not just now.

She went to the kitchenette and sent me into the bathroom to get washed. But if I wanted to go to bed? How come I could not? If I wanted to go I could go. How come I could not? How come?

If I could just go to sleep. I just needed to. Oh if I could get into my room and just oh if there had been a snib on the door so I could snib it but there was none.

But I could just get under the blankets and snuggle under and I would go to sleep. And just pull the blankets over my head. I liked them over my head. And if Matt was reading and the light was on, that was the best, and just going to sleep. I did not want anybody and not him either, if he was not like a brother, if he did not want me for one, well I did not want him, just to go to bed and under the blankets, and pull them over and I would be underneath.

§

Down near the burn there was a high tree with thick thick branches. I saw it when we first flitted to the new scheme and I went with Matt and his pal. But I forgot about it. But now I remembered again and I wanted to see it and just about climbing or what. I just called it that, the high tree. Its branches went down over the burn and if ye got a rope, ye could make a great swing. I would climb the tree and tie the rope. We could knock the rope off the workies.

Me and the boys went. Peter Wylie and Billy MacGregor came with us. Gary McNab went home first from school but was coming to meet us. Before he did we saw a rabbit and chased it. They had wee holes roundabout and they stayed down there. If ye catched one ye could eat it. Mitch had a knife to do it. He got it someplace. Ye made a fire and flung the rabbit on. There was a story and it said how pirates were fighting natives and getting chased on a desert island. If they got captured they got flung in a pot. They were long pigs. That was what the natives called them. Oh we will kill the long pigs.

Some pirates got caught. And if they got ett, maybe they did. Other ones escaped and were hiding down at the beach feared if the natives catched them. Oh but they were starving and dared to try it and out they went, just creeping. They went hunting for their supper and got a rabbit, they bashed its head in. They flung it in the fire then skinned it and ett it. Ye saw the pictures. The grease ran down their chins and whiskers and in their fingers and they were licking it.

The rabbit we saw got away, maybe into its hole. If we had a dog we could have set it on it. Ye got the rabbit in a corner and bashed its head in. Mitch had a knife and could stab it. Maybe if it was in a bush we would fling boulders at it and knock it out. We were looking but could not find it.

Then Gary was whistling on us, running down the hill.

It was a good dry day and we did some jumps across the burn. We sat down on the bank for a smoke, but then it was a w**k. That was Mitch. Oh I am f*****g going for a wank. Who is coming?

We just laughed at him but sometimes we did. Ye went to yer own bit and shut yer eyes and done it. Ye did not want people looking, so if ye were shivering or yer face went red. So if Podgie was there. He did not do it much and just looked at ye and said stuff. Mitch shivered all the time. Oh see Mitch shivering he is f*****g shivering.

Then if it was me and my face. Oh f**k see Smiddy, look at his face, a big riddy! Hoh Smiddy see your f*****g face!

Him and Gary were laughing at ye. He did not say nothing about Gary. But Peter and Billy were there now and they were looking at us when Mitch said it but then they came. We all went behind the bushes. But just when we started Gary saw Peter's c**k and said it, Oh it is a f*****g Gerry's Helmet look! You have got a Gerry's Helmet. Hoh. It is a f*****g Gerry's Helmet! Gary shouted, Peter is a Jewboy.

Peter got a red face. Mitch says to him, Are you a f*****g Jewboy?

No.

Aye ye are, said Gary, yer t****r is cut off at the top.

Cut off at the top?

Aye Smiddy, that is Jewboys. The Gerries f*****g done it to them, so that is how, it is a Gerry's Helmet.

Show us, said Mitch.

No, said Peter.

Because ye are f****g scared, said Podgie.

No I am no.

Gary laughed.

Come on we will get him, said Podgie. He saw Billy looking but did not bother with him, only laughed to Gary and Mitch and me. He wanted to take down Peter's trousers to see. Would we come in if he started? He did not care about Billy.

Except Billy was Peter's best pal so what would he do? Would he come in with Peter? Because if he got a kicking because with us there, we were with Podgie. He would think we were, so we would get him too.

Mitch said it to Peter, Are ye a f*****g Jew?

No.

Well if yer t****r is cut off at the top, said Gary, that is what they do to Jews.

F*****g show us, said Podgie.

No.

Just f*****g do it you c**t! Podgie could go angry and if he did be careful but just now he was not angry and just nearly laughing. Oh we will f*****g strip ye and throw away yer trousers. We will f*****g dump them in the burn.

Gary laughed. We will dump them in the f*****g burn and ye can just go in and get them.

Podgie was pointing to Peter's trousers. Take them down.

No.

F*****g do it.

He does not want to, said Billy.

Oh are you backing him up?

Are ye? said Gary.

Billy had a big red face and was feared. Ye could see it. Peter was too. He looked at Gary, Oh I can fight my own battles.

Gary just was looking, but I said, Oh it is no a battle to fight, it is just to show us, we just want to see.

It is only just to see, said Podgie. He was not laughing now, just watching Peter. Ye saw that with Podgie, how his eyes just could watch ye. But he thought too about Peter, if he was a good fighter, maybe he was. So if he was a best fighter, I did not think so, but he could give ye a good go. So could Billy. We all knew it from football. So if it was the two of them the gether. They were good fighters.

Is your da a real Jew? said Mitch.

Is he f**k.

He f*****g must be, said Gary.

He f*****g is not, said Peter.

What about yer maw?

No.

Oh but maybe ye are adopted, I said, if ye are an adopted child. If it is not yer real da and ye are adopted because then what happens.

They all were looking at me.

Well if he is an adopted child, wee weans get adopted, if ye are a orphan, maybe if yer real maw and da got killed, if it was the war, ye just get adopted.

That is right, said Podgie.

Are you a orphan? said Mitch.

No.

He is no a orphan, said Billy, that is stupid.

Aye but Billy it is no stupid, people do not know if they are orphans. Nobody tells them, I said, ye just find out later.

I am no a f*****g orphan, said Peter.

Aye but if ye are a real one. So yer real da, maybe if he was a Jew.

Or else yer maw, said Gary.

That happens to people. Their real maws and das get killed. The wee babies are left and people adopt them.

They all were listening to me and I said it to them. It is true. Nobody tells ye, ye just find out later. It would be the same if ye were something else. There was a boy that was a Pape and brought up a Proddy. I read it in a story, him and his sister were rightful true Heirs. So they had to journey to faraway lands. Then that was them, they met their real maw. Their da was dead. So then the boy was the King. He had to do it, even if he did not want to. He ruled over all the land.

What age was he? said Mitch.

Thirteen.

F**k sake.

He was a Pape and brought up as a Proddy.

Podgie said, Oh Mitch, get the fags out.

Mitch got them. After he lit one he gived it to Podgie for the first limit. Three draws was a limit. If ye got a limit ye got yer three draws. Podgie always got a limit off people but other ones, if it was you, usually ye just got one draw.

But how come Podgie got it first before Mitch, if it was Mitch's fag? He got more out it than Mitch. Mitch just lit it and got one draw then passed it to him. Then Podgie passed it to Gary. Gary put his hand out and Podgie just gived him it. That was what they done. Podgie and Gary and Gary and Podgie. But they were not bothering about Peter.

I was glad nothing happened to him and Billy. I liked them coming with us. Peter was a good climber. He used the ronepipe. But his house was just one storey up. He knew mine was the top flat. If he wanted to climb it I would let him, he could do it after school, it was just me in the house.

We were going along by the burn and I said about the high tree. I still wanted to climb it and make a swing. It would be a great swing and go right over the burn. We just needed a rope. We could knock one off the workies. Oh aye, said Mitch.

No the now, said Podgie.

Oh come on.

No.

We will go another time, said Gary.

How no just now? I said.

Oh f**k Smiddy, we will go another time.

Oh but we can still go and just see it.

No, said Podgie, I am no f*****g going.

Me neither, said Gary. I cannot f*****g be bothered.

Aye but I can just show yez it. Oh come on. Peter and Billy have not seen it.

Neither have I, said Mitch.

He is the only c**t that has seen it, said Podgie.

We could kick a ball about instead, said Billy.

Aye, said Podgie, six of us, that is three a-side, three a-side is good.

F**k football, said Gary, I do not feel like it.

Neither do I, said Peter, I would f*****g like to see the high tree as well. Oh Smiddy whereabouts is it?

It is just along the burn.

How far have we to f*****g walk? said Gary.

Oh it is no too far.

F*****g better no be, you are a b*****d Smiddy, ye always have to get everything.

I do not.

Ye f*****g do, said Gary.

Him and Podgie were moaners about climbing because they did not do it much. But if they did they would like it. Mitch had started doing it and he liked it. He said about climbing mountains, it would be good to do that. Gary just thought it was daft. If ye said about climbing to him. Oh do not be so f*****g stupid, I am no climbing that. But he was skinny and could have climbed good.

Podgie was just a moaner. Mitch said it too, Oh Podgie is a moaning-faced b*****d. That was him when we were walking. Moan moan moan. It is a f*****g swamp. Oh the grass is f*****g wringing. Oh my maw will kick up f**k when she sees my shoes.

We went along the side of the burn. There was all good trees here with big branches. But the high tree was just the best. But then we got to it and there was no low-down branches and no wee bits sticking out. They all were sawed off too. Somebody had done it like it was just stripped.

If it was men done it maybe for firewood. But usually it was just a tree that was dead, else it was sap and did not burn right. Ye flung branches on the fire and if there was sap it just bubbled out and smoked. Big boys used to set complete fields on fire just burning all the grass and ye thought it was going to come up the hill and burn down yer house. I loved the smell. Me and Mitch made fires and that was what happened, if ye saw the dry grass, ye just lighted the match.

Maybe the men just done it to the tree to stop people climbing. I was seeing how to do it but ye could not see everything the farther up it went. If something was up there, maybe there was. Maybe a tree-hut. Ye got tree-huts. People made them. It was safe. Ye could sit there and ones would be walking down on the ground. They would not know ye were there. Imagine walking down a path in the woods and voices talking up a tree. Ye would be feared. Ye would think it was goblins or evil sorcerers going to get ye. If ye were up the tree and making scary noises, if lasses were walking under and ye were kidding on ye were an owl hooting, the lasses would be screaming and bawling.

But ye had to talk quiet too if gangs came and they heard ye, they would have stanes to fire at ye.

Trees had to be the right kind to build a hut. It was how the branches fitted. Then if ye built one ye had to watch out for people. Gangs came along and smashed it. The Squatters were away now but other ones went about and ye had to watch it. They went looking for stuff. If ye had a rope swing they used it till it fell down. If it was a tree-hut they would just smash it up. So if there was one up the high tree and people were trying to hide it. Maybe there was. The branches went dead thick going up the top and ye could not see past them. Imagine there was one. We could all just go up. I could climb the tree and see.

Oh but if there is no f*****g branches?

Oh but look, ye can get yer foot on the edges! Look!

Ye could. If ye went up a wee bit you would be okay. It was the way the branches got sawed. There was wee toty bits left. Ye could get yer feet on. If ye could climb the first bit, that was all.

I showed them but Podgie was moan moan moan. That was all he done, a true moaner. He would never climb the high tree anyway so how come he was saying it? Podgie always said if ye could not do it. Oh ye cannot do that. That was Podgie. If you said something, he said something else. He kept doing it till ye stopped, so then he done his wee smile. But this time it did not matter because it was no just Mitch, Peter Wylie backed me up and so did Billy. Gary backed up Podgie. I am no going up, he said.

Oh but ye do not have to, I said, I can just go up and see.

Me too, said Peter.

I will go too, said Mitch, if it is a tree-hut it will be f*****g smashing. We can just f*****g hide in it. It will be great.

See the next time, I said, we can bring pieces with us and bottles of ginger. Nobody will see us. Ye are just really high up and all the leaves and branches, it is just all thick, so if they look up, they will not see nothing.

It will just be like a f*****g roof, said Peter.

Gary laughed. I am going to bring up n**e books.

So now everybody was laughing and saying about it. Podgie too. Mitch got another fag and we smoked it.

It was just me, Mitch and Peter going up. Mitch was the worst climber so he went first. Me and Peter put our hands the gether, fingers inbetween, making a strong step so he got his foot on and we hoisted him. He got on our shoulders trying to reach up to the edges of the sawed branches but he was not doing it good and he was heavy. His feet were kicking yer head and yer ear and then on top of yer head trapping yer hair and it was agony. Oh Mitch Mitch!

Oh I cannot f*****g help it.

Aye but ye are kicking my f*****g ear, shouted Peter.

Well I am no f*****g trying it.

The other ones were laughing at us. Oh you stupid c**ts! It is too f*****g high to reach.

No, it is not.

Mitch could not do it. He could not get himself up any further. He tried again but me and Peter caved in and he had to jump down. They all wanted to chuck it but I did not and showed how the good branches started and then right up were the big ones. They grew right over and drooped down the other side of the burn. Ye could see the best branch for the rope swing. And I could see how to climb it easy.

It was a real beauty and went out along and right over and if ye were on it ye could climb right along and tie on the rope and then go down it or even just go on more and dreep down the other side of the burn. I had never done that before. But I had done ones just quite the same. It was a long long branch and went thin at the faraway end so when ye got there and were climbing down yer weight would get it bending.

Peter had not done it before. Him and Mitch gived me a puddy up then Billy and Mitch gived one to Peter and I helped him more so then that was us.

A branch was no good if it went thin too early, it bent too quick and swooshed ye round, so then ye fell off. One time I did it and went into a bush with all jaggy nettles, all tearing me when I was getting out. There was marshy weeds there too so ye had to watch that else ye would be soaked and complete mud all over ye.

Ye had to go careful on a branch. Ye held on in a very tight grip just edging out slow and slow, watching ye did not get turned. The branch just swooshed ye round so then ye were hanging underneath it and just hanging on with yer knees and feet and hands, and yer elbows too, keeping them tight in and yer chest in too, right as much as ye could into the branch else ye would fall. Yer body was heavy and made ye if ye were not careful. And if ye fell through the branches. Or if they broke yer fall. But if ye dropped straight down and it was yer back, oh yer back was the worst. Or yer head so it got smashed in, that was the worst, yer skull got smashed and cracked open. If it was yer back ye landed on it was tough luck for you too because people broke their back and went on wheelchairs the rest of their life, so that was them.

If the branch turned ye ye could not get back to the right way up, ye could only go backwards and yer body hanging down and it was just yer feet and yer hands holding on. Ye could never get back up the branch again. Ye just could not do it. Ye tried and ye could not. So down ye went down ye went and if ye were going to fall it was all ye could do no to, hand by hand by foot by foot going fast fast fast as ye could before ye fell because ye were going to fall and ye were quick quick to see where ye would land getting ready to land, so ye would let go yer feet first so they would hit the ground and break yer fall. The best thing was letting go yer feet first and holding on with yer hands, hanging there, then swinging yer feet, trying to bounce the branch to go near the ground, as near as ye could go.

The farther out ye went the more down it bended till ye got low and could just dreep down or if ye kept yer grip and brought that branch right down onto the ground so like ye captured it. That was what I thought. Mitch or Podgie was there and trapped it down. If they let go it bounced and ye had to jump out the road so it did not clout ye on the way up. That was Podgie. He done that for a laugh. So then the branch battered ye. Who was laughing? Him.

And then the branch was back up the tree again. Hoh Smiddy get that f*****g branch again! But ye would not climb the tree another time so he was laughing against ye. That was Podgie. I did not care. He was just acting it. But if they trapped the branch good ye could get off and hold it down for them then they could get on. I said it. Mitch was going to try it.

I climbed higher into the branches and it was great. The branches were very thick the gether so if ye fell even they could break yer fall, maybe they would. Ye felt the tree swaying now because with the wind and yer body on it, ye just had to cling on tight.

I heard Gary shouting up, Oh can ye see a tree-hut?

I could not see him down through the branches. I just shouted, No.

Up through the branches was just the sky. So there was nothing there like a hut or a den, there was just nothing. I saw Peter and waved down to him. I am coming back down.

Nobody had been up that high before. I thought that. I said it to Peter how we were the first ones. Ye looked down but could not see them on the ground.

It is f*****g smashing, said Peter.

The good branch was there so I went on it just to try it and see if it was good for a rope swing. So if it went right over the burn and just, well then, so we could just maybe dreep down the other side. I thought I would and said I was going to. Peter wanted to come with me so then we went, me first, crawling backwards and out and out waiting for the branch to bend, the boys were all shouting. Fall you c**t!

But it was just a laugh and they just were acting it. Podgie and the boys done that. They all just shouted stuff. If it was you that was doing the thing ye just gived them the V sign back. That was what I done. Except if it was a branch and ye were gripping on, ye had to watch it because if it turned ye. Ye were just watching and going careful for when to let go, so ye would not land on a rocky bit that sloped or ye falled back down in the burn. Ye waited till it was right so to jump out the way and could kick over to land, just kicking kicking. Ye just were waiting, then ye did it, throwing out yer shoulders to get yer body the right way, for yer legs to take it. Peter was gripping on up above me.

Alright Pete! I just shouted, then I done it, letting go the branch, and it jerked hard up swisshhh swisshh. I did not hear it much or if I did, maybe I did, but Peter did not do it right and the bounce turned him and he fell off. I did not see it because I was dreeping. But I could not help it and it was not my fault, if he did not hang on right.

230

If it was two of yez doing it the one left on the branch was to be ready for the bounce. So if he was not ready. Ye had to hang on tight. Ye gripped it with all yer body so ye would stick on so the bounce would not turn ye. I telled him before we went. He did not do it right, ye just had to grip on with all yer body. He fell through the branches and it was in the bit near the bank. Lucky for him it was all marshy so a soft landing. But he could not get up, just his breathing, oh oh. The boys were there and talking, Oh what is going to happen, will we get the doctor, oh what will we do? Maybe we should get a ambulance or what, because Peter, how he just was gasping and gasping no able to breathe and looking up at us. He just was lying there a long while, then ye thought he was asleep till his breathing got okay again and ye heard it, and then he was looking up, his eyes were looking at ye. Oh what happened?

Ye fell off the f*****g tree, said Gary.

Just right down, said Mitch.

The branch bounced ye, I said.

Oh oh oh. It is my back oh and my chest, my chest is sore oh and my back and my shoulders, oh my arms, oh my back, oh it is f*****g sore oh I cannot breathe I cannot breathe.

And all the time it was all his breaths coming when he was talking just sore, ohhh ohhh, hooh hooh, hooh hooh.

He was all soaking and muddy. His jacket was not because we left our jackets on the ground when we climbed up. We were thinking what to do and then just got him up. We walked him up the field and round to his street then upstairs to his house. His big sister was there. She ran to get his maw. Other people were there and what they were saying, Oh Peter Wylie has broke his back. He fell off a tree. They were high up and Smiddy let go the branch.

But he had not broke his back and it was not my fault. That was Gary. Oh Smiddy let go the branch and Peter fell off. What did Gary say it for? He just thought it but he did not know, it was not my fault, it was the branch, just how it jerks right up it just is a real bounce and ye have got to cling on and cling on and just do it with all yer body just gripping because if ye do not ye just fall off and that was what happened. I was saying to the boys.

231

Peter's maw was there and what to do, Oh we will wait for Peter's da to come home from work. Or else run down to do a phone call. Oh if we need to get an ambulance. Or else if there is a taxi. Oh who can get a taxi?

We helped him in the house and lying on top of the bed. So then we were just to go home. His maw said it, Oh away home boys.

We all walked round to Billy's close and were talking. It was past teatime. Gary and Podgie went home and me and Mitch too. He said cheerio and I just ran up the stair and just stepped on the landing and the door burst open and it was my da. Oh come in here you bloody fool!

And he clouted me on the head and it went right on my ear, whohh a sore one. He pulled me right in the door and skelped me and it was on the side of the chin, a real smack. You climbing again? I thought I told you before! How many times, how many times.

Smack smack smack. I was down on the floor and with my hands up shielding from him.

Take yer punishment! Take yer punishment! He was trying to skelp my backside but I was getting away from him so his hand was hitting my legs. I was greeting and did not want them seeing me. I was just greeting and snotters out my nose. My da stopped doing it. Get in that room!

I was still on the floor and covering my face with my hands and it was hiding too, I did not want to see them, Matt and my maw, I thought if I hated them, if I really did.

Get in that room!

My room. Well I wanted to. I wanted to. That was what I said, I just wanted to, no to see them in that stinking house, that was what I said, I hated that house and just hated it all.

So get in then, get in! And he shoved me in the room.

I just really hated them, if I did, I really did, so if I just went away. I would just go. I wanted to. I was not their family. It was all just for Matt, he never got hit and just got everything and I was just wanting to get away and just get away away. They were there where they wanted. But I was not. I did not want to be there. They could just be anywhere, it did not worry me because I would not be with them and Mitch was going too, sometimes he ran away and I was going to go with him, the very next time I was going to.

I did not go to bed but was just lying on top of it. My maw came in after. If I wanted my tea. She was heating it up for me. I did not want it. I was to come and get it but I did not want to.

It was Peter fell off the tree, but it was not me did it, if they thought it was it was not. I telled his maw what it was and so did the boys, it was not my fault if it was the branch. But they were not bothering. My maw was saying about Peter and how he was in hospital, a neighbour came and telled them. Oh that poor woman.

But he was not in the hospital, they did not keep him in. My da went round to see, and his maw and da telled him how it was not my fault and how he just fell off, that was Peter, how he was just climbing all the time. His maw and da were sick telling him and now here he was, lucky for him he did not break his neck.

But mine still got on to me. They did. That was it in my house, I had not even done nothing and I was still getting it. Because the climbing, if I did not stop that b****y climbing. If I fell and broke my d**n neck, that was what he worried about, and what about my maw, what would she do? And that d**n balcony, that d**n balcony.

Because he found out I done it. There were two keys for the balcony and I took one to school. They did not know. I climbed up and came in and my maw saw me through the kitchenette window. She was at the sink, she dropped a good plate when I jumped in off the ronepipe. Oh my heart stopped beating, my heart stopped beating, that was what she said.

She telled my da when he came home from work and it was a doing. The next time was a worse one. The boys knew that one because Mitch was with me and he telled them. Mitch was down watching me and I just climbed up and in and was leaning back over and we were talking. But then the kitchenette door just opened and it was my da and he grabbed me. Mitch said it. I was just talking down to him then I vanished and it was shouting, and it was against me, I got a real doing.

That was my da. He was home early from work for something.

It was a dentist else a doctor, I do not know. But that was the worst doing. It was a horrible one. I just got doings.

So if people ran away, ye knew how, and it would just be so much the better, even in the Bible, the Minister told a story and maybe if it was about brothers, and one goes away and the other one stays home or else kills him and then Jesus and the Devil if the Devil was his brother and got cast out by the Heavenly Father. I did not care so if it was you and you were the Devil and got cast out. I did not care.

Boys ran away. They went to sea as a cabin boy and then to desert islands. When Mitch was old enough he was going in the Army. How no me too? That was what he said. How come I did not join the Army? Then the two of us could go the gether. Other ones were doing it. Podgie said he was so how come I did not?

Oh well maybe I would. It was going to be the Navy but maybe if it was the Army and everybody all went. I did not care about the Navy, if my da wanted me to go in there. Just because he was in it, I did not care.

In my house ye did not get money, just if ye needed it for something, but no for yer pocket. People got money for their pocket and just spent it. Other ones did. Gary's big brother gived him some on a Friday night. That was his milk-job. Imagine a brother giving it. Maybe my grannie and granda would give me some. I needed to get it. Me and Mitch were saying about it. He hated his house too. We would just run away. People ran away.

I was a best climber. If my da thought I was not. I was. People knew. If he thought I would do something and it was to Peter Wylie. It was not fair thinking that. I would not ever do anything bad to people. I just was climbing and Peter wanted to. He did. I did not make him. It was his business. If he just gripped on with all his body. I told him. I said it to Billy and the boys. Peter did not hold on right, ye just have to really grip it tight. He did not so the bounce got him. It would not have got me if it was me, if it was me to do it and I was hanging on, the bounce would not have turned me, so if Peter dreeped down first and me second, it was just how I went first, if Peter had went first.

§

I did not join the Lifies. Other boys did, I did not. My da tried to make me. Oh you are aye moaning about having nothing to do so go and join the Lifeboys. You liked it back in the old place why no here?

Dad I am too old.

You are not too old.

I am going to join the BB.

Oh you are too young for the BB. You can join the Lifies just now.

I do not want to. I am waiting to see.

See what? Eh? See what? You feared of something?

Feared of something. That was what he said. Feared. I was no feared of nothing, if it was in the Lifies, it was just stupid, ye could not be feared of nothing. I said it to him. Dad I am no feared of nothing. I am waiting for the BB.

Oh but then my maw. Oh it is not scared of anything it is not nothing it is anything you are not scared of anything and you have not to say feared it is scared. That was my maw. Oh you have to talk nice. That was her.

I was glad she said it because it made my da stop getting on to me. I did not want to go to the Lifies. It was just daft. My da forgot what age I was. Me and the boys were going to join the BB. Ye were not supposed to join till Secondary School because then ye were twelve but at the end of Primary School ye could be twelve, so then ye were old enough. Some were ready to join. It was just a wee company at the new Church and they were wanting to recruit all new boys so maybe they would let us in the now. It was not the same one as my big brother but I could have went to that too because he chucked it. My da did not like him for chucking it but he just done it. My maw backed him up. Oh it is just too much time, I need to study.

He said that to my maw but really it was his girlfriend because it was Friday night and he just wanted to go with her. I knew it. He did not think I knew but I did. Her maw and da let him into the house. He could sit in and he got a cup of tea, that was him and his girlfriend. She was in his school so it was trains there and back. On Friday night I always got the room to myself.

But some of the boys went to Bible Class. They said if ye did they would let ye in the BB sooner, if ye were still just eleven. My maw wanted me to go there. I went and then I stopped. Billy MacGregor had started going. My maw liked Billy because his maw and da went to Church and acted posh. But I did not want to go to Bible Class. The man that took it was mad. We all knew it. If it was for the BB I would go. It was in the new Church.

My maw wanted to go to Sunday Service with all the grown-ups but my da did not. She would not go without him. Sunday is a long-lie, he said.

Oh but Johnnie it would be nice to go to Church.

But it is the one day of the week.

Well what about me? said my maw.

Oh do I no deserve one long lie?

I deserve something too.

Oh if it is Sunday breakfast, I always make it for ye.

That was my da. He done the breakfast. But nobody wanted him to because it was how he just moaned all the time, it was just moan moan moan, and ye had to eat the breakfast even if ye did not feel like it, so if ye left something on yer plate, ye had to say an excuse. Oh sorry, I am full up.

Somebody does not like my cooking.

Oh dad it was good.

Well why are ye leaving it?

I am just full up.

You are the first man I ever saw that left a sausage on his plate. Maybe I burnt it.

No it was good.

But sometimes he just laughed. My da made jokes if Matt was not there. Matt went out on Sunday mornings and did not wait for breakfast. Where did he go? He did not tell us. Oh I am seeing my pals. He took stuff with him in a bag to play five-a-sides with his pals in school. He said that. Maybe he did not. He was quite good at football but no very good. He was good at other stuff. But no at everything. I did not care if he was anyway. But he did not play for the school team. Best players did. So if he really was good how come he did not play for it? I did not say it to him. It was just really snobby at his school. They all were posh. One time Matt said it to me, Oh it is just a bunch of blasted snobs.

Are they all rich? I said. Eh Matt?

But he did not tell me. Matt only done it when he wanted. His books and jotters were there but just scattered about. One thing he done was a foreign language, Latin, I looked at his book when he was in the bathroom. Now he was just lying on the bed with his hands behind his head, looking out the window.

My da said it to my maw. Oh I think he has got a girlfriend. Have you got one too? He said that to me and was laughing.

But I quite wanted one. I liked two lasses in my class. One was Rona Craig but she liked Billy MacGregor. Him and Peter Wylie went with lasses. Billy was better than me at football. Another lassie was Julie Michaels. One time a teacher came to give us PE. We all thought it was games to get but it was dancing for the school party and it was Scottish Dancing, all just hooching and shouting, but it was a good laugh. Ye were to say girls instead of lasses. Julie Michaels came and got me for a partner. She wore perfume and ye smelled it. She took yer hands and ye jumped up to the right then up to the left, one two three, and then back again. Then she took yer one hand and went round in a circle, hooch hooch hooch. It was just Scottish and hard to get right. Boys were jumping and laughing. Some lasses were angry and telling the teacher, Oh Miss he is kicking me, oh he is pushing me Miss.

The song was like Oh the Grand Old Duke of York but was for Scotland instead, people were saying the name. I forgot what it was. My maw was asking. She liked Scotland, Oh it is your history.

I did not talk to Julie and we were not looking, only if I did not do the dance right. She said what I was to do. Oh it is the other foot. But usually I could do it without her, except if it was too fast. I did not need her to tell me. That was Julie, she liked to boss people. Some lasses were fed up with her.

The boys were seeing who ye danced with. So were the lasses. It was a good laugh but and when we were out on the playground we all were talking about it.

It was funny seeing ones like Isabel Hartley and Sarah Wright. They were top of the class. Isabel was going to be a Dux. The teacher said it. She could be a Dux just now. People all laughed at her, quack quack.

Sarah danced with Robert Wotherspoon. I saw her eyes looking up the way and she had a red face. It was funny seeing her dancing. She could do it good. She was bigger than Robert. Robert was alright. He lived near her. He liked football and lenned ye the ball if ye wanted a game. But he was no one of the boys. He had other pals. They did not do stuff, I did not go about with them. So if ye saw them, ye just nodded. Sometimes they spoke to you. Oh Smiddy are you joining the Lifies? Oh Smiddy are ye going to Bible Class? Oh Smiddy Mitch is looking for ye. But Mitch was not looking for ye. It did not matter about what they were saying. If ye said it to Mitch, Oh were ye looking for me? He did not know about it. These ones only said it to get in with ye. I did not talk to them much.

Lasses did not like if they were bigger than the boy. My da said it too. He laughed if he saw it out the window. Oh this is better than the telly. He saw people walking down the street. Oh look at him. Oh look at her. Oh see his baldy head! Oh look at the size of her, she is like the side of a house!

So if it was a wee man and a big woman. Oh look at the wee bloke with the big dame! Oh come here and see!

He got my maw to look. She did not like doing it. Oh Johnnie that is not nice. They are man and wife.

Oh she is twice the size of him. Look! Then he would be laughing and pointing at her. Look look!

If my maw was not there he wanted me to look or else Matt. Matt did not like it. My da said, How no? It is only a laugh.

What if people see ye?

Matt did not like people seeing him. But they would not see

because we were the top flat. They would have to look up high. People did not, not when they were walking. That was how my da liked it. Matt did not. If my da done it he just went out the room. My da saw him doing it and looked at my maw or else just out the window.

Matt did not talk much. If he did not come home at teatime my da was wondering. Matt was the hungriest in the house. So if he was not there, my da was laughing. Oh he definitely has got a girl-friend.

He is just seeing his grandfather, my maw said, he will get his tea when he comes home.

But I knew it was a girlfriend. I said it to him when I went into the room. He was just lying on the bed. Have you got a girlfriend?

What are ye talking about?

Dad said ye have.

Dad says a lot.

He just said ye have one. So maybe even if ye went into her house.

Matt had his eyes closed and his hands clasped behind his head. So if he did not hear me. He did not talk much to me. Sometimes I wished he would but other times I did not care, he was not like a brother, if brothers were pals, he was not one. That was Matt, that was him, if he wanted he just done it. Even with my da. If my da said something. Maybe Matt would not do it. My da never hit him, he was too old. But he did not hit him when he was young either. No much anyway. But Matt did not do stuff. He used to but no now. Usually he was just in the room and with his radio.

I said to him. Eh Matt, will I put on the radio?

No. But then he said, Aye.

So I put it on. It came on at a place he liked and it was good songs. Matt's eyes were shut but he was listening, I knew he was. Maybe if he was fed up swotting. It was just swotting, swot swot. That was all he done. It was horrible. The house had to be quiet all the time. Even my da. My maw said it to him too. Oh will you turn the telly down a wee bit.

Oh but I cannot hear it.

Matt is trying to study.

So it was the complete house. Even when he finished the exams he still was swotting. He did not go out with any pals much except a Sunday. We did not know where he went, except if it was ones from school. So it was snobs. He did not have any real pals. He used to have ones in the scheme but now he did not. So if he liked going to that school. Maybe he did, if he was a snob, maybe he was, even if it was yer brother.

Then my maw said it about me too, about that school. I thought it was just she was saying it and no meaning nothing. But then my da too. We were up at the hospital and in the corridor walking along and I heard her saying it, Well maybe Kieron can go there as well.

Oh what was that, it was the posh school. I was looking at maw but she did not say nothing else and did not see me looking.

My granda had got took into a unit. I did not know. I heard them talking how a growth was there. Matt was in with my Auntie May when we went into the ward. He went himself and found where it was. He just went into it and said to nurses and they showed him.

Then it was too much people round the bed. The nurse came and telled us.

Me and my da waited outside. He opened his paper and was reading it. Then was yawning and shut the paper. Oh how is school. How is it, is it okay?

Yes.

Ye looking forward to the big school? Eh?

Oh I do not know, maybe.

I was leaving in the summer and going to Secondary. So if it was Senior Secondary or Junior Secondary. My da said, Senior Secondary is the best and when ye leave school ye get the best job. Junior Secondary is just for dunderheids. I should know, that is where I went, do not tell yer mother.

He opened the newspaper and was reading it.

I saw the back page and was reading that, what if Rangers won the League. I thought they would. They could beat Celtic and the other teams. They could win easy. Usually my da did not like me reading the paper when he was and if he saw me doing it he shut it. But just now he did not bother and gave me the back pages to see the football.

The teacher wanted us to read it. Oh if ye can just read the paper, that is a good benefit.

She liked us reading books the best. Oh but just read anything, just read anything. When I was a girl I read sauce bottles.

People were laughing at her but she did it, all the labels and if it was the cornflakes packet. She went round the class on Monday morning. Oh what have you been reading over the weekend? So then ye said it and if it was Lorna Buckle and a book, Oh Lorna will you tell everybody about it.

Lorna Buckle got a big red face. She had to stand in the front of the class. People laughed when she done it but then ye were listening. One time she done a Famous Five story out a book. I knew it because I read it. She told the story and I knew what it was but did not tell the teacher.

I had the book out the library bus. It came round the street and ye just went in and got yer books. It was not like a real library, ye did not get many books. But it was good. The driver was a wee bit grumpy. But ye put yer name down for new books and he liked it if ye did. He showed ye the book names on a paper and ye just said, Oh that one, if a book had a good name, Lost Treasure of the Mountains.

I got that one but was having to skip bits. It was no very good and ye just forgot what it was and then were reading it and all the names of the people, who were they, they were all jumbled up. I saw Danny taking it out and told him no to. Catholics came to the library as well. Some books ye did not read and just gave back. Ye said to people if ye knew a book was good or if it was not. Oh get that one, you will like it. But some books people told ye were good were not good.

Oh but it was great hearing the horn when the library came. It was the same as a bus nearly, a single-decker one. Ye watched for it coming then ran down the stairs to get first in. I tried to beat Danny but it stopped outside his close, so usually he got first choice. A lot of times it came too early and ye were still at school, so ye missed it and had to wait till next week or the week after.

A boy in my class was good at stories as well. Stuart Johnson. He just made them up. It was not from a book and was just daft but ye still listened, ye wondered what was going to happen. Oh there was a young man and he ran away from home to go to the Wild West and he joined the cowboys and they were all in a circus with pirates. So then it was a story about cowboys and indians and pirates as well. How come pirates if it was cowboys and indians? But people liked it. Podgie and Gary McNab just laughed at Stuart and said it was daft. He looked at ye when he was telling the story, he was wanting to see if ye were watching him. So if he was a true show-off. I think he was. I lifted my desk and looked in at the stuff, so he would see me doing it, Oh he is not listening to me.

But I was listening. But Lorna was the best one. Her voice went up and down and was a real lassie voice but what she done too if it was somebody talking, she did it in their voice. Oh where do you think you are going? So it was the baddy. Oh he is growling in his throat. Ohhhhh. Then it is the little girl. Oh please sir I do not know, I am just searching for my mummy. So Lorna done it in a wee squeaky voice.

Everybody liked it when she done them. I could tell stories too but I did not want to. I used to do it with John Davis when we went on the school buses. I just said if I was reading a book, oh it is about a boy who does this. John liked it. Mitch too and Gary McNab. Gary done it if he went to the pictures. He was good at it. So was Peter Wylie. Him and Billy went with lasses and that was what they done. They sat in the close and telled stories. Rona Craig was there. Peter said about pictures he went to. I done it with books. I read books a lot because in my house it was just peace all the time, Oh be quiet be quiet, so ye just read them.

§

Ye saw programmes on the telly too. Horrors. Some were good, except if they were too far-fetched and that happened a lot of times. It annoyed my da. Young lasses especially, if it was old men, if it was a play. How can a good-looking young lassie like her fall for that smelly old codger? He will just be pumping all the time. Pumping was not for s*x but just how my da said pumping for farting. Oh he will just be pumping the place out, it will be pongs everywhere.

It was all far-fetched, that was what my da said, just because of money, if the old codger did not have money no lassie would look at him twice. See the state of him. He is just a wrinkled old man with a baldy head and look, a bad limp, no a single tooth in his gub and he cannot walk without creaking and moaning all the time. No lassie would look at him twice. But would ye credit that, he is getting the woman and look, she is just a lassie, and beautiful, just a young lassie.

Old people are ponging. My da said it. It was not nice but I was thinking then my grannie, it was true, because sometimes she smelled, it was true, not a bad awful smell just maybe if it was whatever it was but ye knew it was her and ye never smelled it off anybody else. Old people on buses and on the train, they could have smells and sometimes bad awful ones. People said it. Look at that smelly old b*****d. Then ye saw an old old man. Oh he is minging, look at the state of him. But all people had smells. Even my maw, it was a milky kind of smell. My da's was just manky if he was home from work then washed but that smell was there, it was like bikes, that was on him, and ye saw his hands, inside his hands, it was the lines and there was black, so how come he did not wash it off?

Then if dogs sniffed ye. They did. They came up and sniffed. So you had one too. If they did not know ye they just went away. The dog just came up and sniffed ye. Oh it is you. Because they did not know it was you till it was yer scent, so that was you.

Cats done it too but they did not tell ye they were, like how dogs done it. Cats just looked at ye. But if they opened their mouth to yawn oh what a smell that was and ye thought about all what they were eating if it was wee mice and old bits of stuff, and old skin off fish and scrapings, that was what cats got, and if they opened their gub for a yawn that was the worst pong ye could get, and ye saw inside their mouths, how it opened like a crocodile, Oh Captain Hook and it was going to swallow ye down. If a big cat done that and it bit yer hand it would just be half of it taken away, ye would just have yer thumb and finger left if granda's big cat bit it. Ye saw its teeth and it was like a crocodile, so then you got a hook to join on yer wrist or if it was yer leg, a wooden leg, that was with pirates, if maybe a shark got them, the pirates made ye walk the plank and ye saw down below all the sharks were swimming just waiting to get ye, just to gobble ye up.

Matt had one too, it was in the room with all dirty socks and stuff. And if it was an old man, that was the worst smell because he was old, but if they had money, thousands and thousands, so they were millionaires, so they got all the lasses. That was what happened. Young lasses and they were just beautiful. It was disgusting and ye saw it on the telly. The celebrities and personalities, they were all millionaires, and ye saw the women they got, and they were all old guys, no teeth.

My da got annoyed about it. If it was not money. Of course it was. Money talks. How does a young lassie go with somebody like that, and if she is a personality, she can get who she wants, it's b****y disgusting. My da went on and on. My maw was knitting, but waiting to speak. So then she did, her fingers and the needles just the same. Stop going on about it, you go on about it too much. She did not look at him but just said it. It is only a play.

Matt was there too. I was about to go ben and make some toast for supper. No now. They were going to have an argument so no supper, da would not want any. That was what he done, he got huffy. Ye waited to see what would happen but usually that was what it was, he brought his feet up on the chair then sat on them, facing away from her. Oh I do not go on about it too much.

Yes you do.

244

Well it is just far-fetched, an old man like that touching the young lassie.

It is only a play.

Well it is far-fetched.

Now Matt came into it. Dad they are married.

No they are not.

They are. In the play they are, that is the story.

It does not matter what it is, a story or a play or what, if it is a load of nonsense. That is what it is. In real life it would not happen, no with him, a young lassie like that.

Well she is getting off with somebody else.

Oh Matt, said my maw.

But she is mum, it is that young fellow, she is getting off with him.

Do not talk like that, it is not nice.

But she is.

Maw did not want to hear and she kept on with the knitting. I went ben to make the toast, just for myself or whatever it did not matter, I was wanting out before something happened. Sometimes I liked it when they were fighting but just now I did not. My head was sore. If something bad might happen, I was wanting away before. It was my head just being sore, I did not like it. My da acted stupid and Matt was going to get him, that was what I thought. It was going to happen. I could see them. Matt was better at talking. He could beat him. He could beat my da. Then if he was shaving, my da said that to him, Oh you think you are a man because you are shaving?

I do not have any option, said Matt, if I shave I shave.

Oh you will need a house to yerself next.

Maybe I will.

I saw them as if they were separate when they done it, it was not the real them. Ye felt like shouting at them just stop it, as if they were kidding on, that was what I thought, it was not a real argument. Even it annoyed me, sometimes it did, just something about it I did not like it it was daft. Stop it. Ye shouted at them in yer head. And what could happen now was if my da picked on me. That was what I expected. Then it was not kidding on. After a wee row with my maw or my brother he sometimes done it, then it was a real one and he just shouted at ye. But no at Matt, he did not shout at Matt.

§

They built a new Chapel, a right big one. Most of the Catholics went to it. It had all wee wee windows and they were in the shape of a Cross. If ye fired a stone, ye could not hit them unless it was a lucky throw. Some boys tried it but not that many and they did not break them. The Cross could put ye off. That was what people thought, because the Cross is God's or else Jesus's so if ye hit it well that was you. I would not have done it. They put them there for good luck, so something bad would not happen. But what bad was going to happen? Nothing bad was going to happen. The place was full of Papes so more like something bad was going to happen to the Proddies. We would get the trouble, the way they were all just breeding, it was like hot cakes, so then what would happen, if they outnumbered us. My da got annoyed or if he laughed how they all went to the Pineapple then they came home and out they all went to the pub. That was funny, because how could ye say that was religious, that was not religious, that was just like they said something at the Pineapple and then came home and done something else, if that was supposed to be Christians, what did their Priests say about that, nothing, because they went to the pub themself or else had a carry-out, everybody knew it, they liked a bucket, but the likes of Ministers, the ones there that drank too much, they were few and far between. My da never went to the pub on Sundays, just Fridays and maybe Saturdays at dinnertime.

Sunday morning was hopeless but the afternoon was good. It was aye a big game of football and that was where the cards happened, after the game or else at half-time. I said to Pat about coming for that, if Danny came too. They knew Catholics played but only in the big game. But even our wee games were good except if we had more players. I telled Pat and he said he might come, but he never. If it was just me out in the street then he came down with his ball. Or else if Mitch came up for me to go and play heidies outside my close.

If it was raining, it did not matter except if it was too heavy. Even if it was snowing, we just went out. We played till I got called up or else if the snow fell too thick. It was my da called me up. He was not working and saw out the window a lot. So if it was us playing, and it was snowing or else heavy rain he opened the window and shouted down, Hoy you! Up here! At once!

So ye had to come. There was a lamp-post on the outside of the pavement. From there to the inside pavement was one goal. We made the other one along a bit with a brick for the other goalpost. The game was just on the pavement but ye could use the street if the ball went out, usually it did.

The other side of the pavement was the front garden and it was a fence. Ye had to watch the ball did not go over too much. I was better at heidies than Mitch. He was a great goalie. But when he heided the ball it went squinty and over the fence. The family that had the garden did not like it. I knew them. They did not give me a row because I stayed up the close but they gave me hard looks.

I saw Pat up at his window watching us. He was good at football. I waved to him to come out but he did not. He could have played the winner except it was Mitch, he did not know him except he was a Proddy. Some Proddies did not play with Catholics and the same the other way about. Billy MacGregor and Peter Wylie would but Podgie and Gary McNab would not. They hated them. So did Mitch but he just played if it was me. If Pat came out Mitch would have played. Pat would have played with Protestants. Other Catholics would not. So we would not play them. Danny was a wee bit like it. If him and Pat were out kicking a ball with their pals from school they looked over and gave ye a wave but would not say to come for a game. Danny was pals with me but would never have come out if Mitch was with me.

A lot of times I went down the shops to meet the boys. If Pat was down a message for his maw he gave me a wave. One time he shouted on me, Oh Kieron, how ye doing?

I just shouted back, No bad Pat, how is yerself?

When he went away Gary McNab said, Who the f★★k is that?

Is he no a Pape? said Podgie.

Mitch was just looking at me, he knew he was. But Podgie and Gary knew he was a Pape as well. They were just acting it. And Gary said, Oh he called ye Kieron.

Oh Kieron! Podgie laughed.

If Papes called me Kieron, that was what they meant, how come? How come they did not say Smiddy? So Kieron was a Pape's name. I did not care. I did not care about my name. If people said Kieron and gave a wee look, well that was just them. One was one, then the other one. That was just me, that was what I thought.

Papes stayed everywhere and beside Gary and Podgie as well. People all knew them. Ye just gave a wee nod and so did they. If ye saw ones coming ye kept out their way. Ye just went on the other side of the road. They did it or else us. Ye saw them coming a long way away so ye just crossed over, or else they done it. But ye done it a long way away. Because if ye did not, if ye waited too long, well ye had to stay. That was Podgie, Oh I am not moving for these c★★ts.

So then if ye just kept walking. So they had to cross over. Ye hoped they would. Ye did not want a fight, except Podgie and if Mitch was there, Oh I will f★★★★★g kill them.

Podgie just laughed but it was a worry. Because then the Papes saw you and how ye were not crossing the road. They thought if ye were chancing it, ye were making them look like s★★★ebags. So they would not let ye. Then ye could not back down, we could not and they could not. When they passed ye had to not give in, ye did not squeeze to the side to let them pass and they did not do it either. Ye kidded on ye did not see them. They done the same. When yez passed ye just walked a wee bit in and they walked a wee bit out and so then yez got through and no an argument and ye were just glad. Except Podgie. If it was one boy walking and he did not get out the way Podgie punched him off the pavement and even a kicking.

Usually it was not to Papes, because ye did not know him and if he was in a gang or had big brothers, so if he came back with a team to get ye.

But people did not want trouble and usually ye just went the other side, if ye were yerself, if ye saw boys coming, ye always crossed over. So did big boys and even men, a lot of men, ye just looked to see who it was, they looked as well so if they knew ye, Oh hullo boys.

But if they did not know ye. I saw men cross over. Except with a drink in them, then they would just walk to ye. Ye heard them in the street if they were drunk. So if it was a Friday night they went to the pub after their work and came home steaming. Some came along the road singing and shouting, Follow Follow, Follow Follow. We are the Peopell. No surrender, no surrender!

People said it back to them. What is the cry? Oh no surrender! Wee boys shouted it to the man and ran after him and maybe went with him.

But then what if it was Papes? If Papes saw the drunk man. Oh who the f**k is that! Maybe they would give the drunk man a doing. Proddy b*****d. We thought that. We went behind them to see. So if people were there, if there was Papes. What were they going to do? If they took on the drunk man. That was not fair, and just wee boys with him. So if we were there.

A lot of times Mitch got angry at Papes. Podgie pointed at him. He liked it when Mitch got angry. But me as well because it just was not fair, people picking on one, if it was one Proddy and a gang of Papes were getting him, so ye were just watching to see who was going to do it, because they would soon find out with us there. What was the drunk man's name? If he was somebody's da, maybe he was. One was Mr Thompson, he stayed in my bit. He had two wee lasses. He came home drunk a lot of times and was shouting and bawling. Oh f**k the Pope, f**k the Pope. Pat and Danny knew him. He did not do nothing except if he was drunk. The worst was a man that got his head kicked in. He was a Proddy too. That man was just drunk and could not defend himself. My da said it, He could not defend himself. And they still done it. So that was the worst cowards.

Imagine it was yer own da and a gang was going to jump him. What would ye do ye would just run and batter them. So it was quite the same. If people were going to pick on one man they had another think coming. They were looking for trouble. That was just cowards because he was drunk. So he could not defend himself. Even if he was a good fighter but now he was not and ye could batter him, just a bunch of weans could batter him. Well if they thought that they were wrong. We were there and would back him up. Fenian b★★★★★ds.

We were not scared if it was bigger ones. It was dark and ye could run away easy through closes. We were not scared of them.

The drunk man did not see us, only the wee boys. We did not walk near him. So it was not us, we were not doing nothing, if people heard him shouting and looked out the window and saw us, well they did not. If it was Papes there and ye knew them, ye kidded on ye did not, just looked the way ye were going. If ye saw two ones sitting at a close and they were watching ye. So you were watching them. Who were they? If ye did not know them, well, if they are Papes. They were just sitting like that. If they were Proddies they would shout to ye. Or what. They would not be there, no sitting like that. If they were Catholics and they said something, well, we were just waiting, we would have jumped them. Who were they looking at. If they did not say nothing and just looked, who were they looking at if they thought they were looking at us. We were no feared of them, never, we would never have been feared of them. And if they were laughing, what were they laughing at. Even if a wee boy flung a stane at them, we would back him up. If it was just a wee boy and they were going to jump him, we would not stand back. But they would not do it with us there. We just stared at them. So if they did say something it would be after we were away, so we could not hear them, they were just cowards, Fenians were just cowards. And then if it was an old drunk man, imagine doing it to him, it was just cowards that done that.

So if a wee boy did fling a stane, the boys sitting would just walk into the close and through the back, we would not chase them, no unless they done something, but ye would just have to watch it because what the wee boy did not think was if the Papes had a gang and came looking for us so then what. Ye turn back or if ye do not, if it is a fight, what else, how many of them are there, so if it is too many ye have to scatter, just run for it.

§

Matt came out to the ward waiting room. I was to go in and see my granda. Matt stayed out with my da.

I just went in myself and saw my maw and Auntie May, and my grannie too. I did not know she was there but she was. In the next bed was a man and he had a very small head, it was just wee, and his eyes just shut.

My maw waved to me so I was to go round the other side to my granda. He was lying with the sheets up and his pyjamas and all white hairs out his chest. He was smiling and I was to take his hand and it was hair at the back too and all up his arm all black hairy. I did not see it like that before. My maw was watching me. My granda was only lying there and his breathing. I stood at the front and my grannie was watching. Granda was smiling and so was I but he did not say anything. I thought about what to say to him but nothing came till then, Hullo granda.

Hullo son, and a croaky wee voice.

Are ye okay?

Oh I am fine.

My grannie was just looking and ye saw her. She was just sad, just looking. And if she was worried too, she was, I saw it, I saw how she was. That was my grannie, I knew how she looked. So if my granda was going to die. Oh.

My maw too, her and Auntie May, just looking to see him. I made a sound and it was a funny one like a big hiccup, oh, I was going to greet just be greeting, I was going to but just managed it, I kept it in.

It was alright after it and I was just to go away from the bed, my grannie looking at me. Oh yer granda is tired son, just say cheerio.

Well cheerio granda.

My da was there and waved to me. He took me and Matt home. My maw stayed with my grannie and Auntie May.

It was a bus from the hospital to the subway then the train. And now a Sunday so hours just waiting for everything. My da was talking about football. It was a game on television.

Matt was just quiet. He was thinking about my granda. I was too. My da said something else, whatever it was, if it was school or else if it was what, I do not know, it was no to me, it was to Matt.

Matt said stuff back to him. To do with things, I do not know, I was seeing out the train window and the people all there in their houses, how they did not know about granda and the other ones all in hospital and all in their hospital beds. People were just walking outside on the street, so if ye took away the walls in the hospital it would just be into the wards, ye would just see in, and all the people lying in their beds, all looking down at the ones on the street. Granda would just smile, that was granda, all what he done. And people would be waving up to them.

Another day after that my maw gave me money for the train and subway to my grannie's. I was trying to skip my fare but the man saw me. I was looking out the window but he came and got me. Oh I have lost my ticket.

But I had to buy one.

Lost yer ticket is just daft, I should have said something else. The man did not even speak, just held his hand out for my money.

But instead of the subway I went down and got the ferry so that was money in my pocket. My grannie gave me some too. Even on weekdays now I went to her house, I went straight after school. My maw wanted me to. My grannie went up to hospital at nighttime. I walked down the stair with her to the main road. She got a bus and I went the other way kidding on to get the subway but I did not.

And when ye got home it was good with the money in yer pocket and ye could put it in yer plank.

My maw liked me going to grannie's with granda no there, it was company for her. Sometimes Auntie May was there but sometimes she was not. She did not talk much to me just smiled a wee bit. I went after school and got my tea there. Her and my grannie were talking about Uncle Billy. He was coming back from England to see granda.

My maw always gave money for the subway. Then I got more off my grannie to go home on it, but I did not. I liked the ferry better anyway, it just took long to go but it was great at nighttime seeing the lights on the water and everything all quiet. Ye could just lean yer elbows on the rail and look out or if it was raining just in beneath the cover and yer back to the wall and it was boiling hot with the engines and the engine smell. All the ships were there that were getting built or else just sitting there in the water, all dark. But if their lights were on along the gangways and ye saw men there, just maybe their heads, they were sailors. Or if ye heard them talking and their voices came out loud although they were not shouting, or if they were laughing. And then too it was pots and pans clinking, ye heard it way down the river and thought what they were getting for their tea. It was something good. My da said how it was big steaks and ham and eggs and as many sausages as ye could eat, if ye wanted more ye just put yer hand up and the cook guy came and gave ye it. They got chips and puddings too if they wanted them. A lot of sailors did not take their puddings, they had enough with their dinner bits, potatos and whatever.

§

The boys were talking about how Mitch was no at school and we would go up and see if it was something, what it was. Two would go. So that was me and who else. Podgie. But I was first, I was Mitch's best pal. People knew that.

His maw answered the door. Oh hullo Kieron. William is away, he is down in England with his auntie and uncle.

Is he coming back?

Oh yes, it is just a wee holiday. Come on in a wee minute.

Oh no.

Just for a wee minute. What is your name? she said to Podgie.

Derek.

Oh yes, that is right.

Derek was his real name. Podgie had been in Mitch's house before, but no much. I did not want to go in now but his maw took us. Podgie was glad. People liked seeing in houses. But I went into Mitch's other times so it did not matter.

He had a room to himself because he was a single brother with all big sisters. If I had a big sister and no Matt I would have got a room to myself. It was great for all yer own stuff.

Mitch did not think it was. He wanted a brother and a big brother. He thought it would be good. But no it was not. Maybe if it was a young brother because then ye got the things, the best sides and the best drawers and all else. But no a big brother. Oh but Smiddy Matt is a good big brother.

Mitch said that. He liked Matt. If he was in my house and Matt was there Matt waved to him. Howdy Mitch. That was what he said to him, Howdy Mitch. Mitch thought that was great. He liked being in my house.

His maw let me and Podgie into his room and it was all just the usual except neat and tidy, all his pictures on the wall.

Just wait a minute, she said and went away back out. So we were just there. It was not good with Mitch no there. I did not like it. Mitch had a knife planked in below his bed. I knew where it was, if it was still there. I would never tell Podgie. Mitch had started doing model airoplanes and two were hanging on the ceiling. Podgie wanted to touch them. I did not want him to. Oh Podge you should not touch them, I said.

Oh I am no going to hurt them.

Yes but if Mitch is no here, it is his stuff.

Oh he will not care, said Podgie. He lifted one down and looked inside it and was touching all its bits and the propeller too, pushing it. Oh it does not go round.

No because it is stuck down, it is glued, it is not a real propellor.

If anything came off Mitch would hate it. He stuck it all with glue and it took ages to do it right. He showed me how to but my fingers could not do it so easy. Oh but if ye keep doing it and keep doing it, said Mitch.

But I got tired with all that stuff.

Podgie lifted another one and was looking at it then looking on top of the cupboard, then at the window and on the ledge, if anything was there. I knew Podgie and he knocked stuff so I was watching him. I would not have let him knock stuff. If he had done it, I would not have let him. Now Mitch's maw shouted on me. Oh Kieron, bring Derek through to the living room.

She had cups of milk and a piece and cheese each for us. She said, Oh sit down a wee minute.

Oh I am fine standing, I said, but Podgie sat down and started eating the piece.

Mitch's da was there reading a paper. I did not like him. He hated Mitch. Mitch said it. Mitch just hated him back. Smelly old f*****g c**t. That was what Mitch called him. I got more doings than Mitch but Mitch got punched, so that was worse. My da never punched me but it was real hard skelps, he done it to yer legs and they caved in. I did not swear at my da, even in my head. Sometimes I was going to but I did not.

If he was old maybe he would punch me. Mr Mitchell was a lot older than my da. He wore big specs and they fell down his nose, so he kept shoving them up. He waited a wee minute reading his paper then stopped and put it down. Oh hullo boys.

Hullo Mr Mitchell, I said.

Oh I know this one.

Kieron Smith.

He is William's friend, said Mrs Mitchell.

Of course ye are, he takes you in his room. Oh but you are the climber. William says you are the best climber and could climb Ben Nevis. But could you climb Mount Everest?

No.

He laughed. But I did not like him saying it with Podgie there. If I was showing off, I was not. It was not me that made him say it. I was not a boaster. Mr Mitchell looked at Podgie now, pushing on his specs. Oh who are you?

I am Derek, said Podgie.

I have not heard of you.

I am his pal too.

Oh, that is nice. And it is nice he has got pals. Mr Mitchell looked to Mrs Mitchell. Where has Margaret got to? Is she not back yet?

No father.

That was Mrs Mitchell saying it. I heard her before. She called Mr Mitchell father although he was her husband. Some mothers called the husband dad. Mine did not. But sometimes she did. But she really just called him by his name. My grannie called granda dad. They all called him dad, my maw as well. But he was her dad. People did things different in families. In my house the youngest did stuff but in this one that was not it, it was the big sisters. Mitch did not do anything. That was the same in Pat's house, he had sisters too, so he did not do stuff.

Mitch only went messages if he wanted to. He knocked money off his family and that was a way he got it off his maw. I done it off mine. But he went into his maw's purse, I did not except only a few times. He went into his da's pockets as well. That is something I would not do because if he caught ye that was the worst. The one way was if it was the ice-cream van, if my da sent me down for fags and chocolate, if it was Saturday night. Oh we will get bars of chocolate.

So when the icey came round I went down to get the stuff and I just knocked money out the change. Ye just had to be careful, if ye took too much and ye waited for him counting. Usually he counted but he did not say if it was too little. How much is that chocolate? He did not ask me. So if he had. Oh I do not know what it costs, I just gave the man the money and he gave me the change.

Oh you should always count yer change. My da would say that. My maw too, Oh you must count yer money. I never asked my da for money. Maybe Matt did.

But Mitch got it off his. That was something. I said it to him. Oh if yer da gives ye money.

Well if he does not I just take it out his pockets. Mitch tried to get me to do it to mine. All the time he tried it. If yer da goes to the pub and comes back, ye just take it, he will no know. That was how he done it. He did not care if his da caught him doing it. If me and the boys were there and we did not have nothing, we got Mitch to get it. Podgie said it, Oh Mitch can you get money?

Mitch went and done it. Podgie tried to get in with Mitch because he got money. But then if he made a fool of him? I did not like it. Oh Mitch, I said, Podgie is just at it with ye, he just wants yer money.

Some Friday nights my da went to the pub after his work and did not come home till late. My maw did not like him doing it. I could have went into his coat pockets then but I did not. If he ever found out, that would have been me. That would have been the worst. My da hated thiefs the worst of all. On board the ship they just threw them over. Man overboard. Oh he was just a dirty thief. So the Captain did not stop the ship. What was worse than stealing off yer shipmates? Oh feed him to the sharks.

But if I did take his money and he found out, so what, I would just run away. I did not care if he gave me a doing. So what? The next day ye were better. I thought I would do it, but I did not. If I ran away I would.

Mr Mitchell was saying to me and Podgie about school but we were not saying much back. I would have if Podgie was not there. I wished he was not. He would tell everything to people. If Mitch's maw and da said stuff, he would just go and tell them. That was what Podgie done.

Mrs Mitchell said, Oh William is enjoying his wee holiday.

Oh yes, he will be coming back in a week or two, said Mr Mitchell. He was looking at me but I did not speak. Then I did. Oh I could write a letter.

Oh that would be nice, said Mrs Mitchell, he would like that.

I could as well, said Podgie.

Oh that is nice of you, she said.

I finished my piece and drank the milk. I gave the cup to Mrs Mitchell. I was wanting Podgie to finish his but he was just doing it slow. I saw him smiling and it was for nothing. I did not like it when he done that. He was not a real pal to people and was just wanting to see stuff about Mitch's big sisters. He had three. The oldest one was married and had two babies. I had not seen her. Margaret was the nearest one to him but that was four years older. She called him wee brother. Oh wee brother, do you want any toast?

I liked how she said it. The other sister was Carol. They did not open Mitch's bedroom door but just chapped it. In my house people opened the door and said stuff to you but his waited till you said it to them. What is it? So then the person came in.

It was because it was lasses, so ye would not see them if they were not wearing their clothes. My maw always said it, Knock before ye enter, but a lot of times ye forgot. She forgot with me and Matt, she just came in and was looking about yer room, and if ye were not dressed. Oh mum, she just went, Oh sorry, and came back out. But if she chapped the door and ye said it, Oh just a wee minute. Then it was alright. My maw just looked in yer room. Even yer private stuff, so if ye had planked something, ye had to watch it. I did not like keeping stuff, so when I used to go up the loft it was good for hiding all what ye wanted. But I was finished with the loft now. I could just never go up again. If ever I did I was finished. That was what my da said, I was on my last warning, he would just kick me out the house. I telled Mitch.

Oh we will just f*****g run away.

Mitch had done it before and talked about it a lot. But where would ye go? I said to him about the highlands. I thought the highlands was the best. But he said England because he had his relations and now that was where he was.

I thought that, maybe he just ran away, if his maw and da were not telling us. Podgie thought that too but I did not say it to him. I liked Mitch's maw. She always gave ye stuff if ye were in the house, biscuits or a piece and something. But Mitch did not like her either. And his sisters. How come he did not like his sisters? They were good. Oh I f*****g hate them, I f*****g hate them. He said it to me. Oh if I had poison I would just poison them all to death, everybody in the whole house.

People liked him saying it, Podgie and the boys laughed when he did. But I did not like him saying it. And no to everybody. If I thought that I would not say it to people. I liked Mitch. I wished it was all better. I thought about John Davis too. It was not fair.

Podgie just sipped his milk. I looked to him but he kidded on he did not see me looking. But I knew he did. I was glad to go away. Oh I think it is time to go home now. Mr Mitchell said it. I was glad, I was ready and went to the living-room door. Podgie stood up and came. Mrs Mitchell took us to the front door. Oh Kieron it would be very nice to write a letter to William, he would love it, you are his best friend.

She shut the door after us.

Oh but I wished she had not said about best friends. Podgie did not like it, he just went down the stair and we went along the street, not talking.

§

I went up for Peter and Billy but they usually just went the gether. They let me come but if I did not go up for them they did not come up for me.

But what they did was comics, I did not bother. They saved comics and went round swopping them. Billy had most comics but his maw was snobby and did not want boys up at her door. He swopped them at Peter's door. People came there to do it. I liked to see the stamps and comics but no too much and I did not save them. If it was raining they stayed in their own street. If ye were passing and they were in a close ye went in to talk and it was about songs in the Top Forty or good pictures they saw. Peter sang the songs and mimicked the people in the pictures, he could do it funny. Ye were just all laughing when he done it.

259

The other real thing was lasses. They had girlfriends and just saw them and if it was you you were the third one and it was just two and two, ye got left outside the close. I did not like that. One was Rona Craig. If her and her pal went messages for their maw Peter and Billy walked them down the shops. I liked Rona too.

Ye did not do that with Podgie and Gary. Podgie just laughed at lasses. He said things that were daft and like a wee boy. I did not laugh at it. Gary did but Peter and Billy did not. I liked going with them, they done other stuff. They listened to the radio. On Sundays ye were playing football and some went away before the game finished. Peter did it but then Billy did. We were playing football and he just stopped. Oh I am away with Peter to hear the Top Forty. I would have went too. I did not ask but if I did they would have let me. But no if Podgie was there.

But on Sunday it was the hospital. I did not like coming to see granda but usually I had to.

It was just in the ward with the other people and him in bed with the blankets down his chest and his head all baldy and his arms outside. He did not look the same and his face had changed, it looked dirty and yellow and just wee, just a wee face. Maybe if the window was open and dirt came in. It was lines in his face, the dirt was in them. I could clean it up, just wipe it if there was a cloot to do it. Then his chest where the buttons on the pyjamas were, the hair poked through, all white hair from his chest, long stuff all through the pyjamas edges and tangled up and just like hair on a head.

What if he passed away and ye were to go in and see him? His face just looking at ye. I did not want to see it. What would it look at ye for? It would just look at ye. It would just be another thing and laughing out at ye if it was creepy, if it was an evil spirit, granda was away and it took his body and then his mouth opened and his eyes too, just a wee bit. What if they opened wide and it jumped out to get ye?

Ye saw something funny and went up close to see. Ye looked in and ye knew it was not the same granda. Phantoms went into bodies then came out. The soul came out if ye passed away. It was my granda's soul if it was him. It flew out yer body and up to Heaven.

Or it flew you away. The spirit came to get ye. Ye were dead. It came to get yer spirit and take it up to Heaven. That was the Guiding Spirit. Ye held its hand and it pulled ye out yer body. And then up up up going over the chimney tops. Ye were holding on going all the way up past clouds and way way up to Heaven to sit beside a Generous Host. Nobody was turned away from the Golden Table, and it was just a feast.

But if he was not passed away, only sleeping. But then he did it when ye were there visiting. Ye would see his mouth wide open, Oh it is the last gasp. It is his dying breath.

People gasped to get it and then could not. That was granda. He just gasped and could not lift stuff, not even a screwdriver. He could not walk and could not do sparring with ye. Oh I need to get a breath son, that was what he said and breathing to get it like hiccups, wee hiccups, slow ones and his eyes big looking at ye, hit hit hit and wee squeaky sounds, hit hit. And ye wished he just would not look at ye. How come he was looking at ye. Until then he smiled. Oh it was granda it was just granda it was him after all, and nearly ye were greeting. Oh what is it son?

Oh it is just you granda.

I knew it was only granda. That is who it was. Him himself. I just did not like it. But when I came home after seeing him I was glad oh just glad I went, I was.

Men came up to see him and were Masons. My grannie told me in a quiet voice. Oh they are good men. And always smart. Oh they have nice clothes.

Granda had old friends from where he worked. They brought him stuff and he gave it to me and Matt. Lucozade and lemon juice. Oh I am no wanting that, give it to the boys.

Oh but granda it is yours, I do not want it.

Do as ye are told son.

Granda could have that voice if my maw was there or Uncle Billy. If he was angry, it sounded like that. They done what he said. My maw did not want to but she did. But he never done the voice with Auntie May. He liked her the best. That was what I thought. Her and grannie.

People liked some and no others. It was no really fair. It happened with me and Matt. No granda but he liked the two of us equal. He did. Most people liked Matt. Oh he is the first-born, said my grannie.

One time granda was sleeping and his hand was lying and I could take it and then he would smile out at me. Oh son it is you. But I did not. If he passed away I would do it and just take his hand, Oh bye bye granda, and his head would not move. That would be him dead. People are dead. My Granda Smith passed away before I was born. He was my Grannie Petrie Smith's husband. I called him Granda Petrie Smith and she checked me for it. Oh he was not a Petrie. I am the Petrie. He was a Smith.

It was just granda's cats, what about them? Grannie did not bother with cats. So if she kicked them out, where would they go? Uncle Billy could take them. Or us. If my maw let us. She did not like cats, but maybe if it was granda's she would. Oh but our house was too wee, that was what she said, you cannot swing a cat in it. There was just no free space for cats and just for nothing at all. Nobody picks up their mess. She shouted at people, Oh pick up yer mess.

But it was Matt that done it. And my da too, he left his stuff lying, his shoes and his jacket. And his cups and plates. He left them beside his chair in the living room so if ye walked by ye stepped on something. A cup. Or if ye stood on his jacket and stuff was in the pocket. Oh my fags my fags, so ye squashed the packet and it was just a stupid big row. But ye could not help it if it was down at the side of the chair. Or his ashtray, ye kicked that and the ash and the dowps all scattered. So then my maw got angry at me. Or if it was a can of beer, that was the worst, the can went flying and all the beer splashing on the carpet. Oh stupid stupid, shouting at me, my maw was shouting at me, but it was my da that left it. Oh it is just asking for trouble with Kieron there. She said that to him, it was my clumsy feet.

Then the worst happened and she was greeting. It was terrible. My maw did not greet much. My da was just looking at her. She went away out the living room. My da looked to me. Oh for G*d sake son can ye no watch where ye put yer feet?

But it was no my feet's fault it was him for leaving it there.

And the shoes down the lobby at the bathroom door. Everybody left them there. If ye needed a pee during the night ye tripped over them. When it happened to my da ye heard the crashing and shouting and if he swore too, B★★★★y d★★n thing.

I tried no to leave stuff lying about, and in the bedroom I kept my side tidy. Ye walked in and saw it. It was not my clothes lying on the floor and a stack of clothes in below the bed. Matt just kicked them under. There was a laundry thing in the bathroom and one out in the lobby so ye could just shove in yer stuff. But he did not do it. If my maw was doing a wash she had to go and find his clothes. Oh if everybody would just put their old clothes in the laundry.

But it was not everybody it was Matt.

Oh do not blame your brother.

But it is him doing it.

Oh Kieron.

But it is no me.

It is not me.

Not and not no. It is not me and not it is no me. I just got sick of it. Matt did not even make his bed. His own bed. He did not make it. So she made it. Not if I was there. She did not want me seeing. So it was still not made when he came home from school. At bedtime he just jumped in and it was all untidy and the sheets and blankets all out. He did not bother. He was just lazy. I said it to my maw.

Oh stop cliping.

So I was cliping because I told what he did. Then getting a row for what I never did. And it was him that did it. I just said it so that was me cliping. It really was not fair. My da never said nothing if it was Matt. Oh Matt Matt. Everything was Matt, he was just the goodie. That was my house.

I did not want my maw making my bed. Maybe I had stuff planked under the mattress. What if I did? I found a n★★e book on the train coming back from my grannie's. I was going to take it into school. People done that, they opened it under the desk, then out in the playground. Sometimes they hid them off ye. Gary McNab did not let ye see. But just for a laugh. He did after.

But having one in the house was a worry. Just if my maw found it. She went into our stuff. She even done it if ye were there and just lying on the bed reading a book. She was a quiet walker. Then the door jumped open and in she came. Ye got a fright the way she done it. She went to the cupboard and poked about. Oh you need clean shirts. Oh this vest is just a disgrace. Oh you do not need all those socks. Oh what happened to your new underpants? Oh see this jersey, it is dad's, dad has been looking for it.

Well I did not put it there.

Oh well somebody did.

Yes but not me. I would not take dad's jerseys, they were too big. We got trouble with socks and underwear. My maw washed them. After they were dry she put them in yer drawer but did not get the sizes right. Then with underpants, if she put my da's into my drawer and I put them on and went to school they were just hanging down all day and it was terrible. He got angry about it, but it was a laugh too when ye said it.

Other mothers did not poke about but she did. So ye could not plank stuff in yer drawers. I done it at the side of the bed and put the n**e book in with stuff like football boots and old balls and games. It was just a worry but. I was quaking. What if she came home early from work and found it? I rushed home from school at dinnertime and got it, I buried it in the backcourt and covered it over with stones. But when I went to get it it was not there, the stones were all scattered. Somebody took it. But what if it was a grown-up? What if they telled my maw? I had that in my stomach for days, what was going to happen?

§

When Gary did not come out it was just me and Podgie. One time he came home from school with me. I brought him in the house. My maw let me. Ye just saw their feet were clean or what and they waited in the lobby or else the living room if my da was no home. But with just me there Podgie went over the whole house and was going to go into my maw and da's room. I said to him, Oh do not go in there, that is my maw's room. So he stopped but he was peeping in. He still wanted to go in. I did not let him and shut the door.

He kept looking to see stuff and then with a wee smile on his face. How come? Maybe if he thought something daft about yer house, if he was just laughing at ye and telled people. Even if it was yer maw. She gave him a piece and he opened it to see inside. He done it all the time. Even she was looking, he still done it. It was rude, I saw her face. If it was a piece and cheese, or just jam, he opened the two slices and looked in. What did he do it for? I got a sick feeling, if he was going to be cheeky to her. So if my maw did not put on enough jam or the cheese was too thin, if he thought that. One time I got a cheese piece off Gary McNab's maw and the cheese was really thick, just the thickest, so even it tasted different. I quite did not like it, just if it was too thick and ye could taste a flavour that was greasy fat and ye only tasted that. Oh is that a cow? It tasted like a cow. Or else a wee baby's milk if sick was coming out its mouth. I did not like cheese too thick. Unless if it was toast and cheese, then the grease came out and tasted smashing. I made it for supper and cut thick slices. My maw did not like me doing it. The cheese melted over the toast and sparked up at the gas, sticking to the grate and the pan, making it all greasy. So if it went hard, how did ye get it off? Ye had to scrape it and watch ye did not waste the pan if ye scraped too hard. I got a row off my maw for doing it. Podgie did not know about it because in his house he did not do the dishes.

In my house ye done them. One time the boys came up for me and I was still doing it. I did not hear the bell and my maw went to the door so then she said it to them, Oh Kieron is doing the dishes.

So they all laughed at me. I did not care.

Podgie did not go pals with people except if he wanted in with them. So if he went pals with me he wanted in with me. If it was to get in my house or what, I did not know. If Gary was not there he had nobody except if it was young ones that stayed near him. He did not want that.

But a lot of times Gary did not come out. Ye went up for him and he just left ye outside. He even shut the door. So ye were sitting out on the landing stairs. He done that a few times. Even he just sat and watched the telly. You were outside waiting. He knew ye were waiting. So when he came out he told ye the programme he was watching. Oh it was a laugh, ye want to have seen what happened. And then he told ye the story about it. He done that and ye just felt, Oh I am never going to come up for him again.

But if he had a fag and shared it with ye. So ye did not know what it was, if he was yer pal or what.

Then his big brother, if he came up the stair and ye were sitting outside the door. Oh who the f★★k are you?

Oh but he knew who ye were, he just said that. He saw me on Sundays after the football and him and the big boys were playing cards. We all watched. He kidded on he did not know ye to make ye feel bad. Other ones liked him. He worked on the milk and made good wages and then got good haircuts and good clothes. If it was good style. People watched to see what he was wearing. Oh Gary's big brother has got good style. Oh it is an Italian suit and his shirt is American. Gary told us about it. Oh see that jacket, it cost a fortune and he just paid it. He is giving me his old one. I can get it taken in.

Gary's big brother gave him clothes when he grew out them. He gave him money too. I saw him do it. Come here ya wee b★★★★★d. And he gave him money. He called him a wee b★★★★★d but he gave him money. Gary saw us looking and winked to us.

My big brother never had money and did not have good clothes except at Christmas or for his birthday. He just had school ones and then if he got something off Uncle Billy but Uncle Billy was bigger and usually they did not fit. Oh you will grow into them. Then if it was trousers. Oh yer mother can shorten them. Oh she can take them in for ye.

My maw did it with her needles and thread. She took the trousers and made the bottoms loose then shortened them up and ironed them. But if Matt did not like them. Sometimes he did not wear them. My da got angry at that. Oh if your mother has taken the time to do it.

But Matt just went ben the room. He did not like fighting with my da. My da just said it was arguing. We are only arguing.

I do not want to argue.

Well why will ye not wear the trousers?

I do not like them.

I was laughing when Matt said that. My da saw me but did not say anything. But I was not laughing at him. I just laughed. It was not at Matt either. One time he got a job but only for one week then he chucked it. Imagine that. Ye had a job and got money and then just chucked it.

Gary was getting a job with his big brother next year. Ye had to wait till Secondary School. That was the same with other jobs. I was getting one too. I needed to because of money, just to get money, I never had any and just needed it. A milkboy job was best, or else the papers. Just anything. I never had any money. People knew that. Oh any fags? Oh do not ask Smiddy. Fancy a bottle of ginger? Nobody said it to me. If Mitch had money or Gary, or Podgie, but I did not unless I got it, so maybe if a woman gave me it for climbing the balcony. But they did not ask much. One time I had my fares to go to my grannie's and I met Podgie and Gary when I was going to the railway station so I did not go. I just kidded on I was out and just walking about. I bought fags with the money and shared them out.

I hated it after. I hated it. Just my grannie and granda. I thought about them. It was just terrible and rotten what I done. I was just rotten. I was a f*****g rotter. I said it in my head, Oh you are a f*****g rotter. And if people ever found out, if my grannie said it, Oh Kieron has not been to see us. And then my maw, Oh but I gave him the money, so ye just spent it on fags. It was just terrible and horrible and granda in hospital. I would never do it again.

It was Gary and Podgie's fault. They said it to me. Oh you have never got any f*****g money.

I did not like going with them when Mitch was not there. They ganged up on ye. I went up for Podgie and his maw came to the door. Oh Derek is out playing.

So he was out and had not come up for me. That was what that meant. I went up for him but he did not come up for me. So if he was out with Gary. But they never came up for me.

Then I thought about pals. Who brought ye into their house and who did not? And who brought people into their house but no you? Because that was Gary, he took Podgie in but no me. How come?

Podgie did not take anybody in. His maw did not let him. Maybe it was his wee sister, if they did not want ye seeing her.

But another time Podgie came home with me after school he just came in my house. He knew my maw was not home till five so he just put his foot in and came in.

But I did not want him in my room because with Matt's stuff, what if he looked in it or knocked stuff? I wanted just to go out but he wanted to stay in. He said stuff in yer house. I did not like it. If it was outside it was okay but no if it was inside. Hoh Smiddy imagine ye had a sister? What if ye did and she was s★★y? Oh if ye were seeing her and she was n★★e. I thought if he wanted to w★★k but I would not have let him.

I did not like him saying stuff. I did not have a sister. But what if I did and she was s★★y? Podgie would just want to see her. That was what he was meaning. If he was there, he would ask all personal stuff about her underwear clothes and what, did she leave her stuff lying, if it was her k★★★★★rs on the floor or if I ever saw her with no many clothes on, n★★e or what, if ever she was n★★e and whatever she was doing or having a bath, if she just walked about the house in her bare feet and if she was wearing a b★a, some lasses did, just her b★a and p★★★★es, if ye saw her t★ts and bare b★m, so if ye got a s★★★★y seeing her, even if she was yer sister so what if she was s★★y? Gary McNab told me. Oh he watches his wee sister getting her clothes off and has a w★★k. Gary said that to me, if Podgie done that, that was just terrible, if it was yer sister, a wee sister. Podgie was just a rotter and a bully except only Gary, Gary could say stuff about people. He done it against me and Mitch, Oh they just go for w**ks, they go down the field to do it. That was what Gary said. I did not care. So if I got a riddy. Oh Smiddy has got a riddy. People said that, Oh if ye get a riddy it means ye done it.

I did not like Podgie saying stuff in my house. He done it in front of people too but that was just to get ye. But if it was just you and he done it. I did not like that and it was in the kitchenette and ye were just thinking, Oh that is where my maw sits. He was sitting in the same seat and saying s**y stuff, but in yer house it was just dirty. I hated him doing it. My maw went here making the tea and doing the washing and all what she done.

He said it to other ones that had sisters, Primary 5s and 6s. Oh I would s**g your sister. He said that to people. Oh your sister has got a big f***y. Oh can I f**l yer sister's t*ts. If I had a sister and he said it to me, if ever he even tried it, even just tried it. I would not have let him if it was mine. If ever he said s**y stuff about her. I would not let him. He done it the worst to wee Rab McKerrow. Then it was Bobby Millar. But he did not do it so much to Bobby because he was in Second Year at Secondary School but it was just how his wee sister was Sandra Millar. People said all stuff about her and got a f**l. She let boys do it. Other boys than us. Bigger. People said, Oh she is a r**e. But she was not a r**e, but she gave people f**ls.

Gary McNab told us. Boys out Secondary School went with her to the back close where she stayed. She let them get a f**l. Bobby was her big brother but he was not a good fighter and not good at stuff. He shouted at Sandra but she shouted back at him. She was in 1st year so a year above me. People came to the close when their maw and da was at work. They just shouted up the close to her. Is Sandra coming out? Sandra! Ye coming out!

They were the same age as Bobby else older. He hated her for doing it. She hated him back. She just went out. People said if she would go with them. But she did. But at first she did not. Oh get away get away. That was what she said but they were going, Oh please Sandra please, oh just for a wee minute, oh please Sandra.

So then she let them do it. She said they all were a bunch of dirty bees but she let them, she just let them do it. She went round the back close with them so they were going to f**l her. They were just going to do it. Ye saw her taking them and she was going to let them. We went to watch. Two of them were on lookout at the back close. and they saw us. They were Second Years, same as Gary's big brother. We played football with them. At football it was okay if we were there but here, if we went over. Well, we would not go over. But if we did? We never would. They just were watching us. We did not see her, she was just up the steps but boys came out the close.

It was only some she let do it. No if ye were younger. Ones that done it just laughed and then if ye were playing football. Oh did ye get a f**l off clatty Sandra? Oh her f***y is f*****g minging, it is minging, it is smelly as f**k. That was what they said. Everybody was laughing. Oh did clatty Sandra give ye a w**k? Boys said that. But she did not, you got a f**l off her but she did not touch you.

Oh please Sandra please, oh just for a wee minute. And then she was letting them. Papes too. Gary said it. He knew ones that did, they went up for Sandra too.

Papes. Imagine that. Sandra let Papes do it. I did not think she would have let that happen. How come? It was no fair. If Papes had their own lasses, they should just have got them. How come they did not? How come they went with her? She should not have let them. She should not have let them. The Papes all would be laughing and she just let them. They should have got their own lasses and no laughing at ours. They all would be laughing. I did not like that. Papes should have their own lasses.

Gary looked when I said it.

Sandra is a Proddy, she should not be letting them. They will just laugh at her.

Podgie laughed at me saying it.

No but Podgie, I said, They should have their own lasses, they should not be laughing at ours. I do not like it if they are laughing. I do not think it is right that they are.

No. I do not either, f*****g Pape b*****ds.

Fenian c**ts, said Gary. That is all they are. Tam Fairley and his pal, I saw them going.

Fairley is a cheeky big b*****d, said Podgie.

He is big-headed at football, I said, he thinks he is the best player.

He is a good dribbler, said a Primary 6, but he is too slow.

Gary said, If she lets Papes do it and no f*****g us, that is not fair either. And then they are just laughing at her, Papes.

Just because they go to Secondary School, said the Primary 6.

It has to be f*****g Secondary, said Podgie. He did not look at the Primary 6. Podgie let Primary 6s come with us but we did not talk much to them.

Oh she is a just a complete r**e, said Podgie, that is all she is, she is a f*****g p**p.

Gary said, Oh but imagine ye got the f*****g pox and yer t****r fell off!

Everybody laughed. But it was stupid. But what if it was not? It was a joke a boy telled when we were playing football. It was about a prostitute and how she was like a film star and was just beautiful. Then the soldier went with her and what happened he got the pox and his p***k fell off.

But it was funny how he telled it, just daft. But it came into my head when Gary said it, just if it did happen, and it was you, if ye were just doing it, and then something else and after it it just fell off, so it was just, it just fell off. Ye tried to imagine it. I could not. If ye needed a pee what would happen? It would come out yer belly button or something. Ye could not imagine it. Ye would have to pee out yer belly button, I said.

Oh would ye f**k. It would just be like a f***y, said Podgie. He pointed at me. Belly button! Gary laughed and so did the Primary 6.

What are you laughing at? I said.

Oh it is just thinking about it.

You have no even got a t****r, said Podgie.

Oh but imagine it was Sandra, said Gary, she is just clatty.

Aye but you telled us ye would go with her, I said.

So did you you c**t.

No I did not.

Oh you f*****g liar Smiddy ye did so.

I did not.

Podgie laughed. I bet ye f*****g would p**p her!

No I would not.

She is a f*****g cow, said Gary.

Well she would not take you, I said.

She would not take you either.

Maybe she would.

Well away and f*****g ask her.

No.

I dare ye, said Podgie. Oh do it!

You do it.

Are ye feared?

Gary said, Oh Smiddy, maybe if ye asked her she would.

Go and f*****g try it, said Podgie.

No.

Oh but I am daring ye! Ye have got to. Just if we can get a f**l, go and ask her.

Oh Podge, no, I am not going to.

Gary laughed. Oh Smiddy what would ye say if ye did? Just if ye did.

I am no going to.

But just if ye did.

No.

We are not asking ye to go, just if ye did, what would ye say?

Podgie was laughing now. I said to him, What would you?

It is f*****g you Smiddy it is no me. Come on, just say it!

Just what they say, oh please Sandra please.

Gary laughed and pointed at me. Oh please Sandra please!

Podgie laughed too. A big f*****g riddy! Look! He has got a big f*****g riddy. Oh please Sandra please!

But that is what they say.

No they do not.

Aye they do.

They f*****g do not.

Aye they do, I heard them.

No ye did not you c**t! Podgie and them were laughing at me.

Two Primary 6s were there. Podgie let them. They stayed near him and Gary. One of them had a sister and telled Podgie about her, Oh she comes out her bath and just with a towel.

Imagine that if it was yer sister. I did not mind Primary 6s coming but if they were there and laughing at ye. I would have battered their head in. They were all laughing. That was Podgie. But I knew about it with Sandra Millar and he did not, only what Gary said. Gary thought it was just him knew but I knew too. I did really. People f**t her t*ts and her legs too. If it was her f***y, maybe it was. Ye were to sit on the step and she stood beside ye and that was it, so ye done it then, that was what she done, and she stood beside ye and ye were just sitting on the step, so that was when, ye just done it, so if ye put yer hand up and she just let ye so ye just did it and I knew what it was.

Oh but if it was yer sister. Sandra's brother Bobby did not come out much, just stayed in his house and done model-kits. Mitch did not like him doing it because he done them too, but no so many as Bobby. Ye could see his from the pavement outside if it was night-time and his light was on. He had them hanging from the ceiling, wee airoplanes. If he came out to play it would be fights all the time. Ye could not laugh if it was yer sister they were talking about and Podgie there. Ye would have to fight him else ye were a s***ebag cause ye would be the worst coward. So if the big ones were feeling her f***y and touching her t*ts.

Podgie could sink ye with one punch. I would not care. If it was a bottle, I would batter him with it because if it was yer sister ye were no going to let that happen. I would not be feared of him. If he was bigger than me. So what. How because they were big so they could beat ye, so what, I was no feared of him. Maybe I was, so if I was, ye just had to move fast. My granda showed me that and to get them off balance, ye stand square and go to the side to shove him and shoving his left arm and he would fall down. Because if yer man is heavy and ye get them off balance they fall to the ground and it is all that weight they carry. And ye just had to boot them. And it was no dirty fighting, it just had to be else they would get ye. Uncle Billy said that. Then if they got ye down, tough luck.

In the old place a fat boy was there and we all were in the park. He was no scared of any best fighters. Me and him were wrestling and we were having to do something and he had on his vest and big fat legs. Older ones laughed at him, Oh fatso, wee Smiddy will beat ye!

Out the wee ones I was a best fighter. But he just was looking at me. But he knew I was a best fighter. So then we were wrestling and he was on the floor and I got on top of him but he threw me over and sat on top of me. I could not breathe. His big b*m was on top of me and his knees on me too. I could not move even a wee bit. He looked down at me, and a big red face. Do ye give in!

No.

Do ye give in?

No.

I would not give in. I tried to throw him off but I could not, he was too heavy, and his knees squashing down on my arms, just sore. My granda said about big heavy ones and ye just watched for balance and were square on with yer feet but side to side to get him and if he came in ye grabbed his arm and pulled him through and down he went because with his big weight, so that was him. For Uncle Billy it was just boot into him. But no my granda. Oh son you are a defender. If somebody comes at you ye just defend yerself. But do not talk about booting into boys else that is the dirtiest fighting. But if it was Podgie and ye were fighting him, ye would have to else he would have gave ye a real doing.

§

I did not like Sandra's face much but it came into yer mind if ye were near her close and looking up at her window or else her brother Bobby was there and he was looking down at ye. He did not like ye there. And ye were thinking it, if she was there on the step and if

274

ye were beside her. Then if ye saw her coming home from school, she did not look at ye. I did not look at her.

Oh but Lyndsey Farrel, she was Sandra's pal. People wanted a f**l off her too but she did not let them. I was down at the shops and saw her. She was looking at me. I thought she was. Another boy was there and we were smoking a fag. She had black hair coming down both sides of her eyes, and her skirt and her legs just like the way she walked and then how she turned round and just how her skirt stuck out, and just swinging. Some lasses' skirts just done that and it looked good just how it went, I thought it was good.

A lot of people fancied Lyndsey Farrel. She came past and they all watched her and if they shouted else whistled. Podgie and Gary done it and said about her because she went with Sandra Millar. So she was a r**e, or a boy p****d her. Oh he p****d the a**e off her. Oh she is just a pure p**p. She is worse than Sandra Millar. I did not like them saying about her. Oh Smiddy fancies wee Lyndsey. Oh Smiddy's got a f*****g beamer.

Other boys were there and they still were saying it. They were not real pals. If they were, real pals would not do that. Oh f*****g b*****ds, I said it in my head.

Gary just laughed at ye too. But take away Podgie. If Podgie was not there. So then Gary would be different. It was Podgie. It was just him. He was just like the worst bully. I thought that about him. I would never ever take him in my house again, never ever. Never. Just never at all.

So if ye were fighting him. I thought about it. If I could. It was not like granda and ye were boxing. For Podgie ye went and got something so ye could hit him. So if it was a brick. Ye just got something. Uncle Billy said that. Podgie was just a dirty fighter. He done stuff to people. Then if he picked on ye. He done it to me. If ever he did it again I was going to get him. He tried to make a fool of ye. I hated him doing it. He could not make a fool of me. He did not know stuff and just thought he did. If he thought I could not get him, I could.

If it was the old place I would have. Ye done things there, he did not know. Oh and if it was boys younger than me and he still said stuff, if it was Primary 6s and they were there. So they could say it as well, if they thought that. If I was just stupid. Oh Smiddy cannot fight. Maybe they thought that. If they were going to laugh at me. They would never laugh at me. So if Podgie wanted to get me, I would get him. I would do it. Even it was a hammer. My granda had one and I used to look at it when I was wee. It had a round bit at one end and the hammer bit at the other. It was a beauty. It was just old and was not dirty at the iron bit, just all shiny where granda used it to bash stuff. I thought that about the hammer, it was like an old man, one that was a smashing old fighter. Ye could not imagine anybody ever beating granda's hammer and just how the iron bit fitted the wood and was shaped there with holes in it so the wood came through. It was better than all the workies' ones. It was all just smooth and how it fitted in, and its smell was just something like oily stuff. The handle went thicker in the middle and ye carried it straight up or else straight down but if it was straight down ye had to watch if it hit yer knee, tough luck how sore it was, it just was a thud and it pinged in yer knee and ye could not walk. I done it when I was wee. Granda had a hatchet too. It was for firewood, ye just split the wood, ye tapped in the blade then battered it. He showed Matt how to do it. He said I was not to until I got bigger.

I did not know if he still had the hatchet. I asked my Uncle Billy. He was up in grannie's house. I did not know he was there. He was playing with the cats. Even the one that did not like playing. It came to Uncle Billy. Oh look at that, the wee traitor. Granda used to say it but just smiling, seeing Uncle Billy petting its head.

He was doing that just now and laughing about stuff. He was taking me to see granda. Grannie and my Auntie May were away up already but we were waiting for Matt.

Uncle Billy made jokes if ye said something daft. But sometimes it was not funny and ye wanted him to hear ye. It was different to a joke what ye were saying, it was no for laughing, ye just wanted him to listen to ye. He done it when I was wee, he tickled ye to make ye laugh. But ye were wanting to tell him stuff. If people done something to ye and were hitting ye and going to get ye and just batter ye, he did not listen, just tickled ye worse and it made ye angry, I got angry. Uncle Billy Uncle Billy. I shouted at him. But he tickled ye more and more till then ye were laughing too, ye could not stop it. But I did not like him doing it and if I kicked him hard then he put me down. Oh you wee buggar ye.

But he just laughed at ye again. Oh Kierie boy, I am a wee brother same as you.

Oh but you just have big sisters, if it was a big brother that just hits ye all the time.

Aye but who is my big sisters?

My maw and my Auntie May.

That is what I am saying, a pair of warriors. Imagine them as big sisters! Dear oh dear oh dear.

But it still was not so bad as brothers, I knew it was not.

And it all was different now from when he was wee. It was. He did not think so but I told him all what was happening out in the scheme. It was not the same as the old place, and fighting too, it was all different. Some had knives, and it was blades, ye just called it blades. Oh he carries a blade. People said it. They hid them in their socks else down their trousers if the cops came or just if other gangs were there. So if they came to get ye ye just took it out and ye stabbed them. Mitch had one and it was planked in his room and I could get it off him if somebody was after me.

Oh Kierie hold it hold it hold it.

Oh but Uncle Billy I am just saying if they are after me and if they have got a blade to stab me. Some do it and then if they do and ye just have yer own one and ye take it out.

Hold it. I shall tell you something Kierie, never you carry a blade. That is one thing never to do. If ye do that ye are in trouble.

Aye but

Listen to me now. What if the guy takes it off ye?

Oh but he would not.

Aye but what if he did?

I would not let him.

But what if he just takes it? Some fellows take out a blade but do not know what to do with it or if they are feared to use it. So then the one they are fighting just grabs it out their hand and stabs ye with it. See because he is not feared to use it. Telling you son that is what happens in this life, ye take a knife to a bad b★★★★★d that is out to get ye and he takes it off ye and stabs ye. So what if it kills ye? It is your knife, that is the one that has done it. So that is you, dead by yer own hand. How would ye like that? That is what happens. Never ever carry a blade.

But what if they have one for you?

Well ye take it off them.

But what if ye cannot?

Ye just hit them with something.

But what if ye cannot get to them?

Oh well ye just run for C★★★★t sake. Kierie boy, ye used to be a fast runner. Can ye no run fast any more?

Oh but Uncle Billy

G★d almighty son do not let yer mother hear ye talking like that. Blades and what have ye, that is just trouble. Do not ever carry a blade.

Uncle Billy stopped talking, he had a paper and started reading it. He was angry. I saw that he was, he did not like about knives but if people had them. He did not think they did but they did. It was different from when he was young.

After that Matt came. Uncle Billy said bye bye to the cats and took us to see granda. He got us chips out the chip shop and we ate them going along the road. He did not get his own ones but just took some off us. He smoked when he was eating them, he smoked a lot, and was saying about granda, if we went to see him a lot of times or what.

Oh quite a lot, said Matt.

Matt was good at talking. Uncle Billy liked him. People liked Matt. I did too, a lot of times, if he was yer brother, ye just liked him. My maw liked Uncle Billy. So did Auntie May. They laughed at jokes and had fun and the same with granda, they talked to him. I liked it when they did. Oh dad do ye remember when ye took us to Glennifer Braes and we went through the puddle?

My grannie was laughing too. She had a funny laugh and with a hankie covering her mouth. She did not want ye to hear her. She kept her mouth closed. And she did not kiss ye. You could kiss her but she never kissed you, she put her cheek to ye. Oh do not kiss my lips, you should not kiss a child's lips. Just kiss me on the cheek son.

Her skin was the softest. People's skin was soft but hers was the softest. Auntie May laughed at her. But my maw did not, but she smiled. My maw did not talk much about their old days, it was just Auntie May and Uncle Billy. But my maw liked when they did, so did my grannie. Sometimes my maw looked as if she should give them a row, Oh that was mischief, we were just scallywags, we should not have done it.

Listen to her, said my Auntie May. Oh Cath.

Auntie May held granda's hand and so did Uncle Billy. But my maw and my grannie did not but just looked. I did not see granda smiling, it was just the breathing all the time ye just heard it and always heard it. People just looked, just looked at one another and that was what they were hearing. Poor granda. Ye just thought that, it was just a horrible shame. Oh he cannot get a breath, said my grannie.

It was his lungs too, no just the growth. Uncle Billy said it. They were just closing up. So if it was skinny lungs there was not much space left for the air to go through. So he was wheeching. Wheeech wheeech. Uncle Billy said, Wheeech.

I did not think it sounded wheeech. It was Hohhhh hohhhh, hohhh hohhh.

Granda done daft things when they were wee and it made them all laugh. My da did not. If they were all talking he just looked and with a wee smile but he did not speak much. It was not his family. I felt sorry for him. But he had his through on the east coast. But he did not see them much. They were mine too. If ye were the boy ye had the two families but yer father only had one. No he did not, he had two as well, it was just another family, it was his father's family, so that was my grandfather, my other one from granda, he died before I was born. He was the Smith. So we were Smiths after him. It was all the Smiths, just all the fathers.

I liked it if granda's old pals were there. One was Shuggy Baird.

He came in and my grannie said it, Oh it is Shuggy, and she went away and gave him a big cuddle. My granda was no big and Shuggy was weer but ye saw how his arms were thick. If he punched ye ye would feel it. Uncle Billy said, Oh that is Shug Baird, he is a hard man on the Clyde. That is nice of him coming to see dad.

A nurse came in beside us, Oh there is too many round the bed, you will need to go away some of you.

Uncle Billy took me and Matt out to the waiting room and outside the corridor so he could smoke a fag.

§

Matt did not watch television much. He stayed in the bedroom reading books and swotting or with his radio listening to music. Just if it was football and sport, so then he came through. It was amateur internationals. My maw was there. She did not look except maybe her head would come up, Ohhhh, if one of the boxers got a right tanking. She read a magazine and was knitting. She did not like boxing but it was amateurs so she quite liked it. Oh your grandfather would love this!

Then it was a darkie fighting against a white man. Just with my da there it was a worry, he got angry at stuff. Sometimes ye went out the room but boxing was good. I kept my head down. I was sitting on the floor. My maw's needles clacked the gether, that was all ye heard. Then came an argument and ye did not know to be glad or sad because it was Matt and my da, my belly just, ohhh and my throat funny. I kidded on I was not listening. My da was saying about darkies and Matt did not like it and ye heard his voice, it was cheeky. Oh but dad, he said, what if the white man gave the Sign of the Cross?

He did not, said my da.

Well but if he is an RC, what if he is? Some do not make the Sign.

No if they are playing at Ibrox they do not. They know better. It would be b****y pandemonium.

But what if he is one?

What are you b****y talking about, said my da, keeping his voice low as if he was not angry. But he was angry. And swearing. My maw hated it. She would not let me and Matt say bad words either. Out the house I said them if I wanted. I did not used to but now I did. I just did. But not swear words. I tried it sometimes but it did not sound good.

My da did not like Matt talking like this, not with me and my maw there. Ye were not to say stuff back to him because he was the father. He was not allowed to when he was a boy and we should not either. Matt said to him, I am just saying what if the white man is a Catholic? What if it is him and a darkie fighting together?

My da's knees came up under him, so he was sitting on his feet. That was a way he sat. His fags were on top of the boiler cupboard at the side of the fire. He reached for the packet and the matches.

Who would you want to win? said Matt. His voice was rushing and jittery and he did not look at my da.

My maw said, Do not be cheeky to your father.

I am not being cheeky, I am just saying.

My da had a fag out the packet now and got it lighted. He stared at the match burning then blew out the flame. He turned to look at Matt. What do you know you do not know nothing. Once ye have been out and seen a bit of the world then ye can talk.

I am just saying.

Oh ye are just saying. Ye are always just saying. Why do you not keep yer trap shut?

Oh John!

My da just blew out loud and then lit his fag.

Oh you are too noisy, said my maw. Both of you.

But Matt said to my da, Would ye want somebody to win?

Pardon? My da stared over at him.

Who would ye want to win?

My maw laid her knitting down. You are just too noisy. The pair of you are.

That was the way my maw done it. But they were not too noisy they were just saying it in low voices. She went back to the knitting.

My maw hated it if people argued and if it was Matt and my da that was the worst. But my da did not bother with what she said and was looking at Matt. Now Matt looked at him. My da said, So what are ye saying? What are ye saying?

Nothing.

Oh, nothing! My da kept looking at him.

Matt said, Do you want it to be a draw so they both lose?

I beg yer pardon? What did you say?

Matt did not talk. It was cheeky what he had said. He had a red face. My da took a long draw on his fag and blew the smoke out slow. I am asking what you said.

It was just a question.

Oh it was just a question.

My maw's face was red too. She had her head bent to the knitting. I could see her eyes from where I was sitting. She said to me, Oh Kieron, who is the teams boxing?

Wales and England.

Yes, said Matt to my da, I did not know you wanted the English before the Welsh.

I do not care.

Oh. Matt sounded like it was a joke.

That is right, said my da. He was very very angry. He did not smoke his fag, just held it in his fingers then saw on top of the boiler cupboard, maybe for his ashtray. His teacup was there but he did not lift it.

My da never took the English before the Welsh and Ulster. Only if it was Ireland. Ireland was the worst of all. He said that, I would rather have the Gerries before them. Oh the Irish, they get everything, just everything. But in the boxing here the wee darkie was in the Wales corner. My da said, Oh he is not Welsh, he is a darkie. You do not get darkies that are Welsh, that is just a joke. And he said about the English boxer, Oh I like him, he is a tough wee boy.

My brother said, Oh but dad what if he is a Catholic?

He is not a Catholic.

Yes but what if he is?

Shut yer d**n mouth.

What if the darkie is one too?

Pardon?

What if he is?

What ye b****y blethering about?

I am only saying what if he is?

Matt's voice sounded funny and was more jittery. What was he going to do? Ye did not know. I wanted to see his face but I kept my head down and did not because my da, if he saw me listening. He would hate me listening. But just his voice, it was just so so angry. It was not the same for me. He just looked at me and shaked his head. Now a thought came to me about Matt, and just if he gret, what if he gret? I had not seen him greeting. When was it last? I could not think of it. He said to my da, There is a coloured boy in my class.

Ye telled me before, said my da.

Yes, well he is, and he is a Catholic.

Oh ha ha.

He is.

Ha ha.

I am telling ye dad he is a Catholic.

So what do ye want me to do?

Nothing.

So what ye telling me for?

Just telling ye.

Ye have a good b****y cheek in ye son that is what I will tell you.

I am just talking.

Oh aye ye are just talking, ye do enough of that.

Oh please stop this fighting, said my maw.

My da looked across to her.

Just stop it, please.

Well, I do not know what he is talking about. He took his feet down off the chair and sat back with his paper and opened another page. The boxing match was still on but he kept reading the paper and was not interested to watch. Matt too, he waited a wee minute then got up and went out the room.

Usually in our house ye said goodnight if ye were going to bed. If ye did not ye were in a huff or it was fighting. That was it with Matt. After he left the room there was no speaking. I did not like sitting there as if it was us three against him. Sometimes he spoke to my da and it was snobby, he just sounded snobby, and my da did not like it. He did not say aye and ye and telled and my da did. Matt did it to get ye. He got in with my maw by doing it and my da did not like it. My maw just liked Matt for talking nice. Me too, if I did it.

Matt was in the bedroom so I could not go there and it was raining out the living-room window so not to the balcony either, it would be raining there too. I went to see if it was. In some countries ye got that, it was raining on one side of the road and ye could just cross over to the other pavement and ye were okay. But here if it was raining it was everywhere, just all the time. Maybe I could go to the bathroom. But if people wanted the toilet ye needed to let them in. So I just stayed and saw the boxing till my da said, Right Kieron. So bedtime. It was only quarter to ten so too soon but it was bedtime he was meaning so I had to go.

It was because of granda in hospital. My maw was sad about it and us too. I was in bed and said it to Matt but he did not speak back.

§

I went to my grannie's by myself. I was glad. I liked it better. I got off the train and down to the river and just which way I wanted. The ferry was no in so I walked and ran along to the carferry. I just wanted to. It was a long long walk and all big lorries went on the road. The carferry took ye across and ye came out by the dumps. People were there and I did not go in, in case it was gangs.

Then ye were at my old park. If ye went the other way ye came to the hospital. I looked for old pals but never saw any, just wee boys fishing round the pond. Ye had to watch it for other ones. They did not know ye and thought ye were a stranger. I went to where ye got a game of football but nobody was there. So into the library. It was the same except a different woman. I was looking at the books. It was great seeing all them after the mobile. But I did not have my ticket and could not get any out. I read them at a table.

And then my grannie, I forgot. I asked the time and it was late. I rushed out and away up the street and up the stair and flapped the letterbox. But nobody. It was dark when I looked through. They were away to the hospital. I did not know what to do but then just I would go myself. Grannie and them would be there. Maybe I would beat them if I ran fast, if they were just walking. They would not go on the bus. I walked and ran. My grannie would not be angry. Oh but Auntie May, she just looked at ye and ye knew it was wrong, ye had just done something. And I had, it was my own fault.

I knew where to go in the hospital and ran along the path. No many people were there. Usually there were. Grannie and Auntie May visited all the time. They were feared for granda. They thought if he passed away. I knew it was that. People all were sad and just quiet all the time.

Oh but I was late. They waited for me and I did not come. Because I went on the ferry then in the park and the library. I had money for the subway but just spent it and frittered my time. That was what I done. The teacher checked me for it. Oh Kieron is a careless boy and just fritters his time. She said it to my maw, Oh if he just did his work, he is bright except he fritters. Oh you are a bright boy. My maw told my da.

Oh but grannie would not mind. If I done stuff she just looked but not giving me a row. But coming late, if something happened to granda. Oh he had passed away. I was late to come and so it happened. I was doing stuff. I did not come and he went. I did not think about him. Just other stuff and all nonsense, Oh his head is full of nonsense, he is just a careless boy, if he just stopped his nonsense. I should not have done it, I just done it and was a stupid, stupid rotter.

My Auntie May was beside the outside door, smoking a fag. She waved to me. Oh Kieron, come here. She gave me a cuddle and said, Did ye go up to the house? Oh we had to leave early. Yer grannie was saying ye were coming. Did Mrs Duncan tell ye? She was looking out for ye.

Oh I did not see her, I just ran up the stair.

Grannie says to her to tell ye. Sorry about that son we just came away fast. Auntie May took a draw of her fag and looked up at the sky. It was white clouds, white clouds. Yer mummy is in with Billy and yer da. Away in. Give me a kiss first, she said.

I did it and she said, Oh but now a real kiss.

So I gave another one. Oh when did ye last wash yer face? she said.

I did not know. But it was just for fun, she was laughing at me. She done it to Matt, now she was doing it to me. She had not done it much. Oh are you shaving yet?

I went along the corridor to the door into the ward. Matt was there with my da. My da waved. I went round behind. Nurses were at the desk and no looking at us. Uncle Billy came out and my da was talking to him. My da came now and put his hand on my shoulder. Go and see yer granda. He said to Uncle Billy, He will regret it if he does not. Oh Matt, you go in with Kieron.

Yes dad.

It was curtains round the bed and I was glad Matt was there. My maw just was looking at me, holding my grannie's hand. I stood down from granda's feet in the bed. His eyes opened a wee bit. I thought they did and he was smiling. Maybe he was. I was smiling at him. I knew about what it was, how come I was to see him, and my da told me. If he was going to die, that was how, he was going to pass away. That was what it was. That was them telling ye, that was the grown-ups, they did not say it but that was it and poor granda, I just felt that, poor granda, it was just a shame for him and the grown-ups did not tell ye. Poor granda. What if he did not know?

I would just tell him. Ye saw the bumps in the bed where his feet were. He would pass away so ye would never see him again. He would go to Heaven because he was good. Ye went except if ye were evil.

If ye believed it. People did not. All white clothes and high voices singing and just smiling all the time. What about? How come everybody all was smiling? Matt said it to my maw. I heard but he did not know. My da was not there. Oh it was all stupid and just white garments, people all just wearing them. How come? And all just looking and, Oh oh, oh oh.

Matt was laughing but my maw said, Oh yes well maybe you will go to Hell for saying it.

Maybe I will, Matt said. Maybe I will. And it was Hell, he might go to Hell and he did not care. Oh my maw was not angry. But maybe she was. Oh but she just looked at him. Yes well Matthew maybe you will, maybe you will.

Oh I am very scared.

It is nothing to be sarcastic about, if it is people's beliefs.

I was sitting at the side of the settee and could not see his face, if he was laughing. His voice sounded it. But if it was to God. Ye could not be sarcastic to God because it was no fair if ye did. I did not like Matt saying about God, no about God. It was not fair, if God could not say nothing to him. He could not. God was fair, and a fair fighter. He would not be a bully or one that booted into ye when ye were down on the ground.

But He would give ye a good go. But He would always beat ye, He just won all His fights. If it was the Devil. That was the only one that could fight God but he always got beat. Was he God's brother and got cast out? Maybe he was. So then he was the wee brother but maybe he was Jesus's brother. He just stayed in the shadows and was not a fair fighter. He lurked below and took advantage. If it was a blade, would he carry one? But God would not, unless for self defence. Then He would.

Matt laughed but I hope it was not to God. If he was just laughing, and it was at God. It was not fair because God would not do anything to him. He could just say it, because God would not get angry and would just see ye and just wish ye would do it better and just be a better boy.

If ye could be one. Ye wished ye could. I wished it. Ye just could not. Except if God helped ye. People said He would oh if only ye ask, just pray and if ye ask it. Oh God help me.

I prayed that. I did not always but a lot of times I did. A lot of times I did not pray at all, ye were just asleep. Now I lay me down to sleep, and ye were, and ye did not wake up and ye just forgot, and then the next night ye thought about it, Oh did I say my prayers last night? Oh I forgot and then if ye said them twice. I done that and changed it for the second one. God bless my father and my mother and my brother and everybody and then I put on somebody like a teacher or a neighbour. One time I thought of doing Pat's grannie, just trying it, how it was if it was a RC, imagine ye prayed for a RC? But if it was just somebody's grannie. I did that.

God did not get angry at ye. But He could if He wanted. He could get ye. He could get Matt if He wanted. He just did not. Just because He did not. Because He did not want to. God was God. He was kind. People said He was not, how it was all diseases and babies dying and then if somebody was murdered, how come He let that happen and the cops did not catch the one that done it?

God is kind.

What did ye say? Hoh Kieron, are you awake? Kieron, are you awake?

Yes.

I thought ye were away to sleep?

I am just no talking.

Ye forgot to say yer prayers.

No I have not, I am going to.

I thought ye had stopped saying them. I do not hear ye saying them. Eh Kieron?

I just say them quiet, I just whisper.

Ye can say them into yerself. Ye can. Ye can if ye want. Why do ye not?

Because.

Then he was saying Because what? But I did not say anything

back. Sometimes I did not like talking to Matt. No about prayers and stuff. He acted it. So he knew everything. Because he was older than me. I did not think he knew everything. He did not say his prayers. He stopped a while ago. But he said he said them. It was just into himself. Oh but I did not believe him. I said it into myself but it did not work. And what if God does not hear ye?

Oh but He hears everything. People said that but I did not think so. Not everything. Not rubbish stuff. Oh Kieron is going to the ice-cream van or down the shops for his maw. God does not know that. Oh he is away down the street to play heidies. God does not know that.

I said prayers into myself but it was just not good. God would not know. He could not hear everything in the world. If it was inside yer head, He could not hear it. Because if ye were not speaking it, just thinking it, then if ye were not and it was just there.

How could He hear things in yer head if they were just there and ye were not thinking them? Maybe He did but maybe He did not, maybe He did not.

So if He knew everything. Maybe He did not want to. If it was bad stuff and ye done it, if ye done bad stuff. Well that was up to Him. If He did He did. If it was God, God was God. If ye believed in Him. I did. Some people did not. They did not believe in Him. It was not fair. He could not fight back. God could not. If people said stuff about Him. Oh well say it to His face and do not just be a coward. Matt was a coward. Maybe he was. It was not fair. Ye could imagine God if He just done something if He was angry but He was not angry. Oh if He is wrathful. But God was not wrathful. God was kind and did not think all bad things about ye and if ye done bad stuff, He did not listen to it all or see it all if it was just wee things and just rubbish stuff.

Now I lay me down to sleep I pray the Lord my soul to keep.
If I should die before I wake I pray the Lord my soul to take.
God bless everybody and make me a good boy
For Jesus sake, Amen.

I did not care about Matt. He could hear me. I could say my prayers. I did not care about him. He knew I did not swear. I did not say any swear words. And what was rude words, I did not say them. I just did not. That was me. And tried to speak good, I did. If they laughed at me. Gary did. Oh Kieron is posh. I did not care. I was not posh. If I was posh. I did not care. I did not care about any of them. I wanted to swear and just say things, anything too and I would have said it, even about my granda if about him I would have said it, anything just about him and even if I was greeting and I would say it because I felt that and my hair was crinkling on my head and I was greeting and it was just quiet but Matt heard me doing it because I stopped it and I heard him in his throat making that noise no to breathe so just to listen and it was me just to hear it, just about granda, if I was saying about him or just thinking, Matt knew it. I did not like it that he did, if he did. It was just all dark outside, ye could see it through the curtains.

§

I thought about my granda, how God took him and not old people ye saw even if it was a Grannie Petrie Smith and ones that were sick. Ye saw an old person and if they were at the train station or walking with a walking stick and they were very old, they were walking and my granda was not, he was just dead or what, passed onto the other side. Auntie May said that. Oh dad has passed onto the other side.

Oh it is just Fate, God wills it. Matt said it was not our fault, God willed it for granda. It was not fair but Fate gave him it. Fate deals a blow to ye. If God wills it. It will be done as it is in Heaven. So then it happens. The same with Kings and Queens in history, they had their Fate, and Princes and Princesses if they were rightful Heirs to the throne, and locked up in dungeons or turrets and then dying there, maybe if they went mad or starved to death, the poor little Prince and Princess, it was their Fate, even if they were on the rack, and getting put to death in the Tower of London, it was God willed it, so if it was Mary Queen of Scots and the English took her. The

Queen of England wanted to get her and put her out the way because of her throne and if God willed it she was a Protestant and Mary Queen of Scots was not, she was a RC. And there was nothing ye could do, even if the people loved her it was just how the Queen's Army was all the Redcoats, she had the best ones and they would beat anybody in the world, the whole world, it was the English Army and the Navy, they had the best ones and if countries were wanting to fight them if it was Spain and trying to take our lands, if it was England and all our treasures, the Spanish were sending all their Navy to fight us and that was England and ye saw the Spaniards and they were all just high-faluting with their wee lace handkerchiefs, Ooohh oooohhh, that was how they spoke, anybody could beat them, and the men kept wee hankies up their sleeves for their noses and if they were fencing they had the sword in one hand and then the hankie in the other just if they were nancyboy poofs that was what it was like, if they thought they could just walk in and take over and just plunder, we would just show them. England would not bow to them and just never surrender, if anybody thought they would, never till the last drop of blood if it was just their Queen or the young Prince they would soon show them, just a wee country but an island nation, that was England, so ye got Sir Walter Raleigh and Sir Frances Drake then if it was Churchill and they were the best Navy. England had the best Navy the world had ever seen. My da said it too, they could beat anybody and we were just there too if it was the kilties marching as to war because we had the pipes and just were the best fighters and helped them because if they helped us too. Maybe if it was grain and oats for eating if ye were having a famine with all the crops destroyed so the people had no food and all were starving to death so if the Queen and the Princes were trying to help ye. Oh if God will save our people, they have no potatos, and the ministers all praying to God Oh be merciful the Heavens forbid ohhh if we are all sinners, ohhh what have we done if it is Thy will, Thy will be done, of the power in Heaven, and all wee babies for their milk and nothing is there. Oh what will happen? And if ye survived ye were lucky, God willed it and His Hand was the guiding hand and it helped ye over troubled waters and all the raging seas. So if ye got the very worst disease that was you. Or if ye lived to a ripe old age. Other ones did not. Wee babies died in their cradles and if children got knocked down and killed and other ones got murdered, wee lasses, it was Fate.

§

My maw and Auntie May done all pieces and sausage rolls and cakes baked out tins the same as Christmas and New Year. But we carried all the stuff down to Mrs Duncan's house, that was where the people came. My grannie did not speak much to people but she did with Mrs Duncan. She stayed the first storey up the same close but her house was bigger and neat and tidy. Her husband was dead and her children were all up in years and away living in places.

My grannie's house was not neat and tidy and all cat smells. She said that. And because it was the top flat where she lived, ye did not get good water for washing, it was just a wee dribble because of low pressure. My maw said, If we did not go to the swimming baths we would have been filthy all our days.

Catholics were at my granda's funeral. My Auntie May said it quiet, Oh there is Mr and Mrs Osborne, that is nice of them, they are Catholics, that is just really nice.

I saw them. They did not come to Mrs Duncan's house after, only the funeral parlour. It was a wee kind of Church place and did not look good. I looked at Mr and Mrs Osborne when the Minister was talking and then we all were singing the Hymn. Other ones that were there were Catholics. They were granda's old pals from work. Uncle Billy told me. He spoke to people outside the door. So did my maw and my Auntie May. Everybody all was shaking hands, and giving cuddles if it was a woman.

All people came back to Mrs Duncan's house. I liked it except there was no many young ones but I liked seeing the grown-ups, they were relations. My da told me to get dirty dishes and take them to a woman at the sink. I did not know the woman but she was washing plates and stuff and drying them. She said to me, Oh son does Mrs Duncan keep ashtrays in the house?

I did not know. I was to get in all what was lying. People were not eating their pieces. They ate bits and left it lying but they still gave ye the plate. I said it to them, Oh you have not finished yet.

I am finished son, just take it. Oh but do not take my glass, do not take my glass. And they were laughing if I took their whisky and they were not finished. But I knew not to do it from my da. Oh do not take my tumbler son do not take my tumbler, I will give it to you.

But people smoked and put their fags out on the saucers and plates and even into the pieces so the fag was sticking out from the cheese and pork luncheon meat. I saw Uncle Billy doing that and nobody could have ett the piece and finished it, so it was just a total waste, and there was good ham too, a woman said that, Oh there is a nice ham sandwich.

But other ones were doing it, and ye saw a piece and it was fag ash all over and just one bite out it. My da was talking to my granda's old pals. Two women were sitting at the window and I brought them sausage rolls. One looked at me, and just looked. Then she said, Oh but he is not a McGuigan. Who are you son?

It is my granda.

Oh are you Lawrence McGuigan's grandson?

Yes.

Oh you are a McGuigan. Oh he is a McGuigan.

They gave me big smiles. So I was their side of the family. My grannie's side was MacDonalds from Ayr. Only two came, a man and woman. They did not talk much to people except my grannie and my maw. My Auntie May sat near them. Our relations from Dunfermline and Fife did not come. Matt said, Oh but Kieron they are da's relations.

Well but if it is granda's funeral. We would go to theirs.

Yes we would go but no grannie and Auntie May, no Uncle Billy. They would not come. They are not their relations, just ours, they are not dad's. They do not even know them.

Yes but if it was our family and they did not come. I did not think that was good, if they were my da's family and my granda was my maw's da then it was just they were all family and here was me and Matt and we were both families so it was the same one. I thought to say it to my da as well but I did not. My da was taking drinks round to men. Some had red faces or white ones, white shirts and black ties. I saw them from the funeral parlour. Uncle Billy and my grannie talked to them but no my maw.

Matt was eating a lot. The food was on the tables and he stood there beside it. I saw him looking at people. We did not go with each other when people were there. If they were talking to him he did not like me hearing. I did not care. He could listen if it was me. He kept away from me. I kept away from him. Then if grown-ups gave ye money, if it was one person, maybe it was better that it was not two. Matt was helping with glasses and tumblers. People were drinking whisky and sherry and wee ports. Oh I will have a wee port, just a wee port. They were saying it to my da.

Oh but if you want a whisky? he said.

Oh no a wee port, just a wee port.

The port was in a big glass and the whisky just in a wee one. My da said that to a man. Oh the port is bigger. My da laughed. It was just a joke. But the man did not laugh back. I saw it. He talked to another man and looked at my da. It was not nice him doing it. I did not know him, if he knew my grannie and my Uncle Billy. It was just for a laugh, my da said it to him, so it was not nice, and it was a hard look.

Women were drinking cups of tea and ports and sherries. Oh just a wee sherry. My da was smiling to them. I was to give them pieces off the plate, just hold the plate to them, do ye want a piece?

My maw was near and she saw me. It is not a piece it is a sandwich, would you like a sandwich. Oh Kieron do not pick up the sandwich and give them it. Give them the plate.

But I was not going to lift the piece up to give them or if it was a sandwich, I was not. I knew what to do and just hold the plate for them. I knew to do it. But then my da said as well, Oh you should know better than that.

But dad I was giving the plate.

Ye never touch somebody else's food son.

But dad.

It is the height of bad manners.

People were looking and smiling at me. But I was not going to touch their sandwiches or what. But my da thought I was, because my maw thought it. It was just stupid, as if I was a wee boy or else how come they said it? Because all other people were there, so they were looking and smiling. My maw hated people looking, if they were looking at you. What were they looking at ye for? Maybe ye done something wrong so they were laughing at ye. My maw thought they did that. If they did, well maybe, but maybe they did not.

Ye just were fed up with it. I wished I was away, I just wanted to go away and if granda was there looking down, he might be, and he would be seeing it. He would be looking down and seeing it all just stupid. I thought it, Oh granda, because it was, because if he was there he would know it, I would never have done that stupid stuff. If he was looking down he would see me.

§

Billy MacGregor lenned me a comic and it was the Undead. One of them came to get ye in the middle of the night and ye had to get a Cross. If ye had a Cross ye would just burn him. But we did not have Crosses, that was RCs. Ye had to be a RC else Dracula would get ye because ye could not fight back if ye were not one. Ye did not know who the Dracula was, ye just looked for a mirror and held it. That was how ye knew if ye met one, ye looked to see their reflection and if ye could not then tough luck, that was him or if it was a woman, a lot of times it was and she came to get ye and ye did not know except her eyes were red like blood and all black inside and she is just looking at ye and then her fangs hanging out. Imagine ye were winching her and then she opens her mouth and out comes the big fangs? Gary McNab said that.

I used to think I was a RC but no a complete one. I could not see myself in a Chapel. Ye would have had to be a complete RC to see yerself. If ye were not ye could never be in a Chapel, no to be doing all the things.

I could not see myself inside it. I tried to and I could not. I could not see my body. So I could not see myself. If I could see my body then I could see myself.

If ye were a complete Catholic ye would see yerself in a Chapel. So if I was one I would have been able to see myself but I could not, so I was not a complete Catholic.

So if ye were in Chapel ye could not see yerself, maybe if ye were a Dracula it was the same. People could not see ye. Ye could not see yerself. Ye just were not there. Where were ye? I do not know. Ye look in the mirror and do not see yerself. So if ye are creeping up behind somebody, they never see ye. But neither do you. You do not see yerself.

But what stops ye? If it is something. Oh you must not do that if you are not a Catholic. You cannot go in there. Only Catholics can go in there.

You cannot see yourself in a Chapel because you cannot be in a Chapel. If I could not see myself. Because if I was not there, I was not there and could not be there, I was a half Protestant and a half Catholic, but trying to do something that was complete Catholic. I was a Protestant on the outside and a RC on the inside. I could not see myself in a Chapel because that was the outside. The outside was Protestant. So I could do all the outside stuff, whatever it was, going to the Lifeboys and the Sunday School then the BB. But what was the inside stuff? That was yer prayers.

I prayed to God to forgive me.

If He thought I was kidding on. I knew He would hate that. But I was not kidding on. He would have to forgive me, if it was not my fault but my maw's and da's for doing it. What did they do it for? Because they did not like Catholics. But if I was one, did they not like me, if I was their son. But I was an adopted child so did not get treated good. That was it in stories, ye were stolen away to another land and chained up so ye could not escape. People took yer rightful fortune, they thought ye were a poor orphan but ye were the young Prince.

I tried to see myself in a real Church too, if it was really me. But I could not. That was funny because I was there with my maw and da. But if I could not see myself in a real Church. I thought it was just a Chapel. But if it was a Church too. So I could not see myself in any of them.

I was just no to be in them. How come? Maybe if I was just half and half. So that was how I was not to be in them.

What was me? What I was? If I was something. What if I looked like something? What did I look like? If it was me, what did ye see? I could not get the things that made it me, just my nose and my haircut or else what. If I was walking down to the shops or going to school. If I could see me walking. My arms and legs and my shoes. I shut my eyes tight to get the picture. But it was too tight maybe, I could not get it. Only just faces in photographs. My old faces from when I was wee. My face as a baby in the pram. I had a big face. My grannie said it. Oh you had a big face son, you were born at the right time. Boys born at the right time aye have big faces.

But ye cannot see faces if they are your own, only if it is from when ye were wee. I looked in the mirror to see mine and I just saw everything there and just everything and it was just the strangest thing and my face could be a Doctor Jekyll and yer eyes oh whose eyes are they, evilly glinting, eyes are evilly glinting, evilly and yer face altogether, whose face is it? Hohhh hahh hahh haahhh. Laughing evil. Uncle Billy always done it for a joke. Me and Matt were in bed and the door would open a wee bit a wee bit a wee bit and creaking creaking, eeeeeehhhhhh eeeeeehhhhhh oh mammy mammy what was that and then Ohhh hahh hahh haahhh.

Oh mammy a ghost a ghost.

Ohhh hahh hahh haahhh.

Oh it is Uncle Billy. Matt knew all the time. He said so. Sometimes he telled lies.

But Uncle Billy was good. We all wished he would come back to stay but Auntie May said he was not. Grannie would have liked it if he did. I went to her after school. That was the best time. She liked to see me. She was there when I chapped the door. Oh come in son, she always liked it. When I was going home later I walked to the subway myself. I telled her no to worry. If granda was there, he would save me. If anybody was hitting me he would be there, just if it was his spirit, it would reach out, I beseech you come hither, in the name of the Father, the Son and the Holy Ghost. There was the Holy Ghost. Because granda would just be a ghost if he was a spirit. Spirits are ghosts, just hovering. He would watch out for me, so if it was bad trouble there he was. And he would just help me, Oh I beseech you, our Father, we are gathered today as the sun does riseth.

My granda was the best. He was. I thought about him and was not greeting. I was not greeting. But the water was coming out my eyes. I must have been greeting. If it was real greeting. I was not sad, if ye are greeting ye are sad, I was not sad. Granda was dead. But I was not too sad. I was just watching to see, and talking about him.

But the times I went to my grannie's meant ye did not go out much with yer pals because ye were late home. Sometimes I did. But usually everybody was away with people, whatever it was, if they were doing something, they were away doing it and if ye saw them ye were lucky. Ye went looking and found them in a close or else down at the shops but if they were in somebody's house ye did not see them. Peter Wylie and Billy MacGregor saw lasses but if ye were not in with them ye could not go up.

§

There was never space to do stuff, if it was yer private business, ye could not do it, ye never got space. I did not anyway. He had all his stuff, I was not to go near it. Oh I do not want ye poking yer nose in. That was Matt. Oh it is my private stuff.

But I was not poking my nose in and I did not care about his private stuff. What private stuff? If he had something I did not care. Else about his girlfriend, if she really was one. So what? I did not care, if she was a real girlfriend or what. Maybe he was just talking to her. People just talked to lasses and then said it, Oh I am winching her, she is my girlfriend.

And they were not, not real ones. Maybe my brother done that. Peter Wylie done it with Rona Craig. People said he was winching her but I did not think he was. He just talked to her. He went round to her close to see her brother because he liked bikes and was wanting to go runs with him. But then Rona was there and he talked to her. So what? Talking to her was nothing. I talked to her as well.

But I saw Matt one time I was going to my grannie's. I went on the subway instead of the ferry. It was raining and strong strong winds. The subway was near the railway station for Matt's school and there was a cafe on the road. I saw him with the lassie. They were sitting on chairs drinking ginger. I looked in and saw him but he did not see me. But he did see me, he told me in the house when I went home. Oh what were you looking at?

I was not looking at him anyway. I was just going down to the subway station, I did not care about him and his girlfriend if it even was a girlfriend. I did not care. I was not spying on him. Oh you wee spy. That was what he said.

Oh he will not be there forever, said my maw. He will be going to college and getting a flat with his friends.

Then I would get the room to myself. That was what she said. I could just do whatever, put out my private stuff and just all the things, once he was away, I could just do it all. And my bed under the window. That is where I would put it, the same as him. It would have been great. When he was not there I sat on his bed and looked out. I loved it. How come we could not switch beds? Just one time if we could. Oh I do not want you in my bed.

I would wait and see because I knew already. He went away camping with his pals, so the next time he did I was going to his bed. I just had to watch it with my maw in case she saw but she would not if I done it right. Then if he caught me. I did not care. So if he battered me. He would not.

So if he saw me passing the cafe, how come he did not come out and get me? If I was his young brother. How come he did not come out. Oh Kieron Kieron! because if he had money too he could have bought me something, just a hot orange or a tea.

He saw me and it was away miles from where we stayed but he did not come out and get me. Because he was with a lassie. He did not want me to see. I was not looking at him. I did not care about him. I just saw him. I was just walking to the subway and I saw him. People saw people. I was not spying. I was going to my grannie's, I was getting the subway. If he thought I was spying. What would I spy on him for? I did not care about him and his girlfriend, if it was a girlfriend, I did not even look at her, she had on a big long coat. Lasses were wearing them, if they had good style, their coats came right down to their ankles. The coats flapped open and their skirts were just short and ye saw their legs right up, then if they were walking, ye just saw them and it was just their legs, lasses done that. Mitch's big sisters wore the same skirts. I saw one out with her boyfriend and her coat was flapping. She waved to me. I shouted, Is Mitch home yet?

But he was not and she did not know when. People said he was no at his uncle and auntie's, it was an Approved School. Podgie thought it too. Oh his maw just told us for an excuse. In the Approved Schools ye got locked up in dormitories. Porridge, bread and water. People talked about it. How come Mitch was there? He ran away too much. He broke into houses and shops. People said he did but he did not else I would have done it too. I would have. I wanted to do it so I could get money. I said it to Mitch. I could climb up and go in a house. Boys done it, burglars, ye climbed up the ronepipe and went in the window.

Mitch could not climb the ronepipe but I done it easy. I could go up their balcony and take their money if they had it there. But what if the people were in the house? They would catch ye.

But ye would just see if their light was on. If the light was on ye would not do it.

If they did catch ye they would just get the cops and give ye a doing. Men done that if they caught ye breaking in. My da too. Oh if it is a thief, the very worst. He hated them.

But ye would just get away, ye would not let them catch ye. If Mitch was in the Approved School he would run away. He would not stay in it. But maybe they put chains on him. They done that in prison, then yer feet too, ye had to get a saw to cut through, just sawing and sawing.

I could not tell my maw about Mitch. If ever she knew she would not let me go pals with him. Approved Schools were the worst, the same as Borstals.

My maw was a snob. We all knew it. My da too. If she gave him a look when he said something wrong he did not like it. She was snobbish and posh. I did not want to go to Matt's school. It was not fair to make me.

My teacher said if I just stopped frittering, frittering and frittering. I was good at my lessons except I did not try. If I tried I would do it. She wrote it in a letter to go with my Report Card. My maw asked her to write it. Then she went to see them at Matt's school. My da did not go, just her. It was the headmaster she saw. Oh Matt is a fine pupil, he is a credit. If Kieron is anything like him he is most welcome. We will see how he does.

I liked the headmaster saying it but I did not want to go. My maw told us on Saturday morning. Matt was not there but my da was. Saturday was usually overtime but today he did not go. He said, Maybe ye are brainy after all.

He laughed but my maw did not. My da said eftir aw and not after all so maybe that was how. My maw said to me, You will have to speak better Kieron and it is not aye remember it is yes.

I know.

Well if you know you should say it.

Sorry.

People that talked like me were just keelies and did not go to good schools. That was what my maw said. But Matt talked ordinary. He did not let her hear but out on the street he did. So if he did talk posh, he done it in school, but no outside. People would just batter him.

Oh forget about Matt, said my maw. Just concentrate on your-self.

People would not batter him, said my da.

Aye but da some would. They would not go about with him. He would not have pals.

Oh of course he would.

Aye but only in school.

Matt? My da's eyes squinted at me.

He does not have them outside.

Of course he does. Matt has plenty of pals. Do not be so stupid.

I am no being stupid I am just.

My maw put her hand on her head. Kieron! Stop your nonsense.

It is not nonsense.

Yes it is.

It isnay.

It is not.

It is not.

Oh for G★d sake. My da got up from the table. I am going down the shops to buy a paper.

My maw looked at me but it was not my fault. He was not angry anyway, not very angry. He was just fed up with it. He was fed up with the arguing. He said that. But a lot of times it was him started it. And if it was speaking bad, it was me that my maw gave the rows. My da spoke bad but it was me she blamed, she never said it to him. He done it worse than me.

He had his coat on and came back in the kitchen to get money. My maw said, Oh Johnny will ye get me a pint of milk and a half stone of potatos.

Right.

Usually it was me went the messages but sometimes my da went just to get a walk. He liked walking. When he went out the door my maw said, Oh Kieron, you must learn to concentrate.

Matt moaned about money. But sometimes he had it. Where did he get it? How come he had money? Maybe his girlfriend gave him it. One time he got a paperboy job before school but he only done it for one week. It was morning papers. He had to start at quarter past six. Just one week then he chucked it. I thought my da would be angry but he was not, just laughed.

My maw was glad. Oh it is interfering with yer lessons.

But I would have loved a job. But Matt still got money. People gave him it. He got a lot more than me. My da gave him some but he got it off my maw as well. From my grannie too. My Auntie May gave him money. I saw her. Sometimes she gave me money too.

My da gave me some now but not much, it was in my pocket to do what I liked, so I could just spend it on stuff or what, I could save it up. But it was just wee compared to other boys.

Gary McNab was getting a job as a milkboy. That was what I wanted and I was going to get one. Milk was the best job because ye got good tips, the best tips. Gary's big brother earned a fortune. Gary was just waiting for it. It was the first vacancy. I asked him about me and if I could get one but he said, Oh it is a long waiting list and ye have got to get somebody to talk for ye.

In our house anything with money was bad. When my da gave me pocket-money it was mine just to spend but he wanted to know what I was spending it on. I hope it is not cigarettes.

He said that for a joke. He did not know I smoked, but I did not smoke much. But it was my business. If it was my money and I spent it, that was up to me.

Once I got a job they could not say nothing, no if it was my money and I got it from my job. I could just spend it and if it was the carnival, I would just go and get shots on everything. Oh and a radio. I telled my maw I was going to get one.

But your brother has already got one.

Well but so what if he had one. So if I was not to get one just because he had one. That was not fair.

Oh it will be too noisy with his studies.

But I will not put it on if he is doing them.

Oh Kieron.

I played his radio all the time. He did not know. He did not let me when he was there. But if he was out the house I just switched it on. He went camping for the weekend with his pals in school and I had it on the whole time. I played about with all different stuff, hearing all the programmes from all over and different ways to speak from faraway countries and then ye heard Morse code. Sailors at sea were speaking to each other, fishermen. Morse code was how they done it. My da knew Morse code. SOS was dih dih dih, dah dah dah, dih dih dih. The complete thing was dots, short dots and long dots. If ye knew it ye could talk and they would not know what it was. If it was yer pals and ye talked to them, nobody could listen. Ye could do it in school and the teacher would not know. Ye could swear.

The radio was great. I went to my bed early and done it. Ye could turn out the light and have it on the pillow and even just fall asleep, if ye had it low.

But I always put it back the way he left it so he would not know. Because he looked. He looked to see. I know he did. One time I forgot and it was just a nightmare. I was up the field for a game of football and forgot to put the radio back where he left it. He would see I had used it. All the things went through my head about what would happen once he came home. So I better stop playing and go home early. But what if he was there already? If he had come back? That happened. Him and his pals were away camping, it rained and they got washed out. So they just came home. That was what I thought. So it was too late. He was there and he knew. But maybe no. No if I ran home and got it.

What if he had set a trap? What if he had set it at a certain station? He could have done that before he left the house and then he would just look and see. There was nothing I could do. I just carried on playing football. I did not want to go home. But when it came teatime I just went. Lucky for me he was not home, and not when I went to bed. When I got up for school next morning there he was. He came home very late.

One day he would leave and I would get the room to myself. It would be mine to do whatever I wanted. I could even put a lock on the door and ye would need a key to get in.

At his school they expelled people. If ye did not do yer lessons they expelled ye. Well I would not do them and get expelled. I did not tell any of the boys about it all. Imagine I did. Imagine Podgie. I was up their bit and we were talking and I just said, Oh I am joining the BB.

So am I, he said.

Gary was with us. Are you joining too? I said.

I might or I might no.

That was Gary. He never done much except just walk about. Other ones were joining the BB too and then there was the Bible Class. I was going to that as well. I did not care.

§

I started climbing back up the loft. I did not need my da's stepladders and I did not need anybody to help me. Ye just watched it when ye climbed onto the landing wall. Once ye were up ye saw yer feet did not make creaking noises. If it was Mitch sometimes he did not do it right and ye thought if somebody heard us down below. I told him all the time, Oh Mitch just watch it or ye will fall through the ceiling. He got worried and went slow but if it was too slow it was no good and ye just creaked on the rafters, so ye had to go quite quick. Imagine they were sitting watching the telly and ye went through the ceiling. Oh look, and it was your leg coming down. Ye saw it in the pictures, the family is eating their tea and the burglar runs across the roof then falls through it and lands on their table right in their food, Oh pardon me, and then he runs away. But if it was yer da and it happened, he would kill ye.

A wee brick wall split our loft from the one up the next close. I climbed over it and went along. I had fags and matches planked in at the edge. I did not usually smoke unless with people and it was draws each, but now I was going to. I went to get them but they were not there. I had not been up for ages so if somebody had stole them. I checked along further, there was a lot of places, but I could not find them. Somebody had stole them. I did not know other boys who went up. Maybe if workies were up, I saw their wee roof ladder, so if they took them. Their ladder was near where the skylight was. I could take it and get up to see out. Maybe I could open it. If I could and went out on the roof. Ye could sit up there and nobody could see ye. They would have to be on an airoplane.

That was the ronepipe, I did not like that about it how people saw ye, then if they telled yer maw. Ye just got bad rows, or else doings off yer da. But if it was the roof they could not see ye. But maybe they could if it was windows and they were looking out.

I heard noises. Usually it was birds ye heard or else doors slamming. I had another look for my fags then went back along to my own bit and the trapdoor was open, I had forgot to shut it. My da was waiting down below. I did not see him. He came home early from work and saw the trapdoor open and knew it was me because it was me that went up. He just kept in at the side and did not speak till then I was dreeping down. I still did not see him, just getting my feet down onto the top of the wall. Ye had to be careful yer feet did not slip off and ye fell right down the landing and all the stairs. But I heard a noise and it was my maw, she was there too, Oh God, and then my feet touched down and I was on the landing wall, and my da just grabbed my legs and had me gripped and got me down and skelped me skelped me, bum and legs, just as hard, bam bam, bam bam, and against the door so I fell right in. My maw there. Oh Johnnie, that is enough now.

He will never learn he will never learn.

Bam bam, bam bam.

Oh Johnnie that is enough.

I did not care. So if he hit me. I did not care. Just if he done it another time, if ever he did. I did not want more doings. Not off of him. If he done it again, he would never do it again, so if he hit me, he just never would or I would just go away, I would just go away. I was too old to get hit by him. I would run away. I was going to. People ran away. Mitch done it. I was going to. I wanted to go to the highlands. Mitch done it there and he done it to England. I could go to England too if it was my Uncle Billy. I could just get a job, if it was a paperboy or a milkboy or just deliveries for something, if it was bacon parcels and sweetie bags, there was all jobs and I could get one and just save my money.

Some ran away and naybody knew where they went. They did not go to anywhere, just over the fields and faraway, miles and miles. They lived out in the wilds, maybe they found a cave. People had caves. Matt went with his Secondary School on a long weekend and they found one. They were in tents. It was away on an island. He said I would love it because climbing, ye could climb down all cliffs and ye saw birds' nests and all birds' droppings where ye put yer hands. They got special diving out in the deep sea. Ye went out on boats away out past the rocks. Ye went in off the boat and swam along just the breaststroke, then ye dived down and down. Ye went in off the back of the boat so it would not capsize. Oh but the water was freezing.

Matt said how they were all chittering but ye just got used to it. Ye all went away to the side and the man shouted yer orders so ye swam along straight and at a steady pace and if ye swam right out it was America next, but then ye dived down and it was slow motion, keeping yer legs straight up, down and down, and yer eyes open under the water then when yer feet came after ye ye just kicked hard, and down ye went to the bottom if ye could reach it, that was what ye were trying but it was dead deep and ye did not reach it. But the water was clear as daylight so ye could see everything, it was just great. They went on treks. Matt said it, Oh they took us on treks, way way along the shore then at the sides of the cliffs and down into it. The best for climbing, it was just great how ye could even just run up the sides, rock to rock and yer feet hit the right one, just watching for slippery stanes if there was seaweed and moss or if the waves splashed in, really it was the best place. In among the rocks there were pools of water, clear clean water, it was the cleanest, and ye found wee crabs and stuff in them and who knows, ye were looking for treasure, it was just how ye imagined. Matt said it. Ye went over one rock and down to another and then at the side ye saw something maybe sparkling, if it was diamonds and buried treasure from a shipwreck. Shipwrecks happened, and if all hands were lost. The cliffs were rocky and made it bad for boats during bad gales. My da said it too. The rocks went way way out underneath so the sailors did not see them. So it was dangerous for swimming too but when it was deep sea surface diving it was okay then, and ye could swim good except for currents.

But then they got the cave, the leader took them, he was a teacher from Matt's Secondary School. It was big and damp and went into a bigger cave and it was where the old highlanders were hiding. The Redcoats came to get them. They started a fire and burnt them all to death. They all were hiding and it happened. They were filled with smoke and laid down to die. If they came out the Redcoats stuck their bayonets into them.

If ye went far in there was bones. Matt said it. Bones were bleached. Other fires were there too, just wee ones for cooking, and that was shepherds and fishermen caught in a raging storm just keeping warm and dry. But there was other stuff too, like old beer cans and litter. And people had done s***es next to the walls. So ye might find other people using caves, if they were on the run, maybe murderers. Or else boys running away, maybe it was, ye could get jobs on a farm or on a fishing boat and just stay here till ye got fixed up or ye could buy a tent.

But if ever I did run away, I would. I was not scared. Just because I did not. If I did Mitch could come but even if he did not I would still do it.

Things could be yer Fate. So what could you do after that, you could not do nothing if that was you, if it was God, so you had to do it.

Peter Wylie was looking at me, he was at the top of the second row now and I was just in front of him. I liked Peter but he wanted to beat me all the time. He still said about when he fell off the tree, Oh if you had not bounced the branch. He laughed when he did but he meant it. I got fed up with him saying it. Now it was the good school. How come I was going there? It is my big brother's school, I said, that is how.

Oh Smiddy is a brainy b★★★★★d.

It is my maw, she done it, it is no me.

How come?

I do not know, because of my brother.

Oh ye want to f★★★★★g go, said Gary McNab.

No I do not.

I did not like them thinking stuff. Billy too, how come he said it? If they knew I did not want to go? Well, if I did not, how come I was going? That was what they thought. How come it was me. Oh he is f★★★★★g top division, said Gary.

But that did not matter, top division was just daft, it was because of my maw and my brother. I told them. It was my maw went and done it and it was their headmaster because he liked Matt. If Matt did not go I would not, but because he did, that was how.

It would be the worst. I did not tell the boys that. I did not speak much about it. It was just yer Fate and ye had to. Oh but I did not want to. How come they thought I did! Podgie did not look to me. He started talking about football but no to me. He was keeping me out. That was him. He done that to people. He done it to me a lot. I wished Mitch was there. Mitch would not have cared. Podgie and them were just no real pals. Ye went to meet them and they were away out. Ye went looking and found them and they were talking about something. Nobody said hullo. Ye just stood and waited till they finished. Then if ye were walking, they did not shout ye over. Usually people did, if ye were walking down the shops or someplace and ye did not see them, they shouted ye, Hoh Smiddehhh, Smiddehhh!

Now they did not. How come? It was no my fault, if they thought I wanted to go to that f****g good school.

It was Podgie. Or else Gary. People waited for them. They did not say hullo to ye so then everybody else, and even Primary 6s, they were just looking, they did not know what to do. Then if they passed round a fag and ye were waiting for a draw. What if they did not give ye one? What if ye were there and they just did not, they gave everybody a draw except ye? Well, if they did, if they did it to me, I would have went home, I would just have went away, I would never ever no have just

Because it was no fair and I was fed up with it. So if it was my fault. Well it was not my fault. I did not want to go to that rotten stinking f****g school, really, I did not. They all were snobs and spoke posh at it. I knew they did. Matt told me. Even the ones that were not posh, they could annoy ye. Some were alright but mostly they were not. Matt said, Oh you will hate it. You will just hate it.

Do not tell him that, said my maw.

She took me to the shop for my complete uniform, ye had to get a navyblue blazer with the school badge, then trousers and proper shoes, and the school tie. I did not want to wear the trousers, they were too wide. My da said they were flannels. Oh son that is a nice pair of flannels.

If it was windy they just flapped about. Even if it was not windy, ye just were running down the road, they just flapped away. Matt said it when we were running down the hill to get the train, Oh you will take off, you will fly away.

Ye could not wear jeans to this school. That was the last thing, if ever ye wore jeans they would just send ye home.

Ye needed a monthly railway-pass. My maw gave me the money for it. I went with Matt on the first morning. It was a full train so we had to stand. All ones going to school, all different schools. Catholics and Protestants. And all their uniforms. Men and women too, going to their work. They worked up the town in offices.

I knew how to get to Matt's school so he did not have to show me. It was a big big building, all bricks and stone. He did not talk much when we walked up the hill from the railway station. He took me into the playground and went away over to his own bit. I saw him talking to big ones. He was in 5th year now. The playground was full of people. Darkies were there, boys and girls. Matt said they would be. They just walked about, coloured ones.

At nine o'clock the teachers came out and one of them was reading out names of people and what class they were in and where they were to go. It went on and on. All people had their names called. It came down to the last and there was only a few. I did not like it. It was a man and he kept looking at me all the time. I had not done nothing. How come he was looking at me? I did not have a school bag. My maw was getting me one. I had an old one but I did not bring it. Matt said I should but I did not like carrying stuff and just left it.

Now it was only me and another two, one lassie. Then it was just me. The whole place was empty except me and the teacher. He was going to go away and folded up his papers but he saw me looking and went, Oh would you come here please. What is your name and where do you stay and how come it is you and what happened if your name is not here.

He did not have my name. It was not down on his lists. Where do you live? Is this the correct school? Maybe you should not be here. Oh but I should. My mother said it, she saw the headmaster. My big brother is here too, I said, Matthew Smith.

Oh I know Matthew Smith. He is your brother. Mm. Come with me please.

He took me to the school office. I saw doors for Headmaster and Nurse. I sat down and then later he came back. I was to go to my class right away. My class was 1G. They gave me a ticket for dinner-school.

So that was that. Everything was horrible. I did not find the class-room and when I did it was a new class, mine all was away to another one. Every time they finished a class they went away to another one. A different teacher for all the classes. I just went after them and saw people and just followed them but every time in the class I had to say to the teacher what my name was so they could write it down. They did not have it on any lists and said, Oh is this the correct class?

People were looking at ye. I hated it. Ye felt stupid. Ye just got a red face and yer voice. Oh could you speak up please, so ye had to say it loud.

Kieron Smith.

Would you please repeat that?

Kieron Smith.

The teachers just looked at ye and thought, Oh he must be stupid. That was what they were thinking and the boys and lasses too because ye were speaking and they heard ye, so they knew how ye spoke. Oh who is he, where is he from? I had to say my name and other things. Yes sir this is my class.

Are you sure?

Yes sir.

Oh well you had better take a seat.

The next night I saw boys down the shops and they told me my name got called out at the right school. Everybody all was looking to see if I was there. Oh where is Smiddy? Oh he is no here he is going to a good school.

And I was going to be in 1B, so that was the second top class. Here at Matt's school I was in the lowest. That was 1G. They said it was not the lowest but it was. They did not even know me, just put me there. I told Matt but no my maw. He just looked. He was in the second top class. He had pals in that school. I did not. Ones went to the same Primary so they knew each other and did not speak to you. Some were posh or were fat or else big. I was wee compared. There was no darkies but two were Jewboys. One came from Belgium and was a Catholic. Somebody said it. He did not do the Sign. Ye got other ones in that school. Imagine Podgie and the boys, if ye told them. Oh I have got a darkie and a Pape and a Jewboy in my class. Oh are ye sitting beside the Pape? That was what they would say. Oh is that darkie yer pal? What about the jungle, are ye going to go there?

I did not care. But it was just how come if the Belgium boy was a Pape and in a Protestant school. Boys in the class made jokes about how he spoke, I am ver angreee, you think I am sillee fool, I am not sillee fool you are sillee fool.

I sat at the desk to the side of him in History. Ye had to sit where ye were from the second day, so if ye had not changed from the first that was it and ye had to sit at the same desk. He was looking at me. How come? I did not do nothing to him. Other ones laughed. Sillee fool, I am ver angreee. I did not. He knew a lassie and talked to her at playtime. She did not talk much, just looked roundabout. She was skinny and quite big. I saw them in the playground. One day she wore trousers but no the next. Girls were not allowed to, only skirts. She had black hair and yellow skin, and he had the same but she was not his sister.

Some were ordinary but had pals in other classes or from where they stayed. Some did not have pals, so ye just went about. I saw Matt in the corridor but we did not wave or go the gether. I got the first train home but he did not. He came home late.

They did not call it playtime, but morning break and afternoon break. There was a part of the playground ye were allowed to play football. It was next to the little school. They had three buildings and called them the big school, middle school and little school. Ye got different classes in the three of them. They played football with a wee ball but too many played. I was counting. Fifteen or seventeen in one side. Ye got the ball and everybody charged. There was nowhere to run, too many of them were there. What will I do? Just kick it. It was good if ye were a dribbler but it was hard to do it. Some boys were good. Or else if ye had a hard shot, some did and could boot the ball hard. Ye had to watch if it hit ye, it was just a wee ball but it was hard and stung yer leg. Most people just ran about and tried to kick it. If ye kicked it twice it was good. Everybody all was shouting. Teachers walked past and shook their head. One came and stopped the game, Oh please men a bit of hush!

The best game was dinnertime, after ye came back from dinner-school if ye went to dinnerschool. My maw gave me the week's money on Friday morning, that was for the next week, but I just spent it and did not go. I made a piece and cheese after my breakfast and just ate that in the playground or else at the morning break. I went and played football. I quite liked it but sometimes it was just daft. If the ball came and ye were running other ones tried to get it off ye except they were in your team. Oh what are ye kicking me for? But still they done it. Just because they wanted a kick. Some were hopeless and could not play right. They did not bother and then just laughed if they got a kick. After the bell rang and ye were going up the stair a boy said, I never got a kick!

So during the whole game he did not get one kick. Ones played from different classes. Some in my class did not play at all. But I liked that. Boys that played saw me and saw I got kicks. They did not know about my name and I did not say it, so if it was Smiddy, nobody knew. They just said yer second name, Smith.

The ball went up on the roof of the playground shelters. People were looking up. Nobody was going for it. I waited to see. There was an easy ronepipe and it was not high up. I thought I would but then not. But I could, maybe.

The buildings were good for climbing. The shelters were next to them so ye could get up on one and over to the school buildings. A gap was between them but it was not giant. If ye took a long run and did the jump and got to a window ye could get yer hands on the ledge and there was another one down below it. There was ways. I saw them. I wanted to climb it. Maybe I would.

It would be good just to do it then maybe for a laugh looking in the top window, if it was your class doing a lesson. But the little school roof was nay good, no like the one in my Primary School. That was flat. So was the roof of the playground shelter. What if I went up? Imagine nobody had done it before. It would be hoaching with balls and stuff, hundreds of things. All over the place. What would be there? Everything. School books and exercise jotters, pencils and pens and sweeties. And money too. I know because I saw ones do it. Halfpennies and pennies. People flung it up for luck or else showing off. There would be a fortune. Ye would just get the money and no anything else, just fill yer bag. One boy that chipped the coins was in my class. He chipped them with his thumb, flick, and then spinning right up. That was the good way to do it. He was not one of the posh ones except talking, if he was English. That was how he spoke. I would rather you, not me. Oh I would prefer not to, I would rather you, not me.

The lasses all liked him. He was nay good at sport. If it was a games period ye had to play what he done was just funny walks and runs down the sideline or else just walked about talking to people. The PE teacher shouted at him. This boy just looked at him then done it but he was not feared. He did not know nothing about football but some about rugby, it was just rugby. But ye saw the lasses and he was talking to them. He was the only one boy there and talking. If he was telling jokes, ye saw them laughing, so he must have been telling them. But his jokes were good, he told them to boys in the class too, things from the pictures or else the teachers, mimicking them, he was good at mimicking. And then tunes, he put his hands up so he was playing a trumpet, twiddling his fingers, and done a tune like a trumpet.

He must have been quite rich to do it with the money. All them that chipped the coins up on the roof. I was going to climb it and get it all. It would be good if I did, people would know. Maybe lasses too except how they did not notice stuff. It was funny how lasses, you noticed them but they did not notice you. Ye saw them in the playground if it was their gym period and they got taken out. Sometimes they did. Other times it was the boys. The lasses wore short short skirts or else navyblue knickers tucked in and ye saw all their legs. If ye had to leave the room and go to the lavatory ye saw them chasing about and their tits bouncing.

Imagine the boys if ye were telling them, Podgie. They walked behind lasses and said stuff. Sometimes I went. They shouted stuff, Oh can I get a squeeze?

It was Podgie said it first, squeeze, can I get a wee squeeze. Squeezing her tit, that was what he meant. It was a laugh. Him and Gary shouted, Squeeze!

Then in a quiet voice, Yer tit.

Podgie said it out loud as well and if the lassie heard, he did not care, and if she got a big red face all the boys were laughing at her. Oh she is getting a riddy! Look.

He done it with Ann Ritchie, a Primary 7 lassie, and she shouted. Oh grow up you, just grow up.

Podgie shouted back, Naw you grow up, just you grow up!

She looked at me now and it was not me that said it. I could not stop Podgie saying it, if he wanted to then he just done it, so it was no my fault.

It was usually weer lasses him and the boys done it with. If it was with older ones ye had to be careful. Then if people were there and they were older than us. Ye maybe did not see them but they were across the street, then they saw ye. Who the f**k are you? F**k off.

Or Papes. Somebody would say it, Oh she is a Pape. So ye were watching for them because if their boys came and ye were shouting names at them.

But usually ye knew the lasses or who they were. Ann Ritchie was one I liked. She was in the class below me at Primary. Usually if ye liked a lassie she was older or else the same age but no always. I saw Ann Ritchie down the shops. I liked the way she looked and the way her legs went. Her house was up a wee hill and her view went over the top of my roof, right away to the hills. Maybe she saw me out the back window when I was on the veranda. I walked round her way when I went down the shops. Maybe she was at the front window and I walked past. Maybe she looked out and saw me. If I was walking along she would, she would see it was me. I was going to wave to her or if she was out her close, just hullo or what. Oh you are going to a good school. And I would just tell her about it. Peter Wylie said she had wee tits. I did not like him saying that. It was just to get in with Podgie, it was showing off.

With girls at the good school it was different. I did not know about them. They did not look at ye. I was talking to my grannie and she said, Oh they will be looking at you. But you will not see them looking.

Maybe ye were at the desk and one was looking at ye. You cannot see her but she sees you. So she is sitting behind ye or at the side and just if it was out the corner of her eye. What if ye saw her and it was true. Oh and the feeling too, ye would get that and it would just be oh ye would just have to go about or walk or what, just shivering. Ye were sitting at yer desk and writing something and the whole class was quiet and ye just saw her and she was looking. What one?

My grannie said stuff to make ye feel it was okay but really, I did not see one looking at me. My clothes were not good. I needed stuff for going out. Peter Wylie had good clothes. I saw ones he wore. People said he had good style. He did have. Him and Gary McNab had the best. But if ye had a job. I was getting one. I just needed it. There was paperboy jobs too. Ye just put yer name down. It was Proddies. If ye were a Catholic ye did not get one except if ye were lucky. Once I got a job I was getting my own stuff. And that was that and my maw and da, it was up to them what they said, if they wanted to say something that was them, but if it was my money. It would be if it was my job.

In the good school the lasses did not care about if ye saw them in their knickers for their PE period. That was them. Oh grow up.

Ye could see them running about, they did not care, their faces all red from running, puffing hard and their sandshoes squeaking, their legs right up. But ye could not walk too slow else a teacher saw ye and ye did not look. Then if ye watched them going up the stair to see up their skirt they shouted at ye. Oh you dirty animal.

Boys pointed at ye and laughed at ye too. No me but other ones. They had two gyms and two changing rooms in this school. After PE class ye got a shower. Ye did not have to, just if ye wanted. Some done it in the nude, people were looking. Bigger boys were there, doing repeat years. They should have been in 2nd year but got kept back. Ye could bring swimming trunks but ones laughed at ye. Some just ran in, covering it with their hand. Ye did not want people seeing if it was what size was it too wee? Or if ye were baldy or what, them just laughing and pointing and ye were getting a red face, that happened. Mine was not baldy but there was only a wee drop of hair. Then they flapped their towel at yer bum and if it hit ye it was quite sore, but they did not do it to me and if they were going to I kidded on I did not see. I was not going to fight them but if they were going to fight me I would. Except there was a wee gang there, I saw them.

But if ye did not take the shower. Really ye had to or they would say stuff. Ones that did not were fat or wee or too skinny. They talked about ye. Oh he is a poof. Oh nancyboy nancyboy. He has got a vaggie. That was what they said. He has got a vaggie. I did not know it except later, a lassie's thing.

Maybe if ye kidded on, Oh I am just in a hurry, I cannot take a shower. The Belgium boy got a note for the teacher so he did not take one. People laughed at him.

Boys were fast into the gym from the changing room. It was good and I liked it. Lasses had their own gym and it was through the wall from ours but it was a partition wall and sometimes the two sides did not close right so ye could see through it and they were doing their exercises wearing their short short skirts or else just knickers, sometimes it was.

There was two climbing ropes and wall bars. The wall bars were good. Ye could climb up the top and look down. Ye were not supposed to climb it except if a teacher was present. In case ye fell off. But it was good grips with the bars. I climbed up and touched the ceiling with my head. Nobody watched me. I just done it. I had a way so that I was sitting down when I was up high. It looked like I was. I got my hands in so they were just nearly jammed at the wrists, but it was not easy to do and ye had to watch the heels of yer sandshoes did not slip.

The climbing ropes were easy. They went to the ceiling. Boys could not climb it if they were fat, they could not pull themself up. Jeremy Brogan was one. People quite liked him. He tried to do stuff and was good at some games. But he could only climb a wee bit. His face puffed out red. I cannot do it sir.

Oh well. The PE teacher did not give him a row. This was Mr Ramsay, he was the one that took us for it and if ever we got football it would be him. He played football. I told my da about him. I thought he might have heard Mr Ramsay's name because my da liked football, but he could not remember. Mr Ramsay liked Jeremy Brogan because he was good at rugby and swimming. People said rugby was better than football. The other PE teacher said it. Only hooligans play football, rugby players are gentlemen. He was old and said how it was superior and if ye played it ye were a gentleman. He had a posh voice and ye had to speak in a posh voice back to him else he kidded on he did not hear ye or else in yer own voice mimicking ye. I didnay dooo it please surr it wisnay meee droaped the bawww.

Mr Ramsay could climb the rope just with his hands. It was a wee bit like showing off. I would love to have done it. He had his legs straight together at one side and sloping out. The rope went through his wrists and his hands different, just like his wrists jutting out. How did he do it? He did not show us how. He just walked back to his seat and looked at his book. Boys were talking about it in the changing room. Ye needed strong muscles to climb that way. Mr Ramsay's arms were like that. I tried to do it but it was right enough how yer arms were no strong enough. But maybe I was fastest. Except a way ye climbed the rope, I started getting funny feelings, then up near the top it was worse and it was like it was just well the rope was rubbing ye in, just how it was between yer legs, and it was a feeling up yer body. I did not know what but then had to stop and no move and to hang on so just hanging on, and ye were having to press and it was coming and what happened ye got the feeling, and even more having to hold on because if ye forgot and ye took yer hands off, ye were very high up, so ye just really had to watch it, keeping tight in till then it happened and ye just came and there was spunk too, so if it showed through yer underpants then it was yer shorts, if people saw it, they all would know except maybe it did not happen to them, maybe it did not, nobody talked about it.

When ye came down the rope ye did not stand straight but turned sideways and bent a wee bit so nobody could see the front. Really because if they saw ye, what would happen? People would just laugh at ye and spread it about, Oh see him there!

Imagine lasses knew. If people said it to them. But they would not, they would never. But just how things spread about. People would just do it. I did not have pals in that school. People did not know me. Even in yer own class, they were not friendly and hardly even talked to ye. Oh what is your name? Nobody said that. I did not say it to them. People were not pals, I was not pals with them. Some were b★★★★★ds, that was what I thought.

The best thing was the swimming. Except it was Monday morning, so after ye got it ye had all the whole week to come and ye were going to be at school, it was just agony. The swimming baths were not in the school. Special buses took ye.

In the scheme I was a good swimmer and a fast racer with Mitch and the boys. But here at school I was slow, I was no even a real swimmer. It was just like I was starting. Boys done it different. No them all but just some, posh ones. Donald Shields especially. He was just the best racer ever. He done the butterfly. I never seen anybody do it except on television. I tried it, I could not. I only done four strokes then that was that. But Donald Shields just done it. We all were looking. Oh that is smashing. Oh jees oh he is great. That is what ye were thinking.

He did not bother but just done it. He had a posh voice from England. The PE teacher said he would show us how to do the butterfly but first was the ones that could not swim. He took all them to the shallow end. Us that could swim just done it. The fast ones went at the side. On the first and the second day that was where I went, I thought I was to because I would be a fast one, but I was not, I was a slow one compared. The ones that swam the real fastest just went past ye, they were sailing, just smooth. Donald Shields done the backstroke as well. He did not even splash, his arms just in and out the water, ohm ohm, ohm ohm. And then he was away past ye. If he was coming up ye kidded on ye did not see him. Same with the other ones. One was Jeremy Brogan, he was very fast and like a man doing it. Fat people could be good at swimming. What about skinny ones? Maybe I was just skinny. Ye could only keep up for three strokes. But Shields was skinny. Him and Brogan had badges on their trunks for a swimming club. They had Galas. That was where they raced and parents went to see them. Girls went as well. Some girls beat the boys. They went swimming at nighttime after school and it was a club. They went five times a week for practising. Ye did not pay money if ye were in the club. Ye were a member. Yer maw and da got ye into it and ye had a wee card so ye got in for free.

For the school swimming ye did not get cubicles for changing. It was one big changing room and ye put yer clothes into a basket so everybody was all just the gether. Lasses were not there, they went another time. They were in my class for ordinary lessons.

Swimming was the first two periods on Monday morning so that spoiled it. Once ye had dressed the special bus was waiting to take us to school. I was quick out the changing rooms so I sat waiting and it was the worst because that was you trapped for the whole week. It was just so horrible, just the worst. I thought about dodging round a corner before I got on the bus then waiting for it to go away. It was a far walk to the river but I would love doing it, get a ferry over to my grannie. She would be glad. I did not go much.

But I got on the bus. I wanted on first so I could sit anyplace and just in at the window. Ye did not get a double seat to yerself, a person had to sit beside ye. If ye were one of the last ones ye had to go and sit beside somebody. I hated it. Who did ye sit beside? I could not sit beside anybody. How come him if ye did? They would just look at ye. What did ye sit beside me for? I did not want to sit beside anybody. Except a lassie, that was who I would have sat beside. But ye could not sit beside a lassie, that even was worse.

Monday morning and it was all to come, all just horribleness. People talked on the bus but I did not, just looked out the window. My pals were at their own school. Here I did not have any pals. I did not care. I did not want any. One day I would not be here.

When the bus got to the school people were out for the morning break and there was a game of football but usually I did not play. My hair was still wet and that feeling ye got after swimming, like a wee bit tired, but a good tired.

People w****d in the toilets. They done jokes about it. If somebody kicked in a door and somebody was doing it they said their name and wrote it on the wall. Ye were just sitting on the lavatory pan and they looked over to see if ye were doing it. Ones smoked in the toilets. When ye went in they looked to see who it was. I heard their voices and they were not posh. It was McEwan and his pals. They were like a wee gang. McEwan was the leader. One of them was in my class. They saw ye and gave a wee smile, Oh he cannot fight.

That was what it was. Ye did not want to go in because they were there. And what if they claimed ye? Well if they did? If they did they did. Sometimes I waited till the bell rang for the end of the break and just ran in then.

In this school ones ye thought were best fighters were not. They did not fight, they let others laugh and did not care. They kept to their own side and saw their own pals. They were posh, even if they did not look posh. My maw asked me did they talk nice. She knew they did because Matt told her. There was not much swearing except bad words, but bad words did not matter, people just said them, some teachers too, Oh it is a bloody nuisance, he is a damn swine, oh for God sake, oh for Jesus sake. The Algebra teacher said it too, but not against people, it just came out. Hells bells. Oh Hells bells.

People said it. Hells bells. Who has blooming farted, Hells bells.

Most spoke good, even ones that did not, they done it the same like me, just watching it and what they said. Aye and naw, nobody said that. Some had upstairs and downstairs houses with their own door and gardens, and motor cars, they talked about them, Oh the Cresta is a heap of old tin. Oh do you know the Rover?

People had good clothes. Their blazers had the school badge sewed on the top pocket. I heard one boy saying it. Oh I can just take the badge off at the weekend and wear the jacket out.

Jacket and not blazer. And he was not posh, just spoke ordinary. He took the school badge off at the weekend. So then he could wear his jacket out. That was what he said. When it came time for school his mother tacked the badge back on. So it was just like a good jacket for going out. And nobody would see what school ye went to. Oh he is a Pape, he is a Proddy. Nobody would say it because they would not know. Or if it was a posh school.

Him and other ones were talking about a cafe they went to and there was a great jukebox. Oh it is all the Top Twenty, it is great.

My jacket had the badge built in at the top pocket. It was not a patch so ye could not take it out. So maybe it was a blazer and not a jacket. My shirt was no right either, the collar was too big. If ye pulled the tie tight it went underneath. The collar came over it and got wrinkled all up. It was hopeless. Some boys did not pull their tie tight, just let them open at the top and their shirts open at the top as well. They had good clothes. Their trousers too. Mine were not. No just me. Others had the same trousers. Flannels. But Matt did not have flannels. I only saw that now. I had not seen it before. How come he got good ones? They were the good grey and smooth and did not flap about. How come I did not get them? Mine just flapped about and just were horrible, I f*****g hated them. I needed new clothes. Oh wait till Christmas, said my maw, it will be your Christmas.

But mum I need them.

You will just have to wait.

That was me, I had to wait, but no Matt. Oh because he is good at his lessons. Maybe my maw would say that. Two teachers said it to me. Oh you are Matthew Smith's brother, and were looking at me. I just said, Yes sir and yes miss. Oh you are not so good as him, that was what they were meaning. I did not care anyway.

Ye got homework to do. I done a lot on the train home and then the train in next morning. I got the early train to school and finished it in the playground. Matt did not like me doing it in the bedroom if he was in it. I still done it if I wanted. But usually I done it in the kitchenette or else on the living-room table. But my da did not like it because my maw told him to turn down the telly. Oh Kieron is doing his homework.

Can he no do it in the kitchenette?

I liked doing it in the kitchenette anyway. But I done most of it on the train or else in the playground.

Me and Matt did not like going with each other. I saw him standing over with his pals. He did not like it if I was near. At dinnertime people went for a walk and I saw his pal smoking a fag. Maybe he was too. He did not see me looking. What if I told my maw? She would have gave him a row but what else, nothing. If she told my da what would he have done. Nothing. He would not have hit him. My da hit me but no Matt. If he knew he was smoking, maybe he would not do nothing. Except give him a fag. Matt was past sixteen. People smoked in the house at that age. Their maws and das knew they smoked and let them do it.

Ye went along a lane to the railway station. It was great going down and horrible coming up. Coming up ye were going to school, going down ye were going home. Boys hung about the lane. They wore ordinary clothes and acted tough. They did not go to Matt's school. If they looked at ye it was to fight. Then ye were cornered because it was the lane, ye could not get by. Open yer bag. They did not say it to me but they done it to others. I heard they did. They made them open their bag and chipped stuff out on the ground. If it was worth knocking they took it. Usually it was just books, pens and yer pencils.

They were not always there. People went the other way round, it took ages and ye missed yer train. These boys were like a gang, older than me. It was lasses they were there for. They shouted stuff and tried to talk to them. I saw them doing it. Some lasses talked to them.

But ye did not like passing them. I found a short cut. There was a big dyke on the right side of the lane coming up from the station. Ye climbed it and walked along the top. It was not tiles but double bricks with concrete over, some chipped off and loose, ye had to watch it. On the other side was a grass backcourt. The building was two storeys high. Ye dreeped down the backcourt side of the dyke. But people saw ye doing it. An old man watched out the window, he just sat there all the time. When ye walked the dyke he waved his fist at ye. I did not bother. Another one was a woman hanging out her washing. She shouted at me, Get down from there or I will call the police.

Oh missis a gang is chasing me.

But she did not care. People were posh and told the teachers. One morning the Headmaster spoke over the Address System. It is reported that boys in school uniform are climbing the walls along Station Lane. If anybody climbs into the backcourt properties it is a dismissal offence, you will be expelled for such persistent behaviour.

I usually done it at four o'clock and if these boys were there I dreeped down the other side and skipped through the back close. There was a gate there locked, ye had to climb it. It was wood and shook like it was going to fall down. One time I done it but when I came out the close these ones were there. I ran fast down the road and in the side way to the railway station. I did not see if they chased me but was glad when the train came.

Some at that school were stupid thinking they could fight ye. They just looked at ye and saw ye. Oh we can kill him. But if they did not know ye. How come they could beat ye? They thought that. But it was just stupid. They did not know if ye were posh or what. If they claimed me I would fight them. I would, I would just get into them. They did not know that but I would, if they thought who I was, they did not know and did not know my pals and ones I knew from my scheme. They could have come down here and battered them all.

Imagine I brought the boys with me. We could just take them on. Whoever wanted a fight, we would give them it. That was my real pals. No like from this place. They did not even talk to ye. So you did not talk to them. Who wanted to talk to them? No me. I did not want any of them.

My maw said it. Oh Kieron who is your friends, do you have any friends. I just kidded on. So then I just done something. I said somebody's name to my maw. Oh I am friends with him.

But I was not. It was just one that sat beside me in the Geometry class. He just came and sat. I did not know him, just his name, but he started feeling me. He did not talk but just done it. It was a worry if people were going to see, ye just worried about it and were not going to do it again, never. I did not like him doing it but he just done it, so if he started ye just let him, just slow, that was how he done it and ye just thought about it. Outside school as well and ye were home in the house, ye did not want to, it just came into yer head. Ye were not going to let him do it again, never, and going to school in the morning ye were thinking it too, never never, ye were never going to let him but then if it was a Geometry period next, if it was and ye were there and he came in and was he going to sit beside ye and then he done it, just sat down and got out his books and what was going to happen, ye were nearly shaking just waiting till then if he done it, ye could not stop him, he just done it, and if you were to do it to him, keeping his knee pressed against ye till ye did. That was like a good fighter. He acted like he was. He was not, he was just posh. But he done it with his knee, just pressing in like he was trying to make ye. He could not make me.

So if he was a good fighter and you were not, if he thought that. I could batter him any day of the week. Who was scared of him? No me anyway. But then he was doing it and his knee pressed hard in and just keeping doing it. So you were to do it to him, that was what he wanted, you were to do it back to him. But I did not want to. What if the teacher saw ye? Two lasses sat at the desk behind. So if they saw? What if they did? Oh but it was all the class, that would just be the worst. The lasses would tell them or else the teacher, so all everybody would know and ye were just a nancyboy and a poof, all just laughing at ye. How come? It was just the horriblest thing and I did not want him to start it so if he did I switched round on my seat till my legs were away but then if he still tried it and just kept doing it and his hand was there.

Outside in the playground he had his own pals. He just went with them and did not look at ye. I did not care. I did not want to stand with him anyway. I did not even look at him. I did not want to. If he thought he could do something with me. I would have battered him. And if it was his pals, them too. Just posh ones. Who was scared of them.

But if he told them. He would not tell them. Because it was him, he started it. I went and watched the football.

Too many were playing. That was that in this f*****g school. People were stupid. They did not play it right. How many were on each side? Ye could not even count them. It was just a bunch of maddies running up and down trying to kick the ball. They kicked it anywhere. They did not even know where to kick it. Oh Smith, are you playing?

That was a boy in my class. He was shouting on me. Do ye want a game? Two of ye could come on.

Okay.

I just said it but then I thought I would, I would just go on. Another boy was there watching. It was one on one side one on the other and I said it to him, Oh do ye want a game?

Okay.

So they took us on and we got a game. But it was just so hopeless with all too many people running about and that wee toty ball. It was the worst game ever ye could get. It was not like real football. We played real games out in my scheme, we had great games. All the boys played and it was great. This game on the playground was just the most stupid stupid thing. Nobody could even see if ye were good. Too many were playing. Who was good and who was bad? It was just complete stupid nonsense, just running up and down. And then people stopped playing. They just stopped. Ye heard somebody saying it. Oh to Hell, I am not playing. And they just went away. I done it like the last time. Ye got fed up and ye just thought, Oh I am never going to play it again. But then ye did, ye just wanted a game. So then if the ball came I went in hard and got it, I started doing that. Other ones did not, just shouted at ye, Oh stop kicking.

Well if it is f★★★★★g football, that is kicking.

Yes but not legs.

Oh well sorry.

§

Then all the homework, it was just all the time, homework, home-work homework. I done it on the train or in the station or next morning coming to school. Some ye only could do in the house, ink-exercises. Matt did not like me using his desk. My da had made him it. He joined it on the side of the tallboy, so it was stuck with nails. It was good how he done it, two shelves up above for yer books and stuff. Oh but my maw hated it. He done it when she was at her work for a surprise. She came home and saw it. Oh Johnnie! What did you do that for?

Because he put the nails in the wall and in the side of the tallboy to join on the top of the desk. So if ye took out the nails and took it away all holes were left behind. My maw hated it. Oh if we want to sell the tallboy, now we cannot. Why did you not tell me you were doing it? Now it is ruined it is just ruined. And we cannot move the wardrobe because the shelf is joined to the wall.

My da's face was red.

Oh Johnnie it is just stupid. I wish you had said first. Oh why did you not say it first?

Oh well, I can put it back again.

You cannot put it back again. Really, it is ruined. It will just be holes in the side. My maw went to the side of the wardrobe and was poking at it. Oh and see this crack here, she said. Look, the wood is cracking, and will just get worse. Nobody will buy it now. Oh I wish you had said first.

My da done the job and she did not know he was doing it. He waited till she went to work then made it all as a surprise. Oh I thought ye would be pleased, he said.

Well I am not pleased, it is just silly. Ye have ruined the tallboy. Ye have ruined it.

No I have not.

Yes you have.

I can fix it.

Oh you cannot fix it with all these holes.

I can.

But you cannot. Oh I wish ye would get a job.

Well I want a bloody job, that is what I want.

My maw did not say anything. Because it was his fault he did not have one. He had a job and then he chucked it. He got fed up and just stopped it. That was what my maw said, imagine having a job and just giving it up, it was stupid. Now he was looking for another one. Oh to hell with factories I need the open air.

My maw just looked when he said that. If he wanted back to sea, that was what she was thinking. He said it if he lost his temper, Oh I am going back to sea.

Oh well go back to sea.

Yes I am going.

Well go.

I am bloody well going alright.

My maw and my da were arguing about it a lot. I kidded on I was reading a school book or else just went into the bedroom. Even if Matt was there, he did not say nothing. I was over in my grannie's and said it to her. Oh he is idle, she said, I do not like to see a man idle. If he gets a job he will be fine.

It was nay good him being home. I stayed out the road. If I still had homework I lay on the floor in the room and wrote it there. Matt kept his schoolbooks on the desk all marked at their places. He hated me using the desk and ye could not touch his books. But for ink-exercises it was no fair having to be on the floor. Yer elbow did not fit right when ye were holding yer pen, ye got smudges. Then if it was ink on the carpet my maw went off her head. I needed the desk. My maw told Matt to give me a chance for it. Latin was the worst. Ye needed two schoolbooks and were to write in real ink and watch ye did not smudge the jotter. So I needed the desk, I just needed it, so I used it, because if it was there and I needed it, how could I no, if I needed it? That was a desk for writing on. So I done it. Matt came home and caught me. He walked right in. Oh you have touched my books! Do not ever touch my books I am warning ye. You have touched my books. Do not ever touch them.

I was not touching them.

Never ever ever, he said.

But Matt I was no touching them.

Never ever. Do you hear me? I am warning you. Never ever ever.

So what never ever ever. Never never never never. I did not care about his blooming nevers or evers. I was no shaking in my shoes. No for him. What was he going to do. If he punched me, so what. I did not care, I did not care. Oh but now he grabbed me round the neck gripping me and my shirt got caught, and at the button-hole just that sound. Oh it is ripped it is ripped.

I do not blooming care if it is bloody ripped. Lucky for you I do not lose my temper, lucky for you!

I was gasping, and if he was going to punch me, if he even tried

329

it, even if he tried it. I nearly swore at him. He swore at me. I nearly did, or else spit in his face. And he was going to punch me, nearly going to, and I shouted at him I do not know what, just shouted. He let me go and the door opened and my da marched in just the angriest ever. I shall bloody well give yez both a doing if ye do not shut up. Just shut up. Shut up! Just shut up! My da now was roaring. The two of yez, just the bloody two of yez!

Then it was to Matt. He was looking right at him, very very hard, and if Matt said something back to him, well, ye were just waiting, but Matt did not. My da turned and went back out. I had never seen him so angry, no with Matt. He did not shut the door. I went out after him but into the kitchenette, out on the balcony, and just stayed out the road.

I did not care about Matt's desk anyway. I did not want any desk. So what if I could get it after him. I did not want it after him. I was not doing any things after him. He could do after himself what he was doing, going to College or what, I did not care what he done, I did not want his stuff, nothing about it or about him. I did not care about anything about him and that school, it was his school, it was not my school, it was just bloody horrible just the bloody worstest worse it ever could be. I never saw him there. I did not look for him. Wherever he was, I did not care. So if people saw me talking to him, Oh Smith has a big brother. Maybe they would have said it, Oh who is he, is he yer big brother? But I did not see him and did not want to see him. I just walked the corridors. Where was I going. Here and there, everywhere, and late for classes. I did not see the buildings right. I did not know them. And ye came in the door and they all were looking at ye. Oh we are very glad you could make it. That was the teacher if he was sarcastic. Or they gave ye a look and nodded their head so ye knew. Oh just go to your seat Smith.

Then if it was the wrong class. I got that mixed up and the teachers gave ye angry looks. Upstairs for one period and downstairs for the next and everybody all rushing about then if it was another building. There were three buildings. So ye were walking up and down and roundabout and where was yer class? Nowhere. Five minutes, ten minutes, fifteen. So I just chucked it and missed the period. I went to the lavvy and read a book.

Then what happened I was walking in the playground and the next thing I was out the gate.

That was funny. I did not mean to do it. I passed the Headmaster's Office. Ye had to pass it to get out. So I went right along the Exit Corridor and through without seeing. The jannie did not see me either. So I had done it, that was me. I went away way down the road to the railway station but no to go home because my da was there, so I just kept walking and along and down to the river and waited for the ferry. It was great seeing it come and just going over, and all the boats. Then up a river-street and going to my grannie's. I told her a fib, Oh we do not have to go till tomorrow.

My grannie smiled, she liked to see me. She sat down and was talking.

I was thinking about boasters, how people are boasters. Who was not one. Even yer grannie. She was saying about her family and how they were good people and high-up with high educations and how they all done their studies. She did not say it before. Now she did. How come? Her family did not want granda, only her. Oh you are too good for Lawrence McGuigan, he is just a working man.

She had a fiancé before granda and he went away. He was her first intended. They all wanted her to marry him but he went to New Zealand to make his fortune. So he did not come back. I was glad. Who wanted him? No me, I hoped his boat sank. I was seeing my grannie when she was saying it. Her eyes were just looking, no at me. Then I saw granda. He was there too. He was. And smiling. Oh son is that her talking about me?

Aye granda.

People that were dead had ghosts. Ones that were not long dead especially, their body was still warm. Granda's was still warm. He could even be in it if he was a ghost.

My grannie had stopped talking. Usually she was at the sink and washing stuff. It was all just quiet. That happened. Ye heard a wee sound and it was like somebody. If it was my granda. Where is granda? It came in yer mind and ye looked for him. Maybe he was at the bathroom. If ye heard the plug getting pulled. Maybe it was him. Granda could not pull it good. A stupid old thing and ye had to yank it up and down. A lot of times he could not work it. He came out and banged the door. Stupid old thing. Ye heard him saying it.

Now this time he would hear her. But he would know she was just sad for him. My grannie was no really a boaster. He would just be smiling. Oh is she talking about me?

Granda could still be here if it was his ghost. It would see ye all the time. If people done stuff to ye it was him and he would be watching. But they did not do stuff to me, if they even tried it, just if they tried it. If they even thought they could.

My grannie's eyes were closed. She did not have her specs on. She sat that way and did not listen to the radio. Oh son I am just thinking about things. It was only granda that put the radio on, to hear the news. She never did. Maybe she was sleeping. But she was not. If I got up she would hear me.

I needed a forgery note for the Registration teacher, how I had a bad stomach. He was very strict and belted people, ye needed it right. My grannie had a book with all hospital stuff and names. If it was diarrhoea ye could spell it. The books were on the cupboard in the front parlour. Her writing pad was there as well. Ye done different writing for yer maw and da and signed their names. I knew how to write them. I done my grannie's too. She did printing and not writing. It was fancy and with wee twiddles on the end of the letters. I liked doing hers. I liked all the different ways people done it, straight up and down, as many ways as ye wanted. Ye could write all the names down and they all were different.

But I had to do the whole forgery note like my maw. Kieron has got diarrhoea and went home early.

Ones in that school had typewriters. Ye could do good notes with them to get off school. How come ye had to go if ye did not want to, if it was something ye hated and ye had to do it. If ye did not want to go, how come ye had to?

It was horrible. Snobs were the worst. I hated them the worst of all. If they thought ye would not fight, if ye were just a coward, they were very mistaken, if they thought I was easy. I would batter their heads in.

Imagine bringing Podgie and the boys into this school, ye could just do anything. Ye would just laugh and batter them. 5th year and 6th year too, just blooming snobs. So if Matt was there, so what. Who did he come in with, them or me? Was he a snob? Maybe he was. One of his pals was, I heard him talking and he had a snobby posh voice. That was Matt. He must have liked snobs, that was his pals. Well he could just keep them and go with them. I had my own pals and if it was my own school. I should have went there. How come I did not? Only my maw, she was just a snob, and a boaster. My da was one too but no as bad. But my grannie too. I did not know she was one but she was, if she said these things about a high-up family.

They were all snobs, everybody. Except Uncle Billy. And Auntie May, she was no one either.

Auntie May was going away from grannie's house. Grannie would miss her, she liked having her. Oh she makes me laugh.

My grannie liked laughing. It was great when she did. My granda made her. Now he was away she sat on the chair a lot. She did not sit on it when he was there. My granda said, Oh wummin will ye sit down for a wee minute.

I have no time to sit down for any wee minutes.

She did not sit in granda's chair, just a wooden one. Her eyes were closed, she maybe was sleeping and her face was just

well it was only just

just the way it was, how she was sleeping, if she was sleeping, maybe she was not

I got up and ben the parlour and got the writing pad and pencil and back in, seeing the door did not creak, and onto my chair, quietly, my grannie did not move. The wee cat was there and just looking at me. The other one was away, it got put to sleep. Poor old cat. That was killed, got put to sleep. Oh we got the big cat put to sleep. We just killed it, they killed it. Ye just got killed.

I went to the back pages of my grannie's writing pad and started drawing her, just how she was sitting like it was just sideways, was she going to fall a wee bit, and her elbows like that how they were just, she was just holding one, they were like they were folded a wee bit, just one arm, her elbow and wrist and just her one hand holding the other and ye saw her fingers peeping out, that was funny, how her thumb, sticking out, it was even dirty, a wee bit. My grannie did not mind being clean. My maw worried, my grannie did not. Then her knees too and her skirt, just coming out, her knees just came out, her legs down and her slippers, they were just daft ones with pom poms. Pom-pom slippers. Oh will ye look at that woman's slippers. It was not woman it was wummin. That was my granda. Look at that wummin's slippers son, ye ever seen the likes, a pair of pom-pom slippers.

That was how my granda talked, wummin and didnay, um nay and will nay, he did not care. My maw said that, Oh do not talk like yer grandfather. Yes but he was not a snob. My granda was not. I did not draw him, I wished I had, if I had drew him, I wished I had. I knew people but could not see their faces. I was not good from memory.

§

I went up for Billy MacGregor for a game of football and his maw answered the door. Oh are you going to a good school?

She knew I was but just said it. She did not like me going, she wished it was Billy. What I noticed was a funny thing, how she did not say my name. She used to say my name, Oh hullo Kieron, Billy is not in. But now she did not. I walked over the field with Billy and Peter Wylie but they did not talk much to me either. Boys were waiting to play. Primary 7s too. A big game was on. A lot of times the big ones let us play but if there was too many we did not get on. Catholics were there as well.

We waited to see if ones went away early then some of us got a game. Billy got took first but me second. Podgie and Peter Wylie got a game too. Gary McNab, Mitch and other ones did not except if the big boys were very short of players.

If none of us got a game we went to another bit and started a game ourselves. Some big ones had left school and worked at jobs. Men played too. Podgie's da used to when we were at Primary. Some men played for real teams. One was Gerry Henderson and he played for Stirling Albion. A man called Tam McLennan had games for Celtic reserves. When they were all there we did not get playing much. If ye did ye just tried for a kick. Usually they telled ye to keep out on the wing. Just f★★★★★g run with it and cross it over.

It was tough games and I did not like it much but if ye got playing ye just said, Aye, because it was the big boys and if they asked ye. Our own games were better to play because ye could play good. But we all liked watching the big ones. Their games were a good laugh. Sometimes they went in dead hard and ones got hurted bad and that was them, they just had to lie down and watch. They done that to the weer ones, if ye were running on the wing, they just came in and crunched ye. They done fancy stuff to show off and shouted all stupid nonsense. And about religion too. Gerry Henderson was a Pape and he was a laugh. He said stuff about True Blues. Oh I am no playing in that c★★t's team, he is a bitter Bluenose b★★★★★d, he plays a f★★★★★g flute for the Orange Lodge.

Proddies shouted too. Oh there will be no Signs of the Cross off you ya Fenian c★★t. Oh look at that f★★★★★g rebel b★★★★★d he is crossing himself, I am no picking him in my f★★★★★g team, what is he the f★★★★★g Pope.

One game they did not even pick sides. One picked up the ball and shouted, Papes versus Proddies! He booted it high up in the air like a rugby kick. So that was the game started. Everybody all was laughing. That was Papes on one side, Proddies on the other. They all just played. Papes against Proddies and it was a laugh.

I did not see who won because me and the boys went to get a game of our own but that was what I was thinking because we did not have full sides, I could have went up and got Pat and Danny and then their pals that were Catholics, we could have had a big game too. Ours was just four against four.

After that we went back to see them playing cards. Then we were just talking about stuff. No me because I did not want to. They were saying about their school and stuff and what was happening. Boys came from all over the schemes to go and there was a lot of tough stuff. There was a fight and one had a blade in his pocket. A teacher took it off him and was lucky he did not get the blade stuck in him. Gary McNab's big brother was pals with that boy and he was just a mental case. He ran about with a gang that all had motorbikes and leather jackets. The boys were talking about it, ye could go a motorbike at sixteen. Gary's brother had turned fifteen and was leaving school soon then he would get a job and save up for one. He ran about with the same gang. That was how ye said it, if one went about with people. Oh he runs about with them.

Podgie said to me, Hey Smiddy, is there any gangs in your school?

Oh aye.

What like are they?

Well I do not f*****g know them.

Are they hard? said Mitch.

Aye. No that hard but.

Do they carry?

I think some of them.

Mitch meant about blades. Gangs carried blades. I did not see them. Mitch had one but no all the time.

There was tough ones in my year but no as tough as all that. Gary's brother would just laugh, him and his pals would kill them. But Podgie and the boys too, imagine them coming to school with me, just for one day, we could walk up the school gates, maybe round the cafe. It would be a laugh.

They did not get Latin. Peter and Billy got French. I would have been in their class. Latin was a dead language of the Roman Empire. Matt got it as well. My da said it was ridiculous if it was a dead language, and if it was the Holy Roman Empire, that was RCs. He just said it for a joke. Matt was no there when he did. My maw was pleased I got Latin. Ye got it at good schools but not at other ones.

I was going to say about the Belgium boy in my class but I did not. Imagine a Catholic in yer class. But I was wanting to say it. Matt had a darkie in his, she was a lassie. I saw her, her wee sister was in the year below.

They got other stuff at their school. Woodwork. I fancied Woodwork. Podgie and them got Metalwork. Lasses got Domestic. They were in the Junior Secondary and did not get a language. And they got Arithmetic. We did not, we got Geometry and Algebra and then Logarithms. Peter and Billy got that too but the other ones did not. Podgie said, Oh we are dumbies.

Gary McNab and the Primary 7s laughed. I did not. Podgie would see if I did. He said it for me. I just knew him. Mitch said, Oh Smiddy are you still joining the Navy?

Oh aye.

I was glad he said it because how they all were looking. Mitch was going in the Army when he was seventeen. For the Navy it was seventeen as well unless it was fifteen, ye joined as a Cadet. Then after two years ye signed on for seven, or else nine. Ye got good wages.

But that was the Royal. My da told me it was best to think about it first. If it was the Merchant Navy ye could just do voyages. He done that, Brazil or Africa, then ye got the South China Seas. It was all pirates down there then if it was Borneo and all headhunters. But he liked it. He was going back in. He said he was but my maw did not want him to. But imagine he did and I was there and on the same boat as him. Ye were just stuck in the same place. What if it was the same cabin?

Me and Mitch talked about it. If I was in the Navy and he was in the Army and it was a War on, if my boat was taking the troops to the overseas, so all the troops came on board and Mitch was one. That would be a laugh. Oh but it would be f*****g great, said Mitch. Ye would just tell people oh there is my pal.

And he would shout on me and wave over. But before that he wanted me to join the Army, the two of us could do it the gether. People done that, they just went in the same bit. Oh but you join the Navy, I said.

I would never f*****g join the Navy.

Well I would not join the f*****g Army.

Oh but Smiddy ye can go places.

Mitch always said that. He loved going on boats and swimming and all other stuff about the Navy but no if ye were there for good and it was just all the time. Because where could ye go? Even just a walk, ye could not go one. Ye could no go anywhere. That was what he hated, ye were just stuck and could not get out. And ye needed to, ye just needed to. So ye could not go anyplace, just round and round the boat, it would just be f*****g horrible, just a horrible nightmare.

I thought that too. I only said Navy. I was no meaning it. We used to say when we were weer but no much now, only sometimes and only if it was Mitch. I did not think about it if he was not there. Something else I was thinking I did not say to people, no even Mitch, because if they thought ye were a boaster, I was not a boaster. It was just how if I could play football, play for a real team. Maybe I could. Billy was the one people said. But how no me too? When we got a game with the big ones they picked him first but it was me second. That was me before Podgie. They picked me instead. Podgie hated it. It did not mean I was better than him. But maybe it did. Podgie was a good tackler but he just kicked people. So people gave him the ball so they would not get kicked. Podgie came in on the tackle so they just kicked the ball away. They were feared. But that was our games, no the big Sunday ones. Podgie could not go in and boot the big boys. They just booted him back, and they done it sorer.

Oh but Billy had a great great shot. How did he do it? How can some kick it hard and other ones cannot? Maybe their leg does it quicker, just boom, or if it is a thick leg. Even at the good school and that stupid daft game out in the playground. Ones there could really belt that wee ball, they just thudded it so really hard, McEwan, how did he do it? I tried to but could not do it good. Except if it was dropping down, just bouncing, then ye could.

Imagine Billy in that playground game. What if he came and played. Maybe he would not be so good. Ye could not be good in that game, too many were running about. Really, it was just s***e.

Billy was a good runner too but maybe I was faster. But he was a great dribbler. But then passing, he was just great at passing. The big ones said that. Oh wee Billy is a great passer of a ball. When they picked sides they picked him first among all us. They even picked him before some big ones. I saw them doing it. Billy was just the best player. But they picked me second of the wee boys and people saw it. I was not boasting, they just done it.

§

There was not much fighting at the good school except football in the playground if somebody booted ye so ye booted them back or went in hard and they just swiped at ye. Or else rugby, if they stuck their arms out and shoved ye so if ye shoved them back or in the scrum somebody punched ye.

We got rugby practice. Ye picked the ball up and threw it back the way, ye ran forward but threw it back. Some boys knew about rugby. I did not, and other ones. Ye ran about if it was windy, or else if it was not ye just stood still and were freezing. Big ones were good at it, fat ones leaned on top of ye. The old PE teacher liked rugby better than football and wanted us to play it. Ye aye got muddy falling down. Some just stayed out the way. I was one except I was no a bad runner. The teacher shouted at me to carry the ball, run with it, get to the byline and leave it on the ground behind the goal, and that counted as a goal. One boy was a fast runner and knew how to do it. Hannah. Oh tackle him, tackle him.

Ye were to dive on top of him but he was good at it and shoved everybody out the road. If it was football it was a foul but rugby ye could shove them, even if it was a slap, I went to tackle him and he slapped me.

Oh f**k off!

I shouted at him loud and people all heard. But Hannah just ran away and got the goal.

The teacher did not give me a row for swearing but then I was passing him and he said, Oh Smith, next time tackle him.

Hannah would have beat me at fighting. He was one of the best fighters. But if ye tackled him he did not fight, he did not care, and not about me swearing at him. Oh it is just a game. The teacher said, There will be no fighting. If there is any fighting to be done it is me that will do it.

He got angry at ones that did not play right, if ye did not try. Oh rugby is a man's game. Be a man, be a man!

He ran beside ye when ye were running. Keep going Smith keep going. I thought he was going to tackle me but he did not. Oh keep going keep going. I just ran fast to score a goal. And him shouting at ye, Oh do not throw it do not throw it!

Ye were just to put it down then dive on top of it. But with some big ones, ye went to tackle them and they just shoved ye away easy. But the way the good ones tackled you was diving. That was big Brogan and Hannah, they just dived in and grabbed ye. A boy called Stewart was running with the ball and big Brogan came to get him. Stewart looked over and saw him and just threw the ball away. The PE teacher made him pick it up and run with it again and then tackled him, the teacher did, he tackled Stewart. Then he got up and was angry again because his tracksuit trousers were completely mud, mud mud right through them. See what you made me do Stewart!

That made Stewart scareder and ye felt sorry for him.

If the ball came and ye dribbled it like football the teacher hated it. Even if ye kicked it past everybody and ran up to score a goal, he just hated it. That is not rugby.

Most people did not like rugby. The Belgium boy got a note from his parents. The teacher tore the note up. Oh then just stay in the dressing room.

So the Belgium boy had to stay in the dressing room and the teacher locked the door so he could not get out.

But what he done, his homework!

He just finished it. Ye got off the rugby. I could do a forgery note from my mother. Please sir could Kieron be excused from rugby practice, so then ye just done yer homework.

Boys done forgery stuff with railway passes. I saw them on the train. The names and dates were on the green cards. Ink from biro pens was best but no for matching. That was fountain pens and black ink but ye had to watch because it smudged easy. Some things were good for changing. A 1 to a 4, a 2 to a 4, a 2 to a 9. Then if it was September to November, December. January to February. Other ones looked hard. The best thing was razor blades. My grannie kept my granda's. Ye got one and scraped out the real date. Ye done it light so ye did not tear the card. If ye scraped too much it showed white and the railway porters would know. Then if the ink blotted.

But if ye done it good they did not see it. The railway porters were in a rush and did not look at them. But if they saw the forged one they grabbed it off ye, wrote down yer name and address.

It was okay for me if it was Pat's da, he collected tickets at the station. When ye got off the train and it was him standing at the gate ye just walked through and he winked at ye and did not look. But if it was another one he did look so ye had to have the pass to show him.

I was going to do it. My maw gave me the money for the pass every week. If I done it I could keep the money and save it up. I could just go and do anything and what else? Anything just I wanted, if it was my money. So it was nothing to do with them. No even my da.

There was a cafe near the school station and people went to it but it was dear to sit in with drinks or else a roll and sausage, but if ye had money it was great. The boy called McEwan went with his pals. One was in my class. He looked over but did not talk to me. They had a jukebox for the Top Twenty. Lasses went as well. People just talked to them. I was in it one time and a lassie from 1C dropped a spoon and I picked it up and gave her it. Oh thanks, she said, just quiet.

I hoped she would not know I was in 1G. Then my nose how if ye looked at one side it was okay but the other side was not, just squinty. Ye wanted lasses to see it the good way, but I did not care, no in that school.

A woman teacher hit a boy on the ear and knocked off his specs.

She was giving him the strap. She was young and with a quiet voice and looked over yer shoulder when ye were writing. She came behind ye and had on perfume. I could not hear her and wondered if she was still there and then just very very quiet ye heard her breathing. I stopped writing to look round and see.

Oh please carry on with your work.

The boy that she done it to, she held the tips of his fingers in her left hand and then swung the strap down but she could not do it right. Her shoulder went up and down in a funny way. The strap went way out and ye knew it was going to miss but then it hit his ear. People were talking about it. If that boy's father got lawyers to the teacher because what if it bashed the glass and splinters went in his eye. She should be sacked from her job. If they got lawyers, lawyers would just sack her. What if that boy went blind?

Others teachers missed ye as well, or if it just hit the very tips of yer fingers, but it was sore and stung ye. Our Registration teacher was good at giving the strap. Other ones hit ye up the wrist but no him. If he caught ye writing forgery notes it was the strap. For persistent absence some sent ye to the Headmaster but he did not, just belted ye. All the teachers were posh and so was he, McKinnon, with curly hair and a red face. Some let ye away with things but no him. He liked the Bible and gave ye prayers. Usually Registration lasted ten minutes then ye went to yer first class but on Fridays it was a real class except ye got Religion. Ye had to read verses and memorize bits while he marked up the Attendance Register for the week. He asked ye questions. The Pharisees and the Sea of Galilee. Who entered and passed through Jericho. The Lord Jesus. And who was hiding up a tree. Zacchaeus, son of Abraham. Was he a rich man or a poor man? Then if anybody could say a verse. And the second one came, saying, Lord, thy pound hath gained five pounds.

If you did not get the answer right he did not tell ye it, just moved on to the next person. People gave the answers. Even ones that acted tough. The Registration teacher did not speak much. Ye went to his desk to give him a sick letter and ye had to stand there when he read it. Ye got a sore stomach. He finished and stared at ye. He did not know if ye had made it all up. He never asked ye. Oh but you were to tell him. That look he done at ye, right in at yer eyes. And ye were to say it to him, Please sir it was not my mother it was me, I wrote the letter.

That was what he wanted. People said stuff to him then got the strap. Ye knew ye were to get it. Ye walked to the middle of the floor. He got the strap out his desk. It was rolled up. Ye were to hold out yer hands. He did not tell ye to, except if ye could not do it. Ye wanted to keep yer hands in yer pockets and see what he would say, but ye did not. He just waited for ye to hold yer hands out and be ready, then he saw ye were ready and Wham, Wham, Wham. Some were too scared to hold out their hand and were greeting even before he done it. He waited for them to stop but if they could not stop he just said, Come on now, and usually they did.

He hit ye on one hand or he hit ye on two. Ye crossed yer hands for two. He done it in an order so ye knew what it was, one smack for a wee thing, two smacks if it was more, then three then four and then it was six. Nobody got five. Four was bad, yer hand went past the stinging stage to numb. Six was for the worst. Nobody got it in my class. McEwan did. He was in 1F so the Registration teacher was not even his teacher.

People talked about McEwan. Ye wondered what he got the belt for, maybe if it was stealing. McEwan stole stuff. Everybody knew it. But if it was stealing he would have got expelled. People said that too. I waited to hear what he got the belt for but nobody said.

After the Registration teacher belted ye ye were to return to yer desk. People were holding their wrists and blowing into their hands, Aaahh, aahh. Or else if ye were greeting. Some teachers wanted ye to rub yer hands and look like it was horrible agony. I would just have laughed at them. But that made it worse. Blind impudence. One teacher said that, Oh this is blind impudence.

The Registration teacher put the strap back in the desk and if ye were rubbing yer hands he stared at ye till ye remembered to go back to yer desk. Ye got one, two, three or four. No many posh ones got strapped. People said lasses did not get the belt but one did, Effie Stewart, and it was the worst ever. She was a big girl and acted tough. Ye thought she would greet when he gave her it but she did not. He gave her two. They were hard ones. That was how he done it.

She walked fast to her desk after he strapped her. Even it looked cheeky the quick walk she done. Then she sat down and stuck her tongue out. But it was no at him. She was looking down at the desk, her hands up at her head and her head bended over. Her eyes were shut and her tongue poking out. How come? Was she greeting? I could not see proper but then did. Just how her head was and her hands up at her eyebrows, just smoothing them, smoothing them, her fingers just doing it. Nobody was looking at her. I just was because I was near her and was wanting to see, just to see. I did not know if she was greeting. Her head was bent over and her tongue poking out, just poking out. It went on a long while. Ye thought if she was sleeping but she wasnay, I knew she wasnay. I got an angry feeling. It was in my stomach and coming up my throat so I was gulping to stop it, what it was, I do not know, if I was going to greet or something, or what, and my stomach. It was not greeting. I thought it was, that I was going to but it was not. Then ye were just wanting away. People quite liked the Registration teacher. Oh he is fair, he only straps ye if ye deserve it. But no now, hitting a lassie, imagine hitting a lassie, that is what I thought, ye just wanted to batter him, if ye were a man, ye would have battered him, he was just a rotten c**t, I f*****g hated him.

Another one went on and on about stuff that was nothing to do with the class and acted tough with everybody. Oh he has got a mental age of three. A boy said that about him, a mental age of three. Ye thought he was going to smack ye on the back of the head. He walked up the passage and stared at ye with big eyes and raised his hand as if to do it, then just pulled at his ear. People said what they would do if he ever tried it, their father would get lawyers. He was a big man. I thought about how ye would get him if it was me and the boys were there, even just Mitch. One could spit in his face then he was wiping himself and the two of ye just jump him. Ye could pick up something and batter him with it. Ye would just keep out his clutches. He had great big hands and if he skelped ye ye would feel it. He had hands bigger than my da, if he hit ye ye would fly across the room.

The girls did not like him. He said to one, Oh you are just a smelly little girl.

He had two wee daughters of his own and told stories about all stuff. People asked him stupid questions because he forgot the lessons and just said stories. He told one about daft people. Boys were tapping their heads at him. I did not, because what if he was daft? Ye had to watch it with daft people if ye were making a fool of them. What if they caught ye doing it? Back in the old place a daftie stayed at the top of my street and guarded his close. He did not let ye in unless ye stayed up the stair. If ye ran through he tried to whack ye. People done it to get chases off him but if he caught ye it was sore. One time he gripped my arm very tight and slapped me on the face. I was not the worst but he could not catch the big boys, his fingers pressing in my arm. My maw was angry but my grannie knew about the man. Oh he is just simple, she said. We had them in the scheme too so ye were careful.

This story the teacher told was just stupid, a grown-up family with two women that were old. They were sisters and had long straggly hair with white faces and red red lips. People were feared of them. Wee ones used to shout at them but they stopped it. Then they were elderly people and at death's door. One day they went to the shops for messages. The teacher passed by and saw them at a lamp-post looking this way and that. How come?

Oh they are waiting for a bus, a man said, making a joke. But it looked like the two old sisters were. They had been to the shops and their messages were lying at their feet. Ye wondered would they walk on and forget about them. What would happen if they did and left their messages lying. So if ye were a Christian what would ye do. Would ye lift up the messages and steal them, or else take them to their house. Would ye just leave them there. Would somebody else come along and steal them. What if they were a Christian. What if ye had no money. What if yer maw and da had none and ye needed these messages for yerself. There was no food in yer house. Would ye take them and give them to yer maw. Or else give them to the cops to feed the poor, if the poor was needy and wanted them. The teacher said about his little daughter, that was what she wanted to do, Oh daddy if we can give the messages to the poor.

The teacher thought how right she was and was proud of her for such a little girl. But instead of doing that he just picked up the messages and brought them to the two sisters' house. That was the wisest course of action. The stories went on and on and made ye late for the next class but they were better than the lessons.

Some teachers ye thought what things they taught just by looking at them. Latin teachers and Maths teachers were the same, then English teachers and History teachers, and Geography teachers and Maths teachers too. Some tried to be funny all the time or made a joke against ye. One boy in the class was good at being cheeky and he done it so the teacher did not know, but then he wondered and ye saw him looking but the boy acted like it was not anything. Then he came out and said something else and it was nearly total cheeky except it was not, just in no more. The teacher was waiting if it would go further but the boy just smiled. He talked very posh and his da was something like a dentist or an architect, that was how ye could see the teacher. If it was me or other ones he did not care at all but that boy he did.

There was none of them I liked. Except counting PE teachers, Mr Ramsay, he played football for a team down in England. We did not get football much. He took us when we did. Usually he just reffed the games. But if it was before the game and he passed the ball ye could see how he done it. He hardly even touched the ball and it done what he wanted. If he booted it hard nobody could have stopped it. He had on football shorts so ye could see it with his legs, how they were just so thick, but no fat and white, just brown as if he was just back his holidays. Then his bulge, it was a very big bulge, people talked about it, Oh he must have a big dick. Ye thought how that would be if it was you if ye were a man. Ye would just do what ye wanted. Nobody would say anything. Ye would have a laugh. And then if ye were playing for a big team and if it was against teams from Europe maybe if it was Italy or Spain and Real Madrid and ye got the ball and it was out on the wing, the ball coming to ye, right up in the air and ye just caught it on yer foot and let it bounce once then ye just hit it round the defender, right between his legs and running onto it, and to the byline and cutting in and people thinking Oh he is going to cross it but ye do not, ye just zoom it right into the net, a beauty, what a goal.

He never talked to people except, You go there and You go there, and everybody done what he wanted. It was just because of football, ye knew he was a very good player. People liked the old PE teacher as well but he was no a real football player, he just hit the ball the same way and did not hit it with all the different bits and that was Mr Ramsay, he could just hit it any way, just how he wanted.

§

Milkboys were loaded. It was the tips that done it. Ye did not worry about the wages. And ye got stuff too. If ye wanted milk ye just drank it and said it was a leaky bottle. Then if a woman came out the house to see if there was any spare milk you just selled her a bottle and did not tell the milkman, ye kept the money to yerself. Gary's big brother had the best clothes and the best style and haircuts. If ye had clothes like that ye would feel good. A milkboy was the best job. Out them all. Ye started dead early and then were finished for the day. Ye were out the house at five in the morning and back in the house for eight then yer breakfast, a sausage piece or else fried egg. Then Friday night ye collected yer money and made yer tips.

When Gary's brother left school he got his milkboy job. I went with him to see if I could get one too. The man was there that drove the milklorry. I waited for Gary to say about me. But he did not, he just jumped up and climbed in the cabin. The door was open and I was looking at him but he did not say nothing, he just was laughing, no at me but just because of the lorry, that was him and he was up sitting in it, he was just laughing, he forgot me. I had never been on a lorry and not much in a motor car except my granda's funeral. Oh Gary! I shouted up at him.

He waved out the window to me. I ran round the front of the lorry and shouted to the man, Oh mister! Mr!

Aye what is it son?

Any chance of a job?

Naw, sorry.

So that was me. He just drove away. I saw Gary the next time and he said, Tough luck, maybe ye will get one later.

He had fags and we smoked one. But I knew I would not get a job later. I would never get one. That was just me, if it was Fate, I did not f★★★★g care. I said it to Gary and he laughed but really it was no funny, it was all just hopeless, if ye thought about Gary and his brother and me and mine, and then if it was jobs or what ye had, what things happened to ye. People were lucky in their life with Fate but I was not. People got stuff. I never. Gary said, Oh if a job comes I will tell ye.

But I knew he would not, it was Podgie he would tell. I did not care. I did not care about Gary and them and just whatever, they could just do it, I did not care. Except if I had got the job. Imagine I did. If I did. I would just be f★★★★g shouting, shouting and laughing. If anybody saw me they would be looking. Oh what is up with Smiddy?

But I did not get a job. I would never. It would just be other ones. Then Mitch told me about one he was getting. Mitch. He was even to get one. His big sister's boyfriend knew a man that drove a van to do with deliveries. He was talking for Mitch. Oh it is my big sister's boyfriend, he is talking for me.

He is talking for me. People said that for a job. So if ye were fifteen and could leave school, people talked for ye and ye got a job, or if it was yer apprenticeship, ye got yer apprenticeship, people talked for ye. My da said that too, Ye need somebody to talk for ye.

Nobody talked for him. He did not get a job. Then if he did it was no a good one. Oh I will join the Masons, that was what my da said. I told my grannie and she said, Oh they will no let him in but they will let in you.

Because my granda was one. They would not let my da in the Masons but for me and Matt we could get in because we were blood. And then we would get a job easy. But only when we were twenty-one. It did not matter for milkboy jobs.

Just if somebody talked for ye. But they did not talk for me, just other ones. So there was Gary and now Mitch. People got stuff but I did not, I did not get stuff. Other people did. I did not. And if they got it they did not want it. That was even my brother. He got a job and then just chucked it after one week. People that wanted jobs did not get them, just them that did not.

Then it was Mitch! He was saying it too. Just how he did not fancy it. How come? What was he saying? He did not fancy the job. He might not even take it, if he got it, if the people gave him the job, he might no even take it. Oh but I might no take it. That was what he said. No take the delivery job. He was meaning that. He could get a job and was not going to take it.

Oh but Mitch, I said, it would be great.

Aye but

Oh see if it was me!

Aye but I do not fancy it.

Oh f**k I would do it.

Aye but Smiddy ye have to go all the time. If ye do not they f*****g sack ye.

Do ye work Saturdays?

I do not know.

Oh Mitch take it.

Maybe.

Oh f**k it would be great. Getting yer own wages, it would just be yer own money. Oh ye have to do it.

Oh but Smiddy.

Oh no ye have to. Ye just have to. I would f*****g do it with ye.

Would ye?

Aye.

Well maybe I will.

Oh Mitch for f**k sake take it.

Well if you do it with me.

Oh of course, just of course, of course. Oh for f**k sake Mitch if it is a job! Oh f**k sake.

Mitch was laughing. You are f*****g mental ya c**t.

F**k sake Mitch.

I just ran hame after that but who to tell, nobody. Nobody.

§

When ye walked to the subway from my grannie's street there was good shops for clothes and I was seeing them for if I got a job, just if I did and could save money. I would be able to. Then I could just buy my stuff. Great shirts, jeans, jerkins and trousers, casual shirts too and smart jackets, and denhim jackets. Just the best denhim jackets and that was what I wanted, one with big inside pockets and they would be great for keeping stuff and how they just looked good, I just liked them. My maw did not. She said I was not to get them. But if it was my money? I would just get them. I said it but she just got angry.

Matt laughed, Ye should not blab. You always blab.

I was just saying to her.

Yes but ye should not. Once ye get a job ye just go and do it, do not tell people. You tell people everything.

I do not.

Yes ye do. Just go and buy it.

But I cannot because I have no got any money.

Well what are ye talking about?

Just when I get a job.

Oh, okay.

It is a denhim jacket, a beauty.

A denhim jacket. Matt laughed. If ye wore that to school they would send ye home.

Oh well good.

Yes ye say that now.

I will say that all the time.

Okay.

I will say it all the time.

Good.

Imagine no letting ye wear a denhim jacket to school. That is just stupid.

Yes.

So if they send ye home for wearing one. I think I would wear it. Then if they sent me home, that would be good, I would be glad. So if ye got out of school, who wants to go there anyway. I would just wear it.

Matt shifted round on his seat at the desk so he would not see me. I was in bed and it was time for the light out but he was wanting to read more. I did not mind. But if I read a book I fell asleep. It was because it was schoolbooks. If I could just read an ordinary book. But if I did I still fell asleep. I was too tired. If I wanted to read a book I done it in the kitchenette so I stayed awake. Sometimes I read it in the living room but if the television was on my da did not like me doing it. He gave grumpy looks. How come, if I was just reading a book. What was wrong with that, if the telly was on. I did not tell him to turn it down. I did not care. I just read the book. My head went in it and I did not hear the telly. I did not care about it.

Matt thought the same as me, he never read in the living room. It was just dad, how he took things like that, as if ye were making him feel bad. I was not. I did not care if he watched the telly, I just wanted to read my book. The telly was boring, I did not care about it. In books ye got anything ye liked. But it was his telly, his and my maw's. She backed him up. Then he backed up her.

That was it with the clothes, because when I got a job. My maw went on and on about it. She did not like it because if I had money I could just do what I thought. So if it was to buy clothes, if it was my pay and my money, well I could just save up and spend it. I could buy what I wanted, if it was new jeans and a denhim jacket, so what.

Oh it is just hooligan clothes, it is hooligans who dress like that. That was my maw.

But if it is my job and my money.

It does not matter.

If it is my money? Well if it is I can buy any stuff.

Kieron!

How no? If it is my money.

Do not be so daft, said my da.

But dad it is not daft. What if I am going to places like the pictures or else to a cafe? Even just walking about. I need my own clothes, outside clothes.

The police will lift ye if ye walk about looking like that, denhim jackets and jeans.

How come?

It is hooligan clothes.

How come?

Because ye are wearing them.

Aye but if I am no doing anything?

Ye know fine well what I mean.

Your dad is right. If you wear clothes like that then you are a boy from the streets, they are just street clothes.

Yes but mum if ye wear them on the street, so that is you on the street, so they are street clothes. What is wrong with that? They are not house clothes.

Do not be cheeky to yer mother.

I am no being cheeky.

Yes you are, said my maw.

No I am no.

No you are not.

No I am not.

Kieron do not be so cheeky.

I am no being cheeky.

You are not being cheeky.

I am not being cheeky.

Ye bloody well are, said my da. Ye are no too big for a skelp, just you remember that.

But I was too big for a skelp. My da would not have hit me. If he did I would just have done something, I would have done something, I do not know what. They could not do anything about my clothes, no if it was my money and I got it from my job, and I was going to.

Oh what about that nice boy? said my maw, I never hear you talking about him.

Who?

You heard, said my da.

That nice boy, said my maw.

I do not know who you mean?

He was in your Geography class.

Richard Carslake, said my da. My da always remembered his name. So did my maw, but she kidded on she did not. But it was Geometry and not Geography.

Are you still friends with him? said my maw.

No.

That is a shame.

Mum I was not friends with Motorpuddle, he is just a stupid boaster.

His name is Carslake and he is a nice boy.

Just because he is posh, that is how you like him. Ye have never met him.

Kieron do not be cheeky.

I am not being cheeky.

Yes you are.

I am not.

You are.

He just tells fibs all the time, just all stupid nonsense.

Oh do not talk like that, it is not nice.

Mum he is a snobby boaster and tells fibs. I am not pals with him. He is not pals with me and I am not pals with him.

Well who is yer pals? said my da.

Pardon?

You heard. Who is yer pals?

Well ye know them, I said, if it is my pals, Billy and Mitch and Peter and Gary, and Podgie.

My da looked at me then turned his head.

You know what your dad means, said my maw.

My pals?

If you have friends in school.

Oh.

But I knew that. My da was a snob too. He was holding up the paper, kidding on he was reading it. That was what he done. But he listened to everything. I did not say any names. They were not meaning my real pals, just ones from the good school. I went one time to Motorpuddle's house and they loved hearing about it. But it was just lies and stupid nonsense. It was to play football at a park near his house, a real football pitch. But there was not a game, he was just a snobby boaster and was lying. He stayed in a big house and his da did a good job. For my maw everything had to be posh. That was how she liked him and when I went up for him. Oh you will be a guest, you will need to act like one.

But mum it is just for a game of football.

Oh but if he takes ye into his house. You will have to behave properly. Do not say umnay didnay and willnay. Please do not. And say bathroom if it is the bathroom, do not say lavatory.

Ye might get yer tea, said my da. He was laughing. A big juicy steak with mushrooms and chips.

That was my da, all just food and dinners. It was stupid. Motorpuddle was a liar. Liar was a bad word in my house and ye could not say it. And if it was about him, oh they loved him. He stayed up an old building, one storey up with fancy walls and painted windows. It was the same as the one near the railway lane where they had grass out in the backcourt and wee flowers roundabout. Anybody could steal them. Grass was in the middle where the women hung out their clothes and inside the house it was all different and giant big ceilings. I had to take my shoes off and go into the lounge. It was him said it. Oh you will have to take off your shoes to go into the lounge.

My maw had to hear about it, lounge. His young sister was there and just lying on the carpet. His da was there too. His mother was out at the shops. Oh this is a friend from school.

His da shook hands with me. His young sister did not look up. I was to sit on the couch. Motorpuddle lied beside her. It was a children's picture on television about farm animals, they were owned by a farmer who did not like them and wanted to sell them to the butcher. Just a complete children's picture. There was a clock up on the mantelpiece. I was waiting for him to say about the football. It just went on and on. The end came and I got up to go to the toilet. He came to show me. I said, Are we going to play football?

No, there is not a game today.

How come?

Oh it is just cancelled.

There was not a game. It was all just stupid nonsense. He thought he was big because it was me, he thought he could do stuff and I would be too scared or what, just because he was posh and I was not, if I would not batter him, but I would have battered him, if he thought he could do things to me. I hated him and just showing off all the time. Other ones too. Then f*****g homework. I did not f*****g care about f*****g homework. They put their hand up to answer and said it if the teacher telled them. Oh please come out and demonstrate. It is triangles and two sides for the equation. They went out and done it because the teacher said it. Oh 6a equals x minus 1z if it is multiplied by 2z. The teacher gave them the chalk and they wrote it on the blackboard. Imagine doing that. Maybe Matt done it too, he was good at mathematics. I was glad, because I was not. So if he went to College, I was glad and if it was his desk, he could just take the desk, I did not want it, I was not going to College, I had my own pals.

§

I wanted my own delivery run. If the driver saw I was doing it good with Mitch, maybe he would give me one. I hoped that. He could do his and I could do mine so the two of us would have our money. It would be great, all just for yerself and what ye wanted to

355

spend it on, ye could just spend it on anything. I needed the job. I needed it.

The deliveries went to people out in a new scheme. It was a big long walk over the field and up the hill and away round past the old Squatters' Camp, away way past. My da thought it was good but my maw did not, if it interfered with my lessons. But if it was two doing it we would just run round and get home fast and it would not interfere.

The man brought the deliveries to the corner of the first street. Ye filled yer bags and he gave ye the delivery sheets. Ye had yer own streets and yer own customers. Other boys had theirs. He gave ye the sacks to keep in the house. Ye were supposed to go home after school and get them to go back out again but I did not, I just took them to school and went straight to the job. Ye had to be there at twenty-five to five. He was waiting but only for five minutes. If ye did not come he went away and took stuff to other boys then came back at five to five. He waited five minutes again. If ye were no there that second time he did not come back till half past five. After that ye were finished and ye just had to go and see the boss.

The first day I got off the train from school and went straight from the railway station to meet the van. I had the delivery sacks inside my school bag. I had two and Mitch had two. But Mitch still had not come and the driver was waiting. He thought I was Mitch and was a wee bit angry. Oh for f**k sake son, I cannot give ye nay f*****g parcels.

Oh but mister.

What is yer f*****g name?

Kieron Smith.

Kieron Smith. Are ye a Fenian b*****d?

No. I am Mitch's pal. We are doing the deliveries the gether.

Well I am f*****g sorry but I cannot give ye the f****rs. The boss goes off his head if ye do something like that. I was telled to give the stuff to a c**t called Mitchell. If you are not Mitchell ye do not f*****g get them.

Oh but that is Mitch, he is my pal. It will be fine, honest. He just went to get his sacks. I have got mines here.

I brought them out my school bag to show him.

Oh f**k. He took off his bunnet and scratched his head. His hair was all flattened down. He looked at his watch. F**k it, he said, and started giving me the parcels. I was putting them in my two sacks but then there was no much room left. Oh for f**k sake, he said, and was looking at his watch. Where is that wee c**t?

He is just coming. If ye give me them I can carry them in the close and just wait for him. He will be here in a minute.

I cannot f*****g do that, I telled ye.

How no?

How no! What if some c**t f*****g robs ye?

Oh but they will not.

How do you know?

Oh because they would not. I would not f*****g let them. Oh mister come on, I can just wait for him.

The driver closed his eyes. He did not want to do it. But if I brought all the deliveries in the first close then he could just drive away and no have to come back again. So that was good for him. So he waited a wee minute then just done it. I stuffed the two sacks full and carried them into the close and walked back for the next load, just to carry them and put them beside the sacks. He shouted at me. For f**k sake man hurry up. And never you leave yer f*****g sacks lying about, there is aye some c**t watching. And it is you pays the losses.

What?

It is you pays the f*****g losses.

Me?

You, aye, who the f**k else? What do ye think the f*****g boss will pay it for ye! It is you. You pay.

But if it is not my fault?

What ye f*****g talking about man if you leave them lying, and some c**t lifts them! Of course it is your f*****g fault.

Aye but if I do not know?

Well ye f*****g should know, it is your f*****g deliveries.

Aye but

Nay aye buts just do not let them out yer sight.

I carried all the parcels into the close and he tooted his horn and drove away. His name was Freddy and he was the worst swearer ever. I could not have told my maw. She would just have I do not know what. She would not have liked it. But he did not mind if ye swore back and ye were just to call him his name, Freddy. Some adults did not like ye calling their name and if ye swore, even if they swore at you. And it was the same with fags, he did not mind if ye were smoking but just asked ye for a fag. You are too young to smoke, give it to me. But he did not like giving you one. But ye felt good working with him. He just talked to ye that way, oh man, f**k sake man f*****g c**ts.

I sat down on the steps to read my school lessons for tomorrow. People were passing along the pavement, lasses too.

Teachers gave ye preparation to do. Ye were to look at pages for stuff and to memorize. It was freezing sitting there. I put the sacks beside me and they were warm.

A paperboy came fast in the close, taking papers out his bag while he went. He passed by folding a newspaper, shoved it through the first letterbox then ran up the stair two at a time. Then was jumping back down and out the close, walking fast to the next one. That was good about newspapers, just folding them up and shoving them through the letterbox. Most parcels were too thick to go through, ye had to chap the door and give it to the person.

I hated sitting there. Mitch was just too late. I could have been away doing the deliveries and getting finished. I brought out the delivery sheets and looked through them. I saw the names and the close numbers and how it all worked, who was to get parcels on such and such a night and then how the parcels checked against their numbers on the sheet. I checked the parcels for the first close. I could just do them. I could just run up fast.

So I did. I ran up and gave them in, and ran back down. Nobody knocked nothing. I would have heard them come in the close. Except if they crept in quiet, if it was a real sneaky robber, then went out the back close.

I looked at my school exercises again but it was freezing sitting on the stairs and my feet and my bum got pins and needles.

Mitch took ages. When he came I had the stuff ready to go into his sacks. I told him all how we done it with the delivery sheets. He had a fag and sat down for a smoke. Oh come on, I said, smoke it when we go.

F**k sake Smiddy I have been walking for f*****g miles, I need a wee seat.

Well I can just start. You can catch up.

F**k sake.

Well I have been f*****g waiting.

Well I have been f*****g walking.

Me and Mitch did not fight much but now we were. It was no fighting but just an argument, a wee one, but the two of us were looking. It was funny. The school I went to was miles and miles away in the town. Ye needed a train there and back. The one Mitch went to was just a walk. But I was quicker. But his was a long long walk. Him and the boys done it the gether, so it took ages. If he went himself it would be better. I said it to him. Do not wait for Podgie and them, just go quick yerself.

But Mitch did not say he would. He just smoked his fag, passed me it for a limit. I took one draw and passed it back. I went and looked out the back then out the front, just looking. What time was it? When did we finish, when did we get our tea and if we had homework. I did not like waiting it was just f*****g horrible. And how come Mitch did not bother, he did not bother. I hated waiting.

Usually ye done a delivery run yerself or got a wee boy to help ye. But no two the same age like me and Mitch because it was no big money and ye had to split it. Then the tips. Some customers were good tippers and other ones were no. Some did not tip at all. Ye went all week with their stuff and they did not tip ye. Mitch said, F**k them, I am not giving them their stuff.

But that was daft, ye had to give them their stuff. That was just Mitch. I said to Freddy the driver about the tips. He told us some customers did not tip ye every week but just saved it up and gave ye a big one for yer Christmas and Ne'erday.

Friday was the collecting night. Friday was when people got paid.

It was the best night for getting the money. But then we done it and were short of money. How come? I did not know. Neither did Mitch. Maybe people had not paid him. I said it to him, Did people no pay ye?

Oh aye, that c**t up the last close. I have to come back and get it.

Well what is their name?

Oh it is up number fourteen, I know them.

But he did not. He forgot who it was and then other ones too. Or if they gave him the wrong money. We counted it all up and it was wrong, it was all just wrong. We walked away down to the office and the boss counted it all again and done sums on the paper. Oh there are big losses, he said. Have ye no got anything more?

No.

Oh ye must have something.

We have no got nothing.

But what is that in yer pockets?

That is my tips, I said.

Yer tips! The boss looked over at another man that worked there. He forgot about his tips. Get them out, he said, get them out.

So me and Mitch had to put everything all out and he counted it. Good tips, he said. But ye still owe me money. I will just have to deduct it.

And it was off our wages. But even when he done it there was still no enough money. So he took what we owed him from next week too. So we would not get any wages for next week, except just tips. I was angry and so was Mitch. Mitch was going to get him. He was going to hide behind the trees and fling a brick at him. It was just daft and I telled him no to. He will know it is us, I said.

Well I will f*****g puncture his tyres.

Oh but he will just f*****g sack us and get the cops.

There was a cop station no faraway. The boss knew them. Some Fridays ye went into his office and cops were there having a smoke or else drinking a cup of tea. A lot of boys did not go in when they were there. Mitch was one.

But it was not just his fault with the money. People tried to cheat ye. It happened to milkboys and paperboys too. People kidded on they paid ye and they did not. Because they were grown-ups, so they could get away with it. Ye knew it was lies and had to say it to them. Oh missis sorry but ye did not pay because I wrote it in the book and the boss has it as well.

I telled Mitch. Ye just had to say stuff. He did not like to. He got a red face and then telled me. Oh she would not pay me Smiddy, I am going to f*****g break her windows.

We have to get her money but.

She would not f*****g give me it.

Well but we have got to get it.

But Smiddy she would not f*****g give me it.

Well I am going to ask for it.

Oh but she will no give ye it.

But it is our money so she f*****g better, I said because I just got angry too because if it was our money and she was just stealing, that was what I thought. So I just went up and chapped her door and said it to her. Oh missis you did not pay for yer deliveries because the boss told us and wrote down yer name.

I did so pay.

No ye did not.

Oh but I did.

No missis you did not. I said it to the boss tonight when he was talking to the cops and I just told him when all the names were there. Look, see, and your name is down, it was me that wrote it, look.

And then I showed her where her name was written down and how much it was. The woman just got grumpy but she paid it because she knew she had to because if it was the cops and she was just lying. Ye just knew she was lying.

Mitch did not like me telling him stuff. But if it was our money. If ye worked all week and ye did not get anything, no even yer tips, just nothing. Well it is no my fault, he said.

Well it is no mine either. Ye just have to watch it Mitch, if they are f*****g lying. Ye just tell them. We have just got to else we do not get our wages.

Oh f**k, I would just f****g batter them.

Aye but no if it is a woman.

Well but if she is f****g cheating us.

Aye but Mitch if it is a woman.

He did not like me saying it but I had to and the same a lot of Fridays because when the money did not add up and if it was him to blame, it was the ones he collected.

But if it was just me I liked Friday night. I liked collecting. Ye got yer tips when ye done it right and all people came to the door, lasses too, and ye were just there and saw them all.

But other days Mitch still came late. I took his sacks to school with me so I could get it ready for when he came. Then I started doing it myself, because even five minutes and I could do two closes. Easy. One night I was away doing the fifth when he came and he had to catch up. Oh f**k Smiddy, you should wait.

But I was just sitting.

Aye but it is no fair if you are doing it all.

Oh but I do not f****g mind.

Aye but f**k sake Smiddy it is my job and if you are f****g doing it.

Well but if I am sitting doing nothing.

How can ye no wait? Just wait.

Aye but if I am no f****g doing nothing.

Well can ye no do yer f****g homework, if ye have got homework, that is what ye say, so just do it.

F**k sake Mitch.

Just till I come.

It is too f****g cold sitting down.

Well that is no my fault.

Well it is no mine either.

He could have been there fast. If I could so could he. Even if he skipped out early. People asked the teacher, maybe if it was the dentist. Ye could just get a forgery note. I would write it for him. Even ten minutes early was great for me because a train came five minutes before the bell rang. I pelted down the road. Most times I caught it. Other ones done it. All fourth or fifth years. Lasses too. Twice I saw my brother. He did not see me.

The early train was great, just sitting at the window. People in my class were still at their desk and I was miles away. Imagine it was forever. Some trains went to the highlands. All mountains, fields and lochs and ye could get a boat maybe and go sailing, right out to sea, away way away. And that would be you. Boys got jobs as fishermen. Maybe I could. It was a hard life but ye made money and ye saved up. It was rough seas up north and that was where the fishermen went, away to Greenland and up the Baltic. So I was not going in the Navy, but I still liked sea stories.

When Freddy came I was waiting for him. I said, If I come earlier can ye bring the deliveries?

Oh aye, quarter past, I can do it for quarter past.

Oh that would be great.

Well ye better f★★★★★g be there man cause I am not coming for f★★k all.

I told Mitch so he could come early too but he did not. Then it was one day he did not come at all, and then the next night. The paperboy passed and we smoked a fag. He said, Oh well maybe he does not want the f★★★★★g job.

I went the whole way. It was heavy with the four sacks but the weight went down every parcel ye delivered. That was two times. Really, it was no fair. He only had to tell me the day before. Then I would not be looking for him. I would have finished faster. After my tea I went up to his house. He said he had to stay home because his maw told him. But I knew she did not tell him. It was just a f★★★★★g fib. I could have said it to him. It was just stupid.

Then the delivery sheets. Mitch would not read them. How come? So then if he took wrong stuff to people and they were there complaining, Oh where is my parcel this is the wrong one.

I showed him how to mark in the delivery sheets and all the stuff but he did not see it right. Oh Smiddy, f★★k sake, if you just tell me.

Oh but Mitch ye have got to do it yerself, look. And if ye showed him, he just did not look so if he was not concentrating. The teacher said it in Primary class how he would not concentrate. But it was true. Then dogs. How come he worried about dogs? Even the second close dog, old scabby chops. Who could be scared of old scabby chops except Mitch. All it done was lie in the weeds in the front garden. It was just an old old dog, nearly dead, just scabby-looking. Nobody could be feared of it. Ye just wondered because it would be dead soon, poor old thing, Oh my time has come. It just lied there and looked at its paws. Another dog was there and Mitch was feared of it too, a wee mongrel terrier. Other people did not like this one. It was a dog that jumped on ye. But what was it going to do? It could hardly even nip ye. I clapped it to show Mitch. That was all ye done. But he hated dogs and would never clap them. I used to put his hand to the dog to pet it but he still would not.

It did not matter about dogs if ye hated them or ye loved them. Freddy the driver said that. If ye got them ye got them. There is nothing except ye have to do it, if it is yer job. Ye have to go up the close. I said it to Mitch, What if a dog is in every house so then ye cannot f*****g do any f*****g deliveries?

No.

Aye but ye would need to if it was yer customers.

Well I would not.

So if ye could not do the job?

I would.

How?

I just f*****g would.

Aye but how, if ye cannay?

The mongrel terrier was the worst of all for Mitch. When it came running he forgot the names of people and all what he was doing. It was a worry. Then too how come he was so slow? He went up closes and did not come back. Where was he? So I done the next closes myself. He did not like me doing it. F**k sake Smiddy ye knew I was coming.

Aye but how long have I to wait?

Just f*****g wait.

No but how long?

I do not f*****g know.

Neither do I.

And I would not wait. Waiting was daft. A lot of times I was half way before he came then if it was stupid excuses. Oh the f*****g teacher made me stay in the class. You can f*****g ask Podgie if ye do not believe me.

But I was no going to ask Podgie. If Mitch came he came, if he did not he did not. I did not care, just if he told me. I was no the boss. I did not care, I went fast without him. Just if he told me I would not be looking for him. What if it was me and I was late, or else did not come? I said it to Mitch. So then nobody would get their deliveries.

Oh but you always come.

Aye but what if I do not?

Oh Smiddy, you always f*****g come.

Aye but if I did not, what would happen to the deliveries? Nobody would f*****g do them. Freddy would have to return the f*****g things to the boss and the boss would just sack us. He would. Because if nobody is there to do the f*****g job, that is how.

I do not care if he sacks me.

Well I do, I do not want the f*****g sack.

Oh you will no get the sack.

Aye but if I do?

Oh but you will no, the boss f*****g likes you.

Because I come and you do not.

Well who f*****g tells him if I do not come?

No me.

Well who?

I do not f*****g know.

Freddy?

I do not know but Mitch it is no f*****g me. What would I tell him for, I do not f*****g care.

Oh no you do not care.

I do not.

Well what are ye always f*****g saying it to me for? Oh you are late you are late, ye always f*****g say it.

Well but ye are late.

F**k sake Smiddy I cannot f*****g help it if the teacher keeps me in. It is no my f*****g fault.

Well it is no f*****g mine. It isnay.

Mitch spat on the ground. I will not be f*****g late tomorrow.

Oh well, I said but really I did not care if he came late or when, if he did not come. I was no the boss. That was how he acted, as if I was. How come it was me to tell him? I did not want to. The only time he was not late was Friday night for collecting and that was tips. Freddy the driver said, Oh he is a f*****g smart c***t, do not worry about that.

That was Mitch, he was a smart c***t. Nobody thought that except Freddy the driver. Then the paperboy said, You are doing all the work and he is getting half the f*****g money.

I thought that too but I wished he had not said it. The paperboy was a Catholic and was older than me. He acted like he could just say stuff. He finished his paper-run first but if ye were fast he waited for ye. He lived in a different scheme so when we got to the field he went the other way.

I said to him about coming for a game of football on Sundays. I did not know if he was any good at football. A lot of Catholics were. He did not talk about it much so maybe he was not. But he was no really a pal. Sometimes I thought he was but he was not. He could go funny. If he finished his run and I was nearly finished mine he would be away over and going home. So he was not waiting for ye. If ye went after him he did not speak when ye caught up. Then if Mitch was there, maybe he did not like Mitch. Mitch liked him except he was a Catholic so he did not talk to him much. I did. I just wanted to. Mitch said, Oh you just tell him everything.

Well how no?

Mitch did not say it but what he was meaning, because he was a Catholic. Even I did not say Pape. How come ye do not say Pape?

Just because I do not, I do not like it. I would no say it to the paperboy, Oh you are a Pape. You are a Pape. I wouldnay. Would you?

Aye, said Mitch.

366

Would ye?

Aye. How no?

I just wouldnay. So you would say it to him, Oh you are a Pape? Mitch laughed.

What is funny?

I do not know.

But I was laughing too. It was just stupid. But I did not care if the paperboy was a Catholic. But what about him to us? He played cards for money on Friday nights, him and other paperboys, all wages and tips. One time he won pounds and banked it for his holidays. Me and Mitch wanted to go. I would have loved just to watch. But the paperboy never took us. I did not know the ones he played with, if they were all Catholics. I did not think so. No if they were paperboys, ye got different ones. In the deliveries ye did not get many. In Gary McNab's milk job it was just Protestants.

I would rather have had a paperboy job. Ye made more tips and it was just the one bag to carry. The paperboy said it was heavier than our four sacks put the gether. That was just s★★★e. But so what if it was heavier? I would still carry it. If he thought I could not carry it. That was just stupid. The paperboy was a year older than me. He acted like that made him better at everything. How come? He was no even bigger than me. It was the same at school. If there was people from the year above ye it was supposed to make them better fighters. They walked to ye and ye were supposed to get out their way. If a boy from 1st year battered a boy from the 2nd, people talked about it.

The paperboy was quite a boaster. He said his school was better than mine. People came from all over Glasgow to it and everybody had to wear uniforms. That was the same as us. Then if a lassie wore trousers she got expelled. It was the same in ours. Lasses had to wear skirts and no too short. But when they sat down ye still saw their legs, ye could not help it. If they saw ye seeing them they gave ye a look, so ye were the lowest of the low. A lassie in 1B said that. Maureen Jones, she had a quite short skirt and ye saw her legs, ye could not help it. Ye were not meaning to see them, just if ye saw her and she was sitting down, so the tops of her legs like that right up her skirt so ye looked, ye could not help it.

She carried her school bag in a funny way. And her schoolblazer too, how she wore that, she rolled up the sleeves and put her hands in her side pockets. Her thumbs came over the top. Ye did not see lasses doing that. Maybe they were not allowed. But she did, her thumbs came over the top of her pockets and it looked good the way she done it and if she stood there too how she just crossed over legs when she was standing. She was just standing when she done it, her legs were crossed over and just her knees and then up and her skirt was there, ye just saw it, and shadows, just seeing shadows, ye saw her and it was shivering. I saw her going to the cafe with her pal at dinnertime and just walking up the street. She said stuff if she caught ye looking. A boy called McNaughton was doing it and she shouted at him, Oh you, McNaughton, you are the lowest of the low.

I thought about if I was dogging school, imagine ye met her, if she was dogging it and ye were someplace up the town. Imagine ye saw her and ye went over, because if ye saw her and she saw you, Oh it is Smith, he is in 1G. Maybe boys were there and shouting at her and you saw her, Oh Maureen come on with me, and she did, then if ye had a fag, Oh here is a fag. But if she did not smoke. Maybe she did not.

Sometimes I did not know I was dogging school till I done it. I just stayed on the train and watched the people get off. Oh I will change at the next station and catch a train back. That was what I thought, but I did not, I went up the town and walked about. But then if it was too cold or wet, ye wished ye had went to school, ye were starving and nay money for a cafe. There was shops where ye could knock stuff but some were waiting to catch ye. Other ones looked at ye. Maybe they were going to tell the cops. Oh that boy should be at school. Well how did they know? Maybe ye were going to the dentist or the doctor or yer grannie. If a cop said it to me I would tell him. I would never run. Mitch did. Oh there is a cop, and he ran up a close. But what if the cops ran after ye? They did if they saw ye running.

Freddy the driver did not say cops, he said busies. Watch out for the busies. These c**ts will f****g do ye. Just walk normal if ye see them. Put yer hands in yer f*****g pockets man just f*****g whistle a tune. But do not say hullo, these c**ts will think ye are being cheeky.

It was hopeless if ye were too early at the delivery run. Freddy did not come until four fifteen. I asked him but he would not. The boss did not give him the deliveries before four o'clock and did not like ye being too early because what if the cops saw. There was a police office nearby and cops came in to see the boss. They took their hats off and smoked a fag and drank cups of tea. I did not like seeing them, then if they watched ye, so if ye got a red face. Oh what have you been doing?

The boss told ye, Keep out the f*****g road.

Other boys went up the town. Ye had to watch if they were going to jump ye. It would have been good if ye had a pal. I went into the big railway stations but cops were there. I kidded on I was waiting for a train. I had my railway pass to show them. They would say Oh this is the wrong station for that train.

Oh I made a mistake, and then I could just get away.

I liked seeing the different towns on the board for departures. London, Plymouth and Cheltenham Spa. Plymouth was right far down. Imagine getting that train. Ye could jump it, except if the ticket collectors caught ye. But if ye waited till the very last minute then ran and jumped on. But how could ye if they were watching. Except if the train was moving. Ye had to wait till it was moving and then do it. And if ye couldnay open the train doors, well ye could just climb up on the roof then lie down flat and wait till the next station, then dreep down and go in a door.

I stopped dogging it too much because if it was Approved School. Mitch was in one at Primary School. My da would have killed me, and my maw would just be greeting and all just whatever. But I liked dogging it. But I just had to stop it. Sometimes going to school and walking up from the station, just at the very last minute, I turned the corner and went along another street. Because I was dogging it and did not even know until that very last minute. But then if ye changed yer mind and just ran back and in the gate before the bell rang.

But coming home after school, if ye missed the early train it put ye back half an hour with the deliveries and that was good time. If ye started late ye got later and later. First it was half an hour then it was three quarters. Then it was an hour. How did that happen? But it did. I told Mitch. He did not like me saying it. But it was true. If ye are early ye are early, if ye are late ye just get later and later.

No ye do not, he said.

But ye did. I knew ye did because when he did it that is what happened and we were always just late and I hated it, and just in late at night. My maw had my tea to heat up in the oven.

People did not know about yer job. If I was home at six o'clock, how come it was no half past? How come it was no seven o'clock? I had to run and go fast and if I did not get the early train I would always be late. If Mitch was no there I was doing the four sacks myself. But that was alright, ye just got used to it. My maw and da did not think about it. Oh how come you are fast home? They never said that. I did not tell them. Otherwise rows rows rows, it would just be rows. Oh dogging it dogging it, they would not let me.

People thought things were good but they were not. What if ye had short money for yer collection? The boss took it off ye, ye did not get yer pay. It was Mitch's fault, he put things in the wrong door or just whatever. Oh that is just helpers, said the paperboy, ye should no f*****g have one, they just keep ye back.

Oh but Mitch is no a f*****g helper. It is his job too.

But if he is doing it wrong?

He is not.

I thought ye said he was.

No it is just mistakes, just sometimes.

Helpers keep ye back, he said.

The paperboy would not have a helper. He used to have one but then stopped it. But me and Mitch were pals. The paperboy was no really a pal. He was like one but was not. He told me there was somebody in the Boys Guild called Kieron. So if really it was a Catholic name, if that is what he was saying, that was just daft and from being a child. People were all different names. In my school

John and Michael and Jim and Brian were Catholics and Protestants, even a Joseph was a Protestant.

It was Mitch's job first. I was sharing it with him. He just should have come more. I wished he did. But he did not. So it was like my job. People thought it was. Freddy the driver said, Oh it is your job man you are the one that f*****g does it.

I liked Freddy saying it but then I did not. It was good because really if it was me doing the job. So if I was. If I was I was. So if I did not need nobody. Maybe I did not. I could just do it myself. But it was Mitch's job first. Except if he did not want it. Well then.

§

Trials came for the school football team. It was one team for the whole 1st year, 1A down to 1G. Ye went straight after school to the sports ground next Tuesday and Wednesday. But that was no good.

People were talking about it. It was up on the Notice Board down the gym corridor. I went to see and there it was, Trials. Tuesday and Wednesday. It was no good. I read it again to see and it was just the same.

The best players all got picked out the Trial games. After that it was training every Wednesday and ye played every Saturday afternoon. Boys were talking about how they were all going. It would be great, but it was no good. I wanted in the school team. Except I had the job and could not go to the Trials. If ye did not go ye did not get picked. So ye had to go. But then if ye could not. And ye needed to, else ye could not play, never ever, how could ye, ye could not, ye would just never be able to play, so that was you and ye never ever could ever ever. How could ye? Ye could never. I telled my da. Oh well, he said, you will just have to go on Friday night.

But da

The BB comes first.

But da it is not the BB

Well the BB comes first

But I am no talking about the BB.

Well what are ye talking about?

Oh I am no talking about nothing.

Do not be so damn cheeky, ye think because ye are twelve!

No dad and I am no being cheeky, it is just not the BB it is nothing to do with the BB it is the school team and how about the Trials if ye cannay go and ye are just well if ye cannay, ye just cannay go.

Well I do not know what ye are talking about, if it is not the BB, if it is the school team, what are ye meaning?

Oh I am no meaning nothing, I said and just went out the room. I could not say to him, I could not say at all to him. What he was talking about, the BB, it was nothing to do with the BB. He just was not listening, people just did not listen. Ye were saying stuff and they just were not listening. If ye did not play in the Trials ye did not play for the school team.

I talked to him again about it. I made toast and beans for supper and brought it through for me, him and my maw. The school had their own team and the boys to play in it would get picked out the Trials. They had the Trial games, so ye played in them and got picked. And if ye did not play in the Trials ye did not get picked. That was what happened. You went to the Trials and ye played the Trial games and then whoever got picked got picked, that is what happened, but if ye could not go then ye could not go and ye could never ever get picked.

Oh but son, no everybody can get picked.

Aye but what I am saying dad ye get picked if ye play in the Trials

There is more to life than football.

Listen to your father, said my maw.

Yes I know but

Oh there is aye a but with you son. My da was smiling.

I know dad I am just saying, it is after school for the Trials. Ye have to get the bus to the school playing fields and ye do not get home till half past six or else even seven o'clock.

Well what is wrong with that, if it is seven o'clock, yer mother will stick yer tea in the oven.

But da it is no my tea it is my job, I have got my job.

My da just looked at me. He did not know what I was meaning. He did not think of me having a job. He even forgot I had one. I told him how if ye did not go for the training and especially if ye did not play in the Trial games then that was you because how could ye get picked and if ye had a job, well, ye could not.

Football is not everything, said my maw.

I know mum but it is just how it would be good to play but if it is Tuesday and Wednesday night for the Trials and if ye have a job well ye cannot go, it is just not fair. And even after that when ye get picked ye have to do yer training one night a week and it is straight from school ye do it, so ye just cannot go, so really, if ye have a job then it just is not fair, so if

Oh for Heaven sake, said my da.

No but dad

Kieron, for God sake.

And my maw just was looking, her forehead all wrinkled up, not knowing what it was, just worried. Oh what have ye done Kieron? Oh you have done something, what is it?

Mum I have not done nothing, except just what I am saying how if it is the Trials.

Oh Kieron.

Mum I have not done nothing.

My da was looking straight at me, just a hard look, as if he was giving me a row. But I had no done anything, so how come a row? I was just saying it, ye just could not get saying it, they would not listen, they just would not.

I went out the room. I did not slam the door, but closed it. I listened a wee minute but they did not speak about me. My maw would not stick up for me, if it was football, it was all just silly. Everything was just yer studies, yer studies, and my da just said it for her, he did not back ye up.

Mr Ramsay was our PE teacher for football. He used to play for a big club. He had good style. His first name was Charles so Charlie

Ramsay. Charlie Ramsay. When our classes went for outside PE it was him reffed, so he knew who was good players. He joined in playing and nicked the ball off ye when ye were running, then hit a long pass way down the wing for the other team, hitting it with the outside of his boot, and how it swerved and went down there for the other players to chase and maybe they would score a goal. It was good how he done it but he was the ref so ye were not expecting the tackle. Maybe if ye knew he was doing it ye could have got the ball past him. So it was a wee bit no fair. But it did not matter because if he done it, if ye were a bad player, well, he never done it. He only done it if ye were a good player. So if he done it to ye, ye knew ye were no bad.

He was used to real training with real teams and probably that was what they did. He did not even tackle, just nicked the ball off yer foot. Ye were running with it and that was what he done, his foot just took it away. If he ran with it ye could not stop him, ye tried but could not. But he ran with his arms out and ye could not get near him else ye would get punched. If the referee saw it that was a foul. He done it with his elbows too. How could ye tackle him. Ye could not. But he was the ref himself so just done it.

He did not talk to ye like the old PE teacher for rugby. He just watched what ye done. Some smiled at ye or said yer name, but Mr Ramsay did not. Sometimes he was looking and did not see stuff. A boy said, Oh he is in a fantasy world, he is dreaming about the Cup Final, he has just scored a goal.

Well if he did, me too, and ye were on the train to school thinking about games, oh if that pass came to me instead of him I would just break down the wing and if somebody comes with a sliding tackle I shall just flick the ball up and jump over and just on and on maybe cut in and slip a good pass through so yer team scores a goal, and they all clap the one that scored but really it was you, it was you done it, and ye just give a wink.

I was going to say to Mr Ramsay about the Trials. When we were going off the pitch he was coming last. I went to do it then did not. I would tell him after, just I could not even go to the Trials. I could not even go. So that was not fair. I would love to go but I could not, because of my job. But I would love to go. I just could not. I would love to. Maybe if I done my own training or if there was other times or else days for the Trials. What if it was Saturday? Only I had to collect delivery money on Saturday afternoon if the folk had not paid me on Friday night. Saturday morning was football for the BB wee team. It was good but just wee. If it was the school team I would rather play for that. So I could do it on Saturday after all. But Sunday was best if it was Sunday. The BB liked ye going to Bible Class then every month was Church Parade and ye had to go marching with the uniform. But I could just chuck the BB. It was Friday night anyway and they did not like me and Mitch coming late because with the job. So I could do it if it was Sunday.

This games period was the last before dinnertime. Ye took showers because ye were muddy after the game. Usually I was out the changing rooms fast and waiting on the bus back to school because if it was ten minutes to wait ye done yer homework. Now I waited round the teachers' gate. Mr Ramsay came out wearing his outside clothes. I went to talk to him. Oh sir, I said, I am Smith in yer class.

Smith?

Aye sir yes, if

Then I could not speak hardly at all and just got a red face. It got worse so I could hardly breathe. I could not. It was in my throat and I was going to choke and having to gulp for a breath I could not get a breath and Mr Ramsay was looking at me and did not know what was wrong, just squinty eyes, how his eyes were squinting. What is wrong, he said, are you having problems? Are boys waiting to get you?

No, no sir.

If it is bullying? Do not be frightened.

No sir.

My voice sounded stupid. He did not know my name. He thought I was getting bullied. In that school, as if it was me, if I would be bullied, I would never be bullied. He did not know it was me. I was the one he nicked the ball off. So I was a good player, else he would not have nicked the ball off me. But he did not know my name. Just son. What is wrong son are boys waiting to get you? No in that school. Never ever. There was nothing in that school it was just a total complete nightmare and I hated it the worst, just the worst, the very very worst, it was the very worst, ye could not imagine how bad it was it was just whatever was the worst thing, worser. Ye could not even talk and if yer voice was just how it sounded and they were just looking at ye and even if the teacher did not hear ye. What did you say? Are you having trouble? Are boys bullying you?

No sir nothing, boys are not bullying me.

Because if they are.

No sir they are not.

Oh well good, and he was seeing his watch now because with the bus waiting and it was dinnertime next.

Oh sir just about the football sir, the Trial games for the school team, I cannot go because I have got a job, how it says on the Notice Board Tuesday and Wednesday for the Trial games how if the teams are going to be selected at the Trial games and I cannot go. Because if I cannot get to the training sir and then the Trial games so then if I have no to get picked that is not fair.

Well, try your best for one of the nights.

But I cannot sir except maybe if the training could happen later on maybe after teatime, that would be the best time sir if it was not straight from school, if it was maybe the evening. Or else the weekend maybe if it was Sundays if it was the afternoon sir.

Well I do not think that can happen but you know it is not me who organizes the Trials training sessions, it is Mr McCutcheon. He is the man you should see.

Now he was looking at his watch. Now he was going for the bus. Maybe you could do your job in the evenings instead. Or do not do it on training nights, even better. Come on now, the bus is waiting.

So that was him. I saw ones looking at me out the bus windows. I did not care about them. What he said was daft. But Matt said it too. Could ye not give it up for one night?

Give the job up for one night. That was just daft. How could ye give up the job for one night? Only if Mitch could do it but Mitch could not. He would not want to do it, but if he did, maybe he

376

would, but it would just be daft, then if it was every week for one night for training, he would never do that.

So I could not go.

After the 1st year Trials it did not matter about football. In 2nd year the same boys were picked. If ye were not playing in the 1st year and going to their stupid training night ye would not get considered.

Them that got into the team acted like the best players, just showing off. And they were not. How did they know if not all had a chance? They were not the best and could not say it but they did.

§

But plenty in the good school were not posh. One was McEwan. McEwan played in the 2nd year team. He played in the 1st year from last year and now he was repeating he just carried on. The teachers did not like it and did not like him but he was one of the best players. He was past fourteen. Boys went about with him so it was like a wee gang. He was not in my class but one of his pals was. Their class was 1F and ours was 1G. Sometimes they put us together for PE and games and sometimes History. McEwan's pal in our class was Webster. Him and another one made a fool of people and were ready to fight. Going along the corridors they kicked boys on the bum for nothing. They tormented them in the classroom, tapping them on the shoulder and hitting them on the head with rulers or else skelping their bum and flicking towels if it was the changing room. We did not have darkies in our class but two Jewboys and he done it to them and the Belgium boy.

But Webster was good at sports so was maybe a good fighter. People thought he was. He acted like it but maybe he was not. But ye were waiting for him to get ye and ye got sick of it, just because he was pals with McEwan. That was Gary McNab to Podgie, how he went with him. But McEwan was a better fighter than Podgie. He was older and just tougher, that was what I thought. But no Webster, I would never be scared of Webster. But Webster was not McEwan's best pal, that was Sabby, and ye would not fight Sabby, I would never, he just smiled at ye, but he would have battered ye. He was repeating 1st year the same as McEwan. Sometimes they played football at dinnertime in the playground. People did not tackle much there but I started doing it just because I did and if somebody was in the school team, I done it to them.

McEwan was a good dribbler and usually beat ye. It was just a wee ball so he could do stuff with it, hitting it through yer legs. I went in and cracked his ankle, I did not mean it, he just turned quick so my boot caught him. Oh for f**k sake, he said.

Oh sorry, I said, but he just shook his head and pushed me, no for a fight but just so he could walk away. He did not come after me and did not kick me the next time. But he could have, he could have kicked me any time. Ye knew with McEwan he was a tough fighter. Him and his pals went to the cafe or else down a back lane to smoke and wait for lasses.

He sat at the back. If the teacher said a question to him he kidded on he did not hear. The teacher had to say it again, Oh Mr McEwan.

What, what is it – sir?

I asked you a question.

Oh, I did not hear you – sir.

Well?

McEwan just looked at him, who was he talking to. Then the teacher would say, I asked you a question Mr McEwan.

Oh, I did not hear you – sir.

And that wee space for sir, I did not hear you – sir. He did not say answers but knew them, just gave a wee smile. He spat on the class-room floor. The teacher knew but kidded on he did not. Once in History it was an old man teacher instead of the usual one and McEwan whispered, This c**t is a f*****g dickie. He done it loud so everybody could hear him. The teacher looked at him but it was maybe he did not hear it, or did he? No, he could not have, no boy would say such a thing. But McEwan did. Then a wee minute after he started laughing. The teacher kidded on he did not hear. Then he pished against the radiator before the class started. The pee streamed down the middle of the floor. People thought what it was but did not think somebody would do it. Then the teacher came in. McEwan just put his hand up. The radiator is leaking sir.

What did you say?

The radiator is leaking – sir.

The teacher came round to see. Go to the janitor's room and get a mop and bucket and ask if he will come and see it.

Yes sir.

When McEwan went to the door he brought a fag packet out behind the teacher's back, took out a fag and winked at his pals. He did not care if other people saw him doing it. Things disappeared out the gym changing room and people said it was him. The old PE teacher came in to tell us. His face was angry and he told us all to sit down. There is no place for sneak thieves in this school. Sneak thieves are the worst dregs and people that steal from their classmates are just filthy scum. He talked about other stuff, how if these were yer friends ye were to be loyal, friends were friends and if people were in yer class that was what they were, friends.

But then McEwan was there behind him and doing wanking signs behind his back. Ye could not believe he was doing it. What if the PE teacher caught him? He was not a coward and would say it. But if he did McEwan would get him. I thought that. I was glad the PE teacher did not see him else it would have been the worse for him because even if he was a man and a good fighter like a PE teacher ye still thought McEwan would get him.

There was shops near the cafe. I saw him and Sabby in one at dinnertime and they were knocking. I done it too with a bar of chocolate, up my sleeve. Outside the shop I took it out and they saw me. Sabby pointed over. McEwan just looked. He was the best at knocking. In one shop they kept the chocolate and stuff beside the fags behind the counter and people were watching ye all the time. Ye could never get anything. But McEwan was big and he stretched his arm right over the counter. He lifted a bar of chocolate and kept it inside his palm with his thumb holding it. A woman saw him. Her eyes flickered to him but she did not say nothing, because she was scared.

Boys in higher classes were scared of him too. I did not know any he was scared of. If one done something to him, he would just wait and get them after. Ye knew that with McEwan. Once I was reading a paper and he grabbed it out my hand and tore it up. I had not done nothing to him. He just walked away. Webster and Sabby were there and saw it. Webster was in my class and was laughing at me. But then McEwan got him. Webster was good at telling jokes. He started off telling one and McEwan said, Going to shut yer f****g mouth! Eh? F*****g shut up.

So Webster had to shut up. I felt like laughing. That was McEwan, he even done it to his own pals. Maybe Webster was not his pal, maybe he just acted like he was.

Then in the cafe it was McEwan sitting behind me and other ones were with him. I was just myself. Two other ones were at my table because it was crowded. Drenching rain outside and just freezing cold. I was thinking about my deliveries because ye had to watch it if it was raining too heavy and the wet got in yer parcels because if they got soaked, if yer customers did not want them, it was you, it just came off your wage. So if I could get stuff off Freddy to put in the sacks and cover them. Freddy was good at helping ye.

But I was going to get soaked too. I did not have a coat, just a jacket. I hated coats. Only they were good for their pockets. If I got soaked I would have to go home from school and change. That made ye late for work. But if I dogged the last two periods.

Maybe I would. Or else right now, if I just went home right now, and dogged the rest of the afternoon. Except the Registration teacher was giving me looks with my forgery notes. When it got bad with people the teachers wrote letters to yer maw and da. If mine did it I would just get his letter off the postman, or else what, I did not care. Or if the rain went off, maybe I would stay in school, or go to my grannie.

I was just thinking about it and something at my back just at my bum, it was like something, I did not know what, but just – and

McEwan behind me. So it was him. It was him doing it. I sat forward.

So it was him and he was doing it to me. So that was that and it was McEwan. It was just McEwan. But it was no sore, just tickly. But he still done it and I could not go more forward.

I kidded on I did not feel it. I heard him whispering, Oh I f*****g told ye, he loves it.

Oh I f*****g told ye, he loves it, scraping my bum with something, a ruler or pencil, that was McEwan and I went total red because I knew it, that was it and what he was doing to me and I had to look round. I had to. And Sabby and Webster and them looking at me. McEwan kidded on he was not doing nothing. But he started doing it again. I turned round to him. Oh, I said, going to chuck it.

I just said it quiet then sat to the front and was waiting for something, whatever, to happen, then the scraping thing again, but only a wee minute then it stopped.

I counted. I was going to count to twenty but after twelve I lifted my school bag and got up and left the cafe. So that was me, so I was not one of McEwan's pals. Well I did not want to be. I did not want to be anybody's pals, no ever. Just going myself, that was what I wanted. Other ones did not care about McEwan. Posh ones. Big Borland and them did not care about McEwan, they did not go where he went. I would be the same.

Boys got called poofs and bumboys. That was the worst. I always thought if Carslake told people. Maybe he did. But I do not think so because they would shout at him too. Bumboys. And that was McEwan doing it to mine. Ye got called that. So if they were going to do it to me, if they just tried it. What if they did? McEwan and them were down the lane having a smoke. I was too and did not see them till I was there. McEwan did not look at me but Sabby said, Alright Smith?

I just walked past and nothing happened. I did not act tough to them but I did not speak because I did not want to and just could not, if they were going to get me, five of them, that was just cowards, I did not care about them, I was just waiting. Other times they waited there for lasses. McEwan went with one and another went with another. The rest stood a bit away and watched if they were kissing. One time I saw McEwan and Sabby down the railway lane and they were standing with the gang that went there. I was going to pass them that time but I did not, I just went round the long way and they never saw me.

Really it was Webster, he was the one in my class, how he acted it, just stupid stuff, flicking the school bag off yer shoulder and slapping ye on the back then dodging roundabout, clicking yer heels when ye were walking. People kidded on it was a laugh. It was not. He did not do it to Brogan and Hannah or Donald Shields. Even ones like Carslake. How come he left them alone? In Algebra class he started doing it to me, just tapping me on the shoulder. I kidded on it was nothing, just a laugh, but he kept doing it and it was on the same spot and getting sore so I was just moving a wee bit, then he said, Please sir he is hitting me.

He done it in a low voice but as if he was mimicking me and I was going to shop him to the teacher. It was just stupid. Then he was tapping me on the shoulder again so I turned round and said, Stop that.

He mimicked me. Stop that.

He stopped it for a wee while then done a couple of more taps. They were not that sore but just how they annoyed me. I turned round to him, Fucking chuck it.

I shouted it loud and everybody heard. I did not care. It was the Algebra teacher, Mad Marty. I did not care who it was, Mad Marty, so what. His eyes went wide. It was complete silence till he said, What was that! Come out here. Did I hear you right. What did you say? What did you say boy? Speak up. You shall go straight to the Headmaster's Office.

He was opening the desk and bringing out the belt. So it was not the Headmaster, just him strapping ye. He gave me four with crossed hands. If ever ye split yer hands with him so much the worse. Two of them were sore ones that went up yer wrist and came out red with white blotches. And ye just had to stand there when he was putting the belt away, yer hands hanging down and a nothing feeling, then all pins and needles.

Please sir can I leave the room? Please sir may I leave the room? He nodded his head.

Ye had to leave the room. Martin belted ye hard and ye could not help it, just water out yer eyes. Ye did not want people to see so ye asked him, and ye had to say it like that. Please sir may I leave the room. If ye said can I leave the room, he did not speak till ye said it right. Sometimes he said, Can I canoe you up the river.

He let ye go to the lavvy if ye got belted, ye did not want to blink because then the water would come. Maybe ye were not greeting but it looked like ye were and then sitting down in front of them all. And yer hands, what ye do with them, if ye leave them on the desk or under the table and ye cannot blow on them just having to sit there then what, just waiting there till the bell goes for the end of the period and yer head is not thinking about nothing except just how yer hands are and how the stinging is going, if ye know what stage it is, is it near the end or maybe another bit to go, white or red. So if ye go to the toilet, getting the cold water for yer hands and yer wrists, yer face too so ye were not greeting, ye were not greeting, it was just water how it came out yer eyes, I hated that it was just so fucking horrible ye just could not, no if ye could manage no to so ye tried to leave the room ye just ran water over them out the tap. They went tingling and ye looked at them and they were curled up and just shaking a wee bit and then up yer wrist the white was away and it was coming up red and ye saw yer veins. What if they burst? All yer veins were there and that was where he belted ye. He did not try to hit ye there but he did.

People were looking at me after the class. I did not care and was happy what had happened. It was no my school and I was getting to fuck away out it. Webster came up to talk to me after the class. I knew he would. I just did. I knew he would just want to and I was nearly laughing.

Oh what did ye shout for? Ye should not have shouted, he said, that was how ye got belted. What did ye shout for? Ye should not have shouted.

Aye but I did.

Well ye should not have.

Aye but I fucking did.

Webster was looking at me and I was looking at him back. Ha ha, that was what I thought, if he wanted to fight me, well I would fucking have him, that was what I thought, I could just fucking beat him. Other people were looking too. Oh is Smith going to fight him. Maybe I would maybe I wouldnay. I did not care about Webster and all them, McEwan or else the posh ones, I just wanted away and just away from them all, all them, I did not care about any of them. I saw the street down the hill and that was me, I imagined walking down it.

Webster was no a real fighter. I would batter him. Maybe if he jumped me he would get me but he would not.

I was glad I took the belt. People all would know. Oh Smith did not care, he just swore in the classroom. Mad Marty gave him four and he just took it. And that was Webster, it was his fault.

So if he jumped me, the best place was walking down to the railway station. But I could climb the wall and get through a close. So what if they caught me, if it was Webster, I would boot him or stick the knee in, that would be him. Except if he had handers, McEwan or Sabby, they would batter me. Maybe if I carried a blade and took it out. Alright then come on, come on. Ye want it, come on. Ye would just be careful no to stick it in the heart or else the eye or the neck. If they thought I was soft and they were going to get me, they would never get me. I did not need a knife for them, just if it was McEwan or Sabby.

I walked down a river-street and jumped a ferry. All the noise from the yards, sawing and screeching sounds, drills and big hammers falling, hooters going off. Only me and two old men were aboard. I stood up with the skipper looking way over to the pier, going on the wide curve out, it just looked wee. How come he never missed? Who would ye save if it sank, a wee wean or an old woman?

Imagine the skipper sailed it right down the river. One done that, he just got fed up. My Uncle Billy told us. A real sailor from the islands, he sailed the ferry down the river and away out to sea, all the people shouting at him, a big teuchter, he didnay care, he was just wanting to sail the boat and just go away because it was all just horrible, everything.

384

My da laughed to hear it and so did me and Matt, seeing the ferry away out to sea and people all shouting at him. Except if the waves were too high, if it was rough seas and all crashing over, people would be scared, so nay wonder.

My grannie's street was quite a long walk. Auntie May was there. I went into the front room where grannie kept the writing paper and I done a forgery note to the Registration teacher from my maw just how I had the dentist.

My grannie made me toast and cheese. I did not stay long. If she forgot to give me my subway fare I had to take the ferry and it took longer. If she forgot I did not ask. I did not like asking with Auntie May there, if she thought I was trying to get my grannie's money. Sometimes she looked at me and I did not like it and just a funny feeling. I did not do anything wrong but it was as if I did. Then if she said about school, Oh how is yer studies? and ye were telling her, ye saw her eyes, no even looking at ye, no even listening.

I could have said about the belt and showed her my wrists. No my grannie, I would never have showed them to my grannie. But I would have showed them to my Auntie May. She would have seen them, then what would she have thought? But maybe she would not have bothered. When I done my granda's wave to grannie she just looked at me.

My grannie said, Oh but May he has got him to a tee.

But Auntie May did not like me doing it. How no, if he was yer granda? Auntie May acted like he was only her dad, it did not matter if he was yer grandfather. My granda used to wear a bunnet and now she kept it in her wardrobe. I was glad when she was not there. My grannie said, Oh son she is just unhappy.

§

Up at the second last close on the delivery run an old man and woman came to stay on the ground floor. She had bad legs and could not climb the stairs. They flitted in from another scheme. They had an alsatian sentry dog and it guarded the front close. It was a real killer dog and everybody was feared. Mitch would no go near that close. He just would not. The dog sat by the steps and stared at ye or else laid down at the side garden. Ye thought it was sleeping then the nearer ye got ye saw these wee eye slits and it growled from the back of its throat, quite quiet, but rough too. If it had something stuck there, maybe, licking its coat. Granda's cats used to do that and had to cough, so then out it came, big lumps of stuff, all hairs and oose, out from the cats' throats. See if there is any money in there! That was what Uncle Billy said.

The alsatian sentry dog's fur was scabby. Maybe the old man and woman did not care for it good. It went for the paperboy and nearly tore a chunk out his arm. Lucky for him he was wearing a new leather jerkin. The old man blamed him because of that. Oh yer jerkin is too glossy. If a dog sees a glossy thing it goes for it, it is like a rabbit running.

But rabbits are not glossy, and the leather jerkin was not either, it was just new. The paperboy had saved up for it. It was good style. Ye saw it and wished ye had it. That was only the third time he wore it out the house.

Oh but how come he was wearing a new leather jerkin if he was doing a paper run? The old man wanted to know that. But it was a Friday night. Ye wore yer school clothes through the week but no a Friday, no for collecting. That was when ye went to people's doors for the money, and ye got yer tips. Ye would not wear school clothes for that, just yer good ones. Lasses were there too, if they came to the door, they saw ye. Carolyn Smart. Her maw was Mitch's customer but I changed her to mine. Because if he did not come I had to do it. So then I just done it. Mitch got the close after to do. He did not mind. Carolyn Smart was a complete darling. She was just a complete darling, really, she was, so ye wore yer good stuff. I went home between the deliveries and the collecting. I took off my school stuff, put on my jeans and my jerkin. Mine was no leather, it was just ordinary.

Sometimes Mitch came home with me instead of his own house.

My maw split my tea with the two of us and made toast and cheese to go with it. My da was usually at the pub on Friday nights after his work, it was a new job he had.

The paperboy had good style. Mitch thought it too. That leather jacket was a beauty. How come the old man did not pay for it if it was his dog done the damage? I said that to my maw. The old man should have paid for it, it was no fair.

Oh but if the paperboy was running, she said.

Well but if ye are late mum, if ye are running, the dog should not attack ye.

Dogs do not know any better.

Yes but it is the man's dog.

I do not know why his mother is buying him leather jackets anyway, she said.

Oh but it is a leather jerkin.

It is the same thing.

It is not the same thing. He bought it himself out his own money.

She did not speak after that because she did not like leather jerkins. And she did not like ordinary jerkins. And jeans too, she hated jeans. Oh they are just for keelies. It was my grannie bought me the jeans and jerkin. The jerkin was too wee and should have been a size bigger, and the jeans had too wide legs, people had tight ones, that was what I wanted. My maw did not like my grannie buying me stuff. My grannie said, He is just a boy, it does not matter.

Oh but mum it does matter.

Boys at that school had good clothes but they were no good style. I would not have wore them, they were just like for the Church and Sunday School, just posh boys and snobs, sports jackets and flannels, I hated them. That was what my maw wanted. But if I had my own money and just bought my own stuff. If it was my own money.

I still got Matt's old clothes. I did not want them, except maybe a jersey. But socks, vests and pants were the same ones, my maw kept them all in the same drawer. Ye had to look for wee ones. She bought them big so he could wear them. But it should have been him and my da because they were nearer the same, no me. I had to look for wee ones and they were just old and shrunk. At gym and the swimming ye had to change fast so people did not see. The socks were too big because with his feet. The heel bit came out the back of yer shoes.

On Fridays after tea I was fast out the house to collect the delivery money. Mitch was slow. If he was coming from his own house I did not wait for him. I was going up the hill when I heard him whistling. I looked back to see him and he was crossing the burn. Smidddeh-hhhh, Smidddehhhhh. Ye heard it echoing across. I waved but I did not stop. It was a long long walk to that scheme. He had to run to catch up with me. Oh Smiddy how did ye no wait?

Because the boss was wanting the pay-in quick. And people went out after their tea. If ye were too late collecting there was nobody in to pay. Mitch did not care. Oh fuck them.

Aye but Mitch if they are paying the money.

I do not care.

But if ye have to come back on Saturday morning?

Well we are no going to run.

But we have to.

Well I am no fucking running.

Well I fucking am.

Oh fuck sake Smiddy you have always got to do the things.

Well?

Well I do not fucking want to.

Mitch was always tired. I was tired too but ye just done it, if ye got yer money, ye just done it. If it was too heavy rain doing the deliveries we did not go home before collecting. Ye finished earlier. The boss liked it because ye did the pay-in quick. And it was good for going to the BB. That started at seven o'clock so ye were nearly on time. But I did not like it. It was good going home for yer tea and then coming back out wearing yer good stuff. Freddy the driver said it too, if ye wanted good tips ye had to look the part. Oh ye have to look the part, that is what Freddy said, ye have to fucking look the part.

When we did not go home we bought crisps and lemonade off the ice-cream van and ate it up the last close. But Mitch was good at getting grub. He chapped people's doors and asked the woman for a piece on cheese or else jam. It was good if the paperboy was coming up the street. We sat down on the steps to eat the pieces when he came in the close. Oh this piece on jam is great Mitch.

Oh aye Smiddy.

Oh you bastards, where did ye get the pieces? Give me a fucking bite?

The alsatian sentry dog stayed in the second last close and we could see it poking its head out to watch the rain. Mitch said to the paperboy, See if I was you I would fucking poison it, I would get a fucking gun.

Well it is no the alsatian's fault, I said.

Oh you always fucking say that.

But it was true. The alsatian was an ex-sentry dog and bred to the security business, trained to attack thieves and robbers. The old man that owned the dog told me about it. He only told me because it was me that listened. He told some good stuff. I liked hearing him. Once the old alsatian got a grip of ye it would never let go, even if ye bust its teeth with a crowbar. It would go for anybody that was suspicious so if ye ran that was you.

Ye never run with dogs. Lucky for the paperboy it was good thick leather else it would be a chunk out his flesh and blood. It was the paperboy's fault for running. If ye do not run sentry dogs will not attack ye. That was how ye trained yer dogs. Ye told it what to do and he done it and if he did not then ye got rid of it, ye sent it away for a pet. Because it was no good if it did no do what ye told it. Alsatians were working dogs. If ye trained them right and they did not conform, well, ye had to train them right, so if they conformed, if they did not ye got rid of them.

The dog lied beside the old man when he was talking. It always watched me coming. Oh do not worry, said the old man, if that dog did not like ye ye would be dead by now. He has yer scent and it is okay.

If the dog came to sniff ye ye just had to let it. Breathe in and do not move. Say hullo son, he is saying hullo to you, just say hullo. But do not clap it.

I thought ye were to clap dogs.

Oh no son, no a dog like him, ye never clap him, never ever clap him.

Its eyes looked up at ye. Sometimes Mitch watched from along the pavement. The old man saw him. What about yer pal?

Oh he delivers the next close.

The other stuff the old man talked about was fights, fights he had with villains out the underworld. In Glasgow there was a big under-world. People were cowards with them but he was not, he just had to deal with them. That was his job. He asked about my da. I said about the Navy.

Oh that is smashing son, yer da is a serviceman. Mind you, nothing against the Navy, but it is not the same as the Army. Ye have to bash heads in the Army. That is yer job. If ye do not like it ye lump it, else ye are out. If ye cannot do the job they boot ye out and quite right too.

But Civvy Street was so much the worse, they were all thieves and robbers and just low-down cheating scumbags. When he was a security guard he had to deal with them. Smack first talk later. They came at him with sticks and knifes and he had to disarm them. The same if they had guns. He had a gun himself and he shot a man but it was in line of duty. It was a service pistol and he had it planked in the lobby press. Usually it was unarmed combat. The old man was trained for it from the Army. Villains did not know what real fighting was. So with his training he could beat the living daylights out them. These villains were all cowards especially if ye got them alone, ye just waited and then ye got them. Oh do not hit me do not hit me do not hit me! They were all just scared and cowards. No unless it was a real fighter. Some were real fighters and ye could spot them a mile away, so then ye had to caw canny. Ye just caw canny.

The old villains were like that, they were rough and ready. They were not sleakit and did not knife ye, that was one thing. They were not fly men cheaters. It was a square go. Ye had to fight hand to hand. That was unarmed combat. If yer training was up to the minute ye were a jump ahead.

The paperboy did not believe it. I was telling him and Mitch. We were waiting for the rain to go off, sitting on the steps of the last close for a last smoke. Oh he is just talking shite, said the paperboy, you believe everything he says.

Do I fuck, I said.

He is just a boasting old bastard.

No he is not.

Aye he fucking is.

He is, said Mitch.

But maybe he was not. The old man told me about sailors down the docks that were foreigners and had their own way of doing it. They walked in and threw ye over their shoulder or else put ye flat on yer back. Ye had to be fast and slippery like them. If ye were nobody could hold ye, ye got out their grasp and slipped away. They had different ways of doing it. The main thing was turning yer man. And that was right because my granda showed me that when I was a wee boy, how ye just get yer man when he is coming in just getting his hand and oh pull him through and knock him over and he is off balance and that is it, he is down and ye just can get him. It did not matter if they were bigger than ye. The bigger the better.

Oh yer granda is right, said the old man. One time he was wrestling a big foreigner and the big foreigner came in and the way he did it the old man got his arm and pulled him through and just turned him and bumped him over so then he got him down easy and had his hand up his back. Do ye surrender? No. Do ye surrender? No. So he done it harder, till, Aye, aye, and the big foreigner had to surrender.

Because if he did not, the old man could have broke his arm in two. Mitch was listening but the paperboy did not believe it. That old cunt is a liar and a boaster. He is a fucking fanny-merchant.

No but my granda too, I said, that is how he done it.

The paperboy just looked. But if he thought my granda was a boaster he was very wrong. My granda showed me and I could do it. So could my brother. One time it was us all and Uncle Billy and we were practising and it was Matt to get Uncle Billy and he did! He got him, Matt got him! We were all clapping, Uncle Billy too. So then granda showed me and it was me to get him the same way and I nearly did. The paperboy just shook his head when I said it, but it was true, it really was.

Smiddy is right, said Mitch.

Mitch knew because I showed him in Primary School. Yer man came in and ye grabbed his wrist and pulled it through and he was off balance, ye just shoved him hard and got him down.

It is just shite, said the paperboy.

It is no shite.

Fuck off man.

Naw, stand up and I will show ye.

Fuck off.

Oh come on.

No.

Come on and I will show ye.

He will just fucking show ye, said Mitch.

Oh for fuck sake, said the paperboy, but he got up. Do not do anything daft, I am fucking warning ye.

But I was no going to. I just showed him how ye push yer man off balance, if he is attacking ye, so ye get his arm to follow through, pulling him and giving him a shove. Kid on ye are going to throw a punch, I said.

No.

Come on.

I cannot be fucking bothered.

Oh come on.

He took a deep breath then laid down his fag and put his hands up, then threw his left. The very one. I went with my side to him and got his wrist to pull him through and got him down easy, right on his side, but all the money came out his pockets, all rolling over the ground. Oh for fuck sake my tips my tips, ya fucking bastard. He jumped up right away and picked up the money. Look at my fucking jeans too, fucking mud all over them!

It was the side of his jeans, damp and some mud over them. Mitch laughed.

Oh what ye fucking laughing at? said the paperboy.

Nothing, said Mitch.

It isnay fucking funny. What did ye no tell me ye were going to do that for? You should have fucking telled me!

I did not mean it, I said.

Look at the fucking state of the jeans!

They are just damp.

The paperboy shook his head and went away. That was him. That was what he done. He went in bad huffs. He done it a lot. Any stuff where ye beat him, he hated it. If Mitch was no there and I finished my deliveries first, he really hated it and it was excuses. Oh I was late starting the night. The papers were late. People kept me back. I was short of papers and had to go and get more. He wanted to know about tips too, if we had the same customer. Oh how much of a tip does she give ye? So he always wanted to go first on Fridays and it was to get the first tip. Freddy the driver telled me that, First one to the door gets the biggest tip.

One time I climbed a veranda for a woman that was locked out and he hated that too. Just because I done it and no him. I telled Mitch. Mitch said, Aye but Smiddy you are the best climber.

Then if it was fighting, if it was real fighting, probably he would have beat me. I think he would have, maybe, but maybe no. But he would never have beat Mitch. I did not say it to him but I knew Mitch would beat him. The paperboy thought because he was older he would win but he would not, it was not ages to beat people. The paperboy was daft if he thought that. He just acted tough and said a lot of stuff. If the alsatian sentry dog went for him ever again he was going to tell the cops and get it destroyed.

Ye destroy a dog is ye kill it. I would never kill a dog. Whose fault is it? It is not the dog's fault. I did not think that was fair.

How come he did not get friends with it? Ye just walked in the close slow, and ye went to it so it saw ye, just slow and if ye talked to it, Oh good boy, good boy, how are ye son, how are ye, are ye okay. And no putting yer hands up, and keeping in full view so the thing could see ye. If ye ran ye would disturb it and ye did not want that. Ye done it bit by bit by bit. If the dog was in the garden that was good. If it was by the steps up the close it was worse. All ye could do was go in slow and no look at it. Ye heard the rumble in its throat and knew its eyes were watching but ye had to carry on. But ye listened for a swishing noise. That was its tail. If ye heard that then it was coming behind ye. Ye did not know till ye heard the swishing. Ye just walked on, not changing yer pace because not to surprise it.

And do not run. Oh never never. Never run. I told Mitch that all the time. He would not even go in the close. With dogs ye must never run, even wee dogs. That was the last thing. The alsatian sentry dog would not have bit the paperboy if he had not run. The old man said that and it was true. If ye were feared of dogs they knew it. That was a thing with them. People said they were no clever but they were. They were cleverer than cats. People said cats were the best but to me it was dogs. Cats were just how they done things but dogs were looking at ye all the time so if it was people that was how they knew, they were always looking at ye.

Ye had to watch it. If ye were feared ye acted like ye were not. If ye could forget about it, that was what ye did. Think about other things. If yer school has their football team and you are playing for them and ye score a good goal or cross over a good ball for somebody. So if it was for Scotland, imagine it was Scotland Schoolboys played England Schoolboys and beat them 5–3, just one complete team from all the boys, RCs too. It was a real football park and ye ran out the tunnel onto the pitch, then sent over the cross and the centre scored the winner. Even just the BB wee team on a Saturday morning if ye are playing for them. But what if they do not pick ye. Oh you cannot play because ye do not come to the Fall In. But I have to do my deliveries. Oh that does not matter.

Ye just thought of all stuff, just whatever it was and went away thinking about it, then ye forgot about the dog.

§

I carried the delivery sacks inside my school bag so there was no much room. But I hated the school bag anyway, it looked like Primary School. Boys in my class had other ones, just better ones. If I did not have the delivery sacks I would not have brought it, just used my pockets. Then if I went over to my grannie's I would no have had to carry it.

I liked no having to worry about things, bags and books and exercise jotters and pencils and pens. It was all stuff ye did not need. But if a teacher got ye it was hard luck. I was to read a passage out a book for English and was going to borrow it from a boy when one saw me. Where is your book?

I forgot it sir.

You firgoat it.

He came up to the desk and looked down at my school bag. What do you keep in there anyway? I am asking you a question boy. Open your school bag! Are you deaf? Open your school bag! Open it when I tell you. Will you open that school bag! Now!

The class all were watching. I did not care. Who cared about him, no me. He knew what it was, that was in my school bag. I saw he did. How did he know? He just did. I opened the school bag and pulled the sacks out. Maybe somebody told him. I did not care anyway. He held his hand out and I gave him one. What is this? he said.

A delivery sack sir.

A delivery sack sir. He took the three other ones and held them up for people to see, then had two in each hand. It was funny seeing them all crumpled and hanging down. It didnay even look like them. I was nearly laughing. One, two, three, four. Four delivery sacks, he said.

And they could even have had names. I saw that when he held them because there they were, the four ones I knew that were mine and they were different from each other, the one with the rips at the bottom so ye had to carry it up the way else a parcel would fall out and the one with the thin strap, just worn away and ye thought of an old man on his last legs, but wondered if it was going to fucking snap so ye didnay walk across a deep puddle because if it did snap what about yer parcels, imagine they were all fucking soaked so that was you and if nobody took them, ye would just have to fucking pay for them because the boss would just look at ye, It wasnay me that dropped them in the fucking puddle son. That was what he would say.

The teacher was looking at me and saying stuff, holding his hand out, looking down at me. His tie knot was pulled tight and greasy-looking. What did he even want? It was my school bag. I was to give him it. His finger just waggling at me, just stupid. So I was to hand it over, that was funny, his finger, and a dirty nail, teachers with a dirty nail. I gave him the school bag and he looked inside it. Two jotters and no books, he said. Two crushed jotters, and no books. Are you laughing boy?

No sir.

You have no books?

I forgot them sir.

You firgoat them.

Yes sir.

He dropped the delivery sacks on the floor. I reached to get them. Leave them there, he said.

I need them sir.

Leave them there.

But I need them sir.

I said leave them there.

It is my job after school.

I know what it is.

Well I need them. I just need them.

I did not say sir and he heard. I did not care. So it was the belt, who cared about the belt. And if people were watching. So what. That was them, they could just do it, whatever, I did not care. No about any of them, no in that class. I did not care about any of them. And the teacher, what he was saying, Leave them there.

Aw fuck him man, silly cunt. It was Freddy the driver talking. I just reached to get the sacks.

Smith, I have said, leave them.

They are my delivery sacks sir and I need them for my job.

Leave them until later, he said and he turned and walked back to his desk.

So I knew. I was just to leave the sacks there for a wee minute, one wee minute, that was all. Then I bent down and folded them up. I done it quiet, and shoved them back into my school bag. The teacher did not look at me doing it. Other ones in the class were not looking, but some were, I just felt good.

§

I went up a close and it was just something, like a special close, it was no children, and the people were quite old. They put a carpet there on the top landing and flower pots too. It was quiet and I sat on the step on the window landing and just had a rest or else a smoke if Mitch was not there. People did not go up much. If ye were wee ye would think it was a hideout. I saw it the best close in the whole street. That was what it was for me. But then it was, what it was, it was just where it was private because it was just, it was the place, well that was where I just sometimes wanked. And if anybody ever found out, ye could not think about it. I did not tell myself, and stopped myself thinking about it. The only thing sometimes was if it was God, just if it could be. I did not care for myself, if it was about myself, except maybe if God was waiting for me and saw me, people are wandering in the darkness unto the light, even if He was waiting for me for the Confession maybe how Protestants done it. Oh Father, I have sinned and been bad and swearing, just how ye done it in yer prayers. Prayers was talking to God, so that was a Confession, I Confess to you Heavenly Father.

Then ye could tell yer worst secrets. The worst stuff. People said wanking but maybe there was worse. And if ye did not tell Him that was you with a bigger Sin. If ye kept the bad stuff a secret it would all just pile up. Sins and evil deeds. If wanking was an evil deed. I tried to stop it, and no thinking about somebody if I was, I tried no to, but it all just came in my head and did not matter if it came on me, it would not go out my head. It started closes before that one and I started going faster or else if I went slower when I got nearer. I did not feel good about it and after I did it I felt bad. Then walking up the road if ye met somebody, maybe a woman customer and she said, Hullo, ye felt horrible and if it was somebody else like the paperboy, that was the worst, ye were just something what it was, people to laugh at ye.

Mitch did not come much and if he did I was nearly finished so he could not do much work. He always came on Fridays and for collecting money. So he got half the tips. I did not tell Freddy the driver and the paperboy. They would have looked. Oh you are daft. But it was Mitch's job and I just done it. After we paid the money into the boss we split the wages and Mitch got his. Maybe he did not like it because he did not do much. If it was me and I could not do it then he would have gave me it. It was not my job it was his. I was going to say to the boss about getting one for myself so to get the real wage but if I did Mitch could not do his.

I still liked the job, how it gave ye the money and ye did not need nothing off people. What could they say. Nothing. It was not their money it was yours. Ye worked for it, so there was nothing they could say, even yer maw and da. If things went right and ye got good tips then that was you. I made more tips than Mitch. I did not tell him. He asked me, Oh what did you make?

Oh it was good. I just said that. I did not tell him the exact amount. People gave ye more because if they knew ye from giving their deliveries. When they saw Mitch for the money, some did not hardly know him. He thought the third last close was the worst because of the old alsatian sentry dog but I did not care and it was only two more closes to go. The paperboy hated it but he had to go for a customer on the first storey. But he was in and away before me.

The worst dog in the street was not the old alsatian sentry it was a mongrel terrier. It was a mental case. People wished it would get run over. It did a circle dance round ye so ye could not walk, jumping up at ye and barking and shagging yer leg, and even if it was trying to bite at yer bolls. Ye had to pat it hard to get it off ye. I slapped it. I hoped somebody would pass so it would forget me and rush after them. People did not like it and wee weans were scared when it came. It was just nuts. Mitch said that, That dog is fucking nuts. He hated it and did not go near it and just watched when I clapped it. I told him no to worry, it would not bite ye, except maybe if it gave ye a wee nip by mistake.

The paperboy said, Oh it is just a fucking pest. He did not like dogs either. They jumped up at him when he pushed the papers through people's letterboxes.

But it was me it came to. I saw that. How come? I felt sorry for it and just clapped it. So it was me. If it saw me or got my scent. The dog did not mean any harm, it was just the way it was. So if it was a pest. There were a lot of pests. People were pests. At school it was everybody, nearly everybody. Ye got on the train in the morning, it was like a journey into a horrible dream, ye saw these pictures about other planets. Maybe there was nothing there except a cold landscape, all stones and desert and a dark sky or else scarlet red and brown. Everybody's breath comes out like steam, they are waiting for the train and it is freezing cold. And what will happen what will happen maybe if ye could just disappear for ever and wake up on a sunny beach and just go in for a swim and the water is just clean and light so ye can see all the fish and the coral reefs. Then if ye did come back it is a year later and it would all be over or if ye are standing there, a year just flashed by like a second and ye are shivering away and cannot stop and then the train is crowded full, all people going to school or their work and everybody is there all pushing to get onto the platform, maybe a woman with a pram and a wee baby inside, and she cannot get the pram up onto the step, the wee baby looking about, eyes popping and everybody all crushing and ye get carried this way or that, yer school bag getting twisted, and what will happen, maybe the Fates are going to do something like from history in the ancient days there was all Gods watching ye puny beings, all laughing to see ye falling about, then sticking stuff in yer road so ye might trip up or even setting down a wild beast, ye turn a corner and out jumps a crocodile, so that is yer Fate unless ye can do something about it, if ye have a knife in yer belt then ye can kill it, plunge it down between its shoulders. Ye jump on top of its back and plunge it right in between its shoulders. Ye have to do it and ye cannot miss because ye only get the one chance and if ye do not take it that is you. Because that is yer Fate, that is what lies in store for ye and ye have to deal with it, nobody else will. Who else is there. Even if there are big sentry lions sitting at the gates and if ye want to get through ye have to pass them, huge big lions, a pack of them, or else a dragon from history guarding the temples, so ye have to pass through, and just keep walking, do not stop, do not stop, the dragons are watching ye, do not stop, do not stop. This is yer Fate and ye have to go through the gate, even if the dragons are there, because if ye stop ye will never get through.

And nobody can help. It is you and only you. Who else could it be? Because if it is your Fate then that is you and just tough luck Everybody has their own. Some have it better than others. But if it is yours it is yours and nobody is going to change it.

People cannot fight yer battles for ye, no yer individual ones. That was what my granda said. If my grannie was giving him a row for something, if it was boxing lessons. Oh Vera, the boy has got to fight his battles.

Vera. That was what he called her. It was right enough if they were married. Vera, she was his wife. Oh Vera. Then he would laugh. So did she, she liked him laughing. Granda was good and ye just how everybody was really just like he was not there or passed over or what, it just was not fair, ye really thought that. And ye saw old people and they were walking down the street and then the old man that had the alsatian sentry dog, he was fat and just with a big red face, but he was there and he was old and he was older than granda if he was still there, so it was no even old people.

With granda it was cats. My grannie liked dogs. I did not really like them. If it was cats or dogs, ye just had to be careful. Ye watched them and they watched you, so then ye got to pet them, and when ye were wee ye smoothed them, then they were alright. Then they liked ye and you got to like them, but ye did not start off liking them.

Except just the mongrel terrier, how it went after me. He came running down the street and was jumping all over me jumping all over me, how come naybody else, if they saw it, just like a magic trick hypnotizing it. What did they think? It came bursting out the close to get me. And it was just me and I knew it how it was the smell and a scent. I started it. It was no the dog's fault. The twinges started on me, then getting near that close, that one where I went so I knew was I going to do it, I was hurrying else going slower no to think about it, if I was going to do it, or would I, maybe no, maybe I wouldnay, trying no to, I did not want to but then the twinges and maybe I was going to have one and if the mongrel terrier got my scent. It did. Ye saw dogs, how they got that smell and how they followed ye or else other dogs, they were trying to shag them, ye saw how they done it, and then if they jumped at ye it was yer bolls, that was what they went for.

I knew what it was. So if other people knew. This time it was happening Mitch was up a close and I just came down one and here it was it was a nightmare jumping roundabout me on its back legs doing a crazy circle dance trying to get at me and I could not stop it it was worse than ever. I swung a sack at its head but it came back jumping. Now Mitch was there and laughing, but he kept away, feared it went for him. I was shouting at the dog. It was just a stupid mental case.

It was Mitch's next close so I shouted the customer names to him and got out the parcels, flung them for a catch. Mitch was great at catching even if it was a bad fling. He caught them and was laughing, then ran into the close, ran into the close. The mongrel terrier jumped down off me and chased after him. He did not know because he was running up the steps. Then it was barking. I ran into the close, left the sacks on the floor and up the stairs. I could hear the noises and it was funny. I got up the second landing. Mitch was just there standing with his hands in the air and the parcels on the floor. His face was all funny, all something, if it was anguish. The dog was bouncing on its back legs with its two front paws hitting in at his chest and clawing up near his chin. And just its loud breathing.

And Mitch's own breath was stuttering like shivering and his body shaking because he was caught there. If I could pull the dog off him. I grabbed at it but it turned and snapped at me. It did not know me, its teeth there nearly biting me, nearly fucking doing it. The collar round its neck but I could not grip it. Oh but Mitch was no in a good state, just no doing nothing except standing and his shoulders tight up and shivering. I did not know what it was or what if maybe I could chap somebody's door or else what I could not think, except I got roundabout it and punched it dead hard on the side of the head and it went right back and landed down the stairs, its paws scrabbling on the steps and its head jerking round and seeing me then that squealing noise like dogs do it was a squealing noise. I had hit it dead dead hard and my hand even was sore, my knuckles, and my elbow too up at my shoulder, and the mongrel terrier's head, it was just a wee head, and I had battered it.

Mitch was nearly as if he was greeting. It was funny. He was leaning against the wall and making gulping noises, getting his breath, how a wee wean does it, if yer da gives ye a skelping, that was what ye done if ye were greeting and yer throat was too sore with it and ye were gasping. Oh Mitch, I said, Mitch. I patted his shoulder. Oh Mitch, alright?

But he did not look at me and went down the stairs. I gave the parcels into the people then I went down. Out the front close he was standing looking up and down, but the dog was away. I lifted the sacks and went out. He showed me his hand where the dog bit him, just wee marks but no blood. Look at mine, I said. My knuckles were a bit bleeding and the skin was tore. My elbow was sore too, down from the bony bit.

Oh, I am just going fucking hame, said Mitch.

Are ye?

Aye. And he just turned and walked away down the street and did not look back. Usually me and him did, and just called it that, last looks, so when ye were going hame ye looked round to see the person and gave a wave if he was looking and ye done it to see who was last. Mitch remembered who it was, so if it was the next day after school, Oh Smiddy I got the last look.

What I noticed too was how he did not say my name. Mitch always said it, Oh Smiddy, Hey Smiddy. He liked saying people's names. Now he just went away. Maybe he was angry at me, but it was no my fault, I could not stop it, until then I did.

I did not meant to batter the dog, I was just feared for Mitch. That mongrel terrier was crazy but ye did not think it was dangerous. This time it was. It did not like Mitch. I thought that but did not say it. Dogs like some people and no others. But it was his fault too. Because he was scared. Dogs do not like it if ye are scared. Ye just had to clap the dog and then that was that. I telled him how to do it. Dogs looked at ye and if ye were alright with them they were alright with you.

It was a shame for Mitch. After my tea I thought to go up for him but then I just waited to see. Maybe he would come up for me. But he did not. It was no my fault. Maybe he thought I would tell the boys but I wouldnay have, never.

§

It was Carolyn Smart's close, the nearer ye got to it, then when ye chapped her door and she came out, and what she had on, just pyjama bottoms and on the top a thin jersey thing else a blouse and making her tits jut out and she just was standing there. What was she she was beautiful, just what, a complete darling, if ye could say that it was her and ye could get randy thinking about her even just coming home from school and on the train or whatever ye were thinking about her and if she came to the door, just a complete darling, so with the pyjama bottoms how she would have come home from school then changed her clothes, maybe to do her homework lying on the bed, that was how some lasses done it, so she did not want to crease her school clothes, so she took them off, changed to the other ones and if her stomach was showing, sometimes it was, at her belly, the top she wore, it was too short and did not reach to her waist so ye always saw that bit and even her actual belly button, I saw that too and there was a wee bit sticking out. Mine went in deep and if water came in a wee puddle got left. Hers was just a wee thing in the middle. How come? If that meant anything, or if it was just cause she was a lassie. But boys had it too, I saw them. The cord got cut off and it sprung back into yer belly and into a wee circle, that was yer belly button.

I stared at the doormat when I went to her house. So if I started getting a stiffy going up the stair or coming to her close, no even thinking about it it would be twinges down below and ye were having to stop it. But it would not go away. I stood down at the landing window to think about stuff and take my mind away because if it was a wank, ye could not do it but just thinking it and it would not go down, just staring out the backcourt window, seeing all the stuff and no thinking about a single thing, if ye could, seeing the back walls and the easy climbs, just the same as mine with ronepipes and verandas and if ye could get onto a roof how ye could run along it. I would love to do that. And go right round the block, if the building came to the corner and went round to the next street so it was a corner building, I would like to go on that roof too. Just thinking about that and how it would be and even oh but if she was there again, just a complete darling, people called her that, a complete darling, and her bare feet too, she went in her bare feet, she just came down the lobby in her bare feet and when ye asked her for the delivery money she just went to get it and smiled at ye, that was what she done, it was just a real smile, she did not speak.

I stood looking out the window for ages till I forgot about it, whatever I would think, anything. Then I was at her door and ringing her bell, wondering how things were, if I had made much tips and if I was getting my customers in or were they out so ye did not get paid and would have to come back later, maybe over the weekend or else what, just whatever till then she came to the door and I was just complete red and the stiffy back and just total it was just oh red,

red red red, complete blushing. Then she went for her maw's purse and how she walked, how her pyjama bottoms were like they were stuck to her bum and it went side to side side to side, oh she was just a complete darling, ye wanted to just maybe whatever, what it was, whatever it was, ye could not if ye imagined it, even just if ye touched her.

People said that how if ye had a theme for a wank. Give me a theme. They just shouted. Maybe if ye were playing football and one shouted, Oh there is a theme, and ye looked and it was a lassie walking by.

Because that happened a lot in the Sunday games, a lassie walked by and she was a complete darling. Oh she is a theme man look at her! And everybody all stopped playing to go and see her. Oh would ye shag that! Oh what a darling. Look at the fucking tits on that!

If it was Carolyn but, imagine it was, it would just be horrible and I would have hated it. But how would ye get them to shut up? Ye could not, it was Gerry Henderson and McLennan, Gary McNab's brother, all the big ones, they would just look at ye, Listen to wee Smiddy.

Because ye were weer than them. But they were older, that was how they were bigger. I was no wee for my age, just normal. Only my nose and my hair, there was a stupid thing with my hair how a bit would not stay down, I patted water on it but it just dried and stood up, then red faces, ye got sick of it, even somebody telling a joke, if it was a dirty one, it just came on and I had to bend down to tie my shoelaces. Oh look at him man he has got a fucking riddy!

How come ye have got a riddy? People said that.

I did not know. But it was no just me. I did not care. I just hated it. Then if it was Carolyn Smart. Oh he is a wee boy, he has a red face. But she would not think that. Ye could even see it the way she smiled.

On Fridays ye lit a fag if it was a house where lasses stayed and ye kept it in yer mouth, saying how much the customer owed. If they paid with a big note and ye needed a lot of change, ye looked through all yer coins. If a woman came she could be wearing something like a dressing gown and have a smell about her, just a different one and a kind of warm thing about her that was a wee bit like another smell except it was not. They did not really notice ye or else gave ye a look if they did not like ye smoking up their close. Go and smoke up somebody else's close.

Older lasses too, they maybe looked at ye but no hardly noticing then if it was their wee brother came with the money, they just sent him, so they did not care about ye if ye were there. But no if it was Carolyn. She came to the door in her bare feet, just right down the lobby, then her pyjama bottoms and just how she walked, just if she was walking, and did not speak to me. I told the paperboy. She went to his school. He said he did not fancy her but I think he did. It did not bother me. But I liked how if she did not speak to ye, she just smiled, she did not speak, she just smiled at ye, so if it was me at the door, she always smiled at me, she did, I fucking saw it how she did, she just smiled at me.

Oh do not be fucking stupid, he said, she does not fancy you, she gets any cunt she wants. Boys in 5th year. She is in 3rd year, she does not want you, you are no even thirteen.

So? I nearly am.

Aye but you are no the now.

But I soon will be. Then next year fourteen. Then fifteen.

She will be fucking seventeen.

I do not care.

Aye but she does, do not be so daft. You are just a fucking wee boy to her.

Am I fuck.

Aye ye are.

So?

So nothing.

I started laughing.

What ye laughing for?

I am just laughing.

I did not care what he said. People were younger than people. Everybody is not the same age. That was just stupid. What class was she in anyway. I asked him, a high one like 3A or 3B or if it was 3G or whatever. The paperboy did not know. He did not even know. Oh but she is in the netball team, he said, she is good at sport.

As soon as he said it I knew, I knew, I knew she was, of course she was, good at sports, of course she was, just of course, of course.

What are ye laughing for? he said.

Just because I knew, I fucking knew. That was the kind of lassie she was ye could just actually see it. That was her, it was just obvious. PE and games like netball and all gymnastics, that was her, swimming too, I bet ye she was just a great swimmer then if it was running races, ye could see her, just how lasses done it, no bothering about people, if boys were watching, she would still do it and just be running. Even how she stood at the front door, if I was getting the money for the deliveries, ye could tell just how she stood. Maybe she dived in if she went to the baths. A lot of lasses did not dive in because of their hair but I thought she would, she would not worry about that, just her hair, that was just stupid, she would just be a girl that dived right in, maybe off the dale. I had never seen a girl dive in off the dale. Maybe one had. Maybe Carolyn. But she would not go to any swimming baths, just her own one, and it would be a club where people had galas and races where yer maw paid for ye. I could join too, if I saved up and paid then I could just go, just myself. Then if she was there, maybe she would be. So I would see her. Nobody could stop ye going, unless it was a club for Catholics. Oh are you a Catholic, say yer Mass, then ye would have to say it. Well I would, I would just try it, and she would know who I was, if she saw me, because it was me done her deliveries, Oh that is the delivery boy. She would just see me and know it was me, she would.

What are ye laughing for? said the paperboy.

Oh just because. It is fucking funny.

What is?

Nothing.

The paperboy was looking at me. He did not know why. Just because. But it was funny, because thinking about her and just how she was I thought if I was going to marry her. That was what I felt, it was just how then I felt it, if I was. So I was laughing, that was how, because if I was going to marry her, maybe I was, I was just going to marry her. Oh I am going to marry her, I said.

What! Fucking grow up you.

No but I am.

She will never marry you, do not be fucking stupid.

His eyes were not moving when he said it, just how he was looking straight at me, just straight at me, and I thought I would burst out greeting. I felt in my chest or in my throat something and I had to gulp and gulp. I was going to say something back but could not because of gulping, I could not. I thought he liked me. I thought he did. But he did not, he did not at all. He was looking at me that way and I needed to get away. He hated me. He was never pals with me. Never. He just never was. How come I thought he was he never was.

She is older than you, he said, lasses will no marry a man if she is older.

Lies. Lies. I knew it was lies just rotten lies. I knew it was, how could he just tell lies like that. Just lies, I knew it. Lies lies lies and I knew it was lies and I did not look at him. Because I did not want to. Because what it was, I knew what it was. I just knew.

Lasses have to be younger, he said.

It is no that, you are just a fucking lying bastard, I said, fucking cheating fucking bastard because I know what it is, how come ye are saying it, just cause I am a Protestant, how ye do not take me to the cards either, it is because I am a Protestant. Nothing else. It just was not anything. Because I was a Proddy. It was nothing about nothing except I was a Proddy. It was not with her being older but she was a Catholic. So if the Priests would not let her. Else her maw and da if they did not like Protestants. Some did not talk to ye. So if that was her family. Oh do not marry him, do not let her marry him. That happened if ye married a RC, they got against ye.

It was okay for lasses but no boys. Lasses married Catholics but no many boys. If the Proddy lassie married one, he could not turn, no if he was a Pape. Papes could not turn. Never. The Priests did not let them. Because they wanted the baby. The babies had to go to Chapel and be Catholics. What happened to the baby, the Priest came and took it away and put it into an Orphanage with all Nuns.

No unless ye turned from a Proddy. It was okay then. People turned. Usually lasses. They went to the Chapel and got Instruction and that was all the stuff ye had to do. It was wee exams they had to pass. The Priests went their teachers and done it to them so then they turned Catholics. Except if they failed. Then the Priests did not let them, so if they said no then the lassie could not. So the boy's maw and da would not let him marry her. So he would have to run away. They would all be against him. So it would just be his girlfriend, that would be him. He would not want everybody else, just her. What would he want them for? It was her, if he loved her. And he would, that would be what it was. Just true love, that was it, ye met the lassie and she was the one for you. My grannie said that, You will meet the right one son, do not worry.

So ye would just pack yer stuff and away ye go at the dead of midnight, waiting till everybody was asleep and creeping down the stairs. Ye would need yer stuff all packed and ready. Then round to get her. If it was me, I would not care about creeping down the stairs. I would just run down, I would just clatter. I would not care. My da would never catch me. It would be too late. He would still be in bed so he heard the door banging – I would just slam it – but I would be away, so he would have to get dressed, putting on his shoes. By that time he would never catch me. He would not know where to run to. Because he would not know the lassie! Oh who is she?

He would not know because I would never tell him or my maw. My maw would have wanted to know but I would never have telled her either. She would try to find out. I would tell the boys no to tell her. Maybe they would not know. Maybe I would no tell anybody, if it was my brother or who? Nobody. Only Mitch but he was not there so nobody nobody nobody. Except maybe my grannie. No. Not even her. I liked my grannie but I would not tell her.

Maybe I would. No if my Uncle Billy was home. He had a pal married a RC and what happened, when his back was turned, away she went to the Chapel, even taking his weans. Everybody knew except him. They kidded on they did not know but they all did. Then too it was in her Will. That was Uncle Billy said, his pal found out the truth, when she passed away it was the Chapel was getting her. The Priests were going to snatch away the coffin and bury her at a High Mass. Uncle Billy's pal was in the Lodge. Now he was going to have to go to Chapel. He did not know he would. But all other people knew. Even in the Lodge. They just had pity for him. Oh they pity him, said Uncle Billy.

He would have to kneel down, Bless me Father, I confess Father, I am a sinner Father.

Even if it is an old man and the Priest is a young one, the old man has to call the young one Father, Sorry Father and then confess all his sins.

And what would the Priest be doing? Maybe he was just laughing. Oh what is this old man saying! He is just an old codger.

So just laughing at an old man. Imagine a Priest done that. But I could not imagine it. Priests were like Ministers except Catholics, it was just what ye were, some were Priests and some were Ministers, it was just religion and what ye were. I fucking hated it. The paperboy too. People were boasters and he was one. I did not care about what he was meaning, Proddies and RCs, I didnay fucking care about them.

I said it to him another time and we were walking home and just stopped for a smoke. I was talking because he did not. He did not talk first, just waited for me to say something then he came in, Oh that is fucking wrong man do not say that, that is pure fucking shite.

Well you say something.

Fuck off.

You do not say nothing, it is just me, then ye just come in and say it is fucking shite, well you say something.

Fuck off.

But he did not say stuff so I could listen. It was just me. That was the same with my brother. It was always me talking, he never said nothing till I did then he just came in, Oh do not talk such rubbish, that is just rubbish.

The paperboy was like Matt. I said it, You are like my fucking brother.

What ye fucking talking about? I am no like yer fucking brother.

Aye ye are.

Fuck off.

I did not talk to him about Carolyn Smart. Never ever. I just wished it was Mitch because then, because Mitch was a real pal.

The paperboy said stuff. All people did. They said stuff and it was just boasting. And me too, I fucking done it and it was just total horrible shite, just horrible horrible shite and boasting rotten rubbish. I spoke about Carolyn Smart to Sabby and McEwan heard. I said about Carolyn Smart and it was all just stupid nonsense and how come I said it, it was just the worst boasting and me doing it, just complete stupid nonsense about truth, dare or promise, and there was never any truth, dare or promise it was all just horrible boasting shite how I was to feel her tit and she had to let ye if it was truth, dare or promise, that was it if ye were playing, a lassie had to let ye do it, and McEwan was there listening too and I showed Sabby how with my hand, just for a squeeze, yer hand was just gripping over and ye just squeezed her tit. But then when I done it McEwan said, Oh for fuck sake, and went away, and Sabby just laughed and went away after him. I would never ever do that again. Never ever. Never.

§

If it was yer Fate to go to Hell how did ye know? Maybe it came into yer head, God put it there. He said yer Fate so ye knew it without thinking. It was inside ye but ye never knew till after ye were dead. Ye woke up and ye were in Hell. Who could ye say it to? Oh here ye are. But ye were, and ye just looked about.

But if it was not fair. What if ye led a good life and did good deeds? How come it was Hell? It would be a big surprise. Except ye were a sinner.

Everybody was a sinner. Ye went to hell because of it. So how come everybody did not go? Because it was no their Fate. Some people had bad Fates. Tough luck for them, they done good deeds but still went to Hell. They could not make up for it. Even if they done all good deeds, that was them.

Other ones done evil deeds, so if they just got away with it. The Registration teacher talked about it. God's way is a mystery to us. If we could but fathom it but we are puny beings.

What about yer own Fate, if that was Hell? Sometimes it sounded daft. Ye could never imagine it. All people burning in big fires and screaming and it was forever, just screaming. Oh you will go to the big fire. People said that when ye were wee. It sounded stupid. Who lights the fire? Oh is it God or the Devil or who else? If it is an Angel how come he is in Hell? Angels do not go to Hell. So it must be an evil Angel and he lights the fire but then if he jumps in after so he will burn.

Other times it did not sound stupid. If ye did evil deeds ye would get punished. That was right enough. Even deeds nobody knew. Nobody saw ye and heard ye and ye did not tell nobody. So they did not know. Not in the entire world. Except God, because God. Ye could not do a single thing except He knew. A Bible Class teacher always said that to us. But He knew anyway if it was Fate. It was Him gave ye it.

Even dogs had their Fate. Some went to Heaven and some went to Hell. Ye felt sorry for the ones that went to Hell because if it was not their fault. What was a dog's evil deeds? What Fate did it have? Some just were stupid, they ran out in front of a car and got knocked down or just the mongrel terrier, I felt sorry for it.

So a wee wean did not go to Hell. So how come a dog? Dogs did not know. So how come they went to Hell? If it was the human trained it, ye could not blame it. It was not fair to have it destroyed, that was not fair, except if it was the human, he got destroyed, it was him trained it if he was the master, so it was him to blame. So it was me, if the dog liked me and then I done something bad, so it was me.

§

Uncle Billy put his money on horse racing. He got beat and talked about it a lot. My grannie just looked at me if his horse was running on the telly and he was shouting, Bloody stupid bloody horse.

Oh he is shouting at the horse, she said, listen to him. He works down in England. But what does he have to show for it? Nothing. Money just slips through his fingers. Oh if he got paid for playing billiards, then he would be alright. He could not even afford to get married, if ever he found a girl.

She said the same things. Uncle Billy just winked. If the horse won sometimes he gave ye money. Oh Kierie boy, there is a wee bung for ye.

He done it when I was wee and gave me the wink so no to tell people. He still done it now I was old. I had money in my pocket but my grannie said, Oh just take it son.

Uncle Billy laughed. Oh mother mother, sweet mother of mine.

My grannie liked him saying daft stuff. She acted like she did not but she did. But she did not like it when he gave her cuddles. She hated cuddles. I done it when I was wee and she said, Oh it is not good for children, if there is germs. Only the forehead son.

So ye could just kiss her on the forehead. That was the same with Uncle Billy. Oh do not come near me, she said, big beery breath.

I am not beery breath, no yet anyway!

He was going out to the pub with his pal and meeting other ones. And then it is the jigging, we are going to the jigging.

Who would dance with you, said my grannie.

Oh plenty, plenty.

He was going back to England on Sunday night. The bus left at midnight and got there in the morning. He went straight to his work. Oh I sleep on the bus, he said. And then I sleep at my work.

When are ye coming back?.

I am no sure. But I will be coming home for good soon. I am sick of it down there. People do not even talk to ye if ye are Scottish. If it was not for my landlady. She is the only one.

Oh maybe you will marry her, said my grannie.

Maybe I will, three square meals and extra helpings. Eh Kierie boy ye have to watch out for these wummin.

He looked at me for a laugh but my stomach went bad. That was it now. I was anyplace at all and away thinking about things and stuff was just there filling my head. What would happen to me? I did not know. I did not know. If it was a girl in the class and she was laughing to her pal, just that one wee second. A feeling struck through me just sudden and in my heart or there someplace, down to my stomach, if it was not my heart. Maybe if it was my soul. It was the worst nightmare. I could not do nothing, and just if I could away and just go someplace away someplace and just stay there. I would never just be

I did not know what to do.

Uncle Billy was going to meet his pal Chick. He got the van from his work when we did the flitting to the scheme. How come we ever went to the scheme, it was just fucking horrible, bloody just horrible. I did not like swearing in my grannie's, even in my head. Swearing in yer head is the same as out loud, if it is you that does it. I liked swearing but no in my grannie's.

Uncle Billy had his good shirt and tie on and his big coat as well. Oh it is freezing out there, he said, it will snow the night. Come on Kierie boy, I will walk ye down to the subway.

Yes, said my grannie, because it passes his pub.

Uncle Billy just laughed, waiting on me to come.

Oh it is okay Uncle Billy, I will stay a wee while yet.

Oh ye will will ye! Are ye sure?

Yes.

My grannie did not say anything. She was glad.

Well

Oh away to the pub, said my grannie.

I will. You are no making me feel guilty.

I did not think I would.

I went to the door and waved to him going down the stairs. But it was quiet when he went. He made grannie laugh and she liked him. He was just always cheery. People smiled, even my maw. Even my da. My da liked him too.

But if Uncle Billy liked my da, he did not see him much. My da said, Tell Billy hullo from me and it is time we went for a pint.

Uncle Billy smiled when I telled him. Say hullo back to him. But he did not come much to our house. My grannie never did. Her and granda only went once to our house. My granda said, Oh it is a wagon train, ye will meet Red Indians over there, it is too faraway.

Auntie May never came either. How come?

People do not do things. Uncle Billy asked how Matt was and said to me quiet, Does he come to visit his grannie?

Aye, I said but I did not think he did. Maybe he did. I did not see him here. I came at daytime as well because with school, I was dogging it a lot, but I did not see Matt.

My grannie just opened the door and let me in. She did not say about me coming. She made me something to eat, boiled eggs or tomatoes and cheese on biscuit things.

She did not buy much bread, but a lot of tomatoes. I went her messages to the dairy and for Mrs Duncan down the stair. She was grannie's pal. If she was not in her house I chapped Mrs Duncan's door and that is where she was, if they were just drinking tea or watching television. Mrs Duncan knitted but my grannie did not, and never watched television in her own house, just in Mrs Duncan's. Sometimes I got her messages too. She gave me money for going. I did not want it but she said to take it. Oh if people give ye things, ye should just take them.

My maw did not think the same. You do not need things from people. You should just smile and say, No thank you.

I liked looking at granda's stuff. My grannie did not mind. She said to take some but I did not. But I would after. I told her. And all his tools, I took them out the box and laid them out on the floor.

So if it was an electric plug and ye had to fix it, ye had the wee screwdriver to open it up. I saw my da doing it and now here was the stuff for grannie, if she needed it. Then the axe and the hammers. Some screwdrivers were sharp, ye could stab people with them. I could have took one.

My granda let me go into the box when I was wee. If he was doing a job he brought me into it and gave me a question. We need tools son, what tools do we need? So then we would go and see in the box. It was all a jumble. When he told ye to find a spanner or a hammer or pliers ye had to sort through everything. There was no order, just all stuff on top of each other. Sometimes yer hands jagged into sharp ends and nailpoints or ye caught a bad skelf or else a tiny wee clip went under yer fingernail or ye pulled out a tool from the bottom and something heavy turned over and landed on yer fingers. But it was still great looking and ye aye found stuff ye had never seen before.

I went to my old library down at the park. It was great and all the books ye got. I could see in the adult library if I liked. Some books ye got in the juniors ye got in the adults. Ye were supposed to live roundabout to get their books. If ye lived someplace else ye were to use yer own library. But it was only the mobile one we had in the scheme. I wrote down my grannie's address.

I read books at a table beside the window. The winter was there and it was good looking out. I had books planked on the shelves so I could just read them when I came. I hid them flatways behind ones nobody took out. There was dust on them.

My grannie read magazines and books too. She read her same ones and kept her place with handkerchiefs. The handkerchiefs were ladies' ones. They were small with fancy edges. If ye opened her book they kept the pages. I wished I could stay with her. There was the swimming baths too. I said to grannie about going but she did not want to. Oh maybe sometime, she said.

But there was space for me in the spare bed. Auntie May was in her own flat now and had a boyfriend.

But I did not like walking down to the subway on Saturday nights because if Rangers were playing in the afternoon. Usually there was trouble or ye thought there might be and were watching for gangs. If ye saw any ye went fast but no running, and no looking back till ye got round a corner. Then ye ran. But if they were in front of ye, what now, down another street through the backcourt but what if they came after ye and caught ye, they would give ye a kicking. They would see what religion ye were. Oh what street do ye live in? What team do ye support? What school do ye go to? Are ye a Proddie bastard?

No, I am a RC.

Well ya daft cunt we are Proddie bastards. Most gangs were Proddies. If they caught ye, really, it did not matter what ye were ye were going to get it. Maybe if some of my old pals from Primary were there they would see me, Oh he is one of us, and we would just shake hands. Oh where are ye staying now Smiddy?

But I never saw pals from the old place. I would have went with them. Maybe they were there and I did not know them. They would not look the same. I could not think of their faces.

I was no good at faces. I tried to see them in my head but I could not, they were just all dim and looking the one way. The same with granda. He came into my head a lot. If it was his face usually it was the same one. He had his own wee wave. So saying cheerio to my grannie I done the wave so she would see then went out quick, shutting the door, going down the stairs, water out my eyes. So I was greeting. Sometimes I was.

Hearing him laugh or else his voice to me.

I tried to see his face different, and he was doing the windmill and I was to box inside and hit him, he was just laughing, waggling his fists and showing his chest to punch him. I even got angry when I was wee. Punch punch, that is good son.

I should not have got angry. Imagine getting angry. No with granda. I could not ever hit him, granda was great, he was just great. I was not.

It was bad things, ye done them and should not. If people knew about them. Maybe I would go away. I would have to. If people ever knew.

Dead people watch ye from the other side. Billy MacGregor had ghost comics with tales from beyond the grave. My da had books from the Navy. Him and his pals read them at sea, they swapped them round. He liked science fiction and cowboy stories. Matt read them too. Some of the science fiction was like horror books and one I looked in was sexy and getting into temptation where the man was getting pulled down into the dank and soggy earth but what was happening to him, I did not know, if he was a RC. It just said Christian but really it was RC because he had the Priest there and making the Sign of the Cross on his chest. Oh keep out the Evil One. Oh my Father I have Sinned. Tell me my Son.

I did not know my da would read that. I confess oh Father.

The Priest says, Oh Edouard beware the Dread Ghost, it is a Dread Ghost.

But it is not like a real ghost, only a tempting devil from a horror world beyond and it was the ghost of a departed spirit but it was not a real ghost from a real person, it was a Dread Ghost of an Alien, or like the Evil Spirit of an Alien or maybe a ghost from a long-lost planet in a long-lost universe where it is all evil and they all are Devil-worshippers and all backward prayers and upside-down Holy Mothers of God, but they are not, it is just the Devil. But it was in the body of a girl with a torn dress and one of her legs was bare all the way up and Oh milky-white skin, it is milky-white skin of a soft thigh, oh oh, and it was just the way it was in the story how she was waving to ye. She beckoned. She beckoned ye. But it was from beyond the grave. Where she was leading ye ye did not know if it was murderous deeds except how ye were reading it, if ye got a wee bit randy, that was what happened. I stopped reading it. My maw was there. I was in the kitchenette and she was making the tea. Matt was in the bedroom doing his studies. My da was not home yet so I went ben the living room.

And the man got put behind a walled tomb, Edouard, and it caves in on top of him and he screams and screams but it all falls on deaf ears. He is covered in the dank and soggy earth, filling up his pores, all in his pores, and he cannot breathe, and it is only silence all around and the dank and soggy earth is all in his mouth and up his nose and that is him doomed for ever if he cannot breathe, Oh I cannot breathe I cannot breathe, if he can offer up a prayer. But he cannot. But he does not die but forever and ever he is a living corpse with a waking death doomed unto Eternity. This is his punishment. He did not heed the Priest's warning. And now he hears his friends walking on the carpet of grass above his horrible tomb and he would want to tell them all what happened and to be on the lookout and saying about temptation, Oh if it comes in a cunning disguise, do not fail me old friends, at what befalls us, if it is this, we are as puny men, only pray to God and do not forget me.

But his pals could not hear nothing at all except maybe the wind just whistled a wee bit through the trees and one of them goes, What was that?

Oh it is just the wind.

But into their mind comes a picture of the man and they see his face, Oh it is Edouard, and they know then it is an awful truth, he is passed onto the other side. Except he is not because he is buried alive and just doomed as a Living Corpse. Now it is all silent, not a bird chirping and not a breath of wind and it is just scary, for in that time night had fallen as before their very eyes and there in the gloom is a ghostly figure, if it is a lassie and she has a torn dress, it is, and one of her legs is bare all to the top and her thigh is milky-white plump. Plump. And milky-white breasts, but her red lips are real blood, for all the time she is just the Mask of Temptation. The book was called that. I went through the pages. Then in the library I went to find if the book was there too but it was not but other ones were. I just looked at them, sexy ones too.

I did not believe in dead people walking about. It was just stupid. A boy in the class said it one time and people laughed at him. I listened, but I thought the same. It was all just daft, if people were walking about everywhere and it was all ghosts and spirits. How did they do it? Oh they are invisible. Ye can just walk through them and they walk through you. If ye feel a wee shiver well that is them. People thought that.

But then at nighttime it came into yer head and ye saw the dark outside the curtains, it just came in yer head. If there were spirits, maybe they did not walk. How come they walked. They just would fly. That was all they needed was air because they were not flesh and blood with the thickness of bodies. They were wisps. Spirits were wisps and just in the breeze, floating this way and that, and it did not matter how high up ye stayed.

Spirits of yer loved ones, there was a space in between, after they breathed their last and before they got to up above. They had to spend their time on Earth to see ye were okay. That was Guardian Angels. If ye were going wrong and ye needed a guiding hand, so maybe ye had relatives that passed on, they were there to help ye. Oh see your path ahead it is straight and narrow.

Once they went up to Heaven that was them and ye would not see them again, no even if they were spirits. My grannie said, Oh son ye just pass to the other side.

But if the other side was not Heaven. If it was the bit in between, ye had to go there first, and then pass over after. In that first bit ye saw humans walking about but ye were a spirit and could not touch them. Yer spirit was suspended. So ye were dead and floated about and did good tasks, ye had to. Ye did not get to Heaven until ye finished them. Maybe ye had lived a bad life. No too bad or it was Hell. But just ye were not good enough for Heaven so God gave ye tasks and once ye done them that was you. Maybe if it was Fate or else whatever it was but ye could not get to Heaven till they were done, so yer spirit wandered the land maybe helping people, or if it was bad ones ye were haunting them. Imagine that, it was bad people and ye were to haunt them. Ye would even quite like that, hiding up closes and jumping out. Ye saw that it in ghost pictures. But it would be strict and serious till after a certain time it was okay, another Angel came down to tell ye or whatever it was, ye just knew deep down, if God said it inside yer head. So then yer time had come and now ye done the real pass over and it was up to Heaven. Ye got it in Hymns as well, Oh when we pass over, if we reach the other side, it is the far shore.

Protestants believed it as well as Catholics, then if the spirits talked to ye in Seance meetings where people brought back the dead. My grannie knew an old lady who went to them. Oh who is there, who is there. They all held hands and one person called out to the spirits.

420

Identify yourself. Who are you who are you? Oh I am a spirit of the dearly departed and it is okay it is a beautiful place on the far shore we have guiding lights to lead us

It acted like magic but it was not magic. But there was a lot of fakers about. But some were true and a spirit came back if it was to tell ye something that was going to happen if ye did not watch it. Something horrible. It had to warn ye and was trying so hard to reach ye, if it was a special spirit from beyond the grave, Oh save me save me.

But then if evil ones were watching, just walking beside ye. Sometimes ye felt it going down the street, one was walking beside ye. Oh who is that? If it is a ghastly presence. People said that in books, Oh I felt it, it was a ghastly presence. And ye passed a close, Oh if they grabbed ye and pulled ye in.

But evil spirits do not murder ye. They cannot. Else they always would. If they did then you would be a spirit as well so you could fight them back. They would be scared of that. But when they killed ye they would escape. It is a split second till yer spirit leaves yer body. If ye could just get fast out it would be okay, but ye cannot. So then they escape and ye have to go looking for them. But how do ye find them if it is all just floating in the sky? Ye are doomed until ye do. Oh I am in torment, I cannot pass over until the Evil One is found.

Then ye find him and what do ye do because ye cannot kill him back, no if the two of yez are spirits, because that just makes more spirits, if spirits have spirits, or else if ye tell God on him. Except God knows already.

And if it is your own spirit, is it good or evil. Ye do not know until ye are dead. Have ye done good deeds? Good spirits come and help ye do good deeds so ye will become a good spirit yerself and go to Heaven.

Ye wanted to do good deeds. I thought about it in bed or what, sitting on the train, Oh imagine I am walking down the street and an old blind man is there and cannot cross over for the busy traffic. I will just run and help him. Or a wee wean is lost, so I would go into the woods or round the streets and there I find it and take it home, Oh it is Kieron Smith.

I done it if people locked themselves out, I just climbed the balcony, opened the window and let her in, except if ye got caught it was a doing off yer da and a row off yer maw. Oh Kieron I do not care if you are helping somebody, they should know better than to ask ye to climb a building, that is just an outright disgrace.

But if the woman was in sore bother cause she could not get in her house. Maybe she had a pot boiling or a frying pan burning. Chip pans caught fire, all the burning oil so then the house burned down. A woman up the next close to my grannie threw a basin of water on the chip pan and the burning oil all came out and went all everywhere and burnt the flesh off her bones. So if it was going to be a fire and ye stopped it, so it would be a good deed. Even if yer maw said it was not one ye would know it was. Then maybe another day ye were walking down the street and ye felt a presence, the wind blowing like a whisper and it is the breath of a good spirit floating beside ye, Oh well done, that was good helping that poor woman, you were brave going up the ronepipe.

Because sometimes it was slippery. I thought that too, if a good spirit was going with ye, maybe if it was granda, he had just passed over and was climbing with ye so it would not go wrong, just helping with yer grips. But what if it was a bad spirit? I used to think that. Oh what if it makes me put my foot in the wrong place. Or else my foot got jammed in between the ronepipe and the wall and I would topple back over, all my body except just my one foot stuck in. And I would be flapping my arms and just seeing my foot come out inch by inch till then I was falling. Maybe a bad spirit would make me do it. Or lift off my fingers if I was going up a tree, one floated up to get me and if it was reaching high and came to my fingertips and just lifted them off one by one by one, or if it was a ronepipe and ye were getting to the very top and the spirit just blew the wind and knocked ye off. So yer granda would be there, his spirit would come to yer rescue, maybe a breath of wind or a hard blowing wind, to stop ye hitting the ground heid first, ye would land one foot at a time, nice and soft, or else in a big pile of sacks and just get up and walk away, Oh that was lucky, and it would be, except if it was him, yer granda.